About

Born and raised in the P... worn many hats over the ... distributor, singer, nanny, and far... proud to add romance author to that list. After decades of dreaming of seeing her name on the shelves next to her favourite romance authors, she finally found the courage to write her first book. Follow her on Twitter @pauliabelgado or on facebook.com/pauliabelgado or at pauliabelgado.com

The Historical Collection

The Historical Collection:

Victorian Games

PAULIA BELGADO

MILLS & BOON

First Published in Great Britain 2023
by Mills & Boon, an imprint of HarperCollins*Publishers* Ltd,
1 London Bridge Street, London, SE1 9GF

www.harpercollins.co.uk

HarperCollins*Publishers*
Macken House, 39/40 Mayor Street Upper,
Dublin 1, D01 C9W8, Ireland

The Historical Collection: Victorian Games © 2023 Harlequin Enterprises ULC.

May the Best Duke Win © 2022 Paulia Belgado
Game of Courtship with the Earl © 2023 Paulia Belgado

ISBN: 978-0-263-31965-1

MAY THE
BEST DUKE WIN

To my parents, Mercy and Danny.
Thank you for your love, support and sacrifice.
I love you both

Chapter One

London, 1842

If Kate Mason could understand men as well as she did steam engines, life would be so much simpler.

Treat a piece of machinery well, and it would run smoothly. With a little bit of fuel, water, and heat, engines could do marvellous things, like pump water from underground or move hundreds of people across miles and miles of track. And if they broke down and turned temperamental, you just needed to look inside and simply fix or replace the missing part. Truly, there was no mechanical problem that Kate couldn't solve.

But men—what made them tick, how their minds functioned, and what fuelled them—were a mystery to her.

Take her father, for example.

Kate wished she could just look inside his head and figure out how he worked. That way, his words this morning wouldn't be catching her by surprise.

'By now you must have realised why I brought you to England, Kathryn.' Her father's hawklike gaze pinned her. 'You must find a husband so we can begin building a Mason locomotives factory here. Marriage to an influential lord will also ensure we can gain the necessary rights to acquire the land needed for our railway lines.'

Kate should have suspected something when her father—despite dragging her three thousand, four hundred and fifty-nine miles from New York to London—would not tell her more details about the new locomotives factory they were building, nor take her to his meetings with solicitors, bankers, even the architects and builders. When they'd arrived in London a few days ago he'd simply deposited her in their suite at The Ritz, in the care of another American family they had travelled with, and had not spoken to her until today as they'd sat down to breakfast.

But, then again, that was how industrialist and business magnate Arthur Mason had grown his fortune from practically nothing into the empire it was today: by being completely ruthless and never revealing his true intentions until it was too late.

Kate, however, would not give up so easily. Taking a sip of tea from the delicate china cup, she composed herself. 'But, Father, you never mentioned anything about marriage. I thought you said you needed me to oversee the building and operation of Mason Railroad & Locomotives here in England.'

There had even been a hint that she might be able to build an engine of her own design once the facility was up and running.

'Did I?' her father challenged. 'I don't recall any such thing. Did I say those exact words?'

And that was when Kate knew Arthur Mason had outmanoeuvred her.

Ever since he had first brought up the idea of going 'across the pond' to take advantage of England's booming railway industry, her father had dangled the prospect of her managing a factory of her own. *'I need you to start the factory, Kathryn',* he had said. *'Your Pap would have wanted you there.'*

And appealing to the memory of her grandfather had worked. There was no one in the world she had loved more. Right after his wife had died after giving birth to Kate, Arthur had left West Virginia to seek his fortune in New York, leaving her in the care of his father. Henry 'Pap' Mason had taught her everything he knew about engines from his days working in the coal mines. Eventually, when she was about seven years old, Arthur had sent for them and established Mason Railroad & Locomotives so his father could put his talents to good use.

Growing up, she had worked side by side with Pap, even helping him with his greatest creation—the Andersen steam engine. It had been one of the most efficient engines of its time, and it was because of the Andersen they'd been able to build farther west and north than any other railroad company, their rails stretching past Illinois as well as into Canada. It was unfortunate that Pap had died four years ago, before he'd been able to see his invention make Mason R&L a true success.

Despite the fact that Kate had helped with the building of the New York factory, the design of the Andersen, and managed operations after his death, all had ultimately been Pap's accomplishments, his pride and joy. So when her father had planted the seeds of going to England she had thought this was her opportunity to prove herself—that this would be her legacy. In fact, she'd even allowed herself to start thinking about her own engine design.

She now realised she had been mistaken. Or rather, misled and outwitted.

'You're twenty-one years old,' her father continued, now barely looking at her as he unfolded the newspaper beside his plate. 'Leaving you alone with only your grandfather for company growing up was one of the worst mistakes of my life. If your mother were alive she would have taken care of this years ago, and you would be wed and bred by now.'

Her father's coarse words shocked her, and yet she shouldn't have been surprised. Despite his vast fortune and great success, Arthur Mason did not make any secret of the one disappointment in his life—that his only offspring was female. And no matter how hard Kate had worked with Pap, and how efficiently she had run the factory after his death, in Arthur's eyes she would only ever be a woman.

'The sooner you are married off, the sooner we can build. And then you can begin producing sons. Healthy, strapping boys who can one day take over from me.'

Kate's heart plummeted in her chest. She knew, of course, that as a woman she had very limited choices in life. But to have her father state the obvious so bluntly nonetheless struck her like a knife to the gut.

After skimming the headlines, he sent her an ominous stare. 'We will be attending a ball with the DeVrieses tonight, and hopefully by morning you will have secured some offers for your hand.'

Little did she know those words were sealing her fate.

Sebastian Wakefield, Duke of Mabury, stared down at the cards in his hand as if contemplating his next move.

'Your Grace?' the dealer asked. 'Do you stand or choose another?'

He placed the cards face down on the table. 'Another, if you please.'

Beside him, Viscount Derry let out a snort. 'Overly confident tonight, aren't you, Mabury?'

Sebastian nodded to the dealer as he accepted the card, glancing at it briefly. With his expression barely changing, he flicked his gaze to Derry. 'There is confidence, and then there is skill.'

The young pup didn't know the difference, and never would if the way he'd been playing in the last hour was any indication. Or even in the last four years he'd been a member of Brooks's. Indeed, Derry was known as an easy mark amongst the more seasoned card players in the club.

The dealer cleared his throat. 'Your Grace?'

'I stand.'

'Thank you. Now, gentlemen, if you please, reveal your cards.'

Without a trace of emotion on his face Sebastian turned his cards over—the jack of hearts, five of spades, and six of diamonds. Twenty-one.

'Devil take you, Mabury!' Derry exclaimed. 'How could you possibly win three rounds in a row and now get a twenty-one?'

The other players around the table grumbled unhappily but did not express their displeasure as vocally as the young Viscount.

Sebastian turned his freezing gaze on Derry. 'Are you accusing me of something, Lord Derry?'

'I—I'm merely pointing out the impossible,' Derry spluttered.

'His luck is extraordinary—especially at *vingt-un*.' Devon St James, Marquess of Ashbrooke, was the only one at the table who held no expression of disappointment, derision, or controlled fury on his face. In fact, he looked amused. 'Good game, Mabury.'

The glint in the Marquess's eyes said he knew Sebastian had been counting cards, and everyone else at the table was just too slow-witted to have realised it. It was something Sebastian had always been able to do—ever since he'd learned the game as a lad of twelve—and for the first few years he'd thought everyone else could do it. And as for Ashbrooke... Well, perhaps he was either bored or a glutton for punishment as he lost round after round.

Sebastian acknowledged the Marquess with a stiff nod before rising to his feet. 'If you'll excuse me, gentlemen? I am running late for my next appointment.'

'Appointment!' said Sir Harold Gibbet, the gentlemen beside him, with a glint in his eyes. 'I can guess what kind of "appointment" His Grace is off to.'

The other men chuckled and elbowed each other. 'Did you not get rid of your mistress months ago?' Derry asked. 'Have you not found a suitable replacement yet?'

'Maybe he's still in the process of taking applications,' Gibbet added.

'I don't recall you being so choosy,' Ashbrooke said. 'What was it we said during our university days? Any flirt in a skirt!'

A cold chill ran through Sebastian. 'I really must go.'

Ignoring the protests from the other men, he strode away from the table to the exit, and accepted his cloak from the waiting valet. He was about to cross the threshold when he heard someone call his name.

'Mabury! One moment!' Ashbrooke was just behind having followed him out. 'Where are you headed off to in such a hurry?' he asked, narrowing his gaze at him.

Sebastian stiffened, wondering if he should walk

away from the Marquess. However, experience told him that Ashbrooke would never let go of a subject until he got his answer. 'If you must know, I'm headed to the Houghton Ball.'

'The Houghton Ball?'

From the expression on the other man's face, one might have thought Sebastian had said, *I'm off to the gallows*. But, then again, to notorious rakes like Ashbrooke, such an event as the Houghton Ball would be the equivalent of death.

'Why ever would you go there?' the Marquess exclaimed. 'Have you finally decided to enter the marriage mart and leave our club?'

Sebastian frowned. 'I'm not giving up my membership at Brooks's.'

'I mean, leave our club of confirmed bachelors.' Ashbrooke let out an exasperated sigh. 'I truly was betting on you sticking around as long as I. In my case, that would hopefully mean they carry me out of Madame Claudette's at the grand old age of eighty, with a smile on my face and my little marquess—'

'Ashbrooke,' he warned. 'I am not looking for a wife.' *Never*. 'I'm simply meeting my mother at the ball. She asked me to escort her.'

'Ah.' Ashbrooke looked visibly relieved. 'Thank God. You're my only friend here, and I'd hate to lose you to the bonds of matrimony.'

'Your only friend?'

Years ago—in another lifetime—he might have considered Ashbrooke a friend. In fact, they'd once run in the same circles and indulged in the same vices. But not any more. Now Sebastian had no friends at all. Acquaintances, yes. Employees, servants, and tenants, definitely.

But he didn't count anyone as a friend. Not in the last five years, anyway.

'Yes. Friend. Confidant. Comrade. Call it what you will.' As if to prove his point, Ashbrooke clapped him on the shoulder.

'I couldn't call it anything. We are *not* friends. We haven't seen each other in years.'

'So?' Ashbrooke looked completely serious.

But, as Sebastian recalled, that was the kind of person he was—Ashbrooke could part ways with someone and not see them for a long time and then would just pick up where he'd left off.

'Good God, man,' he continued, exasperated. 'We've been playing and drinking together since our university days. Of course we'll always be friends.'

Sebastian did the only thing he could think of—he stared back. Ashbrooke was not the kind of friend he wanted these days.

'Anyway, old chap,' Ashbrooke said cheerily. 'How is the Dowager Duchess these days?'

Sebastian didn't know how to answer that question. 'The Dowager Duchess is...well.' That was the truth, he supposed. He cleared his throat. 'Now, if there is nothing else, I must leave now or I'll be late.'

Ashbrooke let out a bored sigh. 'Are you certain you'd rather go to that stuffy ball than stay? I know about a dozen other ways to spend an evening that would be more enjoyable.'

Sebastian knew exactly what those dozen ways were—which was why he was eager to decline. Five years ago he would not have thought twice about joining Ashbrooke. He might even have suggested it himself.

'I'm afraid I can't keep my mother waiting.'

'Of course...of course.' Ashbrooke's head bobbed

up and down. 'Please send my warmest regards to Her Grace, and make sure you avoid those marriage-minded mamas of the ton when they throw their daughters in your path.'

That almost made Sebastian smile. 'I will. Good evening, Ashbrooke.'

'Good evening, Mabury.'

He continued on his way out, towards the waiting carriage emblazoned with his ducal crest, its door held open by a footman. As he settled into the plush velvet seat and the carriage began to move he contemplated Ashbrooke's words.

With the Season in full swing, the Marquess was not incorrect. Many mothers of unmarried young ladies and misses would fix their gazes on him. Indeed, to members of the ton an eligible bachelor like him attending such a ball at this time of the year was akin to declaring his intentions to seek a wife. And that was why Sebastian hardly went to such affairs—not even before inheriting the Dukedom. He had not been eager to find a wife then, and he certainly wasn't looking for one now. *Or ever*, he added silently, bitterness coating his tongue.

And it was rare for his mother to attend any social event—at least since the death of Sebastian's father five years ago. In fact, if he recalled correctly, this was the first time she'd shown any sign of wanting to leave her home at all.

A strange tightness formed in his chest. Thankfully, the coach stopping distracted him, and as he peered outside he recognised the Earl of Houghton's home in Hanover Square. Damn, he was already late. He should have left earlier, but he'd miscalculated how long it would take him to get here. His mother would be cross with him, for sure. She was probably already inside.

Sebastian rushed up the steps into the house. A servant stopped him immediately and, having no patience tonight, he mumbled his name and title. The man had barely finished announcing his arrival before he rushed inside. He scanned the guests crowded into the ballroom for any sign of the Dowager Duchess, all the while ignoring the whispers beginning to grow around him.

'Mabury? Is that you?'

Sebastian's shoulders tensed and he turned around. 'Lady Caulfield,' he greeted the matronly woman who had approached him. 'Yes, it's me.'

Lady Caulfield peered up at him. 'My, my, I thought I had been transported back twenty years.' Her hand went to her chest. 'You look so much like your father. I thought you were him.'

Thankfully, the retort he wanted to hurl at the old crone got caught in the thickness coating his throat. Would he never get rid of the previous Duke of Mabury's long shadow? It was like the stench from something on his shoes he could never scrape off.

'If you'll excuse me, Lady Caulfield? I've just arrived and have yet to greet our host and hostess.'

With a quick nod, he walked away from her and found a quiet corner. Pausing, he unclenched his fists and his jaw, then continued to search the room for his mother.

Minutes ticked by, and despite his calm demeanour he became increasingly anxious as he found no sign of her. He ignored anyone trying to catch his gaze, lest they see it as an invitation to conversation—especially the bright-eyed mamas who, as Ashbrooke had predicted, looked ready to toss their daughters at his feet.

Perhaps his mother was resting in one of the retiring rooms somewhere. Or maybe she had been delayed and had yet to arrive. Or had planned to be fashionably late. In any case, the crowd made the ballroom stuffy and overheated, so he decided to head to the main reception room and wait for the Dowager Duchess to arrive.

A hush followed him as he wove through the crowd. And, try as he might, he could not shut his ears to the whispers around him.

'Mabury's here…'

'Dear God, he's the spitting image of his father…'

'And from what I heard, the similarities don't end there…'

'Well, we know how *he* turned out…'

'Five years,' Sebastian grumbled under his breath.

He'd stayed away for five years and the ton still hadn't forgotten about his father. Forgiven him, perhaps—because he did hold a coronet after all. But never forgotten.

Growing up, his father had been the ideal loving, doting parent, and Sebastian had returned his affection fiercely. He hadn't spent much time with his mother as Charles Wakefield had been his world and everything he'd needed. When he was young Charles had taught Sebastian how to ride and hunt. And as he'd got older there had been a different sort of hunting and riding that Sebastian had learned on his own. As a young man, he'd been a notorious rake and hadn't cared to hide it. He was the heir to a dukedom, after all.

Unbeknownst to him, his father had been pursuing his own pleasures. His world had shattered that day his father had died in a brothel fight. The father he'd adored had turned out to be a womaniser and a wastrel. The Mabury coffers had been drained and the estate in ruins. His love for his father had shrivelled and died.

And what had followed… Well…

Sebastian swallowed the lump forming in his throat. He would never do that to anyone. Could never subject another human being to that. Which was why he had vowed never to marry. No, the Wakefield line would end with him. *It was better that way.*

As he discreetly made his way to the other side of the ballroom, a high-pitched laugh caught his attention. 'How clever you are, my lord!' a nasal female voice said.

Sebastian halted and winced. It was hard to ignore it—surely everyone in the ballroom had heard it.

'That's them, isn't it?' said a man.

The stage whisper caught his attention, and he tuned his ears for more.

'Which ones? The Gardner sisters?'

'No, no,' the first man replied. 'The Americans.'

Americans? Here at the Houghton Ball?

His curiosity piqued, Sebastian turned his head, locating the two men who were just behind him, then following their gaze towards the corner of the room, where two young women stood surrounded by a gaggle of finely dressed gentlemen. He could clearly see the pretty face of the blonde one as she let out another godawful titter.

Sebastian was about to continue on his way when he noticed the woman next to her—and it was as if he had no choice but to continue staring.

The first thing he noticed were her dark locks, swept up artfully and gleaming like burnished mahogany under the light of the hundreds of candles in the ballroom. The same light made her creamy skin glow, adding an ethereal quality to her. She was not beautiful in the classical sense, yet there was something about her striking features that he could not ignore…not even from a short distance. He wondered what colour her eyes were.

'Rumour has it that the dark-haired one's father owns half of Manhattan Island.'

He stiffened as the two men behind him continued their conversation, but he was unable to stop himself from listening in.

'No wonder Newbery is circling her like a hawk looking for its next meal.'

'Hawk? More like a weasel.'

Sebastian scoffed to himself. That did sound like Newbery. The young lord was known to have run up his accounts at all the London clubs. And now he eyed the woman like the aforementioned rodent. A strange tightness gripped Sebastian's chest as she glanced over at Newbery, whose face lit up as he soaked up this minuscule bit of attention from her.

'I must admit she's quite pretty. Not as fashionably beautiful as the blonde. But she is…comely.'

Comely? Were these two men blind?

'Of course, there is the issue of her background…'

'Her dowry will more than make up for her lack of breeding and pedigree.'

'Yes, well…in Newbery's case, beggars should really be no choosers.'

They laughed in unison. And as the two men continued to gossip like a pair of old society matrons, Sebastian forced his gaze away from her. *Another American heiress on the hunt for a titled husband*, he huffed to himself.

Though he steered away from ton gossip, even he hadn't been able to escape the news about the Earl of Gablewood, who had been trapped by a rich American fur heiress two years ago. He wasn't surprised that more of these colonial princesses had now trickled into London's ballrooms and drawing rooms, hoping to lure in impoverished lords with their deep pockets.

Sebastian would never put himself in such a situation. Indeed, the very idea made his insides twist. After all, he'd spent the last five years undoing what his father had done and making up what that wastrel had lost.

And with the reminder of the old Duke his thoughts once again turned to his mother. So, as he'd attempted to do before he was distracted, he strode out to the main reception room, leaving all thoughts of the dark-haired beauty behind.

Once again, he stood to the side, scanning the arriving guests. Half an hour passed, and Sebastian knew he had to face the truth: His mother was not here and was clearly not coming to the ball after all.

Years of learning control—over his emotions, his actions, and reactions—allowed him to prevent the deep disappointment from showing on his face. He swallowed the lump in his throat and marched towards the exit. However, he stopped short when he saw the hostess herself, the Countess of Houghton, giving instructions to the butler who guarded the door.

Sebastian knew that if she saw him he would either have to explain to the Countess why he was leaving, or why his mother hadn't turned up. He had to make his escape—but to where?

It didn't matter where—only that he could wait somewhere until he could slip out unnoticed. And so, on a whim, he pivoted on his heel and headed towards the first door he laid eyes on.

Chapter Two

Because Arthur Mason willed it so, Kate was at the Houghton Ball that evening, dressed in her best ball-gown of blue silk and grey tulle, surrounded by a group of gentlemen who seemed as insipid and uninspiring as the tepid lemonade the hostess was serving.

'Lord Benton, you are so witty,' her blonde, blue-eyed companion tittered as she slapped the handsome young lord on his shoulder with her fan, then let out a high-pitched laugh that sounded like a cross between a goose's honk and a crying cow.

Kate didn't know how Caroline DeVries managed to smile for hours without her cheeks hurting. Or give false compliments to dim-witted men without utterly losing her mind.

But, then again, she shouldn't put anything past the vivacious young woman, who seemed completely set on bagging herself a lord. After all, that was the reason the DeVries family of Pittsburgh had come to London—to secure matches for their two daughters and elevate their standing in society.

Kate fought the urge to curl her fingers into fists. *I should have known it was no coincidence that we trav-*

elled with them. How obtuse she'd been, not realising her father's schemes.

From across the room, Arthur Mason's gaze landed on her with the force of a hammer on an anvil. He had warned her that he would not tolerate any attempt to dissuade the attentions of eligible gentlemen. And so, since Caroline attracted said gentlemen like bees to honey, she decided to stay by the younger woman's side—if only to appease her father.

When the conversation slowed down, Kate cleared her throat. 'Gentlemen, I fear I'm feeling fatigued and parched.'

'Shall I fetch you some lemonade, Miss Mason?' asked Mr George Moseby, who was in line for a viscountcy from a distant uncle.

'Oh, let me,' Lord Wembleton insisted. 'It would be my honour.'

Caroline spoke up. 'Kate, you do look quite flushed and…wilted.' The slightest sneer appeared on her lips. 'Perhaps you should have a rest inside one of the retiring rooms instead?'

Thank you, Caroline.

'A wonderful idea.' Turning on her slippered feet, Kate marched away from the group. However, she had no intention of going into one of the retiring rooms. What she needed was some privacy and some fresh air.

She tried to appear casual as she made her way across the ballroom through the throng of guests. Finally she reached her intended destination—a door on the far side of the room that would lead to the gardens outside. Just before the dancing had started, she'd heard Lord Houghton boast to a few of the guests that he had one of the most beautiful gardens in London, and then he had led them out through this door. Surely by now they would be gone, and Kate would be able to get a much-needed break from the stifling atmosphere of the house and have a few precious minutes alone.

As she stepped out into the gardens she took a deep breath. The crisp, late-winter air was just the balm she needed. Her tutor back in New York had warned her numerous times never to be caught alone anywhere during a ball, and certainly not unchaperoned with a gentleman. Of course Kate had focused on the 'never be caught' part. Besides, surely that rule wasn't strictly imposed. For how did anyone get any rest at these dreadful balls that could go on until the wee hours of the morning?

Kate continued down a stone-covered path. The full moon shone above, and only a few torches had been scattered about, but they were enough to guide her through the rows of hedges. She gasped in delight as she spied a large structure up ahead. Springing forward, she made her way to the centrepiece of the gardens—a glorious white marble fountain. Water sprang from the top and cascaded down to a second level before streaming out from the mouths of the carved lion heads decorating the third tier.

She drew closer—not only because she wanted to cool herself, but also to observe the fountain's mechanics. Taking off her left glove, she skidded her fingers over the surface of the water. She wondered if the fountain was powered by a mechanical pump or simply through hydro—

A prickle on the back of her neck made her halt. She was no longer alone.

Her instincts were proved correct as she turned around.

Indeed, there was someone in the gardens with her. A

male someone. Though she'd never seen him before—
or anyone quite like him.

He was dark-haired, and tall, but unlike many of the
more refined gentlemen of the ton he had broad shoulders that looked barely contained underneath the black
fabric of his coat. The moonlight illuminated sharply
handsome features and dark eyes—and those onyx orbs
were fixed on her. The look he was giving her was like
nothing she'd ever seen from any gentlemen before.

Many men looked at her with adoration, fascination,
even curiosity. But this man... Something about his gaze
made her throat go dry and a thrill crawl down the back
of her knees. An unknown emotion passed fleetingly
across his face, before a hint of a sneer made the corners of his mouth pull back. Kate felt the wave of con-
tempt from his arrogant stare.

Something about this scenario sparked a memory
in her, something in one of the books she'd recently
read. In her haste to pack for the voyage to England she
hadn't considered how tedious two weeks on a steamship
would be, and hadn't brought anything for entertainment except for her diary and a few well-worn engineering books. She had had to make do with whatever
books had been in her suite, including a few volumes
of Shakespeare.

"'Ill met by moonlight, proud Titania.'"

'Does that make you the jealous Oberon?' he asked.

She blinked. 'I beg your pardon?'

'Shakespeare. *A Midsummer Night's Dream.* Act
Two.'

Despite the flatness of his tone, the deep timbre of
his voice brought on that strange feeling again. 'Yes,
I've read it. What about—?'

Oh, dear. He was either a mind-reader, or she had said

those words aloud. The heat of embarrassment crept up her neck, and she prayed he wouldn't notice the flush that must surely be evident on her face.

Silence stretched between them as seconds ticked by. He seemed unaware of the awkwardness, so she spoke again. 'Have we met before, sir?'

'I can't say we have.'

What was that supposed to mean? And why was she scrambling for more words to say to him? Her instincts screamed that this man was nothing like those foppish gentlemen back in the ballroom. There was an air of danger about him, as well as a kind of cunning that told her he was not one to be trifled with.

Which meant that if anyone should find them out here, unchaperoned... Well, her tutor's warning suddenly rang clear in her mind.

'I should make haste and head inside. Since we have not been properly introduced.' Her reputation would be in tatters if anyone found out. 'I shall trust in your discretion, sir.'

Picking up her skirts, she was about to slide past him when he spoke again. 'Yet it was not I who was splashing about in a fountain like some fairy sprite.'

A flash of temper made her stop and turn her head towards him. '"Splashing about"? You make it sound like I was cavorting inside the fountain with water up to my knees!'

She knew one should never mention body parts in polite company—but, blast it, something about this man made her forget about propriety.

His steely gaze caught hers. 'A young foreign miss alone in the gardens would give anyone the impression that she was, indeed, cavorting.'

She bit her tongue to stop herself from saying what

was really on her mind. 'And I suppose you are innocent? Do you make a habit of crawling about darkened
corners quoting Shakespeare to young women?'

'It was you who quoted Shakespeare.' The left corner of his mouth twitched. Almost like a smile, but one
that he caught before it had a chance to become fully
realised.

'I didn't mean to quote the Bard.' Kate bit the inside
of her cheek. 'And if I had, I would have picked something better. Like something from *Othello* or *Richard III.*'

'Something better?' A dark brow quirked up. 'Pretty
girls and handsome Athenians falling in love—what
more could a young woman ask for in a story?'

'Please...' she huffed. 'None of those people in that
play were truly in love—except perhaps for poor Pyramus and Thisbe.' She grinned at the memory of the antics of Bottom and his friends in Act Five. 'Everyone
was "in love" with those who appeared attractive to
them, without much thought to personality or character. Or just with the aid of magic. That's not real love.'

'And do you believe in love?'

'I—' She stopped, her mouth hanging open for one
second before she clamped it shut. The superficiality
of the love between the characters in the play had been
obvious to her. But love in real life...? Did she believe
in such a thing? How did one even begin to understand
such a concept? It was not something she could examine and take apart and put back together again. And
since that was not possible she could not give a defini-
tive answer as to whether she believed in love or not.

His magnetic eyes held hers once again. Another
pulse of a thrill shot through her, starting somewhere
in her stomach and spreading up to her chest.

'Of course you do,' he stated, before she could put

words together to form a sentence. 'A young eligible miss like yourself is always on the lookout for a good match.'

'And you, sir?' she shot back. 'You aren't at this ball looking for a match?'

'No,' he replied flatly. 'I shall never marry.'

'But what about heirs?' Kate inhaled a sharp breath. What in the world had possessed her to ask such a question of a stranger?

'What about them?' The dark eyes turned flinty.

Did he mean he didn't need them? Or want them? *Why should I care?*

But Kate could not help herself. That hard, determined expression on his face only made her itch to know more. 'You're a man. Don't all men have the urge to… uh…go forth and multiply?' Heat tingled up her cheeks, warming them despite the cool evening air.

A giggle and the sound of footsteps made them both go still. Oh, dear Lord, someone would find them here. While she had known it was risky to come out to the gardens alone, the reality that she really could be compromised struck her like lightning. If she were to be ruined, then no aristocratic lord would have her. What her father would do if that happened, she didn't know, but the thought of it filled her chest with dread.

She glanced around, searching for a way out even as the whispers and footsteps grew louder. Fear and panic drove her to do something she would never dream of doing. Pushing at her companion's chest, she cornered him behind one of the hedges. Her breath caught in her throat as his form caged her body.

Dear God, he was a stranger. She had no idea who he was…what he was doing here. If anyone found them, her reputation would be ruined. He was unknown to her.

This man who held her in what anyone would surmise was an embrace—albeit one she'd initiated—in darkened gardens on a moonlit night.

Kate would bet no other young woman would have such a ruination as she.

'Stay still,' he whispered, his lips hovering just above her temple. 'We will wait for them to leave.'

He was so close to her…not quite touching…but she could feel the warmth of his body even through the layers of clothing between them.

She closed her eyes, biting her lip to stop herself from crying out or laughing at the absurdity of this whole situation. Hopefully, things would get better from here on.

'Lord Newbery, please…' came a breathy female voice.

'Please what, sweet? Please stop? Or please continue?' a male voice asked, followed by a whimper and the unmistakable sigh of pleasure.

Oh, dear, things weren't getting better. Not even by an inch. No, they were now on their way to disaster.

Panic rose in her as her instinct screamed at her to flee. But any noise or disturbance would surely alert the amorous couple.

Looks like I have no choice.

'My lord…you must stop.'

'You're so beautiful, Caroline. I can't help it.'

Caroline?

'But you must!' The woman giggled in a nasal tone. 'Please, my lord.'

That was definitely Caroline DeVries.

'One more, darling. Please…'

'Well…since you asked…' The unmistakable sound of passionate, wet mouths meeting followed.

Oh, for heaven's sake!

With a resigned sigh, Kate leaned her head against her stranger's shoulder.

Her stranger? It was an absurd thought, but then again here she was, trapped between a hedge and his chest. The scent of his cologne tickled her nose. Not that it was unpleasant. It was…unnerving, to say the least. She'd never been this close to any man, after all. Not in this way.

'My lord, I must insist… My mother will be looking for me by now.'

'I… Of course, Caroline.' Newbery cleared his throat. 'I know a separate exit that will lead me to the front. You take the door that leads back to the ballroom.'

'You are so wise, my lord.'

There were a few more whispers that Kate didn't quite catch, followed by two separate sets of footsteps fading in opposite directions.

Kate let out a relieved breath. Finally, the couple was gone. Bracing her hands on his chest, she gave the man a soft push. However, he didn't budge.

She frowned, then pushed a little harder.

He remained in position, unmoving.

'Sir?' she said softly. 'The coast, as they say, is clear.' When still he didn't respond, she lifted her gaze to meet his. 'Sir…?'

Dark onyx eyes were fixed on her, and now that the fear of being caught had dissipated a different kind of sensation filled her. One that reminded her of how close they remained, even though their bodies didn't touch. Her lips parted as her dress suddenly felt too constricting, as if her corset had laced itself tighter.

The sudden loss of his warmth told her he had moved away from her. Taking in a sharp breath, she opened her eyes.

A myriad of expressions was crossing his handsome face. He looked as if he had been possessed by some other consciousness and was only now returning to his senses. That arrogant mask soon settled back on his face. Shock and shame at their closeness filled her, making her cheeks flame as if someone had set a match to them.

And for the first time in her life Kate did something she'd never thought she'd do when faced with a conundrum—she turned and ran in the opposite direction.

When Kate saw her father at breakfast the next morning, he minced no words with her.

'You will go to the DeVries suite as soon as you are finished with breakfast,' he stated. 'Since it seems you've no gentlemen callers, no gifts, nor letters or cards, I can only assume your hasty exit during the ball has warded off any potential suitors. So Mrs DeVries and I have secured the services of a well-regarded chaperone—the Honourable Harriet Merton.'

'A chaperone?' she echoed.

Arthur continued as if she had not spoken. 'We have written to her and told her of our requirements, and she has agreed to teach you and the DeVries girls about English etiquette and society. Miss Merton has the right connections to ensure you secure a match with a lord. From now on you will spend every moment of your time with Miss Merton, learning everything you need to know about moving amongst the upper class. Besides, seeing as young Caroline is attracting the right kind of suitors, perhaps some of her charm and influence will rub off on you.'

Taking a delicate sip of her tea, Kate calmed herself

before speaking. 'Father, surely there is another way to get the factory built and establish the railway company?'

'No one wants to deal with unknown Americans,' Arthur stated. 'And they think our knowledge and machines are inferior.'

'Inferior?' The cup clattered loudly on the saucer as Kate set it down. 'Have they never heard of the Andersen?' she fumed. 'Perhaps we should go back to America and continue expanding westward instead. With a brand-new locomotive design we'll be able to scale the mountainous terrain and—'

'Westward?' Arthur sneered. 'And what would expanding the rail out west do? What's out there anyway? Just dirt and rocks and sand. No, with the current upturn in the English railway industry I must get in now, or lose this opportunity to increase our holdings.'

'Of course all you care about is money,' she huffed. 'What about progress and—?'

'Are you trying to defy me, Kathryn?' The air in the room grew thick as Arthur Mason shot her a frigid stare.

'Father, all I'm saying is—'

'If you do not find an English husband in the next few weeks, then I'll consider this whole trip a lost investment.' His voice remained cool, but the force behind his words was unmistakable. 'And you know I do not like it when my investments don't return a profit.'

It stung that Arthur Mason saw her—his only child—as just another number in his ledger, but Kate supposed she shouldn't have expected otherwise.

'Finding a husband—and a titled one—isn't like going to the market and picking up fresh vegetables.'

'Do not be impertinent with me, young lady,' he warned. 'You will find a husband, or we will go back to New York and you will be married to a man of my choosing. And you can bet that, whoever it will be, he won't allow you to set foot in any factory or engine room again.'

Shock made her clamp her mouth shut. Arthur never made empty threats—especially when it came to business. 'If that is all, I would like to be excused.' She would not cry in front of him. Not over this.

His nose wrinkled, but the victory on his face was evident. Then again, Kate had never really stood a chance.

'You may go.'

As she stood up, the butler strode in to announce a visitor. 'Mr Malvery is here, Mr Mason.'

As if her morning could get any worse. Waiting just outside was another man she wished never to cross paths with again. Her second cousin—Jacob Malvery. He had been sent to London a few weeks ahead of their arrival, and Kate counted herself lucky that she hadn't seen him since New York. Of course, she had known her luck was bound to run out sooner or later.

Her father folded his hands together. 'Ah, just in time. Send him in.'

Jacob was a sycophantic, odious toad who hung on her father's every word. His greatest crime, however, was calling himself an engineer. Some years ago he had come to Mason R&L to apprentice under Pap, but from the first day it had become obvious that Jacob had exaggerated his own abilities.

Pap had thrown him out of the factory a mere three days later, when he had nearly caused an explosion. Her father had then put him to work somewhere his skills would be more appreciated—in the boardroom of Mason R&L, negotiating with government officials and landowners to help pave the way for the expansion of their rail lines.

'Good morning, Arthur,' Jacob fawned as he entered.

His suit looked brand-new—probably from one of the fine tailors on Savile Row. Kate heard others refer to him as handsome, with his wavy blond hair and bright green eyes, but then again, she knew what was behind that smile.

'And I must be the luckiest man on earth! The lovely Kate is here as well. How are you today, Cousin?'

Kate gave him a perfunctory nod. 'Cousin Jacob,' she managed to say without choking.

His eyes ran up and down her figure. 'Leaving already?'

'I'm afraid so.' She rounded the table, making her way to the side opposite him. 'I can't keep Mrs DeVries waiting.'

'Ah, how unfortunate for me.'

Her father waved him over to sit on his right side, then turned to her. 'Remember what we talked about, Kathryn,' he said, and then looked at Jacob meaningfully. 'Jacob will be joining us for dinner tonight.'

This time she did not miss the telling glance her father sent her, nor the weight of implication in his words. Jacob would be the man of Arthur's choosing if she did not find an English lord to wed.

She swallowed the bile rising in her throat. 'I shall see you both then.'

Whirling around, she trudged out of the dining area of their suite. Once she was certain she was far away enough, she balled her hands into fists and let out a soft, unladylike shriek.

Damn that scheming, vile man!

If he couldn't get a return on his investment then Arthur Mason would find another way she could be useful— namely, keeping his fortune in the family. And since he didn't have a coveted son, the only way to do that was to marry his only child off to an heir of his choosing.

The thought made Kate want to lose the breakfast she had hardly touched.

While he might be an incompetent engineer, Jacob was as sly and ambitious as her father. Jacob had always boasted about wanting to see his name immortalised on buildings and locomotives. If Jacob were ever in charge of Mason R&L he would turn it into some kind of monument to his legacy, and all Pap's work would be gone like dead ash from burning coal.

Pap didn't work himself to the bone just to have that taken away from him. I would rather never step foot in any factory again than let that egomaniac take over.

Somehow she had to find a way out of this. If Pap were here he would tell her to buck up, use her head, and find a solution.

No, she would not run away from her predicament. For now, she was merely making a tactical retreat, so she could sit down and figure out how to solve her Marriage Problem. While it seemed hopeless now, she was not one to give up. Hell's bells, she could figure out what was wrong with an engine just by listening to it. There was no hurdle too big for her—not if she put her mind to work. But to do that she would have to be just as sneaky and underhand as Arthur Mason.

Heading out, Kate made her way to the DeVries suite, just one floor below. She was not looking forward to spending the day with the insufferable Caroline and her equally insufferable mother, but at least she would be around Maddie, the elder of the two DeVries daughters. Maddie was more like her father, Cornelius DeVries, and father and daughter were just as close as Kate and

Pap had been. In fact, the two men had been the reason she and Maddie had become friends.

A few years ago, she and Pap had travelled to Pennsylvania to visit the iron forges, in order to source materials for their engines and tracks. Eventually they had settled on the DeVries Furnace and Iron Company as her grandfather had got on well with the owner, Cornelius DeVries.

Cornelius was an eccentric and boisterous businessman, and perhaps Pap had seen himself in the other man. Or maybe seen him as the son he'd wished Arthur had been. Pap had been particularly impressed that Cornelius, having no sons of his own, had encouraged his own daughter's interest in metallurgy. Just as Kate had grown up by Pap's side, Maddie had been learning the science of forging at her father's knee.

It was too bad Maddie hadn't been there at the Houghton Ball. According to her mother, she'd been feeling ill. Kate, however, could guess why Maddie hadn't attended. Though she thought Maddie more beautiful than Caroline—both in her heart and her looks—the elder DeVries daughter had always felt self-conscious about her 'unfashionable' stature.

The maid who answered Kate's knock led her to the luxurious sitting room, where Maddie and Caroline were already waiting.

She gave Caroline a perfunctory nod before turning to her friend. 'Maddie, good morning. I'm sorry to have missed you at the ball. I hope you are feeling better?'

'I am, thank you.' Maddie got to her feet and gave her a warm embrace.

Once released from the hug, Kate looked up to meet her friend's gaze. And, truly, she did look up, for while Maddie, too, had received the same stunning looks from their Dutch heritage as Caroline had, she was also the unfortunate recipient of another of their qualities—their towering height. Even in her flat satin slippers Maddie stood nearly six feet tall, a fact much bemoaned by their mother.

As if to compensate, Eliza DeVries dressed her elder daughter in pastels and other light colours, which made Maddie look even more comical—like an overgrown doll. Today, she wore a light blue frock edged with an inordinate amount of white lace, making Kate wonder if it had been designed by a cake maker.

'Caroline? Madeline?' Eliza DeVries called as she breezed into the sitting room. Some might describe her as beautiful, and indeed she was, with her delicate face, flaxen hair, and slim figure. However, Kate didn't care much for the woman's character. Instead of being satisfied with their vast wealth, Eliza was obsessed with seeking a higher status for her family, and hell-bent on using her daughters to achieve this goal.

'And, Kate, you're already here. Good.' Eliza DeVries turned to the woman who strode in behind her. 'Welcome, Miss Merton. May I present Miss Kate Mason, Arthur's daughter, and my own two daughters, Caroline and Madeline. Ladies, this is the Honourable Miss Harriet Merton.'

'How do you do?' Miss Merton's bright blue eyes sparkled as she smiled at them warmly. 'I am so glad to be here and to meet you young ladies.'

Kate hadn't been sure what Miss Harriet Merton would be like, but she certainly hadn't expected this. In fact, she'd rather imagined a stodgy old maid who would slap their hands with her cane if they so much as slouched, not this sweet and charming woman before them. Harriet Merton looked to be a few years younger than Eliza, and though she wore a spinster's lace cap, her bright yellow morning gown and light blue shawl matched her sunny disposition.

'Why don't I call for tea?' Eliza began, then nodded to the young maid standing in the corner. After exchanging a few more pleasantries, they all settled down. 'Miss Merton, allow me to thank you once again for answering our letters. Your assistance in navigating the Season will be utterly welcome and much needed.'

'I must admit I was intrigued when I read your letter, and Mr Mason's.' Miss Merton glanced over at Caroline. 'Caroline, you're just as beautiful as your mother says. And Madeline and Kate,' she said, turning to where the two of them sat together on the sofa. 'Mrs DeVries and Mr Mason were quite…fervent in their descriptions of you both.'

Kate bit her tongue. She could only imagine her father's commentary about her. 'I'm sure he was most detailed.'

There was a gleam in Miss Merton's eyes that Kate did not miss. 'Yes, well… I must admit you all intrigue me. Over the years I've been asked to chaperone and guide many a young miss as she travails the Season, but I've never met any Americans.'

'And what have you heard about us?' Kate bit out, which earned her a reproachful look from Eliza.

'Nothing terrible, I assure you,' Miss Merton said with a laugh. 'Only that you American girls can be quite…spirited. Not a bad thing, mind you. But here in England things are very different.'

'Indeed they are,' Eliza piped in. 'Which is why we need your help. We have been in London for over a fortnight, and yet we have not met any respectable gentlemen. I was told we needed to be seen at the right places, so we used my husband's and Arthur's connections to secure an invitation to the Houghton Ball. Maddie was feeling ill, so she did not attend, but Caroline and Kate were surrounded by a host of gentlemen throughout the evening. And yet not one has sent a gift or come calling. They're both heiresses with sizeable dowries!'

'Mrs DeVries,' Miss Merton began gently. 'To those who did not grow up in England the rules of the English aristocracy can be quite confusing. And sometimes... er...wealth is not always the solution.'

Caroline seemed perturbed. 'What about Cecilia Lefebvre?'

Miss Merton frowned. 'Who?'

'You know,' Caroline said, exasperated. 'Her father made a fortune in the fur trade in Canada. The Lefebvres were unwelcome in many of New York's society parlours and ballrooms. That is until she went to London and came back as the Countess of Gablewood. When she returned to New York with her Earl, everyone fell over themselves trying to get into their good graces.'

'Ah, yes, I've heard of the Countess...' Miss Merton wrinkled her nose. 'I'm afraid she's more of the exception, rather than the rule.'

Eliza pursed her lips. 'Then what must we do if their dowries aren't enough?'

'I'm not saying they are not enough,' Miss Merton clarified. 'But surely you do not want to attract fortune-hunters and scoundrels? There are other methods of finding a good, respectable husband.'

'I don't care if he's good or respectable, as long as he has a title,' Caroline declared. 'I'll go as low as a viscount, but I'm setting my sights on being a duchess.'

'I should like someone gentle and caring,' Maddie added. 'A man who would be a loving father to our children.'

'So, what do you think, Miss Merton?' Eliza said. 'Will you help us?'

Miss Merton laughed. 'Of course, Mrs DeVries. I made up my mind when I read your letters.'

'You did?'

'Yes,' she said with a nod. 'In fact, I am about to tell you one effective way of navigating the Season—and that is with a sponsor. The stamp of approval from an influential patron could lead to many more opportunities for the girls.'

'A sponsor?' Eliza's eyes grew wide. 'Where would we get such a person? And how much would one cost?'

'If a sponsor can help me land a lord, then surely Papa will pay for one,' Caroline added.

'Oh, dear girl, I'm afraid one cannot pay for such a service.' Miss Merton shook her head. 'But I have already written to a potential sponsor. The widow of a distant cousin of mine, who happens to be a dowager duchess.'

'A duchess?' Eliza's eyes gleamed with excitement, and Caroline covered her hand with her mouth.

'Yes, when I read about you young misses I knew she would be the perfect sponsor.' When Miss Merton mentioned 'misses', however, her eyes darted over to Kate and Maddie. 'And, well... The reason I came here right away was to give you some good news. Her Grace the Dowager Duchess of Mabury has agreed to meet you and discuss the possibility of becoming your sponsor for the Season.'

This time Caroline could not hold on to her delight as she let out a gleeful shriek. 'A duchess sponsoring me? This is fantastic news!'

'Oh, dear.' Eliza fanned herself with her hand. 'This is...quite astonishing, Miss Merton. Now I know why you came so highly recommended. I cannot thank you enough.'

'Do not thank me yet, Mrs DeVries,' Miss Merton warned. 'I'm sure you will understand that as her own reputation is at stake Her Grace will want to meet the girls first, before officially agreeing to sponsor them. And so she has invited us all to stay at the ducal estate, Highfield Park in Surrey, for a few days, to assess the ladies'…er…dispositions and suitability.'

Eliza's head bobbed up and down like a cork in water. 'Of course. Whatever she wants.'

'I was actually quite surprised that Her Grace responded right away.' A strained look briefly passed across Miss Merton's face. 'Since her husband died she has not been seen in society. It's quite tragic, actually…'

'What happened?' Maddie asked, leaning forward.

'Madeline!' Eliza warned. 'We do not gossip about people we don't know. Especially not someone who is being so kind as to open her doors to us. Apologies, Miss Merton. We will start preparing immediately.'

Kate stifled the urge to groan aloud at the thought of spending a few days in some lofty English estate. She did not have time to perform like a show pony for an aristocratic society matron. Not when her grandfather's legacy was at stake.

She chewed at her lip. If this was an engineering problem, how would she solve it?

'Not every obstacle is a setback,' Pap had used to say. *'You might find a way to turn it into an opportunity.'*

Right now, however, an English lord sounded much more appealing than Jacob taking over Mason R&L— even if it did mean she might never work on her own engine. While the thought deflated her, just imagining the words *Malvery R&L* emblazoned on the side of an Andersen engine filled her with so much rage she couldn't think straight. It was the lesser of two evils. If nothing else, she could use this opportunity to delay her marriage to Jacob and give her more time to think of a solution to her Marriage Problem.

Chapter Three

The moment his carriage left the crowded streets of London behind, Sebastian blew out a breath. But it wasn't because of the smog and stench of town. Well, perhaps that was part of it, but his disdain for London only grew the longer he stayed there. Usually, he did not linger in the city for long—three days at most, perhaps—but there had been urgent business he'd needed to attend to, which had delayed his departure. At least that was what he told himself.

With his mind idle, his thoughts drifted to the Houghton Ball and, more specifically, to the dark-haired beauty in the garden. How a short, innocent encounter with one girl—an American at that—had somehow burned itself into his memory, Sebastian did not know.

But he needed to forget about her. Forget about those mesmerising eyes the colour of cornflowers and the creamy, soft pale skin of her neck. Forget about how she'd smelled of fresh powder and lemons and the warmth of her body. Though he had not got the chance to find out in detail, he just knew that her curves would fit perfectly into his and—

Devil take me!

Leaning on the side of the plush seat of his coach, he massaged his temple with his thumb and forefinger. *I should have left London earlier.* As he had lingered in town he'd found himself looking over his shoulder or glancing outside his carriage every so often, wondering if he'd see her on the street, coming out of some shop or tea room.

Perhaps now that he had left London those memories of her would fade away and completely disappear. Once he breathed in the sweet air of the country he would stop thinking about the warmth of her body or the weight of her head on his shoulder. And what a pretty head it had been. He remembered glancing at her from across the ballroom and thinking her beautiful, but up close, under the bright full moon, she had been exquisite.

Of course it had turned out that head of hers wasn't empty or—worse—filled with fluff. Hidden beneath those gorgeous layers was a woman who had a mind of her own, and damned if that wasn't what had aroused him the most about her.

A jostle from the carriage wheels going over a stone or a stray tree branch knocked him out of his reverie.

The tightness in his chest loosened even more as they drove further and further away from the soot and grime of the city. One good thing about his thoughts being filled with the mystery woman was that he'd hardly had time to think about his mother's failure to arrive at the Houghton Ball. But, then again, he should be used to it by now. He'd been disappointed many times before, and why he had thought this time would be different, he didn't know.

'The ride over seemed too long, Sebastian.'
'I tried, darling, I did.'

'I just couldn't bring myself to get out of bed.'

So many excuses. Perhaps one of these days he'd eventually be done with her and he'd stick to the vow he made each time she didn't show up: to leave her to her languishing and never attempt to see her again.

Still, she was his mother, and he loved her dearly. How he longed to see her as she'd used to be, before the ugliness of the events of five years ago had drained her of joy. Before his father had destroyed Sebastian's love and faith in him. In everything.

His mind drifted back to the mysterious woman in the garden. He should have left the moment he'd discovered her, but he'd found himself intrigued, even answering her questions. She'd been right about the ball being the place to look for a match. But, as he'd told her, he was never marrying or siring an heir. He had a distant cousin who lived in Hertfordshire. He would leave the title and the estate to him. Sebastian would be the last of the Wakefields to hold the title Duke of Mabury.

When he'd been alive, Charles Wakefield had doted on his only son and heir. Sebastian had been made to feel like the most important person in the world. But little had he known that once he had arrived Charles had no longer needed anyone else—especially his wife. She'd given him the heir he needed, so he'd been free to do as he pleased. To carouse and frolic all over London. It was how things were done in their circles after all. It was what Charles's father had done and probably what Sebastian would have done if he had married.

But the cycle would end with him. That was the vow he'd made to his mother that day that had changed his life, though she might not have heard him say the words.

The coach slowing told Sebastian that they were nearly at Highfield Park, and a few minutes later it halted. A uniformed footman held the door open and he breathed in the fresh air, his boots crunching on the gravel as he alighted. As he made his way to the front door he stopped. *Something was not quite right.* Turning his head, he saw that only half his household staff were lined up to greet him.

He frowned. Not that he cared much for ceremony, but his butler certainly did. The staid and decorous Eames, who had been the butler at Highfield Park ever since Sebastian could remember, took pride in ensuring that the house ran with military-like precision, with the staff acting like his little soldiers and doing his bidding. Indeed, Eames only had to give a wayward servant one glacial stare or the lift of a thick eyebrow to put them in their place.

Today, however, the usually reliable Eames was not even amongst those here now to welcome him home.

'Higgins,' he said to the head footman, who was at the end of the receiving line. 'Was someone sent ahead to tell Eames of my arrival?'

'Yes, Your Grace.'

'Then where is he? And the rest of the staff?'

The man's jaw ticked. 'The others and Eames are... er...occupied at the moment, Your Grace.'

'Occupied? Do you mean sick?' Eames must be deathly ill, because not even the plague would stop the butler from getting out of bed in the morning.

'No, Your Grace. Eames is busy getting the house in order.'

'What do you mean? I've only been gone a little over a week. What could possibly have gone out of order in that time?'

Higgins's brows drew together. 'Your Grace, I thought you knew...'

'Knew what?' he said, his patience running thin.

'Your Grace, she—that is your—'

The door suddenly swinging open interrupted Higgins. 'Who in the world is—?' It was Eames, whose eyes bulged like a day-old fish's eyes the moment his gaze landed on Sebastian. 'Your Grace!' His face turned red. 'Your Grace, I have only just received word of your arrival! Forgive me for not ensuring you were properly welcomed back.' He bowed his head deeply. 'I take full responsibility.'

'You are forgiven, Eames. But tell me—where is the rest of the staff?' Glancing inside the house, he saw two maids scurry by, their baskets filled with fresh linen, while a footman nearly collided with them as he carried an enormous silver candlestick. 'And what in heaven's name is going on?'

'Your Grace… Were you not…informed?'

'Of what?'

'Of the Dowager Duchess's arrival.'

Sebastian opened his mouth, then quickly clamped it shut lest it remained hanging open for all his servants to see—well, half of them. Composing himself, he managed to say, 'It seems Her Grace's visit has caught all of us by surprise.'

Eames straightened his shoulders and his usual cool, efficient mask slipped into place. 'So it seems, Your Grace.' He cleared his throat. 'The Dowager Duchess did ask that you meet her in her private sitting room as soon as you are able. Would you like to refresh yourself beforehand?'

Sebastian ignored Eames and instead strode directly inside. He didn't know what had possessed him, but something inside him had to know if his mother really was here. Because surely this had to be a cruel joke of some kind. Miranda, Dowager Duchess of Mabury, had not stepped foot into Highfield Park in years. Not since she'd left five years ago.

A knot formed in his chest as he made his way to the Duchess's private sitting room on the east side of the manor. Ignoring the tremor in his hand as he reached for the doorknob, he turned it. His hopes for a quiet arrival were dashed, however, by the loud creaking sound of the hinge.

'Oh, dear, we really should get one of the footmen to oil that.'

The familiar crisp voice sounded like hers. And the figure in profile standing by the window looked like hers. Yes, the beautiful face that turned to him was indeed that of his mother. Still, every instinct learned from the last five years prevented him from believing it was actually her. For one thing, this woman was fully dressed in a lovely purple morning gown, her hair pinned up meticulously, her back straight as an arrow. In the few times he'd visited his mother in the last five years she had either been abed in her night rail or slumped in a chair by the fireplace, her hair in disarray.

He swallowed the lump forming in his throat and stepped inside. 'Mother?'

'Sebastian.' Turning forty-five degrees on her heel, she strode to him, her steps light as air. 'Darling, what a wonderful coincidence that we have arrived at nearly the same time. I was hoping I wouldn't have to wait too long for you.'

He searched her face. While the lines of strain around her eyes and the paleness of her skin would have worried anyone else, to Sebastian they at least looked familiar. This told him she was not a spectre of his imagination.

'Mother. I'm glad to see you here.'

A million questions went through his mind. What was she doing here? Why hadn't she shown up at the ball? How had she managed to get herself out of bed this time? And was she going to stay?

'You look as if you've seen a ghost.' A slip of a smile curled her lips. 'I hope you do not mind me coming unannounced?'

'Of course not—you are always welcome here,' he blurted. His mind still reeled at the fact that she stood before him.

'Come, let us sit.'

She dragged him to the sofa and sat him down as if he were a boy in short pants again. And he let her—because, frankly, he was agog to know what had lured his mother out of her hermit-like state.

'You must be surprised at my turning up all of a sudden,' she began, as if reading his mind. 'Are you cross with me about not coming to the Houghton Ball?'

Yes. And all those other times, as well, he wanted to say, but bit his tongue. 'Of course not, Mother. I'm sure you had good reason.' And she needn't explain because he'd already heard all her excuses before. 'But what are you doing here?'

She folded her hands in her lap. 'Did you mean what you said? About my being welcome here?'

Like most ducal estates, Highfield Park had a dower house about a mile from the main manor, but following his father's death his mother had instead opted to move to one of their smaller estates in Hertfordshire, which had been part of her original dowry. Sebastian had buried the hurt that she didn't want to live near him, because he most of all understood *why*. No matter how much he tried, or how hard he worked, the shadow of his father was there—and Sebastian's face was a constant reminder of what her husband had done to her.

'You two are like two peas in a pod,' his mother would always joke in those early years. *'You'd think he was the one that bore you.'*

Indeed, when he looked in the mirror he could see that the only thing he'd inherited from his mother were her eyes. They had been so alike Sebastian would wake up in a pool of sweat some nights, after the same nightmare plagued him: he would be looking in a mirror, and instead of his own reflection he would see Charles Wakefield with a knife in his chest.

'Sebastian?'

He nodded at her. 'Of course, Mother. Stay as long as you please.'

'Excellent.' A wider smile lit up her face, reminding him of a wilted flower slowly coming to life after being given water. 'I hope you don't mind...but there is a reason I wanted to come here.'

'You don't need a reason to come here.'

'Yes, well...' She fiddled with a bit of lace on her gown. 'It's not just for myself, you see.'

'Bring as many staff as you like to make your stay comfortable.'

Eames would probably grumble in private at having to accommodate more servants downstairs, but the loyal butler would find a way.

'No, darling, not servants. I'd like to invite some guests to stay.'

'You mean entertain?' A spark of hope flashed in his chest. The Dowager Duchess of Mabury had not mingled with society in years. However, his instinct extinguished that hope, fearing disappointment once again.

'Not exactly.' Her lips pursed. 'Sebastian, I shall be

sponsoring some young ladies for the Season, and I would like to host them here.'

'Here? Why not at your home in Hertfordshire? Or the London townhouse?'

'My house is not equipped for guests, and I believe they might do better out here in the country. It will allow them some breathing room before being plunged straight into society. And it will give me a chance to make a list of suitable gentlemen to invite to meet them.' Dark eyes met his own. 'You don't mind, do you, Sebastian?'

Mind that his peace would be disturbed by a bunch of giggling young women? That his home would be invaded by marriage-minded misses? That at every turn he'd run into girls twittering about nonsense like gowns and gossip? Of course he minded.

Yet there was something that made him pause. Despite the gauntness of her face, he saw a fleeting glint of life in his mother's eyes as she spoke of these young misses. 'Of course I don't mind,' he blurted, before he could stop himself. 'Highfield Park is always open to you, and you may invite as many people as you see fit.'

Perhaps it was too late now, but Sebastian hoped he would not regret it.

'Thank you, darling.'

'I do have one condition,' he added.

'Of course. Anything you say. What is your condition?'

'That you don't include me in your list of "suitable gentlemen".'

'Darling—'

'I mean it, Mother,' he said firmly. 'The doors of Highfield Park will be open to your guests for as long as you like, and I shall play the perfect host, but I refuse to be the subject of any matchmaking schemes.'

'As you wish, Sebastian,' she assured him.

'All right.' He smoothed a hand down his coat. 'When are these young ladies arriving?'

'Today.'

'Today?' A pulse throbbed in his temple. Why did he already have the feeling he would regret this?

'Yes, they should be on their way as we speak.' She bit at her lower lip. 'I know it's rather impulsive of me, but I thought with the Season already started we don't have much time.'

Sebastian supposed it would make no difference if they arrived today or next month. At the very least, the sooner these ladies were matched, the sooner he could have his peace and solitude back.

'I'll make sure Eames knows about our guests.'

'No need, darling, I've already informed him. He knows what to do.'

'No wonder Eames was running around like a hen trying to gather her chicks.' And it seemed his mother had already known he would say yes—not that he would deny her anything.

She placed her hands over his. 'Thank you, Sebastian.' That spark of life remained in her eyes and seemed to brighten. This time, he let the hope in his chest flare for just a moment.

He stiffened when she leaned over to kiss his cheek—not because he minded, but because it was something she hadn't done since he was a young boy. The small gesture of affection and the scent of her lavender perfume stirred up memories that he had locked away.

Clearing his throat, he said, 'Since you seem to have things in hand, I shall take my leave and see to some matters that need my attention.'

'Of course.'

'If you will excuse me…?'

As he walked out of the sitting room it still seemed quite unbelievable to him that his mother really was here. That if he turned around and went back into the room she wouldn't be gone like a puff of smoke. How many times had he wished for this in the past five years? That one day she would wake up and remember that the world outside still existed. That her son still existed.

Those thoughts were turning dangerous, so Sebastian put them out of his mind. Instead, he headed to his bedroom to change out of his travelling clothes. He'd been away far too long, and he needed to attend to his estate. When he'd inherited the Dukedom, along with it had come all the responsibilities of a failing estate. However, while many of his peers would have found a way to raise cash by selling off what they could, Sebastian had taken to the work head-on.

Yes, the estate had needed work. But, more importantly, Sebastian had discovered that he'd needed the gruelling activity too. To keep him busy. And to keep him from turning into the one thing he hated most. Now, after just a few short years, the estate was richer than it had ever been. Still, no matter how hard he worked, he couldn't help but feel it wasn't enough. That he was still failing. And that his nightmare would come true.

After a quick meal, and a change into riding breeches, a loose linen shirt, top boots, and a light jacket, Sebastian made his way outside to the stables, where his horse, Thunder, was already saddled and ready. While the cacophony and chaos in the house had considerably lessened, Sebastian was glad to escape for a few hours, before his home was descended upon by silly, fluff-headed girls. An afternoon outside in the sun, surrounded by greenery, would prepare him for a long, tedious evening of playing the perfect host.

Hours passed by as he went about his business. Finally, after visiting one of the water meadows, to ensure his improvements were being done properly, he went to meet one of the newer tenants—a man by the name of Fellowes—and checked to see how he and his family were getting along. By then the sun was sinking in the west, which meant he'd have to make his way back to the house. No doubt his mother's guests would be well settled in by now. Though the thought of having to sneak around like a burglar in his own home did not sound appealing, Sebastian hoped to avoid encountering any of the simpering misses who had descended upon the manor.

Bringing Thunder to a stop, he dismounted by a stream to let the horse have a drink of water. Since the manor was only about a mile away, Sebastian decided to take the rest of the way on foot, gently guiding Thunder to walk beside him on the rough path and leading him up a hill. It wasn't a terribly difficult climb, and they'd done it a hundred times before. As he and Thunder ascended, however, the horse slowed and halted, as if sensing something was amiss.

'My hat!' he heard a feminine voice cry.

A strong gust of wind blew by him, and something smacked into his face. As he spat out what seemed to be bits of lace from his mouth, he grabbed the offending item and tossed it to the ground. Sure enough, it was a woman's bonnet.

Where the devil had that come from?

Looking up, he saw what must be the source of said headwear as a slim, feminine figure trudged downhill, coming faster and faster. If she wasn't careful she'd tumble and hurt herself.

'Slow down!' he shouted. 'You'll—'

Sure enough, the female slipped on a wet patch of grass, which made her land on her behind and slide down the rest of the way.

Damned fool!

Striding over to the girl, he stood over her and offered his hand. 'Madam, may I—?'

His breath caught in his throat, and for the second time that day he found himself questioning reality as a pair of familiar cornflower-blue eyes stared up at him. Surprise flashed across her face as he studied those mesmerising orbs.

'You,' he managed to choke out. 'What are you doing here?'

'What am *I* doing here?' Kate shot back. 'I should be asking you that question.'

She was certain she'd retorted right away. At least, she hoped so. Because she had spent an extraordinary amount of time staring up at the darkly handsome stranger.

Her stranger, to be precise.

How could he possibly be here?

But he was not the product of her imagination, nor some spirit conjured from her memory. No, he really was here. In the flesh, so to speak. And there was so much of him—as if he'd grown larger and taller from their last encounter over a week ago. His tall, well-worn Hessians encased powerful calves, while the tan-coloured buckskin trousers clung to muscled thighs. He wore no waistcoat and his white linen shirt hung loose and open at the throat, exposing a tantalising amount of golden skin.

How far did that tan extend?

As her gaze lifted higher she found herself mesmerised by those dark eyes. But the spell was broken when he cleared his throat, and heat immediately rushed up her neck and cheeks.

Realising her current state—dishevelled and lying on the ground like a wayward sack of grain—she scrambled to her feet and brushed off as much of the dirt from her dress as she could.

'Well?' she asked, picking a blade of grass from her sleeve. 'What have you got to say for yourself?'

'What have I—?' He blew out a strong breath. 'And why should *you* be the one asking the questions, madam?'

'It's *miss*.' She straightened her spine. 'And I happen to have been invited here. By the Dowager Duchess of Mabury herself.'

'Really?' An ebony brow lifted. 'And what does the Duke have to say about that?'

She trained her gaze on his again, but kept her expression haughty. Dear Lord, considering how he looked now, he had to be some kind of servant. That night in the gardens he'd been wearing a fine dark coat—but then again, he hadn't been inside the lavish Houghton home. Perhaps he was a coachman who had sneaked inside the garden.

'I imagine he'd have a lot to say about one of his workers speaking so impudently to a guest.'

The corner of his mouth quirked up. 'I'd like to hear what he has to say about one of these supposed guests traipsing about his land like a fairy sprite with no escort or chaperone. Or were you hoping to run into your very own Pyramus?'

If it were possible, her cheeks burned further at this reminder of their conversation from the night of the ball.

'And if I recall correctly,' he continued, 'it was not I who pushed us into one of the hedges in the gardens. Do you make a habit of accosting gentlemen after quoting them Shakespeare?'

She let out an indignant huff. 'I beg your pardon? Are you implying something, sir?'

'According to you, I am no gentleman, so there is no need for such formal language.'

Those bold obsidian eyes raked over her, travelling in a slow, lazy motion that was much too indecent. It set her pulse racing, and once again her dress felt constricting.

'But perhaps you are not seeking a gentleman.'

'Why, I never...!' Spying her trampled hat on the ground, she summoned up all her dignity and courage, marched to where the bonnet lay, and picked it up. Brushing off the dirt at the brim, she hastily secured it back on her head.

He patted his stallion's nose and retrieved an apple from his pocket and fed it to the giant black horse. 'Leaving so soon, miss?'

'Why, yes. The air around here seems to have taken an unbearable turn.'

Before he could say anything she turned on her heel and marched up the hill, concealing her shortness of breath as the slope turned steeper. Still, she could feel his gaze burning a hole in her back, and she shivered at the thought that he continued to stare at her so boldly. It wasn't until she had completely scaled the peak and was making her way down that she allowed herself to slow down and take short, shallow breaths.

Kate, you fool.

Once again, she'd put herself in a compromising position—and all because she'd wanted some fresh air after the long coach ride from London. The bumpy ride in the stuffy carriage had been unbearable, but mostly because she'd had to suffer the company of Caroline and Eliza DeVries. While Cornelius DeVries had napped, the two had gone on and on about the Dowager Duchess and their plans for capturing a lord. Neither woman had seemed to show any shame, even though Miss Merton had been with them.

Maddie, at least, had cringed every so often. And Miss Merton, bless her heart, had seemed to develop deafness... Or perhaps it was English politeness that had prevented her from reacting to the tactlessness of mother and daughter.

As they'd driven farther away from London the scenery had changed, and Kate had had to admit that the English countryside was divine—very different from its American cousin. There was a genteel, almost refined quality to it, unlike the wildness of American terrain. And when they had finally arrived at Highfield Park her breath had caught in her throat at the sight of the splendid three-storey mansion with an archway and four-columned entrance.

The manor was even more beautiful on the inside. She'd practically been able to see dollar signs in Eliza's and Caroline's eyes when they'd passed through the richly decorated corridors lined with paintings and sculptures as they were shown to their rooms. No one had asked about their hostess, but Miss Merton had told them they would all meet the Dowager Duchess in the drawing room, just before dinner. Eliza had rushed her daughters into their rooms to rest and refresh themselves before tonight, leaving Kate to fend for herself.

Not that Kate had minded—nor had she expected more. Her father had told her he couldn't be bothered to go along with them to Surrey, so he had left her in the care of the DeVrieses and Miss Merton, telling them to write to him once a suitable lord had offered for Kate. Though Eliza had fawned over her as they'd departed, and assured Arthur that his daughter would be in safe hands, Kate knew that she had only said that because of the DeVrieses' lucrative dealings with Arthur Mason. In private, Eliza treated her at best as little more than a stranger, and at worst as competition for her daughters.

No, Kate had not minded at all. However, seeing as the afternoon would be the last time she'd be able to have time alone, she hadn't been able to resist snatching that last piece of freedom. The sweet air had beckoned her and, while the inside of her bedroom was lavishly comfortable, she had been cooped up indoors for far too long, so she had headed outside.

Now she regretted her actions. And knowing that her handsome stranger was on this very estate had perturbed her. *No matter*, she told herself as she sneaked back into the house. She doubted she would ever see him again.

Chapter Four

Kate had done her best to forget the incident. After all, she was about to meet their mysterious hostess. After she'd taken a short nap, a maid had come into her room and helped her dress for the evening, and now she was headed downstairs to the drawing room.

The DeVrieses and Miss Merton were already there when she strode in.

'I should have worn the blue gown.' Caroline gave a disdainful glance to her butter-coloured satin dress with black lace edging. With her gleaming blonde hair brushed to perfection and pinned into curls, she looked elegant and worldly. 'I told you, Mother—it suits my eye colour better.'

'The yellow is fine, Caroline,' Eliza assured her. 'And you must save the blue gown for when there are unmarried gentlemen around. Maddie, will you stop fidgeting?'

'Sorry, Mother, but it itches.' Maddie tugged at her pink lace capelet trimmed with velvet ribbon. The sausage curls around her pretty face made her look even more ridiculously childlike. 'Is there anything else we need to know about the Dowager Duchess, Miss Merton?'

'I've already told you all I know,' Miss Merton said. 'It's been years since—'

Before she could continue the butler strode in. 'Her Grace the Dowager Duchess of Mabury.'

Everyone immediately got to their feet and faced the doorway. A reverent hush settled over the room.

When Miss Merton had first told them of the Dowager Duchess Kate had pictured a rather stiff, white-haired old matron. But the woman who glided into the room was not at all what she'd expected. The Dowager was of average height, and elegantly dressed in an amber gown that enhanced her slim figure. Her hair was rich and dark, pinned up to her head, though a few tendrils had been let down to soften the style. And, while her complexion held a trace of pallor, and shadows smudged the skin under her eyes, there was a warmth to her facial expression that made her appear youthful.

'Good evening. Welcome to Highfield Park,' the Dowager Duchess greeted them, her voice smooth as honey. 'I am so delighted that you've all accepted my invitation. I hope you've found your rooms to your liking, but if you have any requests please do approach Eames.' She nodded at the butler. 'Apologies… His Grace seems to be running late, but perhaps—'

'His Grace the Duke of Mabury,' the butler suddenly announced.

The air in the room shifted once more. There was that stillness again, but of a different sort. A tall figure strode inside, dressed in all-black formal wear.

'Good evening,' a voice greeted them, in a familiar low baritone that made Kate's heart crash into her ribcage.

Oh, no. Dear Lord, no.

As her stranger—the Duke, apparently—surveyed

the room, she groaned to herself as dread pooled in her chest.

Father in heaven, she began to pray. *If You open up the ground and swallow me up right this moment, I promise that the rest of my life shall be devoted to prayer, charitable acts, and service to You.*

But before the Good Lord could even ponder her request those dark eyes landed on her, their gazes colliding. She flinched inwardly, waiting for him to say something, but his expression remained unperturbed.

'Sebastian.' The Dowager Duchess walked over to him. 'Come, I must introduce you to our guests.'

Kate's body stiffened, her stomach turning to lead. Would he say something about their encounter at the ball? Or this afternoon, when she'd accused him of being a servant?

Kate, you idiot!

The Duke could send her packing from his estate before they'd even started dinner and she wouldn't blame him—she had behaved abhorrently earlier. Hopefully he would at least allow the DeVrieses to stay, if only for Maddie's sake.

'This is the Honourable Miss Harriet Merton…' the Dowager introduced their companion.

'Your Grace,' Miss Merton greeted him. 'It is an honour to finally make your acquaintance after all these years. Such an oversight, considering our connection.'

'Connection?' the Duke asked.

'Yes,' Miss Merton continued. 'Your father was a distant cousin of mine.'

'I see.' Mabury's face remained neutral. 'An oversight, indeed.'

The Dowager cleared her throat delicately. 'Miss

Merton, if you please?' she said, her eyes darting to the DeVrieses.

'Ah, yes.' Miss Merton clasped her hands together. 'Your Grace, may I introduce Mr and Mrs Cornelius DeVries of Pittsburgh?'

'An honour, Your Grace.' Cornelius took the hand the Duke offered. 'Thank you for hosting us here on your splendid estate.'

'I've never seen such a beautiful home,' Eliza added, her eyes glossing over with awe.

Mabury did not speak, but merely nodded.

'And these young ladies,' Miss Merton continued, 'are Miss Madeline DeVries, Miss Caroline DeVries and Miss Kate Mason.'

Kate took her time with her curtsey, keeping her head low and her gaze anywhere but on the Duke. Beside her, she could practically feel Caroline's giddiness as she struggled to hold in her excitement.

Oh, please, let this all be over soon.

'It is a pleasure to make your acquaintance,' he finally said. 'I believe it's time we began dinner.'

'Of course,' the Dowager Duchess agreed.

As Mabury offered his arm to his mother everyone else followed their hosts out of the parlour and into the adjoining dining room, where they sat around the table with the unmarried misses at the end. Maddie sent Kate a small smile, while Caroline fumed silently—perhaps because they were too far away to make conversation with the Duke.

Kate did not mind. In fact, she could have been seated in the next county and it still wouldn't be far away enough from him.

Each course that came seemed richer and finer than the one before it, all delivered by liveried footmen who lifted the silver dome from each plate with a precise flourish. Rich soups with truffle. Puréed roasted vegetables. Baked pheasant in a creamy, buttery sauce…

Kate couldn't enjoy any of the sumptuous offerings as her thoughts continued to circle back to her encounter with the Duke that afternoon, and mortification churned her stomach.

It was like waiting for the hammer to fall on an anvil. The night wasn't over yet, and there was still a chance for Mabury to reveal their acquaintance. Would he do it over dinner? Lord it over her? Keep her stewing and squirming in her seat until he had revealed what a horrible, ungrateful guest she was? Or, worse, would he tell everyone that she'd pushed him into the hedges at the Houghton Ball?

Conversation was muted, and the Duke only spoke when asked a question by his mother or Cornelius DeVries. The ladies' side of the table was practically silent—except for Caroline, who made comments every now and then.

'This is perhaps the best meal I've had in England,' she declared rather loudly in the middle of the fish course, turning her head towards the head of the table. 'Maybe in the world.'

'Indeed, it is wonderful, Your Grace,' Miss Merton said. 'I've heard you employ one of the finest French chefs.'

'Yes, Pierre is a marvel in the kitchen,' the Dowager Duchess answered.

After what seemed like eternity the dinner was concluded and the Dowager Duchess announced that there would be tea for the ladies in the blue sitting room while the two gentlemen would be heading to the Duke's private study for port and cigars. The men left the dining room first and the ladies followed behind them, and although Kate felt relief that she would be escaping Mabury's presence for the next part of the evening, the dread and anxiety in the pit of her stomach only continued to grow.

'Kate, where is your reticule?' Maddie asked as they trailed behind the other ladies headed to the library.

She looked down at her empty arm. 'Drat.' In her daze, she'd left it behind. 'Tell the others I've gone back to retrieve it.'

'But, Kate, you shouldn't just—'

'I shan't be long.'

Without another word, she pivoted on her heel and marched back into the dining room. In her haste, she dashed through the open doorway—and promptly collided with a solid object. She staggered, and would have fallen back if not for the firm grip on her arm that steadied her.

'I'm sorry! I—' Her throat went dry as sand when she looked up at that familiar onyx gaze. 'Y-Your Grace.'

Mabury quickly released her arm. 'Miss Mason.'

His expression remained restrained and polite—so different from his bold gaze this afternoon, which had sent warmth through her.

'I was just retrieving my reticule.' Bowing her head low, she sidestepped him, intending to rush to her seat and search for the wayward item. But on impulse, she stopped. 'Your Grace?'

'Yes?' He turned his head towards her.

Here goes nothing. Pap had always told her to tackle problems head-on.

'Your Grace, may I speak frankly? A-about this afternoon?'

'Miss Mason, I don't know what you are speaking of.'

Was he jesting? Or was she mistaken and she'd somehow twice run into his twin? She searched for humour in his eyes. 'You know…about—'

'Miss Mason.' His voice was like a sharp, cold knife. 'Perhaps it would be best for all concerned—especially considering propriety and decorum—if we do not speak of anything that happened before this moment.'

'But I— Oh!' It dawned on her that the Duke was saving her from embarrassment. *How gentlemanly.* Perhaps this was her stranger's altruistic and noble doppelgänger. 'Of course, Your Grace.'

With a dismissive nod, he left the room.

As she stared after him Kate knew she should be grateful. Ecstatic, even. She had escaped embarrassment and disgrace without any repercussions.

But a tight ball knotted under her chest, growing as she formed one thought in her head: *she was nothing to him.*

The encounter that had plagued her thoughts and dreams had not affected him. Perhaps he didn't even remember it. The heat from his gaze this afternoon had been extinguished, only to be replaced by a cool demeanour.

You're being irrational, she told herself.

Besides, catching the Duke's eye was not her purpose here. No, she had only one reason for coming here. Preventing her marriage to Jacob in order to save Pap's memory and legacy. And to do that she had to first obtain the Dowager Duchess's sponsorship—which meant expelling the handsome, dark-eyed Duke from her thoughts.

Chapter Five

Kate did not see the Duke of Mabury at breakfast the next day. When Miss Merton enquired about him at the table, the Dowager Duchess explained that her son was very busy running the estate and was usually up at dawn and out tending to business during the day.

Kate told herself she was very glad that she would not suffer his presence.

Caroline, of course, was disappointed. 'His Grace's charming company will be missed,' she said.

Kate knew the younger woman already had designs on the Duke, and not just because of his 'charming company'. He could have been old and decrepit and Caroline would have thrown herself at him just the same.

'Now, ladies,' the Dowager Duchess began, 'after breakfast, I'd like to invite you all for a stroll in the garden. I know it's early in the year, but I do love to see it before it fully blooms. Then we shall have a quick luncheon, and this afternoon you will have a choice of activities: shopping and tea in the village or a quiet afternoon in the library.'

'Shopping and tea sounds lovely, Your Grace,' Caroline burst out. 'Much more enjoyable than an afternoon in a room full of books.'

'We also have a telescope,' the Dowager Duchess mentioned.

'A *what*, now?' Eliza asked.

'A telescope, Mother,' Maddie said. 'A device to look at the stars.'

Eliza looked horrified. 'Heavens, why ever would you need such a thing?'

Maddie placed her hands in her lap. 'I should like to see that.'

'Then Maddie and I shall spend the afternoon in the library,' Kate declared. Tea and shopping with Caroline and Eliza sounded dreadful.

The Dowager's mouth pulled back into a smile, her twinkling dark eyes making her seem ten years younger. 'Excellent.'

As Her Grace had mentioned, the gardens were still in their early stages of growth, as winter had only just finished. It was still quite bare, but Kate could imagine just how beautiful it would be when in full bloom—especially with its variety of trees and plants, from crab apples to cherries, to gardenias and hydrangeas. An orangery had been built high at the top of the garden and the gardeners were busy rushing in and out of the brick and glass structure, tending to the numerous bulbs about to be transplanted throughout the garden and estate.

'It must be heavenly here in the spring and summer,' Eliza stated.

The Dowager Duchess stopped to nod at a gardener, who bowed to her as he walked by carrying a cherry tree seedling. 'The gardens will be splendid indeed, after all the work has been done.' She followed the gardener as he knelt in the earth and placed the seedling into the ground. 'The seeds must be planted in the autumn and cared for and maintained at a precise temperature throughout the winter, until they are ready to be planted. When I look out here,' she said, and gestured at their surroundings, 'I see the potential and know the hard work will all be worth it. Come,' she added, 'let us continue.'

After their tour, they once again headed to the dining room for luncheon, before retreating to their rooms to refresh themselves. Caroline and Eliza were excited about the prospect of tea and shopping, and discussed what they were going to wear for the excursion.

'Do you think we should change our plans and go with them?' Maddie asked as they walked down the long corridor towards their assigned bedrooms—which thankfully were next to each other. She lowered her voice. 'What if the Dowager Duchess thinks I am too much of a bluestocking to attract a husband?'

'One afternoon by ourselves won't hurt our chances.' Kate stopped outside her door. 'Besides, if Her Grace hasn't asked us to leave by now, then surely she considers us strong candidates.'

Maddie seemed to contemplate her words. 'You are pragmatic as usual, Kate. And I really should like to see this telescope.'

Kate, too, was intrigued. 'Well, I think I shall lie down and nap for an hour. See you at the library?'

Maddie nodded, her curls bouncing. 'I shall see you there.'

Precisely one hour later, Kate entered the library. Maddie was already there, standing by a cylindrical brass object perched on a three-legged stand and propped up by the window, peering into one end.

'Maddie?'

'There you are.' Maddie stepped back and turned to her. 'Oh, this device is such a marvel. Would you like to try it?'

'I would...thanks.' Kate took the same position as Maddie had, bending down to look into the eyepiece.

'I thought it would only work at night,' Maddie began. 'But even in the daytime you can see a great distance.'

Sure enough, the telescope did let her see quite far— past the gardens and the parkland to the nearest farm on the estate. As she moved the telescope around, however, the images blurred. She fiddled with the eyepiece until the scene sharpened.

What in the world...?

Kate continued to play with the eyepiece, wondering if it was the telescope or her eyes that were defective. But, no, she was quite certain of what she was seeing. Yes, it was Mabury himself, helping one of his tenants repair a stone wall. He was dressed much as he had been yesterday, except now his linen shirt was opened all the way to his slim waist, exposing his chest, which was covered with a mat of dark hair.

So he was *tanned all the way down.*

'Yes...um...it's a wonderful device.'

Warmth crept up her cheeks and a tightness pulled somewhere low in her belly. The Duke picked up a large slab of stone and hoisted it over his shoulder. Fascination kept her glued to the scene, but part of her was curious too—why would a duke lower himself to work with his tenants?

'Kate?'

The hand on her shoulder made her start and Kate shot upright. 'Yes?' she said, sheepish.

Maddie cocked her head to one side. 'Are you all right? You look flushed.'

'Wh-why, yes. I'm quite fine.'

'What did you see? It must have been captivating, seeing as you didn't hear me calling you the first few times. Can I see?'

'No!' Kate stepped in front of the telescope. 'I mean…uh…there was a…a beautiful blue jay on top of a tree.'

'Blue jay?' Maddie's brows drew together. 'I thought those were only in America?'

Drat! 'Are they?'

'I think so…let me see.'

'Er…let me check again.' Clearing her throat, she bowed down again to look through the telescope. She intended to move the scope away, before Maddie discovered what she was really looking at, but before she did, she couldn't resist one last peek at the Duke. 'It's…uh…'

She gasped as the view came into focus once more and she saw a portion of the wall collapse, barely missing the Duke.

'Oh, no!'

'What's wrong?'

Kate jumped back. 'I need to go.'

The Duke was unharmed, but what had caused the collapse? Perhaps there was something wrong with the way the wall was being built. Did they not have a mason to direct them?

'Go? Wherever to?'

Kate bit her lip. If there was something she couldn't resist, it was a problem that needed solving. 'I can't tell you yet.' Holding Maddie's hands in hers, she stared up into her friend's face. 'But I require your help.'

Maddie's head bobbed up and down, sending her sausage curls bouncing. 'Whatever you need.'

'If anyone asks, will you tell them I spent the rest of the day with you? Please?'

'Of course,' she replied, with no hesitation.

'Thank you.' Releasing Maddie's hands, she pivoted on her heel. 'I shan't be long.'

Chapter Six

'**Y**ou can say it,' Sebastian muttered as he brushed dirt from his once spotless shirt.

'Say what, Your Grace?' asked John Lawrence as he handed Sebastian a clean cloth.

He took it and wiped the sweat from his brow. 'That you were right. We should have waited for the mason to come and mend your wall.' He nodded ruefully at the scattered pile of stones at his feet.

'Well, my wife kept complaining about the sheep comin' in and eating her herbs and such. And you know my Mary when she's cross.' John Lawrence chuckled. 'And far be it from me to say no to a duke—especially one who offers a hand.' He scratched at his chin. 'It did look like a simple job, Your Grace, pilin' stones on top of each other. Besides, I'm grateful for all your help. I don't think I ever seen a farmhand work as hard as you these last two days. Maybe when you're tired of doin' all your dukely duties you can come work for me, Your Grace.'

The corner of Sebastian's mouth quirked up. 'I'll consider your offer.'

John shook his head. 'Still don't know why you bothered with us these past years. You already paid for improvements on all the farms and fixed all the houses and things. The old Duke never bothered with us. Never even met us tenants.'

Sebastian froze, clenching his hand around the cloth at the mention of his father.

'Beggin' your pardon, Your Grace.' John took his hat off. 'Wasn't meaning no disrespect to your father. And I'm happy for the help.'

His shoulders relaxed. 'It's no bother at all, John.'

Most men of his rank went to fencing or boxing clubs to stay fit. Indeed, Sebastian had used to pursue such sport. But he couldn't even remember the last time he'd stepped into a ring or on a mat. Now he was in the best physical condition of his life, as back-breaking estate work allowed Sebastian to stay in top form. Some might say his tanned skin and hulking shoulders were unfashionable, but he had stopped caring about what the ton might say about him five years ago, and he wasn't about to start now.

When he'd first taken over the running of the estate, he'd discovered that physical activity helped distract him. After all, when the body was exhausted, the mind had no time to wallow in grief. Now he needed the physical activity. Craved it. Sought it out. It had become like a balm to him, preventing old wounds from opening.

Today, however, he hoped to tire himself so that he could sleep peacefully tonight—instead of lying awake in bed as he had the last two evenings, thinking about things he shouldn't be thinking about.

Like cornflower-blue eyes.

Hair like a mahogany waterfall.

The scent of fresh powder and lemons.

And because his mind had been consumed by those

thoughts he had dropped the last slab of stone on top of the wall, sending the rest of it tumbling down.

Damn it all to hell.

'You all right, Your Grace?' John asked.

'Yes.' Putting the cloth aside, he buttoned up his shirt. 'I suppose the wall will have to wait until the mason comes. Wouldn't want to muck it up any more than I already had.'

'I can push my cart up to stop those pesky sheep from comin' in. Let's take a rest, Your Grace. How 'bout some water to wash you off and refresh you?'

Sebastian blew out a breath and observed the dirt clinging to his clothes. His valet was used to seeing them in such a state after he'd been working outside, but some cool water sounded like a good idea. 'I shall come with you to the well.'

He followed John Lawrence to the rear of the house and helped him haul up a bucket of water from the well. He washed the dirt from his face, hands, and fingernails as best he could, but the rest of him would require a bath.

After cleaning up, Sebastian went over the list of things that needed to be done in the next few weeks, as well as the concerns of other tenants. Since John Lawrence worked on the farm closest to the estate and had been there the longest, he functioned as a go-between for Sebastian and the other families on small matters.

'All right, I'll see what I can do about procuring a few more ewes for Robert Talling,' Sebastian said as they concluded, adding the task to his running mental list of things to do. 'Now—' he nodded towards the direction of Highfield Park '—if you don't mind, John, I'll be on my way. Do send word if anything else needs repair.'

John nodded. 'Thank you, Your Grace.'

They made their way back to the front of the house, so Sebastian could retrieve his horse from where it was tied to a post. However, when they circled around the building Thunder was not alone. A figure was bent over the damaged section of the wall. A very feminine figure. Sebastian didn't know why, but from the way his body reacted he knew who it was.

Miss Kate Mason.

Hell's bells.

A shock ran through him—the very same sensation he'd felt when she'd appeared before him two days ago, on his own estate, like an apparition he had conjured up. He'd been amused at first, as he'd realised that she was one of his mother's guests while she'd had no idea who he was—even mistaking him for a servant or a farmer. He had even experienced a kind of satisfaction, seeing the horror on her face upon finding out his identity last night at dinner.

However, she'd somehow turned the tables on him—because being so near her, under the same roof, yet untouchable, had made him want her more. Made him wonder what those curves would feel like under him and how those lips tasted. Missing breakfast hadn't helped because she'd still consumed his thoughts.

He let out a huff. Whatever his body might feel about Miss Kate Mason, he took comfort in the knowledge that she was exactly as he had pegged her in the beginning: another crass dollar princess, looking to bag a titled English lord. That was the reason why he'd treated her so coldly—lest she set her cap on him.

John Lawrence cleared his throat. 'Beggin' your pardon, milady, but are you lost?'

Miss Mason whirled around, her eyes widening when they landed on Sebastian.

'What are you doing here, Miss Mason?' Sebastian thundered.

She flinched, but quickly composed herself. 'I was... taking a walk when I noticed your wall had collapsed.'

Sebastian narrowed his eyes at her. Though her tone sounded confident, he'd played enough cards in his life to know when someone was bluffing. And she was definitely bluffing. And doing it badly.

'Really? And how do you know it had collapsed?' he asked. 'Could it not be that we are in the midst of building it?'

Had she been spying on them? How long had she been here?

A blush deepened the colour in her cheeks. 'I...uh...' Glancing around, she poked a slippered foot at a stone by her feet. She picked it up with both hands, as if judging its shape and size, then marched towards the wall and placed it between two other stones near the bottom.

'Aha! A perfect match.' The stone did, indeed, fit snugly into the crevice. Brushing her hands down her skirts, she looked back at them. 'As I deduced, this wall must have collapsed. And, b-based on the state of your clothing, you were probably in the midst of repairing it.'

Sebastian chewed at the inside of his cheek. 'A lucky guess. In any case, Miss Mason, you should perhaps— What are you doing now?'

She had picked up another stone and was placing it on top of the previous one. 'There you go.' Gesturing towards the fallen stones, she asked, 'How in the world did this happen? Is there no stonemason around to help you with the repair?'

'I've sent for him, miss,' John interjected. 'But he won't be able to come for another couple of days. My wife got all in a temper with the sheep comin' in, and wanted it done right away. His Grace and I thought it would be a simple enough job to put it together.'

'Hmmm…' She tapped a finger on her chin. 'Stone-masonry requires knowledge and experience, but I suppose with careful observation and study one could easily work out how this wall was constructed.'

Crossing over to the other side, she bent lower to examine the intact section of the wall.

'The bottom is made of larger stones, which makes sense as that ensures a more stable foundation. Then it's built up in layers, with the middle filled with smaller pebbles and stones. Perhaps to prevent the stones from sliding apart?'

A finger poked at the layers.

'It seems you did one part correctly, but what happened to the rest?'

'His Grace dropped a long flat piece that was supposed to go in the middle,' said John. 'It must have… er…slipped,' he added, looking at Sebastian sheepishly. 'The rains must've made them too wet.'

'Ah, I see.' She crossed her arms over her chest and drummed her fingers. 'I think we should be able to fix this section for now—at least until the mason comes.'

'We?' Sebastian said in an incredulous tone. 'What do you mean "we"?'

'You don't expect me to pick up all the stones, do you, Your Grace?' she replied sweetly. 'Now…' She turned back to John. 'Let's have a further look, shall we?'

'Do you know about wall-building, miss?' asked John. 'Are you a mason?'

She shook her head. 'Only in name. My Pap—that's my grandfather—loved to tinker and build things. Having no formal education, he learned everything he knew from working in the coal mines in West Virginia.' She paused, the corners of her mouth turning up. 'He always had to figure everything out on his own, and one way he did that was by disassembling something to discover how it was made and then trying to replicate the process.'

There was something about the way she smiled—the way her entire face brightened and her eyes sparkled—that caused a twinge in Sebastian's chest.

John contemplated her words. 'Huh… My Mary likes to do something similar in the kitchen. One day we went to the fair and I bought her a mince pie. She loved it so much that she saved half of it, brought it home, and tried to identify every ingredient with each bite. Eventually she made one and it tasted just like the first pie.'

'Ah, if my Pap had been able to cook or bake he would have done the same thing. He loved pies.' Miss Mason laughed. 'Now, let's see what we can do about this wall so we can keep your Mary happy, shall we? Perhaps she'll make you more mince pies once we're done.'

Sebastian wasn't sure exactly what was happening, but one moment they were standing around, and the next Miss Mason was directing them like a general ordering his soldiers. As he and John Lawrence picked up stones for her she examined each one and placed them methodically in certain positions, occasionally checking to see if their construction corresponded with the undamaged portion of the wall. She also answered John's questions patiently, without brushing him off as if he were a child or a simpleton unable to understand the concept of wall-building.

'Place it closer to the centre, if you please, Mr Lawrence,' she instructed John, and he placed a flat slab of stone on top of the stack.

'Why can't we just pile 'em up on top of each other, miss?'

'Making the wall narrower as it gets to the top directs the weight towards the centre,' she explained.

'To prevent it from collapsing,' Sebastian added. 'Two opposing forces, pushing against each other.'

'Exactly, Your Grace.'

She lifted her head, and when that cornflower-blue gaze collided with his that twinge came back. This time Sebastian swore there was a sparkle in her eyes, but she quickly averted her face.

'I believe that one goes on next, Your Grace.'

She nodded at the long slab of stone by his foot—the same piece that he'd dropped, and which had caused the wall to collapse.

'If you don't mind.'

'Not at all.' He picked it up and balanced it on top of the pile, checking the other section of the wall to ensure they fitted the same way. 'Looks like a perfect match.'

She placed her palms on top. 'Seems stable enough.' Her lips twisted, seemingly in concentration, as she checked their work against the remaining wall. 'I believe we need one more layer of stones, and then a top piece to weigh everything down and keep it all together.' She pointed to the rounded stones on top of the wall. 'However, I think those might require specialised tools and skills, so you might have to wait for the mason to complete the task after all. Assuming we haven't botched it—in which case he'll have to start again.'

'I think it looks fine, miss,' said John. 'If nothing else, it'll stop those sheep from ruinin' Mary's herbs. Thank you so much for your help.'

'You're very welcome, sir. Well, I should be going,'

Miss Mason said quickly. 'I can't be late. Good day, Mr Lawrence… Your Grace.'

After a hurried curtsey, she turned and strode out towards the gate.

Sebastian stifled the urge to go after her, instead watching her retreating figure.

What in the world had just happened?

If he had been confused before, he was downright befuddled now. How could she know how to figure out the process of building a wall just by looking at it?

However, his mind drifted back to that first evening at the Houghton Ball, and he recalled how well-read she was for a young debutante. With wit and intelligence. His instinct told him that there was more under the surface. She was like a puzzle wanting to be solved. And his damned curious mind had always been drawn to mysteries.

'Oh, dear, I didn't think Her Grace would invite so many people,' Maddie said as her eyes scanned the room, sinking her teeth into her lower lip.

Once again, the Dowager Duchess had asked everyone to gather in the drawing room, but this time so that they could be acquainted with new guests before they sat down to dinner.

'So many?' Caroline sneered. 'I wouldn't call this many.' Her gaze narrowed on the people gathered around them. 'There's…what…? Eight people here? Three eligible gentlemen, and only one of them even remotely close to a title. Where are the dukes? The earls? I'd even settle for a baronet.'

Unfortunately, Kate had to agree with her. The clock was ticking, and each day that passed without her meeting an eligible lord brought her closer to an even drearier fate with Jacob as her husband—as she had been promptly reminded by the letter that had arrived that morning.

When the cream-coloured envelope with the familiar neat handwriting of her father's personal secretary had arrived in her room, her heart had plummeted in her chest.

> *Kathryn,*
>
>   *I trust that you are settled into the Dowager Duchess of Mabury's home and can now concentrate on securing a match. I look forward to hearing from Miss Merton about the offers you have secured, so that I may review them for suitability.*
>
>   *Signed,*
>
>   *Father*

The cold, brusque note, which sounded as if he was corresponding with a trader rather than his own daughter, was typical of her father. Being used to it, she was not offended, but the meaning behind the words was not lost on her: she must find a titled husband soon.

That's what I'm trying to do, Father.

The Queen of England herself would dance a jig on London Bridge before Kate married Jacob. Hopefully tonight's party would bring her some prospects.

The Dowager Duchess had invited a few people who lived nearby, including a countess and her younger son, but so far no one suitable had arrived.

I'll marry the first lord who walks through the door.

She didn't care what he looked like, or how old he was, as long as he had a title.

At that precise moment the Duke of Mabury entered

through the doorway and Kate's heart leapt up into her throat.

Kate thoughts jolted back to yesterday, when they'd been building the wall. While he had barely spoken while she was there, it had been obvious that Mr Lawrence was used to having the Duke around. Indeed, they'd both acted casually around each other, as if the Duke working on Mr Lawrence's farm was an everyday occurrence. Which had told Kate it probably was.

She'd been surprised, and confused, for what landowner anywhere in the world took the time to help a tenant with such a menial task? None that she knew. They wouldn't even think of how they could help those they deemed beneath them.

Well, not *all* men.

'There's no such thing as an insignificant job,' Pap had always said when he'd talked of the factory. *'Everyone here contributes in some way.'*

Indeed, her grandfather had known the name of every person who worked for him—from the skilled mechanics who kept the equipment in shape to the boys who mopped up grease from the factory floor.

But that was the way Pap had been—tough, but caring and kind to those around him. Was the Duke the same?

The thought had made something flutter in Kate's chest, and she'd been so unnerved she'd quickly left and bolted back to Highfield Park.

'Finally he's arrived.' Caroline beamed, her eyes never leaving Mabury's tall, handsome form. 'Mother, should I have worn this dress tonight? I know it makes my eyes look bluer, but it's much more suitable for a ball.' She craned her head, trying to catch Mabury's gaze.

A different emotion gripped Kate, making her irrationally cross at Caroline's covetous gaze at the Duke. She supposed with Caroline's beauty she would indeed make a fine duchess. However, the Duke barely acknowledged them, and instead crossed the room to be at his mother's side. That tightness around her chest loosened. *Poor Caroline.* She had no idea that Mabury had no intention of ever marrying.

Caroline pouted. 'Mama, this is a waste of time. Perhaps coming here was a mistake. We could have attended a *real* ball if we were in London.'

'The Dowager Duchess has many other friends, I'm sure,' Eliza soothed, trying to appease her daughter. 'Perhaps they didn't have time to make the trip. Or maybe the Dowager is testing us.'

'T-testing us?' Maddie glanced around nervously.

'Yes!' Eliza's eyes gleamed as if she had stumbled upon some great secret. 'That must be it.'

'I thought she'd already agreed to sponsor me,' Caroline grumbled. 'Why do I need to pass some test?'

'Her Grace couldn't possibly introduce us to the upper echelons of society right away,' Eliza reasoned. 'Remember what Miss Merton said? It's not just about how much money we have. We must prove to her that we have what it takes to move in the right circles.'

Caroline seemed to contemplate her words. 'I suppose that makes sense…'

'It makes perfect sense,' Eliza stated. 'Come, I see your father is speaking to Countess Farley and some of the other guests. We should join them.'

The four women walked over to where Cornelius DeVries stood chatting with the Countess and her son William, Viscount Davenport, and Mr Robert Hughes, the gentleman who owned the neighbouring estate.

'Eliza,' Cornelius greeted his wife as he made space

for the women to join them. 'I was just telling Lady Farley about our impressions of London.'

'Such a delightful, exciting city!' Eliza tittered. 'And
the shops! So many fine things on display. I have to say
Bond Street has become one of my favourite places in
the world.'

'Yes, well, I'm sure you were all overwhelmed,' Lady
Farley commented in a haughty tone. 'We are so much
more civilised over here than in the colonies.'

Kate bit her tongue, so as not to tell Her Ladyship
what was on her mind. That these snooty English really
thought they were the centre of the world.

'Our very first venture into one of the glove shops
left me utterly confused,' Caroline said. 'The pricing
is so different… I told the shop manager I simply don't
have the head for numbers.' Caroline placed a hand over
her forehead. 'Dollars…pounds… I can't quite make
sense of it all.'

'You should have let your father take care of it,' suggested Viscount Davenport, gesturing towards Cornelius. 'He's a fine businessman, or so I've heard.'

'Ladies simply do not have the capacity for numbers
or ledgers,' Mr Hughes agreed.

'You're both so wise,' Caroline fawned. 'I shall not
attempt to bargain next time.'

Kate gnashed her teeth before smiling sweetly at the
two gentlemen. 'Indeed, so wise,' she said, hiding her
indignation as best she could.

If they'd been back in the factory in New York, she
would have shown them just how much capacity she had
with numbers. Pap himself had relied on her calculations while he'd designed the Andersen.

'We ladies desperately need men to take care of those

things while we concentrate on shopping and household management.'

Mr Hughes raised a glass to her. 'Here, here, Miss Mason.'

'Thank you,' she said, lifting her glass in mockery.

Caroline cleared her throat, bringing the attention back to her. 'If only you had been there, Mr Hughes.' She fluttered her eyelashes coquettishly. 'I'm sure you could have made sense of it all. With you running such a large estate, I'm sure it would have been an easy transaction.'

Mr Hughes's eyes lit up. 'Indeed, Miss DeVries.'

'My number skills are just as sharp,' interjected Viscount Davenport. The young man had been eyeing Caroline ever since he'd arrived, and it was obvious to everyone that he was smitten. 'I'm sure I could have taken care of it for you.'

With both men's attention diverted to her, Caroline became animated. Kate wanted to throw her hands up in exasperation. As usual, Caroline droned on without really saying anything of substance. Yet these men couldn't see past the—

That's it.

Her mind began to fill with all sorts of ideas.

Could she…?

Would it work…?

Did she dare?

Of course!

Kate gulped in a large breath of air. Who knew that it would be Caroline who provided her with the solution to her Marriage Problem?

Maddie cocked her head to one side. 'Kate, what's wrong?'

'I'm…fine.'

Why she'd never thought of it before, Kate didn't

know, but it was clear to her now that Caroline knew exactly how to attract the male species. Men were naturally drawn to her—and not just because of her beauty. No, it was because she made them feel clever and capable.

So Kate came to the conclusion that those of the male sex preferred not only a meek and obedient woman, but one preferably less intelligent than themselves.

Damned male superiority.

She'd known about that all her life. Except for Pap, every man she had ever encountered in the factory had underestimated her intelligence and brushed her aside. That had only made her want to prove them wrong, which she so often had, and many of them now grudgingly deferred to her. However, it seemed that in order to attract the right mate she must act significantly more witless than him. If she wanted to catch a husband then she had to hide her intelligence and be completely and utterly vacuous.

The thought made her shudder.

But it would only be temporary.

Just until she'd secured her match and removed herself from the clutches of her father and Jacob.

As Caroline continued to entrance the men, Kate couldn't help but sneak a glance across the room to where Mabury stood by his mother's side. She was once again reminded of yesterday, but this time a bolt of heat struck her as a different image popped up in her mind— that of golden skin and a muscled chest, with that shirt undone down to his waist.

Stop thinking about him.

She had, after all, more important matters to attend to—like using her newfound knowledge to find a husband.

He could be your husband, a small voice inside her replied.

The Duke?
Yes.

Kate huffed as she remembered his words back in the garden. *'I shall never marry.'* She couldn't very well drag the man to the altar and force him to be her husband. Besides, she had nothing to offer him. He was titled, and richer than a king, so had no need of an American heiress's dowry.

The very thought made that small voice evaporate. If only the same would happen to her unseemly thoughts of the Duke—especially of his shirtsleeves rolled to his elbows and his forearms flexing as he lifted those stones.

Kate attempted to swallow, but her throat had gone dry. Realising her glass was empty, she spied a footman with a lemonade jug by the door and slipped away from the group. Before she could ask for a refill, however, a latecomer strode in and nearly collided with her.

'Apologies, my lady!' the stranger cried as he steadied himself. 'Oh, dear, are you all right?'

Kate, thankfully, regained her balance quickly. 'No, it's my fault. I shouldn't have been standing in the doorway.'

'I'm terribly late, and I was rushing in, so the fault is mine.' He ran his hands through his blond hair and gave her a sheepish smile.

'If you insist, then apology accepted.'

Kate couldn't help but grin back. The man was quite good-looking, in a delicate way, as if his features had been chiselled by an Italian sculptor. He also had the loveliest light brown eyes she had ever seen. They reminded her of a puppy's.

'Edward—I mean, Your Grace—welcome,' the Dowager Duchess greeted him as she came to join them.

'Your Grace.' He bowed deeply to the Dowager.

'Please do accept my apologies for my tardiness. I had to attend to some business on the estate.'

'We haven't started dinner, so it's no trouble at all. I had thought maybe you'd changed your mind.'

'I wouldn't dream of it, Your Grace—especially since I am one of the first people invited to Highfield Park now that you have returned.'

The Dowager Duchess's lips pulled into a tight line. 'Yes, of course…' She cleared her throat delicately. 'Oh, excuse my rudeness. Have you met Miss Mason? She's one of my guests.'

'We have bumped into each other, but I'm afraid we haven't been introduced.'

'Then allow me.' The Dowager gestured to Kate. 'Your Grace, may I introduce Miss Kate Mason of New York? Miss Mason, this is His Grace the Duke of Seagrave.'

Kate curtseyed. 'How do you, Your Grace?'

'I'm well, thank you. Lovely to meet you, Miss Mason.'

The corners of the Dowager Duchess's mouth tugged up. 'Oh, dear… I was on my way to ask Eames about dinner. Would you think it rude of me to leave you, Your Grace? Perhaps Miss Mason can keep you company?'

'Not at all rude,' he said. 'Your skills as a hostess and attention to detail are impeccable as always.'

'All right, then, if you will excuse me…?' The Dowager Duchess gave Kate a knowing glance before she headed out of the drawing room.

'So… Miss Mason…you're American,' Seagrave began. 'Tell me, what brings you to England? And how are you liking it here?'

Kate stifled the urge to be honest, and before she could give her standard answer she remembered her earlier thoughts. *Meek and obedient. Completely and utterly vacuous.* She had to do it—if only as a means to an end.

Could Seagrave be the one to rescue her from a dreadful marriage to her second cousin and save her grandfather's legacy?

If he wasn't, she could at least practise…

'Oh, London is just so lovely. Especially all the shops on Bond Street,' she began, pitching her voice higher, as she'd often noticed Caroline do when she was around any male. 'And as for why I've come here…my father has business in England, so I came along.'

'Business? What kind of business?'

She shrugged. 'Oh, I don't know… Building and selling things… I'm not really sure I understand it all.' Lord, it pained her to sound so foolish, but she had no choice. 'I could try to explain it…'

'Don't trouble yourself on my account, Miss Mason,' he said. 'But do tell me more about what you think of England so far. And Surrey? I hope life in the country isn't too dull?'

'Not at all, Your Grace.' She batted her eyelashes at him, the way she'd seen Caroline do countless times. 'Everything here is so…uh…green and fresh.'

'Ah, yes. It's the trees and the grass and the clear air, you see,' he explained, as if she were a child. 'London doesn't have a lot of greenery.'

Really? I hadn't noticed.

Kate forced a smile to her face. 'How right you are, Your Grace.'

Oh, dear, this was going to be a long evening. However, if things went right tonight it would not be a loss.

Chapter Seven

'I think they're getting along quite well.'

Sebastian turned his head at the sound of his mother's voice. 'I beg your pardon?'

'Them.' The Dowager Duchess took his arm and then nodded to Miss Mason and her companion. 'Miss Mason and the Duke of Seagrave. They've been deep in conversation since I introduced them.'

'Ah.' No wonder the man looked familiar. *Lord Edward Philipps.* They'd been at Eton at around the same time, and from what Sebastian could recall Lord Edward hadn't been much of a student, so he could hardly believe the man to be deep in conversation about anything. Deep as a saucer, perhaps. 'I didn't realise the old Duke had passed on.'

'About a year ago, from what I've heard.'

'Really? I'm surprised he hung on that long. The old man was ancient—and that was when I was a boy.'

He had outlived two wives, then gone for his third trip down the aisle a few years ago with some young chit. Apparently, the old Duke had been quite loose with the purse strings with her and the estate was now nearly bankrupt.

His mother took his arm. 'Shall we go in to dinner?'

Sebastian nodded and led his mother to the dining room, with the guests lining up behind them. To his surprise, his mother had decided on an informal seating arrangement for this evening. He remained at the head of the table, but the Dowager Duchess sat at the opposite end, while men and women sat interspersed. Unfortunately, Caroline DeVries sat only two places from him. But that wasn't what truly irked him. No, it was the fact that Miss Mason sat next to Seagrave, and the two of them were carrying on whatever conversation they'd been having earlier.

'Your Grace,' Caroline began, as she craned her neck around Lord Clive Sheffield, the gentleman to her left. 'Your chef has truly outdone himself this evening. This is the best food I've had yet.'

Sebastian looked down at his bowl of creamy asparagus soup. It was half empty, so he had had some of it, but he couldn't remember what it had tasted like. 'Yes, the soup is divine,' he lied.

Seemingly encouraged, Caroline continued. 'You are such a generous host, Your Grace. And I've heard your London home is just as beautiful as Highfield Park.' Her smile turned sickly-sweet. 'Perhaps one day I— we—will be lucky enough to see it.'

He highly doubted it.

'Perhaps.' Taking his wine glass, he brought it to his lips and took his time sipping.

'Sooner rather than later, I hope.' Her eyelashes fluttered coquettishly.

Downing his wine, Sebastian motioned to the footman to refill his glass and watched Seagrave fawn over Miss Mason. She was seemingly basking in his attention. While they did make conversation with other people in their vicinity throughout the meal, they would always eventually gravitate towards each other again, which irritated Sebastian. The Dowager caught his eye, but said nothing and merely sent him a cryptic look.

Once the blasted dinner was over, it was time to entertain in the drawing room. Usually Sebastian surrounded himself with the gentlemen, as they drank their port and conversed about politics or business, but this time he hovered near his mother as she mingled amongst the guests, waiting patiently until she finally reached Seagrave, Miss Mason, and Miss Madeline DeVries. The Duke was talking animatedly as the two ladies listened.

'I hope you are enjoying your tea, ladies?' The Dowager enquired. 'And you your port, Your Grace?'

'Most excellent.' Seagrave took a sip from his glass. 'Mabury, your cellar's selection is superb.'

'Eames deserves all the compliments as he selects the wines,' he replied. 'It seems you've found yourself in lovely company this evening.'

'Ah, yes—how truly lucky I am to be surrounded by such beauty.' He smiled at the ladies. 'And they don't even seem to mind that I chatter on about Stonewin Crest. Though I'm afraid talk about the estate probably seems dull to them,' he replied.

'It doesn't seem dull at all,' said Miss DeVries. 'It's so different from where I grew up, and hearing about farming and livestock and how it all comes together is interesting—right, Kate?'

'I suppose…' Miss Mason let out an exaggerated sigh. 'But talking about soil, plots and crops and animals…it all sounds like dirty and grimy work.'

Dirty and grimy? Just yesterday she'd been examining stones with her bare hands and helping him build a wall. He fixed his gaze on her, attempting to catch her eye, but she seemed intent on avoiding his stare.

'I would much rather hear about your townhouse in London, Your Grace,' she continued, batting her eyelashes at Seagrave. 'How far is it from Bond Street?'

Sebastian's instincts flared. They told him that something here was not quite right. Miss Mason was acting more like Caroline DeVries by the minute.

'Not too far, but I'm afraid at this time of year my stepmother is in residence,' Seagrave answered.

'You don't mind?' she asked.

'Not at all. I prefer Stonewin Crest—especially since all my prized horses are there.'

Miss Mason clapped her hands together. 'You love horses, Your Grace? Do tell me more!'

Seagrave chuckled. 'If you insist…'

Sebastian stifled the urge to yawn as Seagrave prattled on about his thoroughbreds and his prized Arabian stallion. While he enjoyed a good discussion on horseflesh, he was certain that no one liked hearing *that* much about it. But what truly irritated him was the way Miss Mason's eyes never left Seagrave's face as he rambled on, nodding and smiling as if she were listening to the most fascinating lecture in the world.

'Are you sure you want to hear more, Miss Mason?' Seagrave asked eventually.

'Oh, yes,' she replied in a high-pitched tone. 'Please go on.'

Why in the world was she acting like some empty-headed fool? There was something going on…

'Seagrave,' Sebastian interrupted. 'I've heard that a company from Bristol has approached you about mining for minerals on your estate.'

'Mining?' Miss Mason piped in.

Seagrave chuckled. 'Ah, yes. Nothing that would interest you, Miss Mason. I'm afraid it's just minerals used in factories and such—not emeralds or diamonds or anything pretty.'

She opened her mouth, then snapped it shut. 'Of course.'

Madeline DeVries spoke up. 'I should like to hear more, Your Grace.'

'You would?' Seagrave asked, quizzical.

Her head bobbed up and down with excitement. 'My father owns an iron forge back in Pittsburgh,' she began. 'And I work with him as a metallurgist.'

'A meta-what?' Seagrave exclaimed.

'Someone who works with metals,' Sebastian explained.

'You...*work*?' Seagrave looked at Madeline DeVries as if she had grown a second head.

She nodded. 'Why, yes. My father taught me everything he knows about smelting and ironworks.' She turned to Miss Mason. 'Much like Kate, who learned from her—'

'Maddie!' Miss Mason burst out. 'Oh, you are so very clever and sweet.' She cleared her throat. 'But His Grace is correct. Minerals sounds like a boring topic. Could we talk about something else?'

Sebastian ignored her. 'If you decide to have them survey your land, Seagrave, you should be prepared.'

'Really? For what?'

'For all the digging machines they'll be carting around.' He directed his gaze at Miss Mason, then spoke slowly and deliberately. 'Machines are large contraptions made of iron that can perform the work of several men.'

'Really?' she replied without missing a beat. 'How... quaint.'

Sebastian continued. 'Anyway, they'll bring boring machines—steam-powered monstrosities that make a lot of noise—to tunnel into the ground.' He did not miss how Miss Mason's nostrils flared when he said 'monstrosities'. 'They'll disturb your peace. If you ask me, industrial machinery is a nuisance to the senses.'

'Indeed,' Seagrave agreed, raising his port glass.

Miss Mason merely huffed, but her cheeks had gone red.

Sensing her frustration, he continued. 'Do you have something to say, Miss Mason?' he asked as he casually took a sip of his wine. 'Any deep thoughts on boring machines?'

The barest hint of outrage flashed across her face, but she managed to control it. She placed her finger on her chin and seemed to contemplate his question. 'Not at all, Your Grace. All this talk of minerals and machines sounds *boring* to me.'

She let out a laugh and Seagrave followed along, his eyes looking at her adoringly, like a puppy's. Miss Madeline DeVries, on the other hand, only looked at her friend in confusion. If Miss Mason was a terrible bluffer, Madeline DeVries was even worse. And now he knew something was definitely afoot with Miss Kate Mason.

Sebastian finished off the last of his port. 'If you'll excuse me... I require a refill.' Turning on his heel, he marched away.

Spying an empty glass, the footman holding the bottle of port immediately rushed forward. As he stared at the ruby liquid pouring into his glass Sebastian's mind ran the gamut of explanations for Miss Mason's odd behaviour. After taking a hearty sip, he glanced back at her and Seagrave, who was once again taking over the conversation. Miss Mason seemed entranced with whatever it was Seagrave was nattering about.

Perhaps he should ignore Miss Kate Mason from now on. Stay away from her. Yes, that would be the best. Let Seagrave have her. Forget about the chit and let go.

But for the life of him, he just couldn't.

Chapter Eight

To the rest of the world, His Grace the Duke of Seagrave was the perfect suitor.

'Miss Mason, you're looking lovely today,' he said as they stepped out into the garden. 'Like Aphrodite, whose face launched a thousand ships.'

Kate bit her lip. *Actually, it was Helen of Troy.*

'You are too kind, Your Grace.' She tugged at Seagrave's arm. 'My lord, why don't we head this way?' She nodded to the right.

'Of course, Miss Mason. It looks like they've finished planting the lavender.'

Kate allowed him to lead her and ignored the strain on her cheek muscles as she fought to keep a smile pasted on her face and prevent the frustration building inside her from seeping out.

Yes, Seagrave was perfect.

Perfectly stupid.

Which made it much harder for Kate to act more dim-witted than him. But other than that he was the right candidate for her husband. Why, if she could, she would propose to him this very moment, even if it was only their third meeting.

After that first dinner he had called upon her the following morning. Well, her and all the other ladies and the Dowager Duchess. After that, the Dowager had invited him once again to Highfield Park, to visit the gardens and take afternoon tea the next day.

Kate thought him quite fashionably handsome, especially today, in his dove-grey coat and trousers, his fine blond hair tousled in the wind and those puppy-like eyes. Truly, he was good-looking—which was not a bad thing at all. She supposed if she were to have a stupid husband he might as well be pleasing to look upon.

Yes, he was exactly what she needed. Not only was he titled, but from what Miss Merton had told Kate after she'd enquired about the Duke's family, he also needed money. Apparently, his stepmother, the current Dowager Duchess, had spent every shilling the old Duke had left upon his death and the estate was now on the brink of insolvency. Being a duke was costly, after all, plus his prized horses must cost a fortune to keep. A bride with a rich dowry would help replenish the Seagrave coffers and keep the creditors at bay.

Now she only had to ensnare him.

Glancing around, she saw Maddie, Caroline, and Miss Merton exploring various parts of the garden. This was the first time she and Seagrave had been truly alone, but it was considered proper as they were outdoors and her chaperone and companions were still in the vicinity. This was her chance.

'My lord…' she began, entreating him with her gaze. 'Do tell me stories of your childhood days at Stonewin Crest. What was your favourite thing to do on the estate?'

'I'm glad you ask, Miss Mason, because— Oh, Mabury. What a coincidence, running into you.'

Kate's head snapped forward.

Oh, dash it all.

Sure enough, there he was, the Duke of Mabury himself, approaching them from the opposite end of the path. Dressed in form-fitting riding clothes and wiping a sheen of sweat from his brow with a handkerchief, he had obviously just come in from a ride, or perhaps from working with Mr Lawrence. She wondered for just a moment if he'd had his clothes on the entire time.

Stop thinking of that!

Oh, no, this would not do at all.

Mabury's dark gaze landed on her briefly, then turned to Seagrave. 'Yes, such a coincidence—considering this is *my* garden. So, Seagrave,' he continued as he put the handkerchief back into his pocket, 'this is your third visit this week?'

'Yes, Her Grace is extremely kind to allow me to visit Miss Mason and the other ladies.'

An eyebrow rose. 'Indeed, she is.'

'Would you like to join us for a walk amongst the lavender, Your Grace?' Seagrave asked.

'I'm sure he is much too busy for such activities.' Kate tightened her grip on Seagrave's arm. 'Aren't you, Your Grace?'

Her heart thumped in her chest as she raised her head to meet Mabury's eyes. Dear Lord, why did this man elicit such a response from her? How she wished he would just leave, so she could continue with her quest to bag Seagrave.

'It's been a while since I've strolled in the gardens. It would be such a waste of all the effort my gardeners have put in if I never see their hard work.'

'Excellent.' Seagrave shuffled sideways to give space to the Duke. Kate had no choice but to let him drag her to the left, which meant Mabury was now directly on her right side.

'Actually...' he began. 'It's chilly this morning. Why don't we go to the orangery?'

'A capital idea,' said Seagrave. 'I'm afraid Stonewin Crest doesn't have its own orangery, though I've visited one at a distant uncle's estate.'

They walked further up the gardens, towards the glass and brick structure. As they stepped inside, the pungent smell of greenery hung in the humid air like a heavy blanket. Exotic plants and seedlings crowded the sides and hung from baskets above as they followed a path marked by colourful tiles on the floor and flanked by intricate ironwork gates.

'What is that smell and that racket?' Seagrave asked.

'Engine oil,' Kate said automatically. 'And that's the sound of a boiler.'

Seagrave's head snapped towards her. 'I beg your pardon? Engine oil and boilers?'

'Ah, how clever you are, Miss Mason,' Mabury piped in, the corners of his lips tugging up.

Seagrave's expression soured, especially since Mabury had exaggerated the word 'clever'.

Drat!

'I mean... I think that's what it is,' she added quickly. 'I have overheard the servants in our house talking about boilers and engines and...things.'

Oh, Lord. Her grandfather would be turning in his grave if he heard her.

I'm doing this for you, Pap.

'I don't recall my uncle's orangery being so noisy and pungent?' Seagrave continued.

'Perhaps it was an older structure, which relied on brick or straw for insulation and heated with open fires or stoves. Highfield Park's orangery was installed a few years ago and uses a boiler to keep the temperature at the correct level.'

Seagrave lifted his chin and sniffed the air. 'There is an unusual heaviness in the air. What is it?'

Mabury's dark gaze flickered to her.

This time, Kate bit her tongue, preventing herself from answering.

'It's the steam,' Mabury explained. 'As Miss Mason correctly deduced, there is a boiler underneath us.'

'A lucky guess,' she piped in. 'Very, very lucky.'

'I could tell you more about how it works,' he said. 'But I would be very afraid of boring Miss Mason.'

Kate pressed her lips together. 'I'm sure the topic will be too complicated for me.'

Mabury flashed her a perfect set of pearly white teeth. 'Ah, yes, such things tend to go right over such pretty little heads like yours, Miss Mason.'

'But perhaps His Grace would like to know more?' She looked up to Seagrave.

The expression on his face said otherwise, but politeness made him say, 'Of course.'

'As you wish, Seagrave.' He turned to Kate. 'But I'll do my best to make the explanation easy for the female mind. Should you find it difficult to follow, I will not be offended if you choose to admire the flowers while we gentlemen continue our discussion.'

'How magnanimous of you, Your Grace.'

Mabury's condescension irked her today, as it had a few nights ago, during that dinner when Seagrave had first come to Highfield Park. It was as if he was a different person from the man she had thought him to be when they had repaired the wall together. Now he was acting like a pompous fop.

But why in the world was Mabury speaking to her as if she was an idiot? Did he—?

Wait.

That condescending tone.

Those pauses in his speech.

And that delighted smug look.

Mabury was not patronising her.

He was deliberately needling her.

The scoundrel.

He was trying to ruin her plans for some reason. Perhaps he'd sensed her deception and didn't want his fellow peer to fall for her.

I shouldn't have helped him build that wall, she thought ruefully.

Narrowing her gaze, she focused her loathing at him for trying to expose her to Seagrave.

Not that it helped, because Mabury continued. 'An orangery is called thus because it is meant to keep citrus fruits warm, but it can be used for almost any type of flora. This is where we house most of our plants during harsh weather, as the temperature here is the same year-round,' he explained as they continued their walk. 'The boiler underneath us creates steam and is released through these vents.' He stopped to point the tip of a boot at an ironwork grate on the floor next to the tiled path.

'How clever,' Seagrave mumbled. 'How does the steam reach the vents?'

'Good question.' Mabury's dark gaze was trained on Kate, as if he were waiting for her to speak.

Kate bit her lip, refusing to answer. *I have to stay on guard from now on, until Seagrave proposes.* She was determined now, more than ever, to have him as a husband. *Think of Pap*, she reminded herself.

'Well?' Seagrave prodded, but he was not looking at her at all.

'Pipes,' the Duke continued. 'Pipes bring the steam up to the vents.' He once again turned to Kate. 'Pipes are long, cylindrical—'

'I know what pipes are,' she snapped. Realising her mistake, she quickly batted her eyelashes and smiled until the corners of her mouth reached her ears. 'Thank you, Your Grace.'

Amusement crossed his face. 'You're very welcome, Miss Mason. Well, that's about as much as I know about the orangery,' Mabury confessed. 'But, Seagrave, why don't we talk more about those mineral rights you spoke of? We can discuss it over some port.'

'That would be excellent, Your Grace. And— Oh.' He glanced at Kate. 'Miss Mason, forgive me. I know I said I would have tea with you and the other ladies…'

'Oh, not at all, Your Grace.' What was she supposed to say? She couldn't very well stamp her feet and beg him to stay like some petulant child. 'It sounds as if you've much to talk about with His Grace. I should go to Miss Merton anyway. She's probably looking for me.'

He tipped his hat to her as he released her arm. 'Thank you, Miss Mason. I shall call upon you again this week.'

'That would be lovely, Your Grace.' She curtseyed. 'If you'll excuse me?'

Lifting her head, she looked up at Mabury. This time there was no amusement. Instead, the force of his stare seemed to knock the air from her lungs, but she managed to keep her composure.

'Miss Mason,' he said with a short nod.

Turning on her heel, she made her way out of the orangery. *Blast it all!* Why was he trying to expose her to

Seagrave? Maybe he didn't like that fact that an American like her was going to marry a peer—and a duke to boot. Well, it didn't matter. She just had to make sure he didn't get in her way.

That dratted man. And to think that just the other day she'd thought him to be like Pap, working with Mr Lawrence on his farm.

'Never give anyone work you wouldn't do yourself,' Pap had always said.

Of course, the Duke could be both a kind landowner to his tenants and act like a cad to women. After all, he'd vowed never to marry. Perhaps he just didn't think much of the female sex. But his actions towards others and those less fortunate were admirable to say the least.

Stop thinking of him as admirable.

Actually, what she had to do was stop thinking of him, period. And make sure he didn't get in the way of her plan to marry Seagrave.

Just because he doesn't want to get married, it doesn't mean the rest of us can't.

Seagrave was in need of a wealthy wife, and she needed a way to save Pap's legacy.

Slowing her steps, she took in a deep, calming breath of the fragrant air. *Think of Seagrave instead.* He was the solution to her Marriage Problem, after all.

Chapter Nine

Thankfully, Kate wouldn't have to wait too long to see Seagrave again, as the Dowager Duchess had announced she was hosting a musicale at Highfield Park the following day, and had invited over two dozen guests, including Seagrave.

Kate decided that she needed more time alone with him, to indicate her interest in his attentions. But how would she accomplish that? Kate had never been alone with a man before.

Yes, you have.

Her mind drifted back to the night of the Houghton Ball. To Mabury and the garden and the hedges. Heat spread all over her body, as it always did when she allowed herself to recall the incident. It was as if it had just happened, and the scent and feel of him were burned into her head.

Think, Kate.

But not about being alone with the Duke.

Surely she couldn't just overtly tell Seagrave to meet her somewhere private? No, that wouldn't do at all. She would have to find other ways of telling him she wished to have a moment alone with him.

* * *

On the evening of the musicale, after her maid, Anna, had brushed and styled her hair and helped her into a peach-coloured satin gown with a low neckline, Kate made her way down to the ballroom, which had been converted into a performance area, with chairs lined up in neat rows. The grand piano had been set in front, as well as seven chairs for the other musicians. Many of the guests milled about, and she walked over to where she spied Seagrave talking to Miss Merton, Mabury, and another man Kate had never seen before.

'Miss Mason,' Seagrave greeted her as she curtseyed. 'How lovely you look this evening.'

'Thank you, Your Grace.' She turned to Mabury and curtseyed again. 'Good evening, Your Grace.'

The Duke acknowledged her with a nod. 'Miss Mason.'

Miss Merton cleared her throat. 'If I may, my lord?' she said to the Duke's companion. 'May I present Miss Kate Mason of New York? Miss Mason, this is Devon St James, Marquess of Ashbrooke.'

She bowed her head. 'A pleasure, my lord.'

'The pleasure is all mine,' the Marquess replied, a hint of amusement in his tone.

Kate allowed herself to look up at him, lifting her gaze from his collar to his face, and was met with the most extraordinary blue eyes—like twin sapphires, glittering with promise. The rest of him was just as striking—stylishly cut blond hair, a straight, aquiline nose, cheekbones that could cut diamonds. His firm lips were set into a smile that held just the right amount of cynicism and made him appear both charming and worldly at the same time.

Miss Merton cleared her throat and embarrassment heated Kate's cheeks at how she was gawking at the handsome Marquess. To his credit, Ashbrooke didn't say a word, but the glint of mirth in his eyes said he had noticed her appraisal. She averted her gaze, but found herself eye to eye with Mabury's dark stare instead. A different kind of heat rushed through her.

'Are you a fan of music, my lord?' she asked Ashbrooke, trying to distract herself.

'Music?' He laughed. 'I suppose I am fond of many kinds of...art.'

Mabury stiffened beside him. 'Ashbrooke is my guest tonight. I invited him here.'

'Or rather, I finagled an invitation from him.' Those sapphire eyes twinkled. 'Especially since I'd heard Highfield Park has once again opened its doors to visitors. I had to see it for myself.'

'And are you satisfied with what you've seen so far?' Kate asked.

He eyed her boldly. 'Indeed.'

'I think we're about to begin.' Miss Merton gestured to the front of the ballroom, where the musicians had taken their places.

'Miss Mason, Miss Merton...' Seagrave began. 'If it would please you, it would be an honour if you would sit by my side during the performance.'

Miss Merton opened her fan and pressed it to her chest. 'Of course, Your Grace, we would love to.'

'Thank you for your indulgence, Miss Merton.' He turned to the gentlemen. 'Mabury... Ashbrooke.'

As Seagrave led them to the second row of chairs, Kate did her best to put Mabury out of her mind—especially since she had started to form an idea on how to get the Duke alone.

According to the Dowager Duchess, there would be a twenty-minute intermission in the middle of the programme, and refreshments would be served in the adjoining room. With so many people streaming out of the ballroom it would be easy enough to slip outside to the terrace for some fresh air. While she wasn't trying to be found in a compromising position with him, surely a few minutes alone wouldn't be so bad? Especially if they weren't caught. After all, she hadn't been the only one to be alone with a man that night at the Houghton Ball and still have her reputation intact. And if Caroline DeVries could manage it, then why couldn't she?

Kate could hardly concentrate on the orchestra as they began their programme. Anticipation stretched her like the bowstrings on the violins. When they'd finished the first *concerto*, she leaned over to Seagrave, who sat between her and Miss Merton. 'That was an amazing piece, wasn't it, Your Grace?'

'Yes, I do enjoy Beethoven very much.'

It had been Mozart, but she stopped herself from correcting him. 'Yes. Lovely. But I don't think I've been in such close quarters with other people in a long time. Being out here in the countryside, I mean.'

'Ah, of course,' he replied. 'I suppose not being in the crush of London has made you forget what it's like to be in a crowded ballroom.'

Before Kate could reply, the conductor raised his baton and the musicians moved on to their next piece. Settling back into her chair, she focused her attention on the music. Halfway through, a strange feeling crept over her—as if someone were watching her. She tamped down the urge to look around her. Besides, she was near the front of the room, so of course there would be people staring at her back.

Near the end of the final piece of the first half, Kate let out an exaggerated sigh.

'Are you quite all right, Miss Mason?' Seagrave asked.

'I'm afraid the air in here hasn't improved.'

'Indeed, it's got warmer. Perhaps the Dowager Duchess should have the footmen open some windows.'

'Or better yet...' She moved her head closer to his ear. 'Perhaps I might go out for a minute or two to refresh myself on the terrace during the intermission.' Shifting her leg, she let the satin of her skirt brush against his thigh.

He patted her hand. 'A capital idea, Miss Mason.'

Kate nearly exclaimed in joy at her success in conveying her message, but thankfully the orchestra struck its final notes and the conductor put his baton down, prompting the audience to break into applause.

'That was truly entertaining,' Miss Merton declared as they stood up and joined the other guests filing out of the ballroom. 'Her Grace has impeccable taste in music.'

'Truly,' Seagrave agreed. 'Shall we head to the next room?'

Kate smiled up slyly at him. 'Of course, Your Grace. But first I should like to make a detour to *refresh* myself.' Surely Seagrave did not miss how she emphasised the word refresh.

'The parlour has been set up as the ladies' retiring room. But don't be too long, dear,' Miss Merton reminded her. 'We only have twenty minutes.'

'I shan't, Miss Merton.'

With one last glance at Seagrave, she broke away from them, walking in the direction of the ladies' retiring room. However, once she was safely away from her chaperone she made an about-face and crept back towards the glass doors that lead out to the terrace.

Slipping outside, Kate shivered as the cool night air caressed her bare shoulders. *I should have brought a shawl.* But it was too late now. She hurried away to the edge of the terrace and wrapped her arms around herself as she stared up at the moon. What a perfectly romantic setting it was. And perhaps this would be the night that would finally help her solve her Marriage Problem and save Pap's legacy.

The sound of the door latch clicking open told her that Seagrave had been able to sneak away. 'Your Grace.' She gripped the railing with her gloved fingers. 'I'm so glad you could join me for some fresh air.' When he didn't reply at once, she pushed away from the balustrade and turned to face Seagrave. 'Did you—?'

Her heart leapt into her throat. It was not Seagrave standing by the door.

'You!' she croaked, staggering back against the cold marble of the railing. What in God's name was Mabury doing here?

A dark eyebrow lifted sardonically. 'Not what—or rather, who—you were expecting?'

No, decidedly not.

'I d-don't know what you mean, Y-Your Grace.' The tremor in her voice annoyed her. 'I was merely trying to escape the stuffiness inside.'

'And you were hoping for Seagrave to join you?' It was not a question, but rather a statement.

'I do not know what you're referring to, Your Grace,' she began.

Blast it. He was going to ruin her plan to be alone with Seagrave. He could arrive at any moment! It would be a disaster.

'But I find the air out here colder than I expected and would like to return inside.'

'Then by all means go.' He waved his hand towards the door.

'You're blocking the only exit, Your Grace.' She ground

her teeth. 'Perhaps, for the sake of propriety, you should go back inside first, and I shall follow in a few minutes.'

Eyes black as midnight gleamed with challenge. 'You talk of propriety, Miss Mason? But this is not the first time you've found yourself alone with a man. One might think there is a pattern emerging here. Or perhaps it is more of a habit?'

'I beg your pardon?' Her fingernails dug into her palms. 'Are you insinuating that I'm some kind of… of…lightskirt?'

He took several steps forward, his strides so long that it took mere moments to reach her. 'Well…here you are again…alone in the moonlight. With me.'

The timbre of his voice sent heat coiling in her. But if she were honest that had been building since the moment she'd realised he was near. Heavens, this would be not just be a disaster but a full-on catastrophe if she didn't stop it now.

'And so what if I am here alone with you again? It doesn't mean anything.' She had to leave. Yet her feet would not move. 'Nothing's happened thus far, and nothing will. I never allow myself to get lost in passion.'

That last word triggered something between them— like the initial spark to a flame. It hung in the air, swirling like the heat generated in a firebox.

He took a step towards her. 'You're trembling.'

'I'm n-not,' she denied.

'Of course you're not.' His gaze burned into her. 'You never get lost in passion.'

His face drew nearer to her, his head tipping to the right. Her body tensed and she sucked in a breath, trying desperately to fill her lungs before the inevitable came.

Oh, Lord, he was going to kiss her.

And she wanted him to.

'Your Grace...'

Oh, dear, her tone didn't sound as if she was protesting. At all. In fact, it sounded almost...needy.

Not to mention the fact that her hands had somehow found their way to his shoulders and were clutching him tight, pulling him closer.

The world around her slowed down as his mouth descended on hers. After the initial shock of its touch wore off she melted into the kiss. His warm lips moved over hers eagerly, and she found herself responding, matching his growing intensity.

In that moment she could pinpoint exactly where the heat had built up in her. Not in her lower belly...no. Much lower. It was between her thighs, in her most private place, where she throbbed and ached. Her clothes once again felt too tight. Her nipples had hardened into points that scraped against her silk chemise, the delicious abrasion fuelling her even more. His hands had somehow moved to her hips, and now were trailing up the back of her dress until they reached the neckline. Warm gloved fingers delved inside, and her skin tingled from the heat radiating from underneath the kidskin.

The sensation made her gasp, and in that brief moment, as her lips opened, he drew her lower lip between his own, sipping on it. She crushed herself to him, wanting to be near him and hating all the layers of clothes between them. Her body was ablaze with a fiery desire she'd never felt before.

Then, in an instant, he pulled his mouth away, and that fire burning between them cooled as they stared at each other, both of them wide-eyed with shock.

Good Lord, what had they done?

Chapter Ten

Sebastian knew he had just made his second mistake of the night.

His first? Inviting Ashbrooke to this damned affair.

He had gone to London early that morning to conduct some business that needed his personal attention at his bank. Afterwards, he'd stopped for lunch at Brooks's, and of course out of every acquaintance he knew he'd *had* to run into Devon St James. Despite trying to tell the Marquess politely that he wanted to eat alone, Ashbrooke had pestered Sebastian throughout his meal, until somehow he'd finagled an invitation to tonight's musicale.

He hadn't expected the Marquess to come. But he had arrived on the dot, dressed in his usual finery, looking handsome and sinful as Lucifer himself. And, of course, with his damned keen eye for observation combined with a tenacious nature, he'd sniffed out Sebastian's unwilling attraction to Miss Kate Mason.

'Aren't they cosy?' Ashbrooke had remarked as they'd sat two rows behind Seagrave and Miss Mason. 'Careful, Mabury.'

'Careful of what?'

'Some might say you're acting like a jealous lover with the way you're looking at Seagrave.'

'And how exactly *am* I looking at Seagrave?'

'As if you want to throttle him. And then drag him out and shoot him. Then skin him—'

'The music's starting,' he had said, hoping to shut up the Marquess.

Sebastian had thought that was it, but throughout the entire performance his blood had boiled as he'd watched their heads gravitate towards one another, seen them whispering like naughty children.

'My, she does look lovely as a peach. And just as ripe for the picking,' Ashbrooke had drawled. 'And she definitely said "terrace".'

'I beg your pardon?'

He'd tapped a finger on his mouth. 'I can read lips. A useful trick.' A slow, lazy smile had spread across the Marquess's face. 'Seems our two lovers are planning a moonlit rendezvous.'

Yes, it was Ashbrooke's damn fault. Sebastian could have continued with the evening—hell, with his life— not knowing that Miss Mason and Seagrave were in each other's embrace.

But, no, the Marquess had had to needle him with that information, thus causing him to be in the situation he found himself now. Under the moonlight, on the terrace, with the last woman in the world he should be desiring.

You could have turned around and gone back inside.

Yes, he could have stopped himself from making this mistake. But at that time he hadn't wanted to.

And now he would be paying for it.

Sebastian swallowed hard as he reluctantly released her soft and pliant body. 'Forgive me,' he murmured.

'I forget myself. Of course I shan't speak to anyone of this.'

Pivoting on his heel, he marched away from her as he attempted to rein in his desire. Now he knew how Orpheus had felt, fighting the urge to look back at his Eurydice.

The ballroom felt even more suffocating after having been outside, but Sebastian welcomed the smell of sweat and perfume in the air. The musicians had returned and were once again setting up. He strode out to the adjoining room, weaving through the crush of people towards the nearest footman to grab a glass of wine and down it in one gulp.

What had possessed him to kiss her? It was one thing to desire her and another to act on it.

I've wanted women before, he told himself.

A tumble or two—and not necessarily with the same woman—often took care of that itch. That kiss hadn't even been half as provocative as it might have been. Indeed, her inexperience had been apparent. But damned if that hadn't made him hungry for more. To see the full potential of her desire blossom under him.

Bloody hell.

'Sebastian?'

His mother's soothing tone cooled his inner turmoil as she came up behind him. 'Mother.' He placed his empty glass back on the footman's tray. 'How have you been this evening? Enjoying the show?'

'Yes, I'd forgotten how music can lift one's spirits.' Her eyes crinkled at the corners as they focused on something behind Sebastian. 'Is that the friend you said you'd invited? The Marquess? Ashton, is it?'

'Ashbrooke. And, yes I—'

'Begging your pardon, Your Grace,' Eames interrupted smoothly as he came up behind the Dowager.

'What is it, Eames?' she asked.

'It's Mr Alton, I'm afraid.'

'Alton?'

The gardener? What the devil did he want at this time of night? Sebastian wondered.

'What's wrong? Is he ill?' his mother asked.

'No, Your Grace. But he's asked me to relay an important message to you. He says there's a problem with the orangery. It seems the...' His white eyebrows drew together. 'The heating mechanism has failed. He's sent word to London to get someone to repair it.'

'Oh, dear...' Worry marred his mother's face. 'I should go and see to it.'

Sebastian placed a hand on her shoulder. 'Mother, there's no need for you to go now.'

'But I—'

'You shan't be able to do anything about it, and Alton has already done what needs to be done.'

'But the flowers. And the trees—'

'Will be fine for now.'

If he remembered correctly, when the system had been installed a few years ago the company that had provided it had said that if it should malfunction the heat would be retained for a day or two, provided they didn't open the doors too often.

'Mr Alton will take care of them. And someone will come in the morning to fix it.'

The line between her brows smoothed. 'You're right, darling. I should stay here with our guests. We are still to have supper after the musicale.'

Sebastian groaned inwardly. The only thing worse than having to sit two rows behind Miss Mason and Seagrave would be to once again watch them from across the table, flirting and carrying on during supper. 'Why don't I go and see Alton?'

'But the musicale…supper…'

'Don't worry, Mother.' He kissed her on the forehead. 'Enjoy your evening and I'll take care of everything.'

'Thank you, darling. Well, I should go. The next part is about to begin.'

'I'll let you know the situation in the morning.'

The Dowager Duchess nodded and strode off towards the ballroom.

'Eames, is Mr Alton at the orangery?' he asked.

'Yes, Your Grace.'

'Good. I shall go and see him now.'

There really was no need for him to see Alton, since neither of them could do anything with the broken heating system, but it was a good excuse to disappear from the party. Leaving the terrace had been difficult enough. Now he needed to put as much distance between himself and Kate Mason as possible, to erase the memory of that kiss that was still so fresh in his mind.

No, he needed to forget everything. Forget the moonlight. Forget the scent of lemons. Forget the feel of peach-soft skin and the taste of warm, sweet lips underneath his and the press of her supple curves.

He couldn't afford to play such dangerous games with her. Kate Mason was here for one reason: marriage. That alone was enough for him to stay as far away as possible. He reminded himself of that day when he had decided that he would do everything in his power never to turn into his father. Reminded himself of his vow to his mother, never to subject another person to what she had endured. The image of her pale, still body as she lay in bed would never be erased from his mind…

* * *

Kate hadn't thought it was possible to turn from hot to cold so quickly. Indeed, even when the Andersen had to be cooled down for maintenance, it took the better part of a day to lower its temperature after smothering the fire and emptying the boiler. But in a span of mere seconds Mabury had gone from fire-hot to glacier-cold.

Forgive me... I forget myself.

Kate braced her hands on the railing behind her as her knees were still weak and her body limp.

Damn him.

Why did he kiss me?

Why did I kiss him back?

She bit the back of her gloved hand to stop herself from groaning aloud. It wasn't as if it was her first kiss. She'd been kissed once before, by the son of one of her father's friends during a ball. The brazen young man had pulled her into a darkened alcove and she'd welcomed the kiss as they had been flirting most of the evening.

That, however, had been nothing like her kiss with the Duke.

'Argh!' She curled her hands into fists at her sides. This madness had to stop. She couldn't let her plans be derailed.

Focus, Kate.

That was what Pap would have told her. The solution to her Marriage Problem was right in front of her. She only had to reach out and grab it.

The shrill sound of a violin coming from inside told her the musicians had come back and were now warming up. She smoothed her hands down her dress and marched towards the door, carefully sneaking in. Thankfully the musicians didn't seem to pay her any attention, and she was able to slip into the adjoining room unnoticed. She spotted Seagrave by the refreshment table, chatting with the Marquess of Ashbrooke.

'Miss Mason, here you are,' the Duke greeted her as she reached them.

'Yes.' Kate forced a smile on her face. 'Here I am.'

And where were you?

'I do hope you were able to soak in a breath or two of fresh air.' He lifted the glass of chilled champagne in his hand. 'Since you were feeling so warm, I took it upon myself to save you something cool to drink upon your return.'

She took it from him, tamping down the urge to swallow it and instead taking a small sip. 'You are so kind, Your Grace.'

Oh, Lord, he really is thick.

Kate wondered what she could have done to tell him more clearly that she'd wanted him to follow her out onto the terrace. Perhaps next time she should draw him a diagram.

'My, my…you do look refreshed, Miss Mason,' Ashbrooke remarked. 'The evening air does wonders for the constitution.'

The Marquess flashed her a hint of a smile that made Kate wonder if he suspected something—which made her take another sip of champagne. 'Yes, it does. Oh, it looks like the performance is starting again. Shall we head back in, Your Grace?'

'Of course.' Seagrave offered his arm.

With a quick nod to Ashbrooke, he led her towards the ballroom. As they walked in she couldn't help but scan the room for Mabury. *So I can avoid him*, she reasoned. Though the Duke had promised not to tell anyone about their episode on the terrace, she still couldn't risk running into him.

When they reached their seats, she sat down next to Seagrave, and Miss Merton appeared not long after.

'My dear, I've been looking all over for you,' the chaperone said. 'You weren't in the retiring room when I went to fetch you.'

'We must have missed each other. I was with His Grace and Lord Ashbrooke by the refreshment table.'

Miss Merton seemed to accept her excuse, and she settled into her seat as the orchestra once again began to play.

Though the second half of the programme was even better than the first, Kate couldn't bring herself to enjoy it. The moment she let the music carry her mind away, it drifted towards the kiss. Mabury's hands on her. The way he'd suckled on her bottom lip. The heat of him pressed against her.

'Bravo!' Seagrave called as he clapped vigorously when the orchestra concluded their final piece. 'Did you enjoy the music, Miss Mason?'

'Yes,' she said automatically, bringing her hands together to clap. Though she could not recall any of the music, the musicians at least deserved applause.

As the guests stood, Kate glanced around. Frowning, she realised Mabury was nowhere in sight. Maybe he had gone ahead to supper.

But he did not appear at the table. His usual seat was empty, and if anyone remarked upon his absence, Kate did not hear it because she was at the other end of the table, on the Dowager Duchess's side.

A stab of an unnamed emotion pierced her chest. Had he found their kiss so unpalatable that he had decided to leave for the rest of the evening? Maybe that was the true reason he'd promised to keep silent about their kiss: because she was so reprehensible he couldn't stand anyone knowing about it.

'Miss Mason? Are you enjoying the food?' Seagrave glanced down at the plate in front of her.

'Yes, I am.' She put a spoonful of the salmon mousse into her mouth and swallowed, not really tasting anything. 'Delicious.'

He dabbed at the corner of his mouth with his napkin. 'I was wondering…hoping, maybe…that perhaps tomorrow I might call upon you? Just you, I mean.' His cheeks went red before he added, 'And your chaperone, of course. During which time I would like to ask Miss Merton for permission to take you on a carriage ride later in the week.'

'That would be…wonderful,' she replied, mustering up as much enthusiasm as she could.

He seemed pleased with that and continued eating his salmon mousse.

Kate knew she should be thrilled. Finally things were progressing in the right direction. The solution to her problem was on the horizon. Jacob would be thwarted, Pap's memory and his contributions to the world would live on, and her sacrifice would be worth it.

Full steam ahead.

Chapter Eleven

Seagrave called on her in the morning and, as promised, asked Miss Merton for permission to take them out on a carriage ride sometime in the next few days. Miss Merton accepted, and when Seagrave left, the chaperone was positively giddy.

'A duke, Miss Mason!' Her cheeks flushed with excitement. 'I knew you would be able to find a man of quality.'

'He is indeed.' Kate bit her tongue so she wouldn't blurt out the qualities that made Seagrave appealing— which were that he was titled and eager to marry into wealth. 'I have grown quite fond of him.'

'And I'm sure in time his feelings for you will grow.'
Maybe he'll even like me as much as his horses.

But, then again, she couldn't fault those poor creatures. Thoroughbreds were expensive to maintain, after all, and Seagrave would do anything to keep his prized horses. That desperation not only made him an excellent candidate for her husband, but would mean he'd keep himself busy after they married and she could pursue other things.

The other day, the jaunt into the orangery and the

smell and the roar of the engine had reminded her of her beloved factory and Pap. Hope sparked inside her. Once she was married to Seagrave, she'd get away from Jacob's clutches. Then Pap's legacy would be saved. But first she had to secure the Duke.

Later that afternoon, as they waited for the Dowager Duchess at luncheon, Miss Merton told the other women about the Duke's visit.

'You really have done well for yourself, Kate.'

Caroline tossed her blonde locks over her shoulder. 'He's a duke, yes. But his estate is so small, compared to the Duke of Mabury's.'

Kate trained her gaze on Caroline. An unknown emotion threatened to leap out of her throat, but she quickly quashed it. Caroline hadn't bothered to hide her aspiration to marry Mabury, at least not amongst their party, so why did Kate feel such hostility towards her?

'Oh, and what about the Marquess of Ashbrooke?' Eliza tittered. 'So utterly charming and handsome.'

'Ah, yes…' Caroline let out a long-winded sigh. 'We spoke at length during supper. I suppose a marquess would be a good second choice. I didn't see him at breakfast, but I believe he stayed the night.'

'And how would you know such a thing?' Maddie enquired.

'My maid shared that bit of gossip with me this morning.' Caroline's eyes positively gleamed. 'And he hasn't left yet. He's out riding with the Duke now.' A devious smile spread across her lips. 'I think I shall wear my other blue gown tonight, Mother.'

Before Eliza could reply, the Dowager Duchess strolled in, prompting all of them to rise and curtsey.

'Apologies for my lateness, ladies.' She nodded at Eames to signal that the servants should start the luncheon.

As they sat down together Kate couldn't help but notice the distress on the Dowager Duchess's face. Though she tried to hide it, Kate observed that she looked dispirited, and there was a furrow between her eyebrows throughout the meal. Despite the lively conversation the older woman seemed distracted and quiet, and not her usual lively self.

After they'd finished luncheon, and everyone had headed out of the dining room, the Dowager Duchess stayed behind to speak with Eames. With her curiosity getting the better of her Kate slowed her steps, allowing everyone else to walk ahead of her. Then she returned to the dining room, stopping just on the threshold. She focused her hearing, straining to hear the conversation between the Dowager and the butler.

'And they're certain no one else can come to repair it?'

'Yes, Your Grace, I'm afraid so. Not for a fortnight.'

'This is terrible news. Whatever are we to do with the heating system broken?'

'Mr Alton says he will do what he can for the plants and trees…but he doesn't know if they will last for more than a few days.'

'This is my fault. I shouldn't have… I mean, if I had been here…'

The butler cleared his throat. 'Your Grace, if I may speak freely? It's not your fault. Nor anyone's fault. These newfangled machines do break every now and then.'

'Thank you, Eames, you are too kind. Do give Mr Alton my thanks and tell him that whatever he needs to keep the plants alive he may have.'

'I shall, Your Grace.'

Kate backed away, lest the butler catch her eaves-dropping.

So, that's what's bothering the Dowager Duchess, she thought to herself as she hurried away from the dining room. However, instead of turning at the main corridor, so she could go back to her room, she headed left, towards the exit to the gardens.

Straightening her shoulders, Kate made her way to the orangery. Surely the steam-powered system used to heat the building wouldn't be that much different from a locomotive engine? Indeed, as Pap had taught her, all steam engines were similar. He himself had first learned from working on the engines that had pumped water out of the coal mines, and the basic principles were the same: heat combined with water equalled steam. She was confident she'd at least be able to diagnose the problem, if not fix it.

As she approached the orangery she walked past the front door—she already knew the heating system would not be inside. It would be too noisy, for one thing, and when she had been inside she had only heard a faint hiss of the boiler as steam rose through the grates. So she walked around to the back of the building. Sure enough, at the far end, where the walls were thicker, was a door that had been left ajar. She slipped inside and took a spiral staircase to the lower level. A familiar smell hit her nostrils. Oil and ash and iron. This had to be the right place.

Reaching for the lone gas lamp burning there, she turned it up, the flame growing brighter. She found the rest of the lights and lit them one by one, as well as a handheld lamp which, thankfully, was working. Swinging the lamp around, she surveyed the room.

'Hello,' she said to the long brick countertop along

one wall. Only it wasn't a countertop. From the grates along the side, and the small tubes rising up the wall to the ceiling, she knew that it had to be the main boiler.

She put the lamp down and pressed her hand to the iron grates of the firebox. Practically cold. The fire must have died out a while ago. Residual heat should keep the orangery warm for the rest of the day, assuming the door stayed closed, but the clock was definitely ticking.

'What went wrong?' she said to no one in particular. It was a habit she'd picked up from Pap, who, when faced with a problem, had always liked to talk aloud.

'Helps me think,' he'd said.

Straightening her shoulders, she unbuttoned her spencer and placed it aside. She frowned down at her white muslin dress. It would get dirty, for sure; the hem would already be covered in soot by now.

Oh, well.

Shrugging, she grabbed the ends of the sleeves and tugged at them, hearing the seams ripping as she pulled them up to her elbows. Taking the hand lamp, she raised it and began to investigate.

'Are you really not going to tell me what happened on the terrace last night with Miss Mason?' Ashbrooke asked as they slowed their horses to a walk.

Sebastian scrubbed a hand down his face. 'Christ Almighty, you're persistent, Ash. Has anyone ever said no to you?'

The Marquess flashed him a good amount of pearly white teeth. 'Not yet. Well…?'

Sebastian ignored him and nudged Thunder to walk faster. Ash, of course, kept stride. 'How do you even know I was on the terrace with her?'

'For one thing, when you realised she had disappeared you tore out of the room like a madman,' he explained cheerfully. 'And then I ran into Seagrave at the refreshments table, all by himself. Although I have to say when Miss Mason did reappear she did not look thoroughly debauched at all. Not even a little bit.' He tsked. 'I'm ashamed to call you my friend.'

'I'm not your friend,' he replied flatly.

That didn't seem to slow Ash down. 'You had her alone in the dark for ten minutes and—' He sucked in a breath. 'Oh, God.'

Sebastian slowed again, then turned to him. 'What's wrong?'

'Dear God, no.' Ash groaned. 'Say it isn't so.'

His patience was starting to dwindle. 'Just tell me what the hell is the matter.'

'You're infatuated with her,' Ash declared.

'What?' His shout startled Thunder, so he grabbed the reins tighter. 'You're jesting.'

The Marquess looked completely serious. 'The only time a man refuses to speak about his romps with a woman is when he truly has feelings for her.'

'I am not infatuated with Miss Mason,' he said.

'Ah, denial is another sign.' Ash shivered visibly. 'Please don't tell me you're going to be shackled soon. I told you…you're my only friend left.'

'We are not—' Sebastian rubbed the bridge of his nose with his thumb and forefinger. 'I am not—nor will I ever be—infatuated with Miss Mason.'

Or with any woman, for that matter. That vow he'd made would never be broken. His very soul depended on it.

'So you care nothing for her? Have absolutely no feelings for her?'

'No. Absolutely none.'

'Then you won't mind if I have a go at her, then?'

A growl escaped Sebastian's throat and the Marquess barked out a laugh.

'I thought so.'

Blowing out an impatient breath, Sebastian turned towards the manor. 'I should check on the orangery and see if Alton has any more news about the repairs.'

The boiler company should have sent someone out this morning, but according to Eames he hadn't even received a message from them yet. His mother was probably fraught with worry over the whole thing—especially since it had been years since she'd seen the orangery in full bloom. Indeed, before she'd left it had been one of her favourite places in Highfield Park.

'Tell me, Mabury, do you do anything else except work on your estate?' Ash asked in an exasperated voice. 'There are more things to life, you know. Live a little. You used to not be like this,' he continued. 'I remember back in our university days you'd be the one asking me to play truant, and you'd be the first one at the public house, buying ale for everyone.'

A spark of nostalgia hit Sebastian, and for a moment he longed for those carefree days when he hadn't had the burden of responsibility on his shoulders. But it was quickly extinguished as a coldness gripped within him. His very being now rebelled at the thought of idleness. After all, he'd seen the consequences of it first-hand.

'By the way,' Ashbrooke began, 'I do have a bit of gossip I'm sure you'll be interested in.'

'I'm sure I won't.'

'Even if it pertains to Miss Mason?'

Thunder let out a protesting whinny when Sebastian reflexively dug his heels into the horse's sides. He muttered an apology to the animal. 'What is it?'

'In the last few weeks there's been this boorish American fellow trying to get into all the clubs in London. Jacob Something-or-other is his name. Anyway, he doesn't know how memberships work and he thinks he can just barge in and pay to join.'

'And what does this have to do with Miss Mason?'

'Well, whenever the club managers politely decline him, he tries to make his case by telling them he's the cousin of Arthur Mason, locomotive magnate of New York, and saying that they'll be begging him to join once he owns half the railways in England.' Ashbrooke's expression darkened. 'I didn't think anything of it until I met your Miss Mason and made the connection. Arthur Mason must be her father and that odious man her second cousin.'

'She's not my Miss Mason.'

And such matters shouldn't concern him. Not after last night, when he'd vowed to stay clear of her.

'You're not curious? At all?'

Ignoring Ash's question, Sebastian brought Thunder into a canter until they'd reached the gardens, then tied him to a nearby tree before dismounting. Ashbrooke followed suit and they made their way to the rear of the orangery building.

'Alton's probably down in the furnace.' Sebastian nodded at the open door that would lead to the lower level. 'You don't have to come. There's nothing interesting down there.'

'I might as well—nothing interesting out here either.'

Sebastian went inside first, holding on to the handrail as he descended the stairs. The lamps were ablaze, which meant Alton or perhaps the repairman himself must be puttering around.

'Alton?' He walked inside and peered into the dim

room, finding a dark shape on the other side. As his eyes adjusted, he realised that it was not Alton, and nor was it a repairman.

'My, my…and you said there was nothing interesting here,' Ashbrooke mused.

Miss Mason turned around. 'Who in the—? Your Grace!' There was a tremble in her voice that set his instincts flaring. 'What are you doing here?'

'Shouldn't I be asking you that?' He crossed the room towards her with ground-eating steps. 'Are you—?' He stopped as she raised a handheld lamp, illuminating herself further.

A sheen of perspiration covered her brow and tendrils of dark hair hung loose around her face, a few of them stuck to her neck. She had taken off her jacket, leaving her in a light muslin dress, and the cuffs had been torn to expose her from wrist to elbow. A layer of sweat had the cloth sticking to her shoulders, but the bright yellow glow from the lamps behind her outlined the curves of her body through the thin folds of fabric.

His mouth went dry at the sight of her looking so naturally dishevelled.

'Good afternoon, Miss Mason,' Ash greeted her. 'Lovely to see you again.'

'My lord.' Her eyes darted from him back to Sebastian.

'Ash,' he said in a warning voice as he heard the Marquess's steps coming closer.

'Yes?'

'Get out,' he growled, and he turned his head to send the other man a menacing stare. Some irrational part of him didn't want Ash to see her like this.

'Ah, right… Of course.' Ash grinned. 'I'll stand watch outside.'

Stand watch? 'Wait, that's not what I—'

Ash saluted him. 'Say no more, old chap.'

And with that he retreated, his footsteps fading as he ascended the metal steps. A loud slam a few moments later indicated that he was gone and Sebastian and Miss Mason were alone.

Damned Ash.

Turning back, he saw that Miss Mason hadn't moved an inch, and those cornflower-blue eyes were widening as she stared at him. Thankfully, he managed to speak. 'Miss Mason, what are you doing here?'

Quickly, she spun on her heel to face away from him. 'What does it look like I'm doing?'

Placing the lamp on the counter, she stuck a foot into one of the iron grates and attempted to hoist herself up—with no success. Her skirts prevented her from lifting her legs high enough to reach the counter.

'Are you insane?' He was next to her in an instant. 'You're going to get hurt.'

She harrumphed. 'I'll be fine. I only need to take a closer look at that pipe over there.' Bracing her palms on the counter, she tried to climb up once again. 'Blast it. Help me, will you?'

'I beg your pardon?'

'Help me up,' she said. 'Just hold my skirts, Your Grace.'

'Only if you let me know why you need to get up there.'

She let out an exasperated sound and turned to face him. 'I think I know why the boiler has stopped working. If I'm right, I should be able to fix it. But to do that I have to check on that pipe up there.'

'You have to check it? Where the bloody hell is the repairman?'

'He's not coming.' She bit at her lip. 'Eames said the company won't be able to send anyone for at least a fortnight. By then it will be too late, and all the plants will have died. Now, are you going to help me or—? Oh!'

Sebastian didn't know why, but he'd grabbed her by the waist and placed her so she sat on the counter. 'There. Now…' He knelt and reached for the bottom of her skirts.

'Your Grace!' she exclaimed.

'You're the one who wanted help,' he reminded her.

Her lips pursed together. 'Fine. Go ahead.'

Gathering the hem of her dress, he compressed the layers of fabric with his arms, then helped her up to stand so she could plant her slippered feet on the counter. 'There.'

She moved closer to the pipe and got on her knees. 'Hand me the lamp, if you please. Thank you.' She raised it towards the wall lined with pipes. 'Hmmm…'

'What is it?'

'I'm not sure. One moment… Ah, just as I thought.' She leaned forward. 'Bulged surface…thick-lipped fissure…'

'In English, please, Miss Mason.'

'The pipe has burst. Scale deposits, most likely,' she explained. 'The good news is that's the reason why the heat couldn't make its way up to the orangery.'

He swore to himself. 'That's the good news?'

'Yes, it means that the boiler itself isn't broken and only the pipe requires changing.'

'I'm afraid I don't employ a full-time plumber.'

She turned to face him and smiled. The first real smile she'd flashed at him that day. 'Well, now, it's a good thing you have me, then.'

His heart rioted in his chest at her words.

'Here, help me down.'

He found himself reaching out to her, gripping her

waist to lower her down, and reluctantly releasing her as soon as her feet hit the ground.

'Now...' she began, dusting her hands together. 'I recognise this heating system. Made by an American, correct?'

'I believe so. My fath— The old Duke had it installed a few years ago. He said this was made by the same fellow who first built a similar system in the hothouses of the Governor of the Bank of England. How did you know?'

'I recognise the pipe socket design.' She grabbed the handheld lamp, then marched to the other end of the room. 'Ingenious, really. Threading on both the left and right side, so that two pipes can be joined together. And that makes them easily replaceable.' Raising the lamp, she swung it around. 'Now, there should be a... Oh, here you are.'

She pulled at something on the wall. He came up behind her and saw she had found a cabinet filled with tools and pipes. She rooted around in it for a few seconds, inspecting each pipe before shaking her head and putting it back. Finally, she picked one up, checked the ends and exclaimed with glee.

'Perfect.' Checking the rest of the cabinet, she grabbed a few tools. 'Now to put it in the right place.'

They walked back to where the broken pipe awaited and he helped her up onto the counter once again. Sweat had begun to build on his brow, so he discarded his jacket and cravat.

After she'd finished arranging her skirts, she manoeuvred herself into a kneeling position. 'If you wouldn't mind, Your Grace, could you hold the lamp up so I may see better?'

'Of course. But, please, I think we should dispense with the formalities.'

She tilted her head to the side. 'I beg your pardon, Your Grace?'

'Considering the circumstances—' he nodded at her, propped on top of the counter, and at the lamp in his hand '—could we call each other by our given names? At least for now, Kate?'

Even in the darkness he could tell that the prettiest blush tinted her cheeks. But she nodded anyway. 'As you wish… Sebastian.'

He did as she'd asked, rounding the edge of the counter so he could lift the lamp up, and then watched her work, eyebrows furrowed with determination, as she sized up the broken pipe, then took a wrench, and began to disassemble the array of tubes.

Sebastian didn't know what she was doing, exactly— in truth, he probably shouldn't just let her start ripping up a very expensive piece of machinery—but there was something about Kate Mason at this moment that made it difficult to say no to her. The Kate Mason before him seemed an unstoppable force, so self-assured in her capabilities that if she'd told him that jumping off a cliff would fix the boiler, he would have done it.

And damned if he didn't find it irresistible.

'Are you sure you know what you're doing?' he asked.

'I've been around steam engines since before I even learned to read, Your Gra— Sebastian. My grandfather started as a coal miner back in West Virginia, but he worked his way up to become an engineer. Eventually, when my father had established his company in New York, he sent for us and then financed Mason Railroad & Locomotives so he could manufacture an engine of his own design.'

Ah, her grandfather… She had spoken fondly of him

to John Lawrence. 'And you've always worked with machines?'

She frowned at something and peered closer. 'Could you lean in a little closer, please? With the lamp, I mean. Yes, that's it… And yes, I've always worked with machines. Pap taught me.'

'Why would he teach you?'

'What do you mean, "why"?'

'You're…well…you're a woman.'

Her plump lips pursed as she picked up a tool from the pile by her knees. 'So?'

No one had ever replied to Sebastian in such an impertinent manner—he was a duke, after all. Yet he had never quite met anyone like Kate Mason, either. But why all her pretence whenever they weren't alone? She was capable enough to build a wall and fix a boiler pipe. So he continued to prod her.

'Shouldn't you have been at home, learning how to run a household?'

She smiled wryly. 'We were poor before my father left and made his fortune in New York. I'm afraid there wasn't much of a house to run except for a shack with dirt floors. Since my mother died in childbirth and there was no one to care for me, Pap didn't have a choice but bring me to work. And since then, I never left his side. Until his death, that is.'

'I'm sorry.'

'Don't be sorry. Ah!' The broken pipe came off in her hand. 'Hand me the new pipe,' she ordered.

He grabbed the piece and handed it to her. 'Why shouldn't I be sorry about your grandfather's death?'

Taking the pipe, she pushed it into position, trying to find the right fit. 'Because for most of my life I got to spend every moment of every day with Pap. I watched him do something he loved, and I was able to share that with him. Every day until he died.'

She paused as she turned away from him to grab a wrench, though Sebastian did not miss the hitch in her voice.

'And every time I work on a steam engine or a boiler or an engineering problem I think of him. It's as if I can hear his voice in my head—as if he were right here, telling me what to do. It's like just for a moment I have him back.'

And there it was again—the same smile on her face as that day when she'd worked on the wall and spoken of her grandfather. He could hear both the sadness and the joy in her voice. Had he ever felt something like that for anyone? Perhaps he would have for his own father, had he been the person Sebastian thought he was.

'And...' She gave the wrench one more turn. 'There you go. That should do it.' The corner of her mouth lifted. 'It wasn't so difficult. Didn't even need joining material for the pipes, thanks to their ingenious design.' More of her hair had come undone, and a smudge of dirt or perhaps oil marred her perfect ivory skin. 'Now we just have to get someone to light the firebox and prevent it from happening again...'

Sebastian stood there, watching her as she rambled on about hard water and ash pans, and his mind tried to reconcile what was happening before his very eyes.

Mechanical genius. Fairy. Sprite. Innocent temptress.

Who *was* this woman?

Whoever she was, she sure as hell wasn't the same person he'd been observing for the last few days. And certainly not the woman putting on that farce for Seagrave.

'Sebastian?' She waved a hand in front of him. 'Are you quite all right?'

He nodded.

She glanced down at her skirts. 'Would you mind assisting me once again?'

'Of course.'

Moving from her kneeling position, she twisted her body to face him. This time as he placed his hands on her waist he moved closer and took his time, letting her body slide down between the counter and his. He heard her sharp intake of breath and leaned forward, his nose lightly touching her hair. The smell of her, mixed in with her sweat, was a heady perfume.

'Sebastian,' she whispered, lifting her head to his as she placed her hands on his chest. 'Please...'

Sebastian wasn't sure if she arched up to meet his lips or if he bent down to hers. Maybe they met halfway, because before he knew it their mouths had met in a soft, sensuous kiss.

Much as it had last night, his body raged with longing and desire. Unable to hold himself back, he slid his tongue across the seam of her mouth, coaxing her lips open. His hands cupped her face as he parted her petal-soft lips and she gasped as their tongues touched. When she pulled back he slid his fingers around her nape, seeking the downy soft hair there.

A moan of pleasure escaped her, and he captured her mouth again. This time she opened to him, tilting her head back instinctively to let him explore her. He deepened the kiss, tasting her erotic sweetness. Her hands moved up to his shoulders, clinging to him as she pressed against him. The touch of their bodies sent his blood sizzling and his shaft hardened. He pushed her back against the counter, rubbing his hips against hers, the friction making them both groan aloud.

He slid one hand down to the back of her neck, and when he found the top buttons of her dress he undid them deftly and slipped his fingers under the fabric. Her skin was perfect and smooth and warm and everything he dreamed of. And he wanted—needed—more. He opened the rest of the buttons and then loosened the ties of her stays.

She gasped again and he devoured her lips, thrusting his tongue between those soft petals as he pulled down her garments. She cried out into his mouth as his hand cupped a soft breast through her thin chemise and rubbed a nipple to hardness.

'Kate...' he groaned, as he pulled his mouth away.

She shivered as he made his way lower, nibbling and kissing the soft skin of her neck and collarbone. His tongue teased at the delicate lace edge of her chemise, licking down to where the hard point of her other nipple poked through fabric. When she let out a frustrated whimper he wet the silk with his tongue, then drew her nipple into his mouth, making her mewl.

His hand released her other breast and reached under the layers of her skirts until he touched a slim stockinged leg. He looked up, watching her face twist with pleasure as he continued to suckle on her nipple, then moved his hand up, feeling for the slit between her drawers. When he found it, he parted her thighs, and his fingers inched towards the apex of her womanhood.

'No!' she cried, and then pushed him away. 'You can't...'

The heat of passion fizzled out and Sebastian leapt away from her, cursing to himself. How the hell had this happened? And why had he done it again?

She crossed her arms over her chest. 'I'm... We can't...'

'We shouldn't be together.' He raked his fingers through his hair. 'This isn't right.'

She stiffened, but nodded in agreement. 'Yes. I can't. Not with you.'

Those last three words hit him as if he'd been struck with an axe to the chest. *'Not with you.'* But she would with someone else.

'Of course. Your duke.'

Seagrave didn't bloody deserve her.

Despite her attempts to hide it, she was smart and witty. Capable, too. And she wasn't ashamed of her humble beginnings. Seagrave was so far beneath her in many ways. The thought of them together sent his blood boiling.

Then again, he knew all about men who didn't deserve the women they married. And what happened to those women when they stayed in such unions. He'd seen it with his own eyes.

And then it struck him—a memory from long ago that he'd tried so hard to repress rose to the surface of his consciousness. His mother had loved her husband so much that his betrayal had driven her to do the unthinkable.

He'd been wrong about Kate all this time. She wasn't chasing after a title, but something else.

'That's not real love,' he recalled her saying that first night in the gardens at the Houghton Ball.

'So you do believe in love.'

Her mouth parted as a breath escaped it, her chest heaving.

'And you seek a love match,' he concluded.

She didn't say anything. She didn't have to. He already knew the answer. His bubbling rage froze into ice in his veins. Had she merely wanted a title to elevate her social status, he could have given her that easily. But anything more was out of the question.

'Whatever this is between us, we must ignore it from now on.'

Her head bobbed up and down vigorously as she hauled her stays and her dress over her torso. 'Yes.'

'We must stay apart and avoid each other as much as possible.'

'Of course.'

She reached behind her, her arms bending unnaturally as she attempted to button her dress. When he approached her, she shrank back.

'I only wish to assist you. Please.'

She eyed him with suspicion, but nodded and turned around. Though he had more experience in undoing women's clothing, he somehow managed to quickly lace her stays and button her up.

'Th-thank you,' she stuttered, and then turned to face him. 'And for not—'

He raised a hand. 'No need. And forgive me for—'

'Let's not speak of this ever.'

'Agreed.'

They stared at each for a few more moments, then broke away at the same time.

Sebastian gestured to the staircase. 'After you.'

She gave him a nod and marched towards the stairs, smoothing her hair into place. He grabbed his jacket and cravat, then followed behind her until they reached the top.

The bright sun temporarily blinded him as he staggered out, and he squinted against the light. Much to his dismay, once his vision cleared, he saw that the Marquess stood outside, hands on hips. His lips twitched, as if he was trying to suppress a laugh.

'Well, now…' Ashbrooke began. 'That didn't take too long.'

Kate's face flushed. 'We were… I mean, I just… We fixed the boiler. That's all.'

'Of course, Miss Mason. I believe you.' The Marquess winked at her mischievously. 'And please do not fret. Sebastian is my dearest friend. He—and you—can count on my discretion.'

'It's not… We didn't… You don't…' she blustered, her face turning even redder.

'What Ash means is that you needn't worry about anything because nothing happened,' Sebastian said smoothly. 'You should get back before anyone sees you.'

Her lips pulled into a tight line. 'Thank you, Your Grace…my lord. And please do tell Mr Alton to start the firebox at once. It will take a few hours to get it up to the proper temperature to heat the orangery.'

'I shall inform him personally.'

'Thank you.'

He kept his gaze on her as she turned towards the house and marched off, unable to look away. But he had to. And not just look away, but also to remember his vow never to be like his father, to break the cycle. Now that he knew what she was really after it was more apparent than ever that he could never be with her lest she suffer the same fate as his mother.

Ash chuckled. 'Now, *this*, my friend, is what thoroughly debauched looks like.'

'I did *not* debauch Miss Mason,' he said through gritted teeth.

The Marquess grinned at him maniacally. 'I wasn't talking about her.'

Chapter Twelve

Somehow Kate managed to sneak into the house without anyone seeing her. She quickly made her way up to her room, her heart threatening to escape her chest, and slammed her door behind her.

She rushed to the washstand and poured some fresh water from the jug into the porcelain bowl, then wet a clean washcloth and scrubbed at her face. Streaks of soot came away on the white cloth. The dirt was easily washed away from her skin, but when she recalled what had happened with Mabury she felt marked all over again. Not with grime, but with his mouth and hands.

Another rush of heat went straight between her legs and she staggered away from the washstand. While she was a virgin, she wasn't totally ignorant in the ways of men and women. Once she'd begun her monthly courses, in the summer she'd turned fourteen, their old housekeeper, Mrs Hargrave, had taken her aside and explained how children were conceived. Indeed, it had been quite pragmatic of the woman to take the task upon herself, as Kate had had no mother or other female figure in her life to explain such things.

So, yes, she knew what might have happened. She'd

just never thought it would be so…exquisite, or that she would feel like that. Now she had experienced a taste of it, she longed for something she'd never had before.

You shouldn't have kissed him.

It was a good thing she'd come to her senses before they'd gone too far. Well, they already had gone quite far, but at least she wasn't ruined, and things could go on as planned.

Dear Lord, how could she have forgotten about the solution to her Marriage Problem? And Seagrave? If she and Mabury had been caught, even a nitwit like Seagrave would have been smart enough to avoid a scandal.

Nothing is lost, she thought with grim determination. She and Sebastian were at least in agreement that they needed to ignore each other. He was a duke who didn't need the dowry of an American heiress with no name and no breeding. It was a bitter truth that she quickly swallowed.

'So you do believe in love.'

In that moment he'd caught her off guard with his conclusion that she wanted a love match. Kate wasn't sure, but seeing as nothing could ever happen between them it was better if she let him think that she wanted to find love with Seagrave so he would leave her alone.

She couldn't risk her match with Seagrave—not when she was so close. Besides, had she forgotten that Sebastian had vowed never to marry? Those were some of the first words he'd uttered to her at the Houghton Ball. A dalliance with him would not help her with her problem. And she was not unscrupulous enough to force him into marriage—especially when he was so vehemently against it.

At least Seagrave wanted to be married. There would be no force involved. And she wanted marriage too—if only to protect Pap's memory—though the deception made an uneasy emotion settle in her stomach like a lead stone. But perhaps she could slowly show Seagrave that she knew quite a lot about engineering. Though she knew there was very little chance of it, she had hope that he might even allow her to work on the building of the factory or run it.

Or maybe not, she thought glumly. *Duchesses don't work, after all.*

But it would be worth it. Future generations would remember Henry Mason's work and how his engine had changed the world. Never running her own factory or designing an engine would be a small price to pay.

Reaching behind her, she managed to undo the top buttons of her dress and ripped off the rest, tossing the garment aside before crawling into the massive four-poster bed. Her naked skin against the silk sheets made her think back to Sebastian and their encounter. How his hands had felt on her…his lips…that tongue.

She rolled onto her back and blew out a breath.

Kate, you fool! How could you lose sight of your goal with just a few kisses?

Well, they hadn't been just kisses.

Kate sat up quickly and crossed her arms over her chest. She couldn't let a few moments of passion over-rule her mind. Indeed, if losing herself and her control was the result of a few of Sebastian's kisses and an embrace, it was better that she forget about him and focus on Seagrave. While she didn't feel the same blazing and intense emotions with Seagrave, there was every chance that once they were married he'd show a different side of himself to her.

In a few days she would go on a carriage ride with Seagrave. She would have to make certain to ignite his interest enough for him to propose, and then Mason R&L would be away from Jacob's clutches. Once she was married to the Duke of Seagrave, Pap's legacy would be safe.

For the next few days Kate focused all her attention on securing Seagrave. As promised, they had gone on their carriage ride through the beautiful Surrey countryside, and since then he'd been invited to almost every event at Highfield Park.

Seagrave had been the perfect gentleman every time. And they were never alone, as they were always accompanied by Miss Merton or surrounded by the Dowager Duchess and the other ladies.

Kate was thankful for them—especially Maddie—because the truth was, being around Seagrave was monotonous. In the time they had known each other Seagrave had only ever spoken of his horses, and whenever anyone introduced a new topic he just showcased how obtuse he was. Only yesterday the Dowager Duchess had been talking about Napoleon, and he'd revealed that he thought Waterloo was in France.

But he would be the perfect husband for her. She had come so far, and there was nothing that could stop her. Nor distract her, for that matter. Not even Sebastian.

So far no one had found out about their encounter, or that she'd even been in the orangery. The Dowager Duchess had been told that a plumber had come and repaired the boiler, and she hadn't seemed too worried about the details, simply happy to know that her dear plants and trees would be saved.

Sebastian had also kept his promise about staying away from her, and Kate hadn't seen him at all. It was unreasonable of her to feel slighted, but his rejection still stung. To think that he'd found his attraction to her so disagreeable that he had to slink around his own home… Still, it saved her from the awkwardness and embarrassment of having to see him again.

Yet whenever she had her thoughts to herself, she found her mind would wander to that day in the furnace. But just as quickly as the passion between them had dissipated she'd dismissed those thoughts. Although that didn't stop them from creeping in…especially at night as she lay alone in her bed. And sometimes… sometimes she allowed herself to think of what might have happened if she hadn't stopped him.

'My dear, there's a letter for you.'

The Dowager Duchess's voice jolted Kate out of her scandalous thoughts. *Blast it.* Now she was thinking about him during breakfast, too.

'Another one?'

Her stomach was tied into knots; she knew who it was from. Her fingers trembled as she opened the cream-coloured envelope.

> *Kathryn,*
> *Since I have not heard from you, and Miss Merton has not relayed any offers of marriage, I can only assume that this venture is on the brink of failure. Thus, I have accepted Her Grace's open invitation and will be arriving at Highfield Park in one week with Jacob, so we may discuss your future prospects.*
> *Signed,*
> *Father*

The only reason Kate didn't crush the letter in her hand was because the people around the breakfast table were looking at her expectantly. 'My father wishes to accept your invitation to visit,' she told the Dowager Duchess. 'He will be here in one week's time.'

'Of course,' the Dowager said graciously. 'He is welcome.'

Kate lowered the letter to her lap. Her father coming here with her second cousin to discuss her 'future prospects' only meant one thing: he was going to force her to marry Jacob.

Desperation clutched at her chest. *Oh, why hasn't Seagrave proposed, or even asked for permission to court me?* Time was truly running out now. At this point Seagrave was her only chance, since she hadn't entertained any of the other gentlemen the Dowager Duchess had invited to the house.

'Kate?' Maddie whispered, a look of concern marring her face. 'What's the matter?'

Sweet, sensitive Maddie. Of course she knew something was wrong. 'Nothing. It's fine.'

She didn't look convinced, and continued, 'You know you can tell me anything.'

Not quite everything. 'Yes, I know, Maddie.'

Maddie lowered her voice even further. 'If you're not occupied after tea, you should join me in the library.'

'The library?'

'Yes. We can speak in private there. I've been spending some time there by myself, to get away from Caroline and Mother. I had meant to invite you...but you've been busy.'

With Seagrave, Kate added silently, as Maddie would never say it aloud. She'd been such a dear friend all this time, never complaining or expressing envy at Kate's success while she remained a wallflower at every event.

It had never even occurred to Kate that she'd ignored her until now.

'Of course I'll be there.'

It would be nice to spend time with Maddie without anyone else around—especially Caroline and Eliza.

As she'd promised, Kate sneaked off to the library after tea. Maddie was coming down the corridor at the other end and they met outside the door.

'Kate, you made it.' Maddie grabbed her hands and led her inside, directing her to sit beside her on a settee by the fireplace. 'I'm so glad you came.'

'I'm glad you invited me, Maddie.' Smoothing her hands over her lap, Kate decided to get straight to the point. 'Maddie, I'm sorry if I've been too occupied to spend time with you. I have left you at your mother and Caroline's mercy.'

'I am quite used to them,' Maddie replied, 'so think nothing of it. And as for your being occupied, I certainly understand—especially since you have caught a duke's eye.'

Kate's heart jumped, but then she realised Maddie was talking about Seagrave.

'May I speak frankly, Kate?' Maddie continued, when Kate didn't respond. 'Since we are friends?'

'Of course.'

'Seagrave is a wonderful catch, of course. Caroline is boiling with rage that you are so much closer to a match than her. But perhaps…you should not be in a rush?'

'I shouldn't?'

'Er…yes. I mean…' Maddie paused. 'Seagrave is handsome and titled. But he seems quite…er… He's…' Her cheeks turned bright pink.

Kate knew what her friend was trying to say, so she spared her the trouble. 'He's as thick as porridge.'

'Yes.' Maddie giggled, which made Kate burst out laughing. They continued to roar and howl in the most unladylike manner, until tears were streaming down their cheeks.

'Oh… I…' Maddie inhaled a deep breath and sat up straight. 'I thought you would be offended, but I just wanted to make sure—'

'I know.' Oh, dear, sweet Maddie. 'It's just…' It was time to tell her friend the truth. 'It's my father…' Taking a deep breath, she confessed her father's ultimatum, and her own plan to thwart him. 'And so you see… I have no choice. I must get Seagrave to propose, or my father shall force me to marry Jacob. And once he has control of Mason R&L I won't be able to stop him.'

'No. Oh, no.' Maddie shook her head. 'We can't let that happen.'

'We?'

'Yes. We.' There was a determined steely look in Maddie's eyes—something Kate had never seen before in her sweet, mild-mannered friend. 'Your Pap worked so hard. Kate, *you* worked so hard. I won't allow anyone to take that away from you.'

'Oh, Maddie…' A tiny flare of hope sparked inside her. 'But Seagrave hasn't even hinted at a proposal, and my father and Jacob are arriving next week.'

'Then the Duke must make haste in proposing. Or we can help him hurry.' Maddie's teeth sank into her bottom lip. 'I think you should get him alone tomorrow…during the picnic.'

The Dowager Duchess had arranged for a picnic in the grounds and Seagrave had agreed to come.

'Get him alone?' she repeated.

'Yes—and you should k-kiss him,' Maddie stammered, the colour returning to her cheeks once more. 'I mean, you h-haven't kissed yet, have you?'

The memory of Sebastian's kisses flashed in Kate's mind. 'No,' she replied hesitantly.

If Maddie noticed her hesitation she didn't mention it. 'We'll find a way to get you alone. I'll distract the others if I have to. Then you can get him to kiss you. That should make it very clear that you want a proposal.'

'What if I'm wrong? And he really doesn't want to propose?'

'Kate, please—you're much smarter than that. You know he wouldn't be spending this much time with you if he didn't have intentions.'

'But a kiss…'

'Is just a kiss—or that's what Caroline says,' Maddie said. 'If we are wrong, and no one else finds out, then there's nothing to worry about. You can still move on to the next suitor and ensure you don't have to marry Jacob.'

Maddie's words reminded her of why she was doing this in the first place. 'All right. I'll do it.'

Still, her insides twisted at the thought of kissing Seagrave. And she couldn't stop thinking about kissing Sebastian. Would Seagrave kiss her with the same passion? Would he make her feel the way Sebastian had? Ignite something in her—something scary, but at the same time something that made her feel alive?

But then she remembered that Sebastian didn't want her.

And I don't want him.

His kisses might have awoken something in her, but at the same time she'd felt like a spinning top, losing all her senses and her mind. And like that top she would eventually run out of momentum. She could not afford to lose control like that. All her life she'd been under her father's command. This time, at least, she would have a say as to who she was going to marry.

It's just nerves, she convinced herself.

Once she had Seagrave alone she would find a way to kiss him. Then he would have no doubt that she would accept a proposal from him.

It'll be all right, she told herself. *Everything will go according to plan.*

Chapter Thirteen

The following morning started out well enough, with the Dowager Duchess gathering everyone at the manor and explaining that the picnic would take place in a lovely meadow on the estate. The servants had gone on ahead to set up tables, food, and some amusements like archery and nine pins. The guests would have a lovely stroll to the picnic spot.

The food was scrumptious, as usual, with plenty of cold sandwiches, salads, teacakes, and lemonade and ginger beer to go around. When they'd finished the meal, the Dowager Duchess invited everyone to go for a walk in the wooded area nearby.

'I have an idea,' Maddie whispered to Kate. 'You, Seagrave and I will stay in the rear of the group. When we get deep into the woods, pretend that you've lost something. A piece of jewellery, perhaps. Tell Seagrave that it has much sentimental value to you. He'll offer to help you find it, and you can retrace your steps to lead him back. Once you're alone, then you must kiss him.'

'All right…' It was worth a try.

The party gathered and marched towards the dense woodland. One of the guests, Sir Elliot Mimsby, was somewhat of a nature-lover, and pointed out various flora and fauna along the way. While everyone was engrossed by Sir Elliot's lecture about the difference between a chaffinch and a bullfinch, Kate brought a hand to her ear, unclipped her earring, then dropped it into her pocket. Then she gasped and covered her mouth with her hand.

'Oh, dear, where is it?'

'What's wrong, Miss Mason?' Seagrave asked.

'It seems my earring has fallen off.' She tried to sound distressed. 'It was my dear grandmother's, too.'

'A priceless heirloom,' Maddie added for effect. 'Whatever will you do?'

'I must find it,' Kate replied. 'It's the only thing I have left of her.'

'You must help her, Your Grace,' Maddie urged Seagrave. 'Please.'

'But what about the others?' He gestured at the rest of the group, who had gone on ahead as Sir Elliot dragged them to a tree to point out a nest of baby birds.

'I'm sure the earring must have fallen somewhere behind us on the trail.' Maddie smiled sweetly at him. 'You can catch up with us.'

'Oh, please, Your Grace?' Kate batted her eyelashes at him. 'It would mean so much to me.'

He seemed to hesitate, but then nodded. 'Of course, Miss Mason.'

When Seagrave had turned and retreated down the path Kate straightened her shoulders and followed as he craned his head left and right, looking for the lost earring. When the path turned a corner, she retrieved the earring from her pocket, then tossed it halfway between them.

'Your Grace!' She strode closer to him. 'There!'

He swung round and looked down. Spying the earring, he bent to pick it up. She did the same thing, hoping he would accidentally bump into her, even angling her body sidewards. He moved much faster than she'd anticipated, however, and when she leaned down he raised his head, knocking their foreheads together.

Seagrave let out a curse and slapped a hand over his right eye. 'Ouch!'

Pain shot through her temple and she staggered backwards. While she didn't fall over, she also didn't realise what was behind her—until her left foot sank into a shallow pool of water. The sensation of her boot sinking into wet mud made her cry out in surprise and completely lose her balance. Before she knew it she had landed on her back with a loud, wet *splash*.

'Heavens!' Seagrave exclaimed as he stumbled forward, catching himself before he also took a dive into the water. 'Dear me…is that a pond?'

No, it's the Atlantic Ocean, you nitwit, Kate fumed as she sat up.

'Why, yes, Your Grace. I believe it is.'

Her hair was soaked and the water had reached her hips, and was now quickly seeping in through her garments, making them stick to her skin. She braced her hands beneath the surface, feeling the mud squishing through her fingers as she somehow managed to hoist herself up.

'Oh, dear…' The Duke continued to stare at her. 'You're wet.'

'Yes, that tends to happen when one falls into water.'

Seeing that Seagrave was making no move to assist her, she grabbed at her skirts and hiked them up as she trudged out of the pond. When she heard the sound of voices approaching, she let out a loud groan.

'Kate? Where are—?' Maddie's blue eyes widened.

'What is going on?' Miss Merton rushed forward, huffing and puffing, then stopped when she saw Kate. 'Miss Mason, what in heaven's name has happened to you?'

'I… I fell.' There was no other way to explain it, really. Just her luck that she hadn't seen the pond a few feet away from the trail when they'd walked by it.

Glancing behind the chaperone, she saw the Dowager Duchess, Caroline, Eliza, and the rest of their party approaching.

Oh, blast it all.

'My dear, why are you so muddy and wet?' The Dowager Duchess's mouth formed a perfect *O*.

Behind her, Caroline sniggered, and Eliza clucked her tongue in disapproval.

'I slipped and fell.' Kate grabbed a handful of her skirts, peeled most of them off her legs, and wrung out the excess water, not giving a whit that there were other people around.

'We should head back,' the Dowager Duchess said. 'Before you catch a cold.'

'I'm fine.' She waved a hand away.

And I am done.

Obviously, today was not the day when everything would go according to plan. And, considering her bad luck, she wasn't about to tempt fate further.

'Please don't cancel the rest of the day's activities because of me.'

'But you'll get ill,' the Dowager Duchess countered as she came closer, and offered Kate her shawl.

Kate waved the shawl away. 'I'll walk back to the manor and get changed. It's a warm day. I'll probably be quite dry by the time I arrive. Please, Your Grace,' she added in a whisper, 'I've embarrassed myself enough for today.' She glanced surreptitiously at the Duke. 'My ego can only endure so much.'

'Ah, I understand.' The Dowager Duchess patted her hand. 'Let me get a footman to accompany you.'

'It's not that far, Your Grace. I'll be faster on my own. Thank you very much for your concern, though.'

After sending a sheepish smile to Maddie, Kate trudged away, her wet walking boots squelching as she made the journey back. When she saw the manor ahead, she sighed with relief and picked up her pace. When she reached the front door she didn't dare enter with her muddy boots, so she took them and her stockings off and went inside on her bare feet.

Kate stopped and glanced at her reflection in the hall mirror. *Oh, heavens, I look a fright.*

Her coiffure had come undone, and her wet tresses trailed down her shoulders and back. The entire bodice of her yellow gown remained wet and now stuck to her torso. Her corset could clearly be seen underneath the almost transparent fabric.

I need to get to my room before anyone sees me!

Grabbing her sodden skirts, she hurried as best she could up the long staircase, thanking her lucky stars that only some of the servants were at home, since most were still at the picnic. She cheered herself on as she neared the top without having been caught.

'Almost there,' she muttered. 'Just a few more—'

Her breath stuttered when she looked up and found herself staring at a pair of familiar dark eyes.

When he'd arrived at the manor, after another long day helping John Lawrence, the last person Sebastian had expected to see was Kate Mason. And certainly not a bedraggled, wet, yet still lovely Kate Mason, with her dress moulding indecently to the luscious curves of her body. A body that had been torturing his every waking and sometimes sleeping thought for the last few days.

Cornflower-blue eyes grew wide as saucers. 'Y-Your Grace.' Somehow she managed a curtsey on the step.

Stunned, he said the first thing that came to mind. 'What the devil happened to you?'

'I—I fell.' Her cheeks heightened with colour.

He peered closer to her face and noticed some discolouration above her eye. 'Is that a bruise on your forehead?'

'A small…mishap. If you would excuse me…?' Straightening her shoulders, she continued to trudge up the stairs. When she reached the top she attempted to brush past him, but he blocked her way.

'Kate, you will tell me exactly what has happened to you this instant.' Lord, he was exhausted from physical activity, and all he wanted was a bath and a nap. But seeing her like this had his emotions swinging from lust to rage.

She attempted to sidestep him, but with his great bulk it was impossible. 'Please, Sebastian, I need to—'

'Kate, I won't repeat myself.'

Anger flashed in her eyes. 'Why in heaven's name would I say anything to you? I do not owe you an explanation.'

His jaw hardened. 'I want to know.'

'I am tired and wet and I have no patience to argue any more.'

'Then stop arguing and *tell me*.' He searched her face. 'Was it Seagrave?'

Her expression faltered. 'It's not what you think.'

Bloody hell, he didn't *want* to think about it, because

in the time he'd been away thoughts of what might be happening between her and the Duke were the only things plaguing him.

'Did he force himself on you? Try to kiss you?'

'Did he what?' she spluttered. 'I told you—it's not what you think!'

'Enlighten me, then.'

She hesitated, then said, 'If you must know, *I* was the one trying to kiss him.'

Rage tore through Sebastian and his fingers curled into his palms. 'And did you succeed?'

'That's none of your business.'

He had almost convinced himself that he would find a way to overcome this foolish attraction to her and keep her at a distance. But now here he was, in exactly the position that he had wanted to avoid all this time. It was too risky. There was too much at stake. And he wouldn't be able to give her what she wanted. A love match was out of the question, because after the events of five years ago he didn't even know if that was an emotion he could ever feel.

'I can't stand it,' he said.

'Can't stand what?'

Her breathing came in deep pants, and it was difficult to ignore the rise and fall of her chest as it thrust up towards him, her cleavage clearly outlined through the wet fabric.

'Seeing you. Being around you—'

'Then allow me to leave your sight immediately.' She sidestepped him and began to walk away.

'I can't stand being around you but not being able to have you.'

And that was the truth he hadn't been able to admit these past weeks. The truth he had been running away from. But maybe it was time to stop running away from the inevitable.

His words seemed enough to stop her in her tracks, as her frame went rigid. Slowly, she turned on her heel to face him again.

He continued. 'When you're around, I can't concentrate on anything else.'

She took a step closer.

'The only thing I want to do is take you in my arms and kiss you until every bit of breath has left your body.'

And closer.

He couldn't hear anything except for his heart pounding madly in his chest, but he couldn't stop all the words spilling out of his mouth. 'It's driving me mad—you're driving me mad.'

She was so near now, their bodies nearly touching.

'It's as if I might burst from the inside if I wait one second more to have you.'

They stood there, just staring at each other, for what seemed like the longest time.

'Why, Kate?'

'Why, what?'

There were so many 'whys' he wanted—no, needed— to be answered, so he asked the first one that came to mind. 'Why him? No matter how much you may…care for him, he's not the right one for you.'

'You don't understand.' Her voice hitched. 'Never could understand.'

'Why not?'

'You never want to marry,' she began. 'And you'll never have to if you don't want to.'

'So, this is about what society expects you to do?'

'I'm a woman.' A wry smile touched her lips. 'From the moment I was born I've always been under a man's control, and I will continue to be so until the day I die. At the very least I can have some choice in *this* matter, limited as it may be.'

Something in him wanted to shout *You have another choice aside from Seagrave*. Unfortunately, the bigger demons he'd been keeping inside managed to wrestle him down. Even if he could marry her, he wouldn't. Not when the memory of his father's deeds haunted him.

'You men have it so easy. Everything just drops in your lap. You can do whatever you want. You can choose to be anything you want to be. You are free.'

Sebastian ground his teeth together. 'If only that were the case. Men aren't as free as you think. Sometimes we're bound by society too. We must play by its rules and be what other people expect us to be or suffer the consequences. Or have our loved ones pay the price.'

She tilted her head to the side. 'What do you mean?'

'Nothing,' he replied quickly. 'Nothing at all.' This entire conversation was turning futile, so he decided to end it. With a quick nod, he tore his gaze from her and stepped back. 'I should leave—'

'Wait.'

His head snapped back to meet her eyes. 'Why? What do you want from me, Kate?'

The question seemed to stun her for a moment. But then to his surprise she reached out and once again crossed the distance between them.

Lord, he couldn't stand it any longer. She didn't fight him when he leaned down. No, she pushed herself up and fully opened to him, lips parting to welcome his kiss. Lord, he'd missed this. Missed her. The entire time he'd stayed away from her his body had been akin to a wound spring, ready to snap if he did not see, smell, and taste her again.

Tearing his mouth away from her, he trailed kisses down her jaw to her neck. She sighed and leaned her head back, exposing more of her soft skin to his mouth. Tentatively, he touched his tongue to the spot behind her ear. She mewled when he grazed his teeth over her skin, so he pressed his lips there and sucked. That sent her body buckling forward, so he caught her and then slipped a hand to the back of her dress, undoing just enough buttons to pull the garment down and peel the fabric from her chest. Moving his lips to her front, he reached the tops of her breasts and nibbled on the soft, white flesh, inhaled her distinct, sweet scent.

She cried out when he popped one breast from her corset and wrapped his lips around the nipple, licking it until it puckered in his mouth. He drew it in deeper, enjoying the sounds of her whimpers and moans as her body writhed deliciously against his. Her fingers dug into his hair, and the sensation of her nails raking on his scalp sent tingles down his spine.

'Please,' she moaned. 'I…'

He released her nipple. 'Please, what?'

'Please…we can't be seen out here.'

He slipped his hand under her knees, lifting her up into his arms.

'You're right,' he murmured against that spot again. Her pulse jumped, sending a surge of excitement straight to his manhood. 'I'm taking you to my rooms.'

She didn't protest. Instead she wrapped her arms around him, then nuzzled at his neck, and his shaft hardened painfully against his constricting clothing.

Sebastian wasn't sure how he managed it, but somehow they made it to his rooms undetected. Setting her down on the floor, he clicked the door shut and locked it, then turned to face her.

The sunlight streamed in through the windows, bathing her in an ethereal light that made her skin glow. However, it was the haze of desire in her eyes that had his own simmering lust boiling over. Seizing her once again, he backed her up towards his bed, stopping just at the edge.

His hand trembled as he reached up to tip her chin with his finger. 'Do you know what's about to happen?'

Her lashes lowered, but she nodded, her skin flushing prettily.

'And you still want it?'

Lord, if she said no he would turn back right now. If she told him she loved Seagrave and he loved her in return he would send her packing before they did something that they couldn't undo. The thought strung him tight, but all she had to do was say she didn't want this.

Slowly, she raised her gaze to meet his. 'I want...you.'

And with those words Sebastian knew there would be no turning back.

Chapter Fourteen

Kate's world had turned upside-down at her admission. When Sebastian had confessed his desire for her on the staircase she hadn't quite been able to believe it—not because she didn't think it was true, but because he had described her own emotions so perfectly.

'It's as if I might burst from the inside if I wait one second more to have you.'

How could he possibly have put it so succinctly? Every feeling, every ache, every longing had been encapsulated in his words, as if he'd reached into the depths of her soul and plucked them out. This raging attraction between was like a runaway locomotive, a powerful force neither one of them could stop.

And, Lord help her, she didn't want it to stop.

But, more than that, it was as if something had changed between them. In that moment she'd seen a side of him that had made her want to know more about him. Made her want to be closer to him.

'What do you want from me, Kate?'

She wanted him. She wanted this moment. To grab this intense passion by both hands, like a hunk of burning coal, and hold on to it for as long as she could. And damn the consequences.

His head swooped down, his mouth devouring hers, while his hands made quick work of the rest of the buttons at her back. Fabric pooled around her ankles as he shoved her dress down, then undid her corset until it too met the floor. Somehow her petticoats and hoops had also joined the rest of her clothing, but she didn't notice as he once again found that delicious spot under her ear with his talented mouth.

'Lovely,' he whispered, as he stepped back to look at her.

Despite still being dressed in her damp chemise and drawers, she felt exposed under the gaze of his dark eyes. A hand cupped her chin, tilting her head back as he pressed his lips to hers again. This time his kiss was surprisingly gentle, though his hands roamed lower, over her breasts and down her hips, before grabbing handfuls of her chemise.

'Oh!' she gasped, when their mouths broke contact so he could lift the undergarment over her head.

'Kate…' he began as his hand spanned her abdomen. 'Have you ever…touched yourself?' He moved lower, his fingers leaving a trail of heat in their wake. 'Down here?'

She sucked in a breath when his callused palm covered the downy triangle between her legs. 'I… A few times.' The sensation had been pleasant, she recalled, but it had felt entirely too wicked, so she'd refrained from exploring further.

'And did you…?'

'Did I what?'

A finger slid up to the top of her mound and brushed

against the swollen bud there. A cry tore from her mouth as the most delicious sensation rippled through her body.

'From the look on your face I can guess you did not.'

'Did not...what?'

He murmured non-committally and continued to stroke her, his pace increasing, and at the same time those pleasurable shocks came faster. Kate's knees buckled, so she clung to him, her fingers digging into his forearms for support and her face pressed against his chest as he switched to a circling motion.

Her body tightened and tensed and felt hot all over. Unsure what to do, she rolled her hips against his hand, wanting more... She didn't know what, exactly, but she just knew she had to have it *now*.

'Sebastian...' She whimpered against the linen of his shirt as her body climbed a peak. Higher and higher. Until she was sent reeling over the edge. Falling. Drifting. Sapped. Back to earth. Her legs shook when she tried to straighten herself out, so he pushed her down on the bed.

'That.'

Obsidian eyes filled with promise bored into hers, and the heat she'd thought had drained from her body came rushing back, making her feel dizzy.

Mrs Hargrave never said anything about this feeling so good.

'Is there more?' she asked breathlessly.

'Oh, yes. There's so much more.' He stared boldly down at her naked form, spread on top of the covers, leaving nothing unseen.

A sense of shame and mortification washed over Kate, and she reflexively crossed her arms over her breasts and cupped a hand over her mound. 'Please, you— Sebastian…' She shut her eyes tight. 'Could you…draw the curtains?'

'No.'

A rough hand held her ankle, then planted it on top of the mattress, then did the same with the other. Kate could imagine how she looked—what he was looking at, at this moment—and her entire face, all the way to the tips of her ears, heated with embarrassment.

'I want to see all of you, Kate.' He brushed her hand aside. 'And taste you.'

Oh, Lord, he couldn't possibly…

'Oh!' His tongue slid up the crease of her sex. Teasing and licking at her. Sending shocks of pure pleasure up and down her body. It coiled in her, winding tight like a spring, and just when she thought it couldn't possibly get any better she felt something—his finger—slip inside her. The sensation made her claw at the sheets with her fingers.

The maddening rhythm of his tongue and the deep carnal thrusts of his finger were too much. Too incredible. Too pleasurable. They sent her to dizzying heights once more, and this time her entire body convulsed and shook with ecstasy, making it hard to breathe. She let out a hoarse cry, trying to get as much air as she could, until her body collapsed back on the mattress and her lungs learned to function once more.

'You are exquisite.' He nuzzled at her thighs, sending a few aftershocks over her skin. 'Look at me, Kate. Please.'

Somehow, she found the strength to open her eyes and glance down at him. The blurriness of her vision faded until his face appeared before her. He looked entirely too wicked, kneeling between her thighs, dark eyes burning as their gazes crashed into one another.

Slowly, he stood and discarded his jacket, then began to unbutton his shirt, exposing all that golden skin. Mortification coloured her cheeks as she remembered that day when she'd spied him similarly undressed. The view from the telescope, however, had not done him any justice. His shoulders were broader than she'd imagined, the muscles bulging and flexing as he continued to discard his clothes. A thick mat of dark hair covered his wide chest, trailing downwards towards...

She couldn't stop the gasp from escaping her mouth as he pulled his loosened trousers and his drawers down in one motion, freeing his manhood. Heat rushed up her cheeks as she watched the heavy, jutting member rising from the nest of dark curls between his legs.

He came forward, the mattress dipping under his weight. Slowly, he moved over her, slipping his arms under her and then hauling her body higher on the mattress. When he nudged her knees apart instinct made her clamp them together and turn her head away.

'Shh... Kate...' He leaned down and pressed his lips to her cheek. 'Relax.'

A hand slid up her thighs, coaxing them to open. Once again, his fingers did the most delicious things to her most secret part. Kate allowed herself to calm down and unclench. He breathed a sigh, too, as if he'd been just as anxious as her.

'This will hurt,' he warned her as his body covered hers, his heavy sex jutting against her belly. 'But only for a short while. And then it will feel so good.'

She wanted to trust him. No, she *did* trust him. At least in this, she did.

Nodding, she spread her legs even more to accommodate him. He gathered her against him, then planted soft kisses on her neck, moving up to capture her lips again.

She welcomed his mouth on hers, his ardent kisses making her shiver with pleasure. She hardly noticed the blunt tip of his sex as it nudged against her cleft and pushed inside her.

Oh.

The sensation was like nothing she'd ever felt before. It wasn't terrible, but she couldn't describe it. His hips moved further, and she gasped. There was more…so much more of him. Her passage clenched at the intrusion, and she let out a soft cry and squeezed her eyes shut.

'I'm sorry.' He kissed her again. 'I need to…'

'Please…not so fast.' It was overwhelming. The sensations. The invasion. The building pain.

'Shh…' A hand moved between them, searching for the bundle of nerves right above the place where they were joined. He teased her there again, his fingers playing her expertly, until she felt a rush of wetness. 'It will be over sooner if I just…'

'If you—? Oh!' She hadn't expected the immediate thrust.

He continued to brush the crest of her sex with his rough fingertips. The burning hurt terribly, but as he promised it was over quickly. She found herself relaxing, and then rolling her hips at him.

'You feel…incredible…' He groaned when she pushed up, and seated more of himself inside her. Shifting his weight, he drove his hips back and then pushed inside her once more.

The sensation jolted her eyes open. He did it again, the pressure from his pelvis rubbing her just right, eliciting from her a hoarse cry.

'Kate?'

'It's…good.'

Hands slid under her buttocks, lifting her up to meet him. 'Better?'

'Much.'

He buried his face in her neck, whispering soft words that she didn't quite understand. He drew back, then thrust inside her again, each time driving deeper. His mouth found that spot under her neck once more and the pleasurable sensations intensified. Still, she wanted more. A greedy craving grew exponentially inside her with every stroke.

His mouth caught hers again in a savage kiss. Their tongues danced, teeth clashed, his hips all the while continuing that maddening rhythm that provoked sensations she'd never felt before. She wrapped her arms around his torso, fingers digging into his back as she arched up into him, urging him to give her more. He stroked parts of her that no one else had, parts she'd never even known existed inside her.

With each thrust she sobbed and cried out in joyful surrender. A wave of pleasure pushed her once more to the edge, sending her soaring. His arms tightened around her, his thrusts turning erratic as she continued to plummet to the blissful depths. He let out a guttural groan and she felt the oddest sensation of him spasming inside her, then warmth flooding her, before he slumped forward with a deep shudder.

They lay still for what seemed like eternity. She should have been bothered by his body on top of hers but, truth be told, the weight of him was rather pleasant. She felt…enfolded and cherished at the same time.

He breathed deep, then rolled away. Disappointment flooded her as he left her body, but before she could protest he tucked her against him and brushed the hair at her nape to the side.

'Rest,' he whispered lazily, to the column of her neck.

She was about to protest, but only a yawn escaped her mouth. Her body, drained from the physical and mental exertion of the day, relaxed in his arms and she let blissful sleep take over.

When Kate woke up, the first thing that registered in her mind was the strange sensation of sheets on her body. *How odd.* It was as if she was naked.

Bolting upright, she glanced around her. She was *definitely* naked, and that was *definitely* Sebastian behind her.

Dear Lord, it hadn't been a dream.

Her head snapped towards the window. While the last time she'd been awake the sun had been high in the sky, it was now slowly sinking beneath the horizon, casting the room in the glow of twilight.

Oh, heavens.

She slid to the edge of the bed, wincing as pain throbbed between her legs.

Another realisation smashed into her brain.

They had—

'Kate?'

His low baritone was enough to make her knees weak—especially when she remembered the wicked things he'd whispered in her ear.

'It—it's getting late,' she stammered. 'Everyone must have come back from the picnic by now. They're all probably getting ready for dinner.' She scampered off the mattress and grabbed at the clothes on the floor. 'If I can sneak off—'

'What the devil are you going on about?'

He sat up in bed, eyes fixed on her. There was no

time to feel shame or mortification at her current state of undress—or his—so she tore through the pile and picked up her chemise and drawers. 'If I'm found here—'

He was beside her in an instant. 'Kate, what's done is done. Do you regret what happened between us?'

The question made her pause. *Did she?* Perhaps if she considered only the pleasure they had given each other she could say she didn't regret any of it. But now, as the light grew even fainter, the consequences of her actions came crashing into her. Her plan to save her grandfather's legacy was in peril.

But not everything was lost.

Shrugging, she tugged and tied her drawers on and threw her chemise over her head.

'We cannot undo what we did.' He was behind her now, his presence looming over her.

'Yes, that's generally how time works.' She smoothed the chemise down over her body. 'But as long as we are discreet no one will find out.'

'No one will—?' He blew out a breath. 'I've ruined you.'

'No one needs to know. We haven't been caught.' But she had to get out of there before anyone did see them.

A dark look crossed his face. 'You are—*were*—a virgin. I think your future husband will be able to tell if you come to his bed in this state.'

She gritted her teeth. 'I'm sure Seagrave won't mind.' *Blasted nitwit probably wouldn't be able to tell, anyway.*

'Seagrave?' he thundered. 'You still think to marry him?'

'Of course.' She spied her corset in the clothing pile and bent down to pick it up. He was supposed to believe she loved Seagrave, right? 'Who else am I supposed to marry?'

'Me. Marry me.'

The words had flown out of his mouth without thought.

She stopped moving, her limbs frozen in place. 'You're jesting.'

'I am not. I have ruined you and now I must pay.'

Yes, that was it. That was the only reason that didn't sound insane right now. Because, despite his vow never to marry, Miss Kate Mason was the one person in the world who had managed to make him say those two words.

'You must *pay*? Like…like having to recompense a shopkeeper for breaking a trinket on a shelf?' She snorted. 'My, what a romantic proposal, Your Grace. It's what every girl dreams of.'

'That's not what I meant! You simply must marry me now.'

'Oh!' She threw her hands up. 'So now you are ordering me to marry you?'

'For God's sake!' He scrubbed his hands down his face. 'Kate, I know I can't give you what you want—'

'At least we are in agreement on that!'

Pain plucked at his chest, but he ignored it. 'But we have no choice in the matter now.'

'Only if anyone else finds out.'

'If you are with child, then they will definitely find out.'

She opened her mouth, but nothing came out. She clamped her lips shut. Silence hung between them until she finally spoke. 'Well, we will find out soon, I suppose. My courses will come…or they will not…and once we are certain we can deal with it.'

Deal with it? Was she insane?

'Listen, Kate—'

'No, *you* listen!' She waved her corset at him as if she were brandishing a fencing foil. 'This should be a boon to you. A tumble with no consequences. Why must you insist on doing the right thing when it's quite apparent that you want to marry me about as much as I want to marry you?'

That pain in his chest spread, making it difficult to breathe. He could only watch as she slipped the corset over her chemise and tugged on the ties at the back. He couldn't move, couldn't speak.

By the time she had finished knotting her corset, the throbbing in his temple had stopped. 'You will tell me if you are with child.'

She didn't answer. Instead shook out her gown on the floor, then stepped into it.

'There will be no child,' she stated.

'You don't know that.'

Kate pulled the dress over her torso, reached behind her to close the top buttons, then arranged her hair to cover the rest. 'We can't know for sure either way, so let's assume for now there is no child.'

Damn her logical mind.

'This discussion is not over,' he said.

'Oh, I think it is.'

Finally she was somewhat fully dressed, and she strode over to the door. She opened it and stuck her head out, glanced around to check if anyone was outside, then slipped out and tiptoed away down the corridor.

Why he'd slept with her, he didn't know. Actually, he damned well *did* know. He'd wanted her. And it was quite obvious she'd felt the same way. Kate had been a virgin—she was not the kind of woman who took a tumble in anyone's bed for no reason.

So why had she said no?

Why had he proposed in the first place?

Because I did *ruin her.*

Despite Kate's protests about being a trinket, that was the truth—at least, that was how the ton would see it.

In the past it had been easy to avoid virgins. Hell, even when he'd been a thoughtless rake he hadn't dared seduce virgins so he could avoid being forced to marry too early. But now his actions had consequences.

Just as with his father's actions, someone else would be paying for them.

He'd done exactly what he'd been trying to avoid all these years. Which meant he had to put right this mess he'd created. Unlike his father, he wasn't going to bury his head in the sand. No, he would face the consequences and take responsibility for his actions.

Kate had to marry him. There was no other way.

Chapter Fifteen

Kate's heart hammered so loudly she feared it might burst out of her chest. But by some miracle she managed to make it all the way to her room without being seen by anyone. When the door clicked shut behind her, her limbs weakened, as if all her energy had been drained from her very bones.

She leaned against the door and closed her eyes.

What had she been thinking? She had been swept up by passion and his kisses. By pleasure she'd never imagined she could feel. Even now her sex clenched at the thought of him inside her.

I'm no longer a virgin.

She didn't feel different at all—except for the stinging between her legs. Speaking of which…she needed a hot bath, and then she'd have to get dressed for dinner. While she considered begging off tonight, and pretending she had caught a cold, she knew it would be a waste of an opportunity for her to spend time with Seagrave—especially now that her father would be arriving in six days, with the odious Jacob in tow.

A thought made her heart crash into her ribcage.

Mabury had wanted to marry her.

And, God help her, for a brief moment she had wanted to say yes.

But she hadn't.

Some might think it a stupid decision to reject him, but his impulsive proposal had done nothing to sway her. In fact, it had felt like an insult—as if she now had even less value as a person because she'd lost her virginity, and only he could bring her back from perdition.

'I have ruined you,' he'd said. *'Now I must pay.'*

Her chest had tightened at those words. Words that had made what she had thought a beautiful, passionate experience into a sordid affair.

And then he'd made it even worse, ordering her to marry him! Why, he was no better than her father, forcing her to marry.

She couldn't afford to lose this one choice—this one bit of control she had over her life. Seagrave was the right husband. She had thrown caution to wind with Sebastian, and now look where she was. With Seagrave she might never experience that intense passion, but she wouldn't get burned either.

Nothing would stop her from getting him to propose. Not her father, not Sebastian, nor—

Her hand went to her abdomen. Surely she couldn't be... If she were...

Kate straightened her spine and curled her hands into fists at her sides. She would deal with that later. If Seagrave asked her father for permission to court her, then that would at least ward off any notion of her marrying Jacob. Should she be with child, her second cousin would surely never agree to marry her anyway.

Feeling resolved, she rang for her maid so she could dress for dinner.

* * *

Somehow, Kate kept her composure for the duration of the meal. However, she couldn't help but feel that anyone who looked at her would know what she and Sebastian had done—as if a visible mark had appeared upon her person to indicate that she was no longer a virgin. Still, she kept her mind on her goal and focused her attention on Seagrave.

For his part, Seagrave seemed genuinely apologetic for what had happened and not helping her sooner. She, of course, forgave him.

'It was an accident, Your Grace. No harm done.'

No harm except that she had lost her innocence to another man.

And, speaking of Sebastian, he seemed to have no trouble at all in keeping his countenance aloof. Indeed, he acted as if Kate didn't exist at all. When he entered the room, after being announced, he greeted everyone with a nod, his gaze passing over her as it always did. And when he sat down to dinner he spoke only with his mother and the guests around him, but only if they asked him a question first.

This is what he's really like, she supposed.

Maybe, like her, he'd been caught up in the blazing passion between them. It was hard to believe this cold, imposing figure was the same man who had kissed her so wickedly on the neck and the shoulders and well… everywhere.

Everything had changed between them. She was a fool to think otherwise. But it wasn't just their making love. She had glimpsed a side of him she'd never seen before—something he usually hid behind that cold and aristocratic façade.

'Men aren't as free as you think… We must play by

its rules... Suffer the consequences... Or have our loved ones pay the price.'

What did he mean, exactly? She'd been too caught up in their passion to think about it then. Now she couldn't stop thinking about it, and another instance afterwards. It had been the one moment when she'd thought that there was something more driving his proposal. When she'd told him that she didn't want to marry him there had been a subtle change in his expression, but Kate hadn't been able to ignore it. He'd looked almost...hurt.

But he was the one who didn't want to marry at all. Why would her rejection affect him?

'Are you all right, Miss Mason?' asked Miss Merton. 'You seem listless all of a sudden. Are you coming down with a cold?'

'Oh, dear.' Seagrave clicked his tongue. 'Perhaps you should have stayed in bed.'

At the word 'bed' the Duke of Mabury's head snapped towards her and a jolt of excitement shot straight to her abdomen. 'I—I'm perfectly all right. It's just rather... warm in here tonight.'

'Indeed, the weather is changing,' the Dowager Duchess remarked.

'Your Grace,' Caroline began, 'don't you think we should celebrate? Celebrate that spring is here, I mean,' she added quickly. 'Maybe you could host a bigger gathering?'

'Oh, yes!' Eliza clapped her hands together. 'That would be lovely. A large soirée. Perhaps you could invite more people to attend?'

The Dowager Duchess seemed to contemplate the idea. 'Well, I suppose that could be arranged...a ball, perhaps?'

Caroline squeaked. 'Oh, yes.'

'A ball sounds wonderful, Your Grace,' Miss Merton said. 'If you are amenable to such a thing.'

'A small, intimate ball...a party with dancing, really,' the Dowager Duchess qualified. 'We could invite everyone who's already come to Highfield Park.'

'Hopefully we can all dance?' Caroline sent a hopeful look at the Duke.

'It's settled, then,' the Dowager Duchess declared. 'Five days from today—that will be enough time to prepare. Eames, what say you? Are you up to the task? There is no one else I would trust to help me put together an event like this.'

The butler stepped forward and gave the Dowager Duchess a nod of his head. 'It would be my deepest honour, Your Grace.'

'Thank you, Eames.' She turned to the rest of the table. 'And of course everyone here is invited.'

Excitement buzzed amongst the guests.

Beside Kate, Seagrave cleared his throat. 'Miss Mason?'

'Yes, Your Grace?'

'I...uh... I hope I am not overstepping my bounds, but I overheard Miss Merton tell Mrs DeVries that your father is expected to arrive.'

'Oh. I mean...oh, yes.'

'I was wondering...if you think it would be wise... if I might speak to him...perhaps...' He looked around and motioned for a footman to refill his glass.

Just say it! she wanted to scream at him as he took a big gulp of his wine.

'Yes?'

'Um...' He breathed in. 'What I mean to say is... I would like to approach your father about the possibility of courting you.'

Kate paused, waiting for...she didn't know what. It felt as if she'd been anticipating this moment for eternity, and now that it was here she had imagined it would feel more...well, just *more*.

'Miss Mason?'

'Yes...?' she choked. 'I mean, yes, of course.'

When his face lit up, Kate breathed a sigh of relief.

'Miss Mason, I am so glad to hear that.' He wiped his lips with his napkin. 'All these weeks I have been trying to gauge your interest, and I'm glad my feelings are returned.'

She forced a smile on her face. 'Of course, Your Grace.'

The doors opened once again and the footmen came in with the third course. A hush fell over the table as the trays were set down and the silver domes lifted to reveal a scrumptious pheasant dish.

Kate cut into her roasted fowl and put a morsel in her mouth, but it turned to ash on her tongue. Yes, her plan was coming along nicely, but there was an uncomfortable sensation in her stomach—an uneasiness that told her something was not quite right.

Unwillingly, she glanced towards the head of the table. Her chest tightened as she looked at Sebastian, so devilishly handsome under the glow of the candlelight.

'Marry me.'

If he'd said those words under different circumstances would she have said yes? If he had used softer tones, or if he hadn't said that he'd ruined her and therefore had to pay?

She didn't dare let her fantasy play out. It only made her chest constrict. Besides, what was the point of mulling it over now that it was done?

Seagrave was her best choice, she reminded herself.

And now that marriage to him was finally within her reach she couldn't afford any missteps. Pap's legacy was at stake.

Kate didn't know how long she'd been staring at him, but when those dark eyes met hers a slow heat began to build low in her belly. Unable to keep looking at him without losing herself, she quickly turned away.

She had to remind herself of the plan. All she had to do was wait until her father arrived. She couldn't recall ever in her life looking forward to seeing Arthur Mason or Jacob the way she did now.

Sebastian fumed silently, wishing for a cloud or a thunderstorm or a cyclone to spoil the beautiful clear weather outside. *Or perhaps a lightning strike would be better*, he thought. But only if it could be directed to the current object of his ire—the Duke of Seagrave, who as of this moment was helping Miss Kate Mason into his carriage.

It was as if God or the Devil himself had cursed him, so that he'd happened to look out of the window of his study just in time to watch her flirting with Seagrave. The only thing that stopped him from storming outside was the fact that Miss Merton was accompanying them, even though it was perfectly acceptable for Kate and Seagrave to drive together in an open carriage.

At least someone around here has some sense.

'Your Grace?'

Clearing his throat, he turned and faced his solicitor, Mr James Hall. 'Yes, James?'

'The machinery, Your Grace?'

'What machinery?'

James nodded to the papers on his large oak desk. 'The new machinery you ordered. I just wanted to make sure the amounts were accurate so I may release payment to the company.'

'Ah, yes.' Sebastian glanced outside one last time, grinding his teeth as he watched the carriage drive away, before striding back to his desk. After a quick check of the numbers and a few calculations in his head, he knew something was off. 'There's an error in the addition... I think your accountant must have mistaken that seven on the third invoice for a one.'

James took the papers. 'I shall have him redo this.'

'Now, is there anything else we need to discuss?'

'No, Your Grace.' The solicitor stood up. 'Thank you again for your time.'

'Thank you for coming all the way here, James; I do appreciate it. Allow me to walk you outside.'

'I'm sure you have more business to attend to. There's no need—'

'It's no trouble at all.' Sebastian rounded his desk. 'Come.'

He would not be able to concentrate on his work in any case. For the last five days his thoughts had been plagued with only one thing—or rather, one person. His damned emotions were scattered all over the place, swinging from lust to anger to frustration, and it was all because of one slip of a girl.

His burning desire for Kate he would eventually be able to conquer. Even the anger would eventually subside. But Sebastian's frustration stemmed from the one thing he just couldn't understand: why she was insisting on marrying that buffoon.

Granted, Seagrave was young and handsome, but his estate was in near ruins. The match would obviously be advantageous to the Duke, but for the life of him Sebastian didn't know how Kate would benefit—especially when she could find better prospects. Anyone who had even a modicum more sense and intelligence than Seagrave would suit her.

Like you? a voice inside him mocked.

He quickly quashed that thought. Besides, she had made it perfectly clear from her rejection of his proposal that she wouldn't even consider him for a husband, despite what had happened between them. Really, he should be rejoicing. He'd already tried to do the right thing by offering for her, and if she hadn't accepted that was not his fault.

I can't give her what she wants.

Love.

She wanted love. She hadn't denied it when he'd asked her outright in the furnace room.

She believed in love. Sought it out. And, despite her obvious attraction to Sebastian, somewhere deep inside she must know that he had no capacity for such an emotion.

In fact, no emotion could move him, and he was convinced that all sentiment had been removed from his person five years ago.

His throat went dry as the vision in his head became clear. As if he were reliving the nightmare again.

The candles burning.

The empty bottle on the bedside table.

His mother, lying motionless in her bed.

He was no better than that cad who had sired him... who had seduced and whored his way through London. Sebastian had sworn an oath never to marry and sire a child so that he would stop the cycle. So that he would never turn out like his father. Yet he had done exactly that, and that was why he had to make it right.

He'd ruined Kate. That he'd taken her virginity without even thinking of the consequences for her left a terrible dread in his stomach. But even though Sebastian should regret taking Kate into his bed, for the life of him he couldn't. They had both wanted what had happened between them.

'You don't understand. Never could understand.'

What had she meant when she'd said that, exactly? He understood that, as a woman, she didn't have a lot of choices. Lord, he understood that most of all, after what had happened with his own mother. But there was something else. Something she wasn't telling him.

'Thank you once again, Your Grace.'

James's voice yanked him from the grip of the past. Sebastian had been so deep in thought that he hadn't realised they'd made it all the way outside. 'Of course. I shall see you in a fortnight, James.'

'Have a good day, Your Grace.'

Sebastian turned back to the manor and walked inside, nearly bumping into Eames.

'Apologies, Your Grace.' The butler stepped back and bowed his head low.

'It's quite all right, Eames.' Looking behind the butler, he saw two maids carrying large white bundles, their faces turning pale and eyes widening as soon as they realised he was there. They both nearly fell over, trying to curtsey. 'What the devil is going on, Eames?'

Eames gave the two maids a stern look. 'Mrs Grover forgot to inform the maids that they need to prepare two bedrooms in the east wing. They are pressed for time, so I'm escorting them through the front of the house instead of via the servants' entrance. Apologies. It won't happen again, Your Grace.'

'Why are they preparing two bedrooms in the east wing? Who are we hosting now?'

'Mr Arthur Mason and his cousin are arriving in the morning, Your Grace,' Eames answered smoothly.

'Arthur *Mason*?' Even the sound of Kate's surname had him responding like a dog hearing its master call.

'Yes. Miss Kathryn's father is coming for a visit, along with his cousin.'

'Her fath—?' A throb pulsed behind his eyes.

Kate's father was arriving tomorrow. And Seagrave had visited every day since the night of the picnic, sometimes staying for dinner. This only meant one thing: Seagrave was going to ask Mr Mason's permission to court Kate. He must have made his intentions known, which was why Kate's father was coming to Highfield Park.

'Bloody hell!' In his own home, too!

Eames's face drained of colour. 'I'm sorry, Your Grace! I shall tend my resignation and—'

'For heaven's sake, Eames! I wasn't cursing at you!' The throb was now a painful hammering, growing by the second. 'Send word to John Lawrence and all the other tenants that I'll be indisposed for the rest of the day.'

'Of course, Your Grace.'

Whirling on his heel, he stormed down the corridor and made his way back to his study. He went straight to the table by the fireplace, where he kept a bottle of brandy. After filling the snifter halfway, he swallowed the entire contents and then poured himself another before sinking down on the nearest chair.

So, Seagrave has found the bollocks to make his intentions known. Bloody fantastic.

Why in God's name should he give a damn, anyway, when she didn't want to marry him?

There could still be a child.

Yes, that was the reason he should give a damn. From the way Kate had spoken, Sebastian thought it would be some time before she was certain whether or not she was with child. Or perhaps she did already know and had accelerated her courtship with Seagrave as a result. Maybe she'd already slept with him so he could take responsibility for any child she bore.

That she would be bound for ever to someone else had him gasping for breath—as if his body couldn't bear the thought that he would never see her again. Or, worse, see her beside another man.

But why should she bring such emotions within him?

He took another sip. The smooth liquor slid down his throat, straight to his belly. While the alcohol should have dulled his mind, it only brought more questions to the surface. Questions he should have asked himself in the first place.

Kate wanted a love match, and yet she had slept with him. If she was in love with Seagrave, why had she willingly come to his bed?

Something about this whole thing did not make sense. There was something that he had missed. And, dammit, the nagging urge to find out what wouldn't go away.

One way or another, Kate would tell him the truth before the day was over.

Chapter Sixteen

Despite his earlier state of intoxication, Sebastian was clear-headed and sober by the time the ball began—thanks to Robeson. His valet had tutted disapprovingly at his master's inebriated condition, but worked hard to make Sebastian presentable for the ball. To do that, however, the valet had forced some vile concoction down his throat that had him swearing off liquor for the rest of his life.

Miraculously, the foul potion seemed to have worked and he was now sober as stone.

Frankly, Sebastian didn't know if he should fire Robeson or give him a rise.

'It's been a while since I've seen you in your finery, darling,' his mother remarked as he escorted her towards the ballroom. 'You do look so handsome in black and white.'

'And you're ravishing, as always.'

'Thank you. And, darling…?'

'Yes?'

'Thank you for everything.' Her smile seemed to light up the room. 'I know my guests have disturbed your peace.'

Sebastian bit his tongue so he wouldn't ask if she

knew anything about one particular guest and her possible engagement to a certain duke. Thankfully, Eames announced their arrival before he could speak, and they headed to the middle of the dance floor to open the ball.

When they were in position, Eames nodded to the orchestra's conductor and they began their dance.

'Are you looking for someone, darling?' his mother asked, lifting a brow quizzically.

'Looking for someone?'

'Yes. Your eyes are roving the room, I thought perhaps there was someone you were hoping to find?'

'I was simply wondering who you had invited. Apologies. I have been too busy and didn't look over the guest list.' He focused his attention on the dance steps, hoping his mother would accept his explanation.

When the dance finally ended, he bowed to his mother, then escorted her to the side of the room, where a group of their neighbours had congregated.

For the next hour, Sebastian did his duty and stayed by his mother's side, engaging in conversation and dancing with a few matrons. This 'small' ball was much larger than he'd anticipated, and while he used his time whirling around the dance floor to search amongst the guests, he hadn't spied Kate nor Seagrave yet.

It was as he led his latest dance partner back to her husband that he saw the Duke escorting Kate to the dance floor for a quadrille. He couldn't take his eyes off her. Kate looked even lovelier tonight, in a green satin ballgown, her mahogany hair pinned in curls around her head, her creamy skin glowing under the light of the chandelier.

His jaw hardened as the couple took their positions. Unable to stop himself, he watched them like a hawk, each smile and whisper making his ire grow.

Finally, the dance finished, and Kate and Seagrave walked to the corner where the DeVries ladies were waiting. He excused himself from his current companions and strode over to the group.

'Good evening, Seagrave...ladies.'

'Mabury,' the Duke greeted him. 'Splendid ball tonight. It seems half the county is here.'

'It was all my mother's work.'

His gaze fixed on Kate. The low neckline of her dress displayed her creamy skin and a generous amount of décolletage. He couldn't help but remember how she'd tasted, and her soft mewls as he'd suckled on her nipples.

'Your Grace, are you ready for your next dance?' Caroline batted her eyelashes at him. 'Because I am.'

'Indeed, I am ready.' Sebastian cleared his throat. 'Miss Mason, may I have the honour of the next dance?'

'I'm afraid I'm otherwise occupied, Your Grace,' she answered in a sweet tone.

'With whom?' Seagrave asked. 'You said your dance card was completely empty until I asked you.'

A flash of exasperation crossed her face, but she held out her hand anyway. 'Thank you, I would love to, Your Grace.'

Taking her hand, Sebastian led her to the dance floor. When a waltz was announced, she flinched. Sebastian, on the other hand, relished the closeness the dance required.

He slid his hand around her waist and pulled her to him. 'Put your hand on my shoulder.'

She did as he asked, but turned her head away as the dance began.

Undeterred, he continued. 'How lovely you look tonight, Kate.'

'Just because we are dancing, it does not mean we must talk.' She craned her head further away from him.

He leaned down, dangerously close to her ear. 'That's quite all right, because all I need is for you to listen.' She stiffened in his arms. 'Once our waltz is over I will escort you back to Seagrave and your friends. When the next dance finishes you will make up some excuse and meet me in the library.'

Her eyes snapped up to meet his gaze. 'I will do no such thing.'

'Yes, you will.' He lowered his voice. 'If you do not, I shall tell Seagrave that there is a possibility you are carrying my child.'

'You wouldn't dare!' she breathed.

'Would you like to put me to the test, Kate?'

Her plump lips pressed tight as she seemed to contemplate her choices. 'All right.'

'Good.'

The rest of the dance went by in silence, but he couldn't help the satisfaction he felt, holding her close in his arms. It seemed like a lifetime ago that she had been in his embrace.

When the music ended, she curtseyed to him and he led her back to the side of the room. 'Remember what we talked about.'

'Yes, Your Grace,' she mumbled.

'Thank you for the dance,' he announced loudly to her group. 'If you would excuse me, Seagrave, ladies? I think I see my mother waving at me. I must fulfil my duty as host.'

With a final nod, he turned on his heel and disappeared into the throng of guests. He greeted a few people, chatted with some long-time neighbours, and once the current dance was halfway done slipped out of the ballroom and made his way to the library.

Inside, he lit a few of the gas lamps, then settled on one of the chairs by the large oak table in the middle. Anticipation thrummed in his veins, and when the audible click of the door echoed through the empty room he got to his feet.

Kate emerged from out of the shadows, her arms stiff at her sides as she marched towards him with a determined stride. 'Tell me what this foolishness is about this instant.'

While the thought of riling her further tempted him, he decided he'd waited long enough. 'Your father is arriving in the morning.'

'So?'

'What convenient timing—considering he has not come for a visit these past weeks. Tell me, has Seagrave finally found the courage to ask his permission to court you? Or perhaps something has happened in the last five days to give him reason to speak to your father?'

'I beg your pardon!' she spluttered. 'What are you implying?'

'What do you think I'm implying?'

Her eyes narrowed into razor-sharp slits. 'How dare you imply that I would…? Seagrave is a complete gentleman and would never try anything untoward.'

That knot that had seemed permanently lodged in his throat since that afternoon loosened. *She hadn't slept with Seagrave.* Not yet, anyway.

'Then what are his intentions? Did you summon your father here? Did he?'

'Ha!' Her hands flung in the air. 'As if Arthur Mason could be *summoned* by anyone. For your information, my father wrote to *tell* me that he would be coming to Highfield Park.'

Ah, so it was a mere coincidence.

'But if you must know,' she said snidely, 'His Grace does intend to ask permission to court me.'

'He will do no such thing. What if you are carrying my child?'

'If His Grace wishes to speak with my father then that is out of my control. Besides, we agreed to wait until we are certain that I am… I am…in that way.'

'I don't recall agreeing to anything.'

'Before I left, I said the discussion was over.'

'I recall saying it was not,' he countered. 'Tell me, Kate, is your plan to string Seagrave along until he is so in love with you that he would marry you even with another man's child in your belly? Or perhaps you are going to sleep with him during your courtship so he has no choice?'

'You rotten scoundrel of a—'

'Tell me what your grand scheme is, then! What is the purpose of all this deception?' His fists slammed on the tabletop behind her, making her start. 'Make me understand why you would lower yourself to marry a man who's not worthy of you. Why are you hiding your intelligence, Kate? No—' He held up a hand when she opened her mouth. 'I'm not a feather brain like Seagrave. I know you are clever and skilled, despite your obvious attempts to conceal your knowledge. You helped rebuild that wall and you repaired that boiler by yourself. Do you love Seagrave so much that you would pretend to be stupid just so you can marry him?'

Her eyes grew wide, and her lower lip trembled. 'N-no.'

'Then tell me why!' His frustration made his entire body tense like a wound coil. Because the truth he didn't want to say aloud was ready to burst out: he would move heaven and earth and give his very soul to the Devil to stop her from marrying Seagrave.

The muscles in her throat bobbed as she swallowed hard. 'It's not what you think.'

Tension seeped away from his muscles as he recognised the look of defeat in her eyes. Now was the time to push further. 'Then tell me, Kate.'

'I'm not in love with Seagrave.'

'Why lie to me, then?'

'I didn't lie to you. You came to that conclusion on your own.'

His thoughts went back to that day in the orangery furnace. *'So you do believe in love.'* She hadn't confirmed or denied it. 'Why let me keep on believing you wanted a love match, then?'

'It just seemed simpler.' She bit her lip. 'I need to get married to a titled lord or…'

'Or what?'

'Or my father will force me to marry my second cousin Jacob, and I can't let that happen!' She drew herself up to her full height. 'I told you about my grandfather and Mason R&L. After he passed away, I took over the management of the company. So when my father brought me here I thought he meant for me to start our England factory, like we've been discussing for the past year.' She let out a rueful snort. 'But I was made a fool; he never intended me to run a factory here—or any factory. He brought me here so I could find a lord to marry. See, he hasn't had any luck starting Mason R&L in England because he can't even get his foot in the door. My marriage to a lord would help smooth things over in Parliament and allow him to acquire the land he needs to build lines for the railway. Should that plan fail, then he'll marry me off to my cousin.' A fire blazed in her eyes. 'And if that happens that vile man will destroy everything my grandfather built. All Jacob wants is to take the credit and reap the rewards without doing any of the hard work.'

He searched her eyes and face for any signs of deception and found none.

'So, you see, that's why I have to marry Seagrave,' she stated fervently. 'To protect my grandfather's legacy. I want to see his name live on for ever, even if it means having the Duke spend my dowry on his estate and horses. I would rather fulfil my role as his wife and never work on an engine again than have Pap's hard work destroyed. I owe Pap that much.'

So, that's what it is.

She wasn't looking for a love match. No, she needed a powerful name and a title to enable her father to gain a foothold in the English railway business and dissuade him from marrying her off to her cousin. All to protect the name and legacy of the man who'd raised her.

Now, those things he could give her.

'Marry me, Kate.'

'Wh-what?' Her jaw dropped.

'Marry me.' He moved closer. 'Marry me and you'll have everything you want. I'll use my influence in Parliament to make sure your father's railway lines are approved. Your dowry will be put in trust for you to use however you please. You can pour it back into the factory. I don't care. I have no need of it. Nor will I do anything to destroy your grandfather's legacy or name. We'll call the factory whatever you wish.' A thought occurred to him, as he remembered how brilliant she was at engineering. 'And once it's built, you can even design your own locomotive.'

Her expression shifted. 'My own engine… I've always wanted to… How did you know…?'

There it was. The spark of interest in her eyes. He had no doubt she could create an engine of her own. 'Spend all day working at the factory if you wish.'

As long as you spend your nights with me.

'But what about your vow to never marry?' she asked. 'I will not force a man to do something he doesn't want to do.'

'Forget I said it.' Desperation clawed at him. 'Forget every damned word I said about not marrying. Besides, there could already be a child on the way.'

'We're not sure yet. I could still get Seagrave—'

'Damn bloody Seagrave to hell!' he roared. When Kate shrank bank, he immediately regretted it. 'Kate, please…'

This time, she pursed her lips and crossed her arms over her chest. 'You brought me here and forced me to reveal my plan, and now you're telling me to forget you ever said you didn't want to marry? Are you a liar, Your Grace? Did you lie to me about not wanting to marry? Or are you lying to me now, with your proposal?'

'No,' he said through gritted teeth. 'I wasn't lying then and I'm not lying now.'

'But the two concepts conflict with each other. You shouldn't have to marry me—'

'That's not the point.' He raked his fingers through his hair. 'Kate, when I said those things to you I didn't know… I hadn't thought…'

'Hadn't thought what?'

Sweat beaded on Sebastian's forehead as he tried

not to let the memories come back. But perhaps telling her the truth was the only way she would understand.

A heartbeat passed before he began. 'When I was a child, I absolutely adored my father. He doted on me, and I thought him to be the most wonderful man on earth. Then, when I grew up, I realised who he really was…' Swallowing hard, he fought the tightness in his throat to continue. 'I realised that when he died five years ago.'

She reached out and placed a gloved hand on his cheek. 'I'm so sorry.'

The touch soothed him, so he covered her hand with his, closed his eyes, and focused on the warmth of her palm through the silk. 'I'm not. It turns out he wasn't the most wonderful man on earth. He was a wastrel who let the estate decline. It was barely surviving when I inherited the Dukedom. But worst of all was what he did to my mother.'

Kate gasped. 'Did he…hurt her?'

His grip on her hand tightened. 'He did not strike her, but he might as well have. You see, he died during a fight in a brothel. Turns out that after my mother gave birth to me he decided he was done with her. Made his way through every brothel in London and perhaps most of England, too. She never said a word about it, and I was too blinded by my adoration for him to know any better. I think she hid it from me because she saw how much I loved him.'

'You were a child,' she whispered. 'You didn't need to know that.'

'Maybe I should have,' he said bitterly. 'Then I would have seen the truth. That she loved him so much and so deeply that it drove her to drink a whole bottle of laudanum in an attempt to take her own life.'

'Oh, no.' Kate's face turned completely ashen. 'You were the one who found her, weren't you?'

It hurt to breathe, but he continued. 'Mrs Grover, the housekeeper, had fallen while reaching for some linens on a top shelf, so a doctor was already at Highfield Park. Had Dr Hanson arrived a minute later she would have died that day. She survived, but barely, and she hasn't been the same since. The scandal and the gossip drove her away from society, and she's kept herself locked up for the last five years.'

Taking her hand away from his face, he placed her arm back down at her side.

'She survived death, but that didn't mean she came back to life. She withdrew from public life, then eventually moved to Hertfordshire. And I know it was because she couldn't stand being here, in the home she had shared with her husband, and being with the son who reminded her so much of him. From that moment on, I promised myself I would never be like my father. I did everything in my power to undo everything he'd done by working on the estate and restoring it. But that didn't seem enough. I knew I couldn't let the cycle perpetuate, so I also vowed never to marry or have offspring, so that no woman would have to suffer the same fate as my mother.'

'I see.' She stepped back and leaned against the oak table. 'Then why ask me to marry you? What would you get out of it if you don't even want an heir? Our match wouldn't be advantageous for you.'

Why did it feel as if she were slipping through his fingers? No, he would not let that happen.

'When this…situation between us arose, I came to a conclusion. You have an honourable reason for getting married and, like me, you don't believe in love, which means you won't become like my mother,' he reasoned. 'Also, I've heard about your father. Anything Arthur Mason touches turns to gold, and I would profit handsomely if I went into business with him. Should we produce an heir, then that will be an additional benefit, but not a requirement. I already have an heir—a distant cousin, who would inherit the title. But don't you see, Kate? Our marriage will be a mutually beneficial arrangement, which is much better than one built on something as unsteady as sand, like love.'

For a moment, he thought he saw hesitation in her eyes, but then she said, 'Yes, Sebastian. I will marry you.'

Thank God.

Feeling emboldened, he leaned down to her ear. This close, he could smell her wonderful scent.

She moaned when his lips clamped over that spot under her ear. She braced her palms on his chest, then moved them up to his shoulders.

Dear God, he'd missed this. Missed her touch, her taste, her scent. He nibbled at that spot until she was melting against him. Sliding his hands into her hair, he pulled her back so he could kiss those luscious lips. Immediately, she opened to him and he dipped his tongue to savour her sweetness. He could take her here, right now. Make love to her on top of the table and say to hell with the ball. To hell with the entire world.

However, she pulled away. 'We can't…not here.'

'Of course.' Reluctantly, he released her.

'What do we do now?' She took a step away from him. 'We need to get back to the ball before someone discovers we're missing.' Her hand went to her chest. 'Think of the scandal…'

Frankly, he didn't care what anyone thought, but she

was right. 'Will you wait here a moment?' He knew what he had to do. 'I'll take care of this.'

She nodded. 'Of course.'

Walking past her, Sebastian strode out of the library and made his way back to the ballroom. He stopped the first footman who passed by and whispered instructions. The footman bowed and scurried away. A mere moment later, the footman came back, his mother trailing behind.

'Sebastian?' Lines of worry wrinkled her brow. 'Dalton says you require my assistance. What's the matter? Has something happened?'

'Thank you, Dalton,' he said, dismissing the footman. 'I do require your assistance, Mother.'

Before she could ask anything else, he guided her back to the library by the elbow.

'Sebastian, why are we in the—?' She gasped when she saw Kate inside. She looked back to Sebastian. 'Are you trying to ruin Miss Mason's reputation? Taking her in here with no chaperone?'

'I'm sorry, Your Grace.' Kate covered her face with her hands. 'I didn't—'

'I wasn't trying to ruin Miss Mason, Mother,' he stated. 'I was trying to convince her to marry me.'

'You were trying to—what?' For the first time in his life—and probably hers—his mother looked completely flabbergasted. 'Oh. *Oh.*' She took in a sharp inhalation of breath. 'And did you say yes?' she asked Kate.

'Of course she did.'

Kate shot him a rueful look, but answered, 'Yes, I did, Your Grace.'

'That is…wonderful news!' The Dowager Duchess clasped her hands together.

Sebastian hadn't even thought of what his mother

might say about his relationship with Kate, but her wholehearted approval was nonetheless a welcome reaction. 'Thank you.'

'My dear…' Coming closer, she took Kate's hands in hers. 'I never thought…' Her eyes shone with tears. 'I was hoping he would…and you… Oh, no.' Her face fell. 'Seagrave… I thought— I mean, Miss Merton said that he was on the cusp of asking your father for permission to court you. Was she wrong?'

'Ah, yes.' Kate's shoulders sank. 'Right… This was… unexpected.'

Sensing her embarrassment, Sebastian draped an arm around her shoulders. 'But not completely out of the blue. I saw Miss Mason from across the room at the Houghton Ball. It was there that I became acquainted with her.' That part was true. 'I couldn't stop thinking about her afterwards.' Also true. 'And then, to my surprise, she turned out to be your guest. You could say that I've been keeping my feelings hidden because… because of my initial request to you about not involving me with your matchmaking schemes.'

Yes, that was it. He congratulated himself on coming up with such a brilliant explanation on the spot.

'I am a duchess, Sebastian. I do not *scheme*,' she said haughtily. 'And so all this time…?'

'Yes, all this time.'

He sent her a warm smile and pulled Kate closer, hoping it would be enough to convince his mother that this was not merely a case of unwarranted lust.

'And Seagrave's attentions spurred you to take action?'

'It wasn't my intention to use the Duke to make Sebastian jealous,' Kate said quickly.

'Of course not,' Sebastian assured her.

'My feelings for Seagrave were genuine.'

'Yes, I'm sure they were.'

'He is an honourable man, and I would be lucky to—'

'That's enough, darling.' He gave her shoulders a squeeze. 'I believe what Kate is trying to say is that she was unsure of my intentions as I had given her no indication of my feelings for her.'

She bit her lower lip. 'I must tell the Duke… He was to speak with my father tomorrow.'

'There, there, dear.' The Dowager Duchess patted her hand. 'It will be all right. The poor man was besotted with you, but I'm sure he'll take the news with grace.'

'I shall speak with him as soon as possible,' Kate said.

'A capital idea.' Sebastian tightened his grip on her shoulders. 'Mother, would you be so kind as to find Seagrave and escort him here?'

'Here?' Kate exclaimed, shrugging his arm off. 'Have you lost your mind?'

'You think I would allow my future wife to speak to another man alone?' he thundered. 'If so, then you are the one who has lost your mind.'

'Why, I—'

The Dowager Duchess tsked. 'Now, now, lovebirds. Calm yourselves. I shall bring the Duke post-haste.'

'Thank you, Mother.'

'But he and Kate will speak out in the corridor and, Sebastian, you will stay in here.'

'Here? I think not. What if—?'

She held a hand up. 'I shall ensure they are properly chaperoned. No more arguments.'

'But—'

'I said, no more arguments,' the Dowager Duchess

declared. 'Now, darling, try not to maul Miss Mason before I get back?'

However, Sebastian could have sworn he saw the corners of her lips lift before she turned and left the room.

'What in heaven's name were you thinking?' Kate whacked him on the shoulder with her palm. 'Coming up with that...that lie about the Houghton Ball?'

'Lie?' he asked. 'Tell me, what falsehoods did I tell my mother? I did see you across the room at the Houghton Ball and we did make each other's acquaintance that night.'

'And what about...about...?' The loveliest blush stained her cheeks. 'The part about not being able to stop thinking about me?'

He answered her by planting his hands on her waist and drawing her closer. 'Who said that was untrue?'

She shivered visibly, but then pushed away from him. 'Sebastian, why are you making it appear as if this is a love match? I thought that was the last thing you wanted?'

A strange twinge plucked at his chest at her words. 'Because...because I am trying to preserve your reputation. And my mother's,' he added quickly. 'Your father sent you here under her protection. What would he say if he found out I'd swooped in like some predator to seduce you?'

She let out a rather unladylike snort. 'He doesn't give a whit about my reputation or whom I marry, as long as my future husband is able to advance his business interests.'

For some reason he found himself getting unreasonably angry with this man he'd never met. 'In any case, I was also doing it to protect you from the wagging tongues of the ton. They're already going to gossip because I want us to marry as soon as possible. In one month.'

'One month? But that won't leave us time for courting, and then a proposal, plus all the preparations...'

'One month,' he said firmly. 'The sooner we marry, the sooner we can come back from our honeymoon and begin the construction of your factory. If we delay any longer, we might have to wait until Parliament reconvenes after the summer. Besides, you might already be with child. Think of the scandal if the child is born too soon after our wedding.'

She seemed to contemplate that. 'All right, then.'

Thank goodness she was American, and not familiar with the prevalence of 'premature' babies amongst the newlyweds of the ton, most born eight, seven, or even six months from the wedding night while still being suspiciously healthy. Since the couples were already safely shackled anyway, even the most notorious of gossips didn't think that kind of news juicy enough to spread.

'Come, Kate.' He planted a soft, innocent kiss on her lips and let his hand drift to her waist. 'Tomorrow I shall speak to your father, and all will be well.' He led her towards the door. 'Now you must let your erstwhile beau—' Lord, his mouth turned sour even as he said that word '—know about this turn of events.'

Snatching Kate away from Seagrave should have left him feeling completely triumphant. And his plan to have a marriage based on business interests and mutual needs should allay his fears that Kate might end up like his mother. He would at least ensure that she would never worry for money for the rest of her life and that she would have her factory. And as long as they felt nothing except lust for each other he needn't worry, even if he did become like the man he hated.

* * *

Kate was still in a state of shock as Sebastian led her out into the corridor. This was not where she'd expected the events of tonight would lead.

He planted a kiss on her temple. 'I'll be just inside the library, so do not fret.'

'I'm not fretting,' she retorted.

'Then why the frown on your pretty face?'

She pursed her lips together. 'It's just… I worked so hard to even get Seagrave to approach my father, and—'

'How hard, exactly?' he asked, an edge to his voice.

'Oh, please, there is no need to feign jealousy—your mother isn't around. But I do owe him an explanation. Maybe—'

The sound of approaching footsteps made her halt. Her chest tightened and dizziness came over her, as if she were standing on the edge of a cliff. She looked ahead, and as the forms of Seagrave and the Dowager Duchess came closer she thought, *He would be the safe choice*.

It was not too late yet. With Seagrave, she'd know exactly what to expect and how to plan her future. With Sebastian, on the other hand, it would be like starting a project without a blueprint. Or leaping into the unknown and hoping she would not end up broken and battered when she plummeted back to earth.

But everything Sebastian had promised her was too tempting. She could run the factory. Heavens, she'd be able to build her own engine! But, more importantly, Pap's legacy would be safe.

'I think Her Grace has returned.'

He bowed his head and turned on his heel. 'I will give you your privacy.'

She stared after him as he disappeared into the library, but before she could further process what had happened she heard voices coming from the opposite end of the corridor.

'Are you sure she's all right, Your Grace?'

'Yes, Miss Mason is unharmed.'

They're here!

Kate quickly ran a hand over her coiffure and down her bodice, making sure everything was in place. 'Your Grace,' she greeted Seagrave, and then the Dowager Duchess. 'Your Grace. Thank you for your assistance.'

'Of course, Miss Mason. Now, I shall stand over here...to admire these paintings...while you have your little chat.'

The Dowager Duchess turned away from them, then strode a few feet away to stop and look at the picture hanging on the wall.

'Miss Mason?' Seagrave searched her face. 'The Dowager Duchess said you had to speak with me. Are you hurt or ill?'

'I'm quite fine, Your Grace. I just wanted to see you as soon as possible.' Taking a deep breath, Kate considered her words carefully. 'Your Grace, I want you to know that I have truly enjoyed our time together these past weeks.'

'As have I.'

'I am grateful for your attentions, but I must ask that you not speak to my father tomorrow.'

'Not speak to your father?' He gave her a flummoxed look. 'Why not?'

'Because...because I'm afraid I have accepted an offer from another.'

He paused, then blinked twice. 'Oh. I didn't realise you had other suitors.' His shoulders looked deflated. 'Who is he?'

There was no use concealing it from him as he would find out anyway. 'His Grace the Duke of Mabury.' She waited for a violent protest, but none came.

He let out a resigned sigh. 'I should have realised a prize such as you would not be ignored. Perhaps it is my fault that I waited too long. If only I had acted sooner.'

Kate did not know if she should be relieved or vexed that he seemed to accept the news so easily. 'Let's not talk about ifs and buts, Your Grace. It is not your fault. He and I were acquainted before I came to Highfield Park and I found myself...' She scrambled for the appropriate words to say. 'Infatuated with him. But, as you know, the Duke can be quite reserved, and he did not confess his...er...feelings for me until today.'

'I understand.' He patted her hand. 'Your heart had simply been fixed before we met.'

'How...er...perceptive and wise you are, Your Grace.' She was glad he had said it, because she didn't want to lie to him any more than she had to.

He swallowed hard. 'If you would excuse me, Miss Mason? I shall bid goodnight to our hostess and be on my way home.'

'Of course. Goodnight, Your Grace.'

'Goodbye, Miss Mason. I wish you well.' He walked over to the Duchess. 'Your Grace, I thank you for your invitation, but I must cut my evening short. I'm sure you understand.'

'Of course, Your Grace.'

He gave her a deep bow and then walked away, disappearing down the darkened corridor, along with the safe, reliable future Kate had striven for.

'Are you all right, my dear?' asked the Dowager Duchess as she hurried over to Kate. 'I hope you aren't too distressed.'

Kate wasn't sure how to describe how she was feeling at this moment. Relieved? Not quite, as the gravity of her new situation weighed heavily on her. In the morning, her father would arrive, and Sebastian would be speaking to him.

'Is he gone?' Sebastian asked, seemingly manifesting from nowhere.

'Yes, he's gone.'

He frowned. 'Did he cause you worry? Did you argue?'

'No, it's fine. I am just…glad it's over.'

'Well, now…' The Dowager Duchess's smile practically lit up the room. 'It seems we must plan a wedding.'

'Please, Mother.' Sebastian groaned. 'Do control yourself for now. I still have to speak to her father.'

'Pish-posh, let me have this moment,' she teased. 'Don't look at me like that. I know how to keep a secret.'

'Of course you do, Mother.'

'Now, let's go back to the ball before anyone notices our absence.'

'Must we?'

'Yes, we must—for appearances' sake.' The Dowager Duchess shook a finger at him. 'And don't even think about having a midnight rendezvous with Miss Mason.'

'Mother—'

'I am deadly serious. I will not have anyone gossiping about your future duchess.' She cast an apologetic look at Kate. 'Forgive me, my dear, we are being awfully rude…speaking as if you are not here.'

'Not at all, Your Grace.' Her stomach had flipped at the words *future duchess*.

'Now, Sebastian, promise me you won't give anyone cause to speak ill of Kate.'

'Mother, may I remind you that this is my house, and

I will do as I please?' Coming from him, it wasn't a re-minder so much as a statement.

'You have said it yourself: you still have to speak to her father.' The Dowager was equally determined. 'Sebastian…?'

'Oh, all right.' His teeth gnashed together. 'I promise.'

'Good.' The Dowager Duchess seemed satisfied. 'Come, now, let us rejoin the guests.'

Looping her arm through Kate's, she pulled her along and they made their way back to the ballroom.

This was it. Her fate was sealed. She was going to be his wife.

This was what she'd wanted, wasn't it? Sebastian wanted to marry her, instead of being forced to marry her. They would be on an equal footing. She would save Pap's legacy, and he would never have to worry about repeating history. This was her choice. Finally.

But there was still something else—something that felt unresolved. And because her logical mind was tuned to solve problems, she just couldn't stop thinking about it.

Her stomach knotted and her nerves felt frayed, as if she stood on the edge of a precipice, facing an un-known future.

Chapter Seventeen

Just as Kate had predicted, convincing her father to accept Sebastian's suit was not difficult. However, being the businessman that he was, Arthur Mason could not resist bargaining, even if the terms already suited him from the onset.

'Never accept the first offer,' he always said.

'So, you want to marry my daughter?'

Arthur Mason's countenance had been cool and collected from the beginning, and he spoke as if he were asking about the price of a hat at the milliner's.

The moment he and Jacob had arrived, early that morning, Eames had immediately ushered her father to Sebastian's private study, where she and the Duke had been waiting.

'If so, should she be here while we discuss this?'

'Yes, I believe that is what I said,' Sebastian replied, equally composed. 'And, seeing as she happens to be the subject of our talk, her presence is required.'

'Shouldn't you be asking my permission to court her first?'

'I should. But why waste my time or yours when we know the outcome will be the same anyway?'

That seemed to mollify her father enough to continue their conversation. Or negotiation.

While Arthur complained about the date of the wedding, and Kate's dowry, Sebastian was just as tough. In the end, Arthur relented on having the wedding in a month, as Sebastian planned, in exchange for a percentage reduction on her dowry, plus an extra seat on the board for someone of Arthur's choosing once the London company was established.

It seemed that at some point the two men had decided to pursue the railway business together, along with their marriage discussion.

'I feel as if I'm a side of beef at the market,' Kate muttered to her new fiancé. 'Did you really have to bargain so hard?'

His mouth turned into a grim line. 'It was he who began the bargaining, Kate. And I would have given him his every demand, except that he acted as if you were an inanimate object. He doesn't know it yet, but you're a great loss to him and the factory back in New York. With you staying here in England, I'll be gaining a brilliant engineer and manager.'

A nagging thought materialised in her mind. 'How can you be sure of that? You've never even seen me on a factory floor.'

What if he decided that her style of management didn't suit him? What if they clashed on the way things would be run?

'I meant what I said when I proposed. While I know how to run an estate and deal with tenants, I won't be able to absorb everything about factories and engines before the ground-breaking. It's obvious to me that you will have to be in charge of everything from the beginning.'

The sincerity in his voice and eyes told Kate that he was telling the truth. Still…

'But you fought my father so hard about retaining your majority ownership of the company. You could have allowed him to invest more of his money, like he offered, and reduced your own personal risk. He would have given you something of value for more control.'

'But that would mean you wouldn't be able to do what you want.' Dark eyes met hers, pinning her to the spot and boring straight into her. 'And he did give me something of value—even if he didn't know it.'

The words made Kate's heart stutter in her chest.

She couldn't quite remember what had happened for the rest of the day, as she'd felt as if she were floating on air. And now here they all were, having refreshments in the parlour during the usual pre-dinner gathering. Sebastian and the Dowager Duchess had yet to arrive, so after introducing her father and Jacob to the other guests Kate stood with Arthur by the window.

'I must admit, Kathryn,' Arthur began, 'you've done much better than I expected.'

And from Arthur Mason that was the best compliment Kate could ever hope for.

'His Grace the Duke of Mabury,' Eames announced. 'And Her Grace the Dowager Duchess of Mabury.'

As everyone bowed and curtseyed, Kate sneaked a glance at Sebastian, who looked devilishly handsome in his evening clothes. When she caught the Dowager Duchess's eye, she sent Kate a knowing smile.

'Good evening, everyone,' Sebastian began. Tonight, only the house guests were dining. 'Allow me to welcome our newest guests to Highfield Park, Mr Arthur Mason and his cousin Mr Jacob Malvery.' He gave them a brief nod of acknowledgment, which they returned. 'Now, before we begin our dinner, I have some news to share with you. Mr Mason, Miss Mason, if you please...?' He held out his hand to them.

Every single pair of eyes was riveted on Kate, leaving her unsettled. But she kept her head held high as her father led her towards Sebastian and the Dowager Duchess.

'After speaking with Mr Mason today, it is with pleasure that I announce my engagement to Miss Kate Mason.'

A stunned silence hung in the air, and the guests' faces held varying degrees of surprise, shock, and befuddlement—except for Jacob, whose face showed no emotion. She guessed her father had already told him about her engagement to Sebastian.

Perhaps he didn't wish to marry me after all.

'That's such wonderful news,' Miss Merton exclaimed, and clapped her hands.

Thankfully, everyone else followed, and surrounded them to offer their congratulations before Eames announced that dinner was served. This time Sebastian led Kate to the head of the table, where she took the highest position after her father. She was glad—not because of the honour it brought, but because she would have time to collect her thoughts before being bombarded by questions from everyone.

When the scrumptious dinner had concluded, the men and women separated as usual. As soon as they arrived in the parlour for tea Eliza dashed towards Kate, dragging Caroline and Maddie behind her.

'Miss Mason, my deepest felicitations on your engagement to His Grace.' She curtseyed low. 'I always knew you would make a great match. And because you are the best and closest friend of my dear daughters, we hope you will welcome us to the many social gather-ings you will have once you take residence in London.'

'She's not a duchess yet, Mother.' Caroline's mouth was pressed into a straight line. 'My, my, you've done well for yourself, Kate,' she said, her tone laced with snideness. 'And I thought you had Seagrave wrapped around your little finger, too. What has happened to the poor Duke?'

'We simply decided we weren't suited,' Kate stated.

Caroline lifted an elegant blonde brow. 'And you and Mabury are?' She let out a mocking huff. 'I didn't re-alise he even knew you existed. After all, why would the bumblebee hover over a daisy when there are so many roses around?'

Before Kate could retort, Eliza interrupted. 'But now the other bumblebee…er…the Duke of Seagrave is un-occupied, perhaps we can ask Her Grace to invite him back to Highfield Park. Or maybe Miss Merton could arrange for us to visit him.'

'Assuming he would even want to associate with more Americans,' Maddie said under her breath.

Caroline's pretty face twisted. 'As if I would take Kate's leavings! I would be a laughing stock back home.'

'Caroline…' Eliza warned. 'Come, I must sit down. My knees are bothering me. Then you can fetch me some tea. Excuse us, Miss Mason.' She sent Kate an apologetic look before dragging her younger daugh-ter away.

Maddie actually chuckled. 'That was absolutely de-licious.'

'Hopefully you won't bear the brunt of her anger,' Kate said sympathetically.

Maddie smiled wryly. 'In private, maybe, but Mother won't let her disrespect you—not if she wants to be in your good graces. Caroline may actually have to be nice to me now, seeing as you and I are good friends,' she added with glee.

The rest of the evening continued as they usually did—although Caroline's mood only grew more sour, and she continued to send subtle jabs towards Kate— and not so subtle when Eliza was not within hearing distance. She ignored her as best she could. Especially since, at least for one evening, Maddie wasn't her sister's target.

When the hour grew late, the Dowager Duchess declared she was weary, which was the signal that the evening was over. The ladies retired and went to their separate rooms, and after her maid had helped her out of her dress and into her night rail Kate slid under the covers. She had barely closed her eyes for five minutes when a soft knock came at the door. Had her maid forgotten something?

Climbing out of bed, she trod towards the door. 'Anna? Do you need something?'

No answer.

'Anna...?'

'It's me,' came Sebastian's voice from behind the door. 'Don't make a sound.'

Sebastian? She opened the door a crack and sure enough there he was, standing just outside. 'What are you doing here?'

'What else? A midnight rendezvous.'

'I thought you promised your mother you wouldn't come to my room?'

'I promised to wait to speak to your father,' he countered. 'And now I have.'

She didn't know what to say. On the one hand, her body had started vibrating with need the moment he'd declared his intentions. After all, they had already made love before, and another few weeks wouldn't make a difference. On the other hand, her instinct told her to be on her guard. While she was seemingly about to get everything she wished for, and continue Pap's legacy, there was still something not quite right. Again, there was a feeling that there were things left unsaid and unresolved.

'Well? I can go—'

'No!' Reaching for the lapels of his robe, she dragged him inside. 'I mean…don't go.' She slid her fingers over the silk material, feeling his hard muscles underneath. 'Stay.'

Perhaps just for tonight she could lose herself in his embrace and that feeling would go away.

Chapter Eighteen

The room was still dark when Sebastian opened his eyes, but the familiar feeling of dread slid into his stomach like a heavy stone.

'Sebastian?' Kate murmured, her voice rough from sleep. 'Is it time?'

He shut his eyes tight. It was, unfortunately, time. Time to go. However, the press of her warm body against his had him protesting. So he held her tighter and brushed away the hair at the nape of her neck to press a kiss on her soft skin.

'Oh…' She half-moaned, half-yawned. 'Please…'

'Please what?' His hand slid down over her abdomen to the triangle of curls between her thighs.

'Anna will come soon to light the fire.' And yet her legs opened to give him better access. 'You must— Oh!'

His finger slipped into her tight passage, now growing slick with her desire. 'I must what?'

She let out an annoyed grunt, then pushed his hand away. 'Sebastian…' she warned, twisting around to face him.

Though he could only make out the outline of her head, he could picture the admonishing expression on her face. Those cornflower-blue eyes would be narrowed, plump lips pursed together. He let his gaze wander lower, imagining her naked breasts on display.

'Are you ogling me in the dark?' she asked, miffed.

'What do you think?'

That was a rhetorical question, but before she could answer he rolled her onto her back and covered her, rubbing his hardening shaft against her belly.

'Sebastian…' she warned again.

'What? It's been two weeks and we haven't been caught.'

Two glorious weeks of sneaking into her bed each night, exploring every inch of her body. Sebastian had thought that surely, by now, the edge of desire would be dulled. But if anything he wanted more of her. All the time. What Kate lacked in experience she made up for in enthusiasm, and he was eager to keep pushing her limits.

'Haven't been caught *yet*, Sebastian…'

'Oh, all right,' he grumbled.

Despite the fact that he'd had her twice last night, he still wanted her. *Two more weeks*, he told himself. In two weeks they would be man and wife, and he would have access to her any time he wished. They would spend all their nights together. And he'd be able to wake up next to her and watch the morning light…

The idea made him pause. *Wake up next to her?* For the life of him, he couldn't remember ever having done that with a woman. Nor had he ever wanted to. He'd made it a rule always to leave the bed before dawn. He couldn't even recall having breakfast with any previous mistress.

'Sebastian?'

His chest tightened, but he rolled off the bed and reached for his discarded trousers.

'Are you cross about something?' she asked.

'I'm not cross with you, Kate. I am just...' He searched for the right words as he finished buttoning his trousers but could not find them.

'Grumpy?' she offered.

He reached for the candle by the bedside table and lit it. Turning to face her, he let his eyes greedily soak in the sight of her—head propped up on one hand, naked torso aglow in the candlelight, like a half-clothed reclining Venus in one of those scandalous Italian paintings.

'I don't mean to be grumpy.' He leaned down and allowed himself one kiss. Anything more and he would say damn her maid, and damn any potential scandal, and climb back into bed with her. 'It's the lack of sleep, that's all.'

'And whose fault is that?' She chuckled. 'By the way—your mother asked me to remind you that you are to be dressed no later than half past six tonight.'

'Half past six?'

'You've forgotten, haven't you?'

'Er...'

She rolled onto her back, making her breasts jiggle deliciously. 'Tonight is our engagement ball.'

'Ah, right.' *Damn.* 'Why do we need to make an announcement to the ton about our upcoming marriage? Can't we just go straight to the ceremony without all this pomp?'

'I would agree with you,' she said wryly. 'But apparently news of our nuptials has set the ton ablaze. After the wedding, tonight's ball is the most sought-after invitation of the Season, despite being miles away from town. Besides, aren't you looking forward to seeing your friends?'

'I have no friends.'

'What about the Marquess of Ashbrooke?'

'Unfortunately, he is the only one who has declined the invitation.'

Ash had begged off, saying that he was occupied that night. *God knows with what.* But the Marquess had promised to be his best man for the wedding, despite the fact that Sebastian hadn't actually asked him to fulfil such a role.

'What do you mean, you don't have friends?' She frowned at him.

'I don't have any real friends. Not the kind who would be happy for me.' As sad as that sounded, it was the truth. He didn't know anyone who truly cared about him who would come to celebrate his triumphs.

'Who are all these people coming to the wedding, then?'

Sebastian scoffed. 'The same people who spread all the nasty gossip about the old Duke five years ago. If I had my way, none of them would be invited at all, but then it would be a very small party.'

'Sebastian,' she began, placing a hand over his, 'we don't have to invite any of those people to the wedding.'

'Unfortunately, we do, as we will need many of those peers on our side once Mason R&L begins the process of applying for permits for its railway lines.'

'Are you sure?'

'Absolutely. In any case, it doesn't matter. There are other things to worry about. And I promise I will be dressed on time. My mother has surely conspired with Robeson anyway. Now, try to get some sleep.'

'Mmm-hmm,' she murmured drowsily, then hugged a pillow to her torso and closed her eyes.

After he'd finished dressing, he allowed himself one last glance at her beautiful form and committed it to memory, hoping the image would be enough to sate him until tonight.

As he made his way back to his rooms, his mind clicked onto the business of the day. He had a meeting with Arthur Mason after breakfast about plans for building the factory, which might possibly run on until early afternoon.

One might think that after spending two weeks with him Sebastian would have got to know his future father-in-law better. But he still didn't have a clue who the real Arthur Mason truly was—the person, not the industrial magnate. When he'd mentioned this to Kate she had merely scoffed and told him that the hard-nosed business-man *was* the real Arthur Mason. And after a fortnight of discussions and meetings Arthur had yet to even enquire about the wedding plans or his daughter's future as Sebastian's duchess, prompting him to think Kate was right.

While he found Arthur's treatment of Kate appalling, he could see why her father was the successful businessman he was today. Whip-smart and completely ruthless, Arthur Mason did not stop until he'd got what he wanted. He rather reminded him of Kate and her determination to save her grandfather's legacy, though without the bloodthirsty edge. Sebastian guessed that had Kate been born a man she would have taken her father's place in his empire. Unfortunately, Arthur's closest male relation was Jacob Malvery.

Sebastian's mood darkened, as it always did when his thoughts turned to Malvery. While it was unjustifiable to abhor a man on sight, Jacob Malvery had nonetheless elicited from him only feelings of intense loathing. Malvery was a spineless sycophant, whose one skill in life was to obey his rich cousin's orders like a trained dog. He now understood why Kate would have preferred someone like Seagrave over being married to Malvery.

When Sebastian reached his suite and entered Robeson was already there, choosing his clothes for the morning. The valet didn't bat an eye at his dishevelled state.

'Good morning, Your Grace,' he greeted him in his usual serious tone. 'Shall I fetch your paper and your coffee, or would you like to nap for half an hour first?'

The man didn't even have the decency to pretend not to have seen Sebastian sneaking into the room, or that he didn't know his master had been out all night.

'Coffee would be fine. Thank you, Robeson,' he said, dismissing the valet.

As soon as he was alone he began to strip, but stopped halfway as he lifted his shirt over his head. A lingering trace of Kate's scent tickled his senses and brought back memories from last night. He'd been so eager for Kate that he hadn't even bothered to remove all his clothes. He'd pushed her up against the door and unbuttoned his trousers, lifted her nightgown out of the way and made love to her.

He dropped his hands to his sides. *Made love to her?* he scoffed. He'd never called it that before. Not with anyone. Yet he couldn't bring himself to use the typical words for the sexual act with Kate. *Screwing. Tupping. Diddling.* Somehow the thought of those words made him irrationally angry.

Idiot, he told himself. They were just words. Many words had different meanings. And what had transpired between them had no meaning at all. It was just an act between two people—a release for their pent-up energies.

Surely after the wedding the newness of their sexual congress would wear away…like the polish on a pair of new shoes. He reminded himself that their marriage was a mutually beneficial business arrangement. His estate would be enriched further with the profits from the railway company. And once the factory was running she would be preoccupied with its day-to-day business and designing her own engine.

The thought that she wouldn't share her days with him made him regret the bargain they'd struck. While before he hadn't been able to fathom being with the same person day in and day out, now the thought of being away from Kate made him feel lost and lonely.

But if he tried to stop her from running the factory that would surely make her unhappy, and he couldn't have that. Kate couldn't end up like his mother. She was brilliant and beautiful. And he didn't deserve to have her all to himself.

Chapter Nineteen

Though Kate knew that today was the day of her engagement ball, the reality of it didn't quite solidify in her mind until she saw herself in the mirror dressed in her new gown—a gorgeous blue-grey concoction made of silk and taffeta. The low neckline and bodice were trimmed in delicate French lace, while the full skirt featured flounces on the bottom half that revealed a darker layer of silk underneath.

'A perfect fit, Miss Mason,' exclaimed the dressmaker, Mrs Ellesmore, as she turned Kate around to face the mirror. 'We don't even need to make any adjustments.'

'Oh, Kate, how marvellous you look.' The Dowager Duchess's smile was reflected in the mirror. 'You're a genius with fabrics and sewing, Mrs Ellesmore,' the Dowager said. 'Thank you again for entertaining us at such short notice. I know this is the busiest time of year for you.'

'Anything for you, Your Grace,' she fawned. 'It is my honour to create Miss Mason's engagement dress and her wedding gown.'

'I am also very grateful that you've agreed to come

to Surrey to make all the arrangements instead of having us travel to your shop on Bond Street.'

'My pleasure, Your Grace.'

With what Sebastian was paying her she could probably afford to set up shop in Highfield Park for the rest of the month, Kate thought wryly. And, of course, the dressmaker would become even more sought-after now that she was making the future Duchess of Mabury's trousseau.

But Sebastian had wanted the best dressmaker in London, and Mrs Helena Ellesmore was the best of the best.

Mrs Ellesmore offered Kate a hand and helped her off the dais. 'My assistant will press and hang the dress for you. She will also remain here to assist you before tonight's ball, as I must be off back to London. Is there anything else you'd like to discuss before I leave?'

Kate shook her head. 'I don't have any changes since the last time we spoke. Your Grace, do you have anything to add?'

'No, no...' The Dowager Duchess strode over to her, the sunny smile still on her face. 'It is your wedding. Please do not let me interfere.'

'Not at all.' Kate chuckled. 'I'm afraid out of everyone here I'm the least experienced in this particular field. Your Grace, surely you have some advice to give? Did you have nerves on your wedding day?'

The Dowager's smile faltered for just a second, but Kate noticed it. 'I'm sure you'll do just fine, dear.'

A feeling of dread formed in Kate's stomach. *Why did I bring up her wedding day?* The Dowager Duchess didn't need any reminder of her failed marriage or her bastard of a husband.

'Well, then, let's get you undressed, Miss Mason.'

Mrs Ellesmore helped her out of the dress and into her lavender morning gown. When she emerged from behind the screen Kate could still feel the strain in the air. She hated that feeling—couldn't stand it.

I must make things right and apologise.

'Your Grace, if you're not busy, may I have a private word?'

The older woman paused. 'Of course. Why don't we go to the orangery? It's quite lovely there in the mornings.'

They bade goodbye to Mrs Ellesmore and made their way outside into the gardens and to the orangery.

'This is my favourite time of year in here.' The Dowager inhaled the humid, loamy scent in the air then turned to her. 'Now, Kate— Oh! Do you mind if I call you that?'

'Not at all, Your Grace.'

'Thank you, Kate. And you know you may call me Mama after the wedding. If you would like to.'

Mama. The word sounded strange, even in Kate's mind.

'Or not,' the Dowager Duchess added quickly.

'Oh, no—please don't think I don't want to,' she assured the Duchess. 'It's just that I've never called anyone that in my entire life. My mother died in childbirth.'

The Dowager Duchess took her hand and squeezed it. 'I am so sorry.'

'It was a long time ago; I don't remember her.' And that was the truth. It was difficult to mourn a woman she hadn't even known. 'I was raised by my grandfather.'

'And what a lucky man he was, having such a granddaughter as you.' A few beats of silence went by before the Dowager Duchess spoke again. 'Kate, dear, what is it that you want to speak with me about?'

Oh, right. Maybe she could still salvage the situation if she chose her words carefully.

'I couldn't help but notice that when I asked you about your wedding day, you seemed…sad.' Kate took a deep breath. 'If I said or did anything to offend you, I apologise.'

The Dowager Duchess's expression turned inscrutable. 'What has my son told you about his father?'

'He…mentioned he had passed away five years ago.'

'And?'

Oh, Lord, what else was she supposed to say? Should she tell the Dowager what Sebastian had confessed to her? It was such a private matter. Perhaps she should lie. Pretend not to know anything else and save them from embarrassment.

The older woman's complexion turned pale as she read Kate's silence. 'He has told you everything. No need to deny it, my dear. I can see it on your face.'

Blast it, I've mucked it all up.

'Forgive me, Your Grace.' Embarrassment made her want to run away. 'We needn't speak of it.'

'So, you know what happened. With his father. And what I did afterwards.' Recovering quickly, the Dowager tucked Kate's hand into her arm. 'But not the entire story. At least, not my side.' The Dowager Duchess led her deeper into the orangery. 'When we met, Charles completely swept me off my feet. I fell so deeply in love with him I even threw away a chance at…' She shook her head. 'Let's just say that I gave up something very important to me. We were happy for a few years. But… Well, it turned out that I didn't know my husband as well as I thought.'

They stopped in front of the fountain located in the middle of the orangery, and the gurgling sound of the water filled in the long pause.

'I'd long suspected he was unfaithful to me, but I didn't say a word. I didn't even want to admit it to myself.'

The awkwardness grew heavier than the humidity in

the air. 'Forgive me, Your Grace,' said Kate. 'You don't have to continue.'

'But I must.' The Dowager's head snapped back to her. 'You need to hear this.' Those dark eyes, so familiar, captured her gaze. 'So you can understand.'

'Understand?' she echoed.

'After his father died, Sebastian changed. He had always been a precocious child, but growing up he was easy-going and carefree, with a devil-may-care attitude. Very much like his father.'

Kate couldn't imagine Sebastian as the Dowager had described him. That person seemed the exact opposite of the man she knew.

Her future mother-in-law continued. 'He had no idea what Charles was really like. I thought I was being a good mother, trying to hide his father's flaws. Sebastian loved him so much, you see… I should have told Sebastian, but… Anyway, Charles's death affected him deeply and I don't think Sebastian has fully recovered. I'm partly to blame, too, because these last five years…' A vacant expression took over her face. 'I was too swallowed up by my own grief to see that my son had turned into a hard, bitter man.' She paused. 'This match between the two of you… I know there's more to it than you are telling me. And I'm happy with that. I just hope…'

Kate held her breath. Was the Dowager Duchess going to tell her she didn't approve of her as Sebastian's wife? Perhaps she'd decided Kate's social standing was too low or her money too new. Or maybe she thought Kate would be unfaithful to Sebastian, like his father had been to her. Her stomach tied into knots at the thought of all of the things the Dowager Duchess might object to.

'I hope…you give him a chance.'

Now, *that* Kate hadn't expected. 'A chance?'

'Yes.' The Dowager Duchess smiled warmly at her. 'I think you are the best thing to have happened to him. The fact that he has confided in you fills me with much confidence. And while I'm proud of what he's accomplished—restoring everything his father lost and growing it tenfold—I would rather have my carefree son back.' The line between her eyebrows deepened. 'Now, I haven't told you all this so you will pity him— or me. But I think he believes that he is incapable of anything more with you than just an amicable partnership. Because he's afraid.'

'Afraid of what?'

'Of getting too close to someone. Of emotional intimacy. I suspect he doesn't want what…what happened to me to happen to him.' She took Kate's hands in hers and squeezed them. 'But now you've given me something to look forward to. Given me hope that maybe you can help bring back my old Sebastian.'

Kate wasn't sure how to respond to that. But, looking at the Dowager Duchess's face, she couldn't dash the other woman's hopes with the truth: that she and Sebastian had agreed their marriage would be one that was merely mutually beneficial.

The Dowager Duchess thought that Sebastian confiding in her meant his cold façade was melting. That he was ready to bring down the walls he'd erected after his father's death and his mother's attempted suicide. But Kate had a feeling that wasn't true.

If there had ever been a major problem at the factory she and Pap had always found a quick fix to prevent the production line from completely halting and putting them behind schedule. However, a patch here or a fastener there had only temporarily assuaged the situation. No, they'd had to find the cause of the problem and solve it—or else it might turn into a disaster.

Perhaps humans weren't very different.

But what did it matter to Kate, anyway? Theirs would be a marriage of convenience. It would be better that Sebastian didn't think he was capable of any emotional entanglement. And perhaps it was time that she started guarding her heart around him—because it would be so easy to fall in love with someone like him.

Fall in love? she chided herself. *Don't be ridiculous.* Love had no place in their arrangement.

The Dowager Duchess's face crumpled. 'Oh, dear, I haven't upset you, have I?'

'What—? Oh, no, not at all,' she said reassuringly.

'Excellent.' The Dowager Duchess straightened her shoulders. 'Come, let's see how the trees are doing, shall we?'

Swallowing the growing lump in her throat, Kate smiled and nodded.

'Oh, it's so beautiful!' Maddie exclaimed as she looked around the ballroom. 'The Dowager Duchess has really outdone herself.'

Kate would have replied with her agreement, except her breath had been taken away by the marvellous sight before her. The ballroom had already been an opulent space, with its polished wooden floors, glittering crystal chandeliers, and walls decorated with intricately carved twisting vines and leaves in bronze with a gold trim, but now it was a magnificent fairy-tale wonderland.

Potted trees and shrubs from the orangery were dispersed across the room. Cream and gold-coloured bunting intertwined with gauzy white fabric hung from the ceiling. A sixteen-piece orchestra played while the footmen,

donned in their finest livery, roamed around as they offered guests titbits and refreshments.

'Kate, who are all these people?' Maddie asked.

Remembering what Sebastian had said that morning
about his guests made Kate's blood boil. *Snakes. Scan-
dalmongers. Sycophants.* Clearing her throat, she said,
'Mostly other peers from London.'

Everyone tonight was beautifully dressed and turned
out. And every single one of them had their gazes fixed
on Kate and her father as soon as they were announced.

On the surface, they were all polite, even enthusiastic
about being introduced to them, but she could already
guess what they were thinking: who was this American
heiress who'd managed to bag one of the most coveted
bachelors in England?

Kate didn't care much for these vile people, and didn't
even bother to remember their names. Her father, of
course, seemed to have committed their titles and faces
to memory, and after he'd deposited her with her friends
he'd promptly left to mingle with the Earl of What's-His-
Face and Viscount No-Distinguishing-Features.

Still, these people were peers and, as Sebastian
pointed out, they'd need their approval for the factory
and the railway lines. But she didn't have to like them.

'Where is your fiancé, by the way?' Maddie asked,
glancing around the room.

'He's not my fiancé yet,' Kate reminded her. 'Not
until the announcement at midnight.'

That was why she and Sebastian had arrived sepa-
rately and he'd opened the ball with his mother—they
were not officially betrothed yet. However, the news of
the Duke of Mabury's engagement had spread through
the ton like wildfire, even before the ink on their con-
tract had dried. Kate wondered if there was a way to

harness that mode of communication and use it for the signals on train tracks…

'Cousin Kate, Miss DeVries…how are you this evening? I'm so glad to see you both.'

Kate expelled a breath as she turned to face Jacob, who had seemingly appeared from out of mid-air. 'Cousin Jacob, you are…here.' She couldn't quite bring herself to lie and say she was pleased to see him, because he was the last person she wanted to see right now.

'Such a beautiful party.' His greedy eyes lingered a little too long on Maddie's décolletage—which unfortunately, at her height, was nearly at eye level for him. 'Are you enjoying yourselves?'

'Yes, we are, Mr Malvery,' Maddie said politely, though she cast a wistful look at the sea of dancers.

'I don't think I have personally congratulated you on your engagement, Cousin,' Jacob began. 'I've heard nothing except how fortunate you are to have made the match of the Season. Indeed, we are blessed to have someone such as the Duke joining our family.'

'Thank you, Cousin.' Kate was taken aback by Jacob's words, and she didn't know how else to react.

'Cousin, would you do me the honour of joining me for the next dance?'

Kate cursed herself, because she knew she couldn't find an excuse to say no. Not when everyone in the ballroom had their attention on her. 'Of course.'

She let Jacob lead her to the floor with the other dancers. When the galop was announced, Kate sent out a prayer of thanks to the heavens. The lively, energetic rhythm of the dance usually left little time for conversation. Not that it stopped Jacob from trying.

'Cousin, I was wondering if we could speak in private?' Jacob asked as they slowed for a turn.

Kate paused long enough for the beat of the music to change, indicating a change of partners. She stepped away, reached for the woman on her left, and continued on with another gentleman until she returned to Jacob and they once again started the brisk steps of the main dance.

Thankfully he did not attempt any more conversation until the dance had ended.

'Such a…spirited dance,' Jacob huffed, his cheeks red from exertion. 'As I was saying—'

'May I have the next dance?'

Every fibre of Kate's being lit up at the sound of Sebastian's voice. Turning around, she looked up into those magnetic obsidian eyes. 'We are not supposed to dance until after the announcement,' she said under her breath.

His expression remained cool, but the energy vibrating from him felt barely contained. 'And who set this rule? This is my home, my ball. I think I'm entitled to dance with whomever I please.'

Kate could feel several pairs of eyes on them and so, not wanting to garner any negative attention, said, 'Of course, Your Grace.'

She nodded to Jacob, who stepped away. Sebastian took his place without even a glance at the other man, and placed a hand on her waist and pulled her close, as if they were starting the waltz.

'Your Grace, they haven't yet announced—' She stopped short as Eames called out the waltz, then lifted an eyebrow at him. He said nothing, but merely smirked at her as they began the dance.

'What were you and Malvery talking about?' His expression turned stormy. 'What did he say to you? Did he upset you?'

'Jacob? Nothing. We didn't have a chance to talk during the dance.'

Wait—was he jealous? Over Jacob? Her heart fluttered in her chest. *Don't be ridiculous*, she scolded herself. He could never be jealous over another man dancing with her.

As they danced, she glanced around the ballroom. Everyone was definitely watching them now, so she tried to focus her attention on something else. Her gaze continued to roam, and she paused when she saw Maddie standing off to one side, swaying to the music as she drank some lemonade, a forlorn look on her face as she watched the dancers whirling about on the ballroom floor. A group of girls behind her giggled and pointed, making gestures that obviously mocked her height and childish dress.

Irritation pricked at Kate. Maddie was perhaps the one person tonight who was genuinely happy for her. She understood, in a way, what Sebastian had been saying about real friends. And she would be grateful for ever for Maddie's friendship.

'Kate? What's the matter?' Those dark brows furrowed together. 'Tell me what's bothering you and how I can make it better.'

Her heart did a somersault at his words.

'Ah…'

'Ah?'

'You are concerned for your friend.'

'It's unfair, really.' She let out a huff. 'Maddie is worth ten times as much as these insipid, vapid debutantes. Just because she doesn't fit the mould of what a young lady should be, society thinks she should be shunned. These people really are horrible, and I can see why you despise them. Frankly, I don't care any more. They can all go…jump off a bridge.'

His dark brows drew together, but he remained silent for the rest of the dance. Kate wondered if she'd offended him with her defence of her friend and her denouncement of the ton. But that would be strange because, as Sebastian had said, he didn't care much about the guests here tonight.

Once the dance had ended, Sebastian bowed to her and then led her back to where Maddie was waiting.

'Everyone's talking about you,' Maddie said excitedly. 'Mostly in a good way.'

'"Mostly" good is a positive thing with these people,' Sebastian said drolly. 'Miss DeVries, may I have the honour of the next dance?'

Maddie's jaw dropped. 'M-me?' She looked around. 'If you mean my sister—?'

'No.' Sebastian shook his head. 'I mean you, Miss Madeline.'

Kate's breath caught at the look of pure joy on her friend's face. *Oh, Sebastian...*

'Th-thank you. I mean, yes... Yes, Your Grace.'

Sebastian offered his hand and the two of them made their way to the dance floor for a lively reel. Maddie was surprisingly light on her feet, and graceful, her steps keeping good time with the music. With Maddie being only one or two inches shorter than Sebastian, Kate thought that being tall wasn't bad at all if it meant not having to crane one's neck up at a dance partner.

Maddie's delight at the dance was obvious, and even when they came back her pretty face was still all aglow. Kate knew it was not just because of the dancing, but because now half the gentlemen in the room were looking at her.

'You were wonderful, Maddie,' Kate gushed. 'I had no idea you could dance so well.'

'Thank you,' she said. 'Your Grace, thank you.'

'Thank *you*, Miss DeVries,' Sebastian said. 'You were a delightful partner.' He cleared his throat. 'If you would excuse Kate and I…? I believe my mother is getting ready to make a certain announcement.'

Kate looked at the large grandfather clock nearby. It was nearly midnight. Nerves twisted in her gut.

'Of course, Your Grace,' Maddie said, then leaned towards Kate. 'Good luck!'

She grinned at her friend, then followed Sebastian as they walked to the centre of the ballroom, where the Dowager Duchess was giving instructions to Eames.

'Have I made it better?' Sebastian asked.

'Made what better?'

'I told you.' His hand drifted to her lower back. 'I was going to make what bothered you better.'

Her heartbeat stuttered as everything came crashing into her like a wave. He hadn't just danced with Maddie because he'd enjoyed it, or to be a good host.

He did it for me.

'Well?'

Her throat burned as she felt moisture gather in the corners of her eyes. 'Yes,' she managed to whisper. 'You made it better.'

'Good. Now, let's go to my mother so we can make this bloody announcement.'

Kate's unladylike laugh dislodged the blockage in her throat.

As she and Sebastian strode towards the Dowager Duchess a feeling of dizziness came over her—but not in an unpleasant way. It reminded her of when she was a child and she would hang upside-down from the railings on the porch of their tiny shack in West Virginia, then quickly pull herself upright. It was heady, and it sent a thrill down to her toes.

'Ladies and gentlemen,' the Dowager Duchess began, and the guests lowered their voices until silence blanketed the room. 'Thank you for joining us here on this momentous occasion.'

As the Dowager continued her speech, Kate looked up at Sebastian—truly looked at his face, from his freshly shaven jaw to the line of his nose to the crinkles at the corners of his eyes. Her stomach turned topsy-turvy as she came to a realisation.

'And now...' The Dowager Duchess clapped her hands together. 'It is with great delight that I announce the engagement of my son, Sebastian, Duke of Mabury, to Miss Kathryn Mason of New York.'

Applause and cheers rang in Kate's ears, and as Sebastian lifted her hand to his lips she tried to decipher who this man really was. This stubborn, frustrating man, who annoyed her with his high-handedness, yet also made her melt with his kisses. Who loved his mother so much he'd do anything for her—even disturb his quiet life. Whose stare could turn a grown man to ash, but who had shown nothing but kindness to a wall-flower everyone else had written off.

Oh, drat. I have feelings for him.

Impossible. She couldn't be developing any emotions for him.

This is supposed to be a business arrangement.

A marriage based on a solid foundation of mutual benefits. They were both getting what they wanted. That should be enough to make them happy and solve their problems.

Her thoughts turned back to her conversation with the Dowager Duchess that afternoon.

'The solution to a problem isn't just a quick fix,' Pap had always said. But for once in her life she wished he'd been wrong.

Chapter Twenty

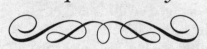

Sebastian could not recall the last time he had enjoyed a ball so much that he'd danced until dawn. He had never even made it to the end of a ball, as he'd either left to continue carousing with his compatriots or been too inebriated to remember.

'You know, you really didn't have to dance with Maddie twice tonight,' Kate said.

Though many of the guests had left, a few still lingered, so he had whispered in her ear, telling her to join him outside the ballroom after he'd slipped out first.

'I know,' he replied. 'But she seemed to like dancing.' And, more importantly, it had made Kate happy.

'She loved it.' Kate was positively glowing. 'Thank you so much.'

He would dance with the Devil himself if he could see her smile as she did now.

'Though maybe you are right and it was greedy of me to take her out for more than one dance. Many other gentlemen were clamouring to get on her dance card for the rest of the evening.'

'All thanks to your stamp of approval.'

The grin she flashed him sent a warm feeling to his

stomach, and it wasn't just from all the champagne he'd drunk. Glancing around, he realised they were truly alone now, so he gently guided her along the corridor.

'Sebastian, where are we going?'

'To your room, of course. Where else?'

'My room? But you said you were tired.'

'That's what I told Sir Elliot, so he would shut up about those damned goldfinches,' he groused. 'But I'm never too tired for you.'

How prettily she blushed, even after all this time.

'We must not let anyone see us.'

Quietly, they made their way through the darkened corridors and up to her rooms. Thankfully, the servants knew everyone would be having a late night, so they would not disturb any of the guests too early. But, frankly, Sebastian did not care if half the staff walked into Kate's room to see him in her bed, naked as the day he was born.

They were going to have to get used to it, anyway.

In two weeks she would be his wife.

He'd hated seeing her across the ballroom, unable to dance with her as he pleased and having all those men look at her covetously without him being able to stake his claim.

Especially that vile cousin of hers.

When he'd seen her dancing with Jacob Malvery, he had decided to hell with propriety and claimed his dance.

And he was glad he had. Initially, he'd abhorred the idea of having an engagement ball, or even a big wedding. If it had been up to him he would have said to hell with it and eloped with Kate to Gretna Green. Imagining all those people who had caused his mother pain being there, in the same room, had made the anger from five years ago flood back.

However, seeing Kate out there, focusing his attention on her and making sure she was truly happy, he'd found that he was actually enjoying himself. With Kate by his side, nothing else mattered.

After what seemed like an eternity, they made it to her room. He pounced on her the moment the door closed, making her giggle. After battling with the layers of petticoats and silk, he succeeded in removing all of her clothing, then his, and they tumbled onto the mattress.

He worshipped her body, trailing kisses all over her naked skin, giving her pleasure with his mouth and hands. First he turned his attention to her breasts, pressing them together so he could lave the pert little nipples with his tongue. He teased her, making her whimper and protest. That only fuelled him, so he suckled at her harder, drawing one nipple deep into his mouth until she thrust her fingers through his hair and tugged hard. But he refused to relent and continued his sweet torture.

When he was done with her breasts he moved lower, his tongue tracing a path straight down over her ribcage and smooth belly to the valley of her sex. He tasted her sweetness, licking at her nether lips, then teasing at her button. Lifting his gaze, he stared up at her while continuing to feast on her. How he loved watching her sigh and shiver, especially from his vantage point between her legs, looking up as her moans and cries escaped her plump lips, her thighs pressing against the sides of his head.

When she was spent, he moved over her, covering her body with his. 'Do you trust me, Kate?'

She nodded.

'Good.' His hands slipped under her, then he rolled onto his back, settling her on his hips.

'S-Sebastian?' Her mouth rounded. 'Can it be done this way?'

'Oh, yes.' His hand traced up her ribcage to cup a breast, and he rolled the hardened nipple between his thumb and forefinger. 'There are many ways it can be done.'

'What should I do?'

'You're a clever woman.' Using his other hand, he reached for her mound, brushing the soft curls aside to seek out her slickness. 'You know what to do.'

Kate arched into his hand, mewling as he brushed his thumb against the bundle of nerves above her entrance. Nodding, she wrapped a hand around his now hard shaft, giving it a tentative squeeze before pointing it at her wet entrance.

'It's… Ah…'

Her head rolled back as she sank down onto him. Slowly, maddeningly, he filled her to the hilt. Neither of them moved for what seemed like the longest time, until she squeezed him. The sensation nearly had him losing his control.

Sebastian held onto her hips as she moved, slow and tentative at first. But when she pushed her hips forward and found a position that gave her the friction she was seeking, her mouth parted in a gasp. Then she began to move in earnest.

Lord, she was stunning, with her dark hair spilling over her creamy shoulders, breasts bouncing, and those small pants escaping her lips as she sought her pleasure.

A realisation swept over him—an emotion building in his chest that he could not recognise. He thought that for a brief moment a voice in his mind had whispered what it was, but he was too deep in his own pleasure to understand it. He needed more of her. No, he needed all of her. Now.

Her body let out a shudder, but he pulled her off him before it could go further. She let out a whine of protest, but Sebastian quickly rolled on top of her and once again filled her, making her moan as he moved his hips rhythmically to push them both to the edge. That earlier thought rushed back into his head, stronger now, but before he could say it aloud he bit the inside of his cheek to stop himself.

He gathered her in his arms, surrendering to the rapture of being deep inside her, filling her with his seed as ecstasy made his body convulse. Afterwards, he crumpled on top of her, fully drained. As the taste of iron filled his mouth he realised how close he had been to saying things he might regret later.

Much too close.

His body had barely recovered from the mind-numbing pleasure before a different kind of emotion ran through him.

Panic.

Anger.

And a coldness that gripped his insides like a vice.

He could only attribute it to one thing.

Fear.

With an inward curse, he pushed himself off her and onto his back, then swung his legs over the side of the bed.

'Sebastian?' Kate said in a breathless voice. 'Are you all right?'

'I'm fine,' he grumbled, then bent down to pick up his discarded trousers.

'Are you leaving?'

'It's almost daylight. I should go before your maid comes in.'

With a determined grunt, he pushed himself off the bed and continued to dress.

'Yes, but if there's something the matter—'

'I told you. I'm fine.' Half the buttons on his shirt still had to be done up but he left her room anyway, as the tightness in his chest threatened to suffocate him if he didn't get away that instant.

Swiftly, he escaped back to his rooms, and air only began to fill his lungs when he collapsed in the leather chair by the window.

Dear Lord, what had he been thinking?

Reaching towards the table beside him, he picked up a crystal decanter filled with amber liquid. He unscrewed the top and took a swig, hoping the burning path the liquor took down his throat would also raze the memories from the past threatening to overwhelm him here in the present.

The candles burning bright in the darkened bedroom. His mother so still and pale and barely breathing.

And once again he was transported back to that moment five years ago. The moment that had changed his life.

'Your Grace?'

Robeson's voice flung him back to the present. Sebastian blinked, then quickly shut his eyes as sunlight burned them. When the devil had it become so bright outside?

'Robeson?' he rasped, his throat feeling dry. 'What time is it?'

'A quarter past nine, Your Grace.'

'Quarter past—?' He clamped his mouth shut. He'd

been sitting here, decanter in his hand, for nearly two hours.

'Do you need a few more minutes, Your Grace?'

'No.' He tucked the empty decanter into a corner of the chair and then got up. 'Please have a bath prepared, Robeson. As quickly as you can. Don't bother heating the water.'

The valet didn't even blink an eye. 'Of course, Your Grace.'

Once he was alone, Sebastian strode over to the washstand and splashed his face with clean water.

This has to stop.

He could not let what had happened this morning— what had almost happened—happen again. Could not lose control. After half a decade of keeping a tight rein on his emotions he'd been on the cusp of letting all that hard work go to waste. Only he had the power to stop it. He could not be alone with Kate—not until their wedding. No more midnight visits, no more intimate glances, no more worrying about if she were happy or not.

Surely by then he would have put enough distance between them that he could get a hold on his emotions before they ran away.

He shut his eyes tight, drawing up an image of his mother in his mind. An image of what might be his future if he did not stop this insanity now.

Despite his weariness from lack of sleep, Sebastian managed to go through his usual routine for the rest of the day. He met with a few tenants, conducted another long meeting with Arthur Mason and the solicitors, then finally changed into his dinner clothes.

'You're looking a little the worse for wear,' the Dowager Duchess commented as they walked to the parlour.

'Aren't we all?' he muttered in reply.

She laughed. 'Indeed. I don't remember staying up that late in a long time.'

A fleeting expression of sadness crossed her face. Sebastian knew she was remembering what it had been like before her husband had shattered their lives and left her to pick up all the pieces. His resolve to keep his distance from Kate grew stronger. But of course his chest tightened in anticipation as they stood outside the parlour, at knowing she was mere feet away. When they entered, he could not help searching the room for her, his gaze stopping once he did find her.

'Come, let's begin dinner,' the Dowager Duchess said, leading them towards Kate and Arthur.

'Your Grace.' Kate's greeting sounded unsure as she curtseyed, her body wavering slightly. Still, she looked stunning in a violet evening gown, its modest neckline showing only the minimum amount of skin. Skin that he wanted to—

'Good evening,' he said, getting hold of his lust.

Lord, this would be a long meal.

She looked as if she wanted to say something, so he offered his arm to her and spoke first. 'Let's go in for dinner, shall we?'

The meal seemed longer than it really was—perhaps because he kept his eye on the clock on the mantel for most of it. He thought no one had noticed, but the Dowager Duchess raised a delicate eyebrow at him, the corners of her lips tugging up.

When they'd finished dessert, and the men and women were parting, Sebastian breathed a sigh of relief. It had taken all his strength to treat Kate as he had before, when all he'd wanted was to be alone with her again.

As they were leaving the dining room, Kate leaned over to him and whispered, 'I shall see you tonight, Your Grace.' She disentangled her arm from his and followed the other ladies back to the parlour.

His resolve nearly crumbled as he watched her walk away, hips swaying gracefully. Thankfully, Arthur and the other men hadn't noticed, and ushered him towards his study for port and cigars.

'Your Grace,' Arthur began, 'now that we are making headway in our plans for the factory, have you thought what to do for iron?'

His head snapped towards the older man. 'What about iron?'

'As you know,' he went on, pulling Cornelius DeVries forward, 'Cornelius here owns one of the largest iron forges in America. He's the best in the business.'

DeVries let out a jovial laugh. 'You are too kind, Arthur.'

'Nonsense,' Arthur snorted. 'If you weren't, I wouldn't be working with you. Though he and his family are only here for the girls, I think we can convince him to partner up with us in our little venture.'

'Is that so?'

Sebastian normally hated talking business after dinner—and with Arthur's enthusiasm for anything that had to do with making money, this might take all night—but it would be a welcome distraction from his urge to be with Kate.

'Tell me more, Mr DeVries.'

Chapter Twenty-One

Kate glanced at the door as she sat up in bed, fully awake, her body thrumming with anticipation, waiting for Sebastian to enter her room. She had nearly gone mad during dinner, acting as if everything was as it had been before last night, making polite conversation and keeping a modest distance.

Yet she knew things were not the same and nothing could ever go back to the way it had been before.

Now that she had a clearer picture of Sebastian's past, and the baring of her own growing emotions, the reality of it crashed into Kate like the rolling waves on the shore, smashing into her mind and sending her into a tizzy. But then, once it receded, she got her bearings and was able to think clearly.

This was a mutually beneficial arrangement. She needn't be concerned for him this deeply. This foolishness had to stop now.

She metaphorically straightened her shoulders and dug her heels in.

Then the wave came crashing back again, knocking her into the sand.

Oh, Lord, what was she to do?

Sebastian had been adamant that emotions could not be part of their marriage. And after her talk with the Dowager Duchess she could guess why. He'd been hurt because of what had happened with his parents, and his mother in particular. She couldn't even begin to imagine what it must be like to be in love with someone and then have them betray you.

But I would never betray him.

Once again, she found herself smashing onto the shore.

The worst possible scenario she could imagine would be Sebastian discovering her feelings, as then he might break off their engagement. That would mean her having to marry Jacob and wiping away all traces of Pap's legacy.

No, Sebastian could never find out about her feelings.

A noise from outside made her jolt. Her fingers clutched at the sheets, as she waited for Sebastian to enter her room. But the doorknob didn't turn, and the door did not open. She guessed it had to be past midnight, which was later than he usually came. In the past two weeks he'd arrived not too long after Anna had left as, when the men and women separated after dinner, Sebastian usually cut his evening short so he could be with her.

While she wished she could be a part of those discussions—because, knowing her father, they would be all about business—she knew she only had to bide her time and then her father would be thousands of miles away and she would be free to do as she wanted with the new factory and her engines. Indeed, her mind was already filled with ideas on how she was going to improve the basic design of a locomotive so it could run more efficiently.

She reached over to her bedside table and pulled out

a leather-bound notebook with a pencil attached to the strings that held it closed. Untying the knot, she opened it to the first blank page and began to sketch. Graphite flew over the pages as Kate's ideas materialised into rough designs and initial calculations.

Yes, that would work!

Her teeth sank into her lower lip.

But only if the factory floor space were doubled…

Then she'd double it.

Her hand paused. Sebastian had said she would be in charge of everything. From start to finish. The possibilities would be endless.

Filled with excitement, she continued to draw and plan, flipping the pages so fast they were nearly ripped out.

Oh, Pap, this is really happening!

When Kate reached the last empty page, she halted and looked up. Morning light had begun to filter through the gauzy curtains.

Goodness, I stayed up all night.

But it had been worth it. She clutched the notebook to her chest, her head light and dizzy from excitement.

But then her heart plummeted when she realised Sebastian hadn't come to her bed.

Maybe he was tired last night.

Feeling her energy drain from her body, she relaxed and sank back into the pillows. Yes, perhaps that was it.

I'll show him my plans later, she thought before closing her eyes and allowing sleep to take over.

Kate could understand it if Sebastian had felt tired for a night or two—Lord knew, she could use some rest from all this excitement herself—but it had been nearly a week since Sebastian had visited her at night.

I should have trusted my instincts.

Something was very wrong. She had felt it the last two times they had made love, and then on the morning of the engagement ball and the day after.

Her gaze went to the stack of notebooks on the bedside table. Each night she had sketched and planned until she was exhausted. She'd told herself that it was a good thing he was busy, so she could finish her work, and she couldn't wait to show him all her plans. But after a week she'd already revised all her ideas. And now all she could do was wait.

Leaning over the bedside table, she blew out the candle. With the room blanketed in darkness, she sank deeper into the covers. Perhaps it was better if they didn't sleep together any more—at least not until their wedding night. With her feelings causing chaos within herself, who knew what would happen if they were intimate and she suddenly confessed?

No, she had to keep it to herself. They were not married yet, and if it should fall through Jacob would be waiting to swoop in.

She turned on her side and hugged her pillow. The maid must have changed the sheets that morning, because they no longer had that trace scent of Sebastian's cologne. She closed her eyes tight, trying to convince herself to go to sleep. Not that it helped.

Kate found herself wide awake until the early hours of the morning, and it was only pure exhaustion that had her finally drifting off. By the time Anna came in to bring her some tea and toast, her eyes felt dry and swollen, her head was throbbing, and her chest was ready to burst with… With what she didn't know. But if she didn't get to the bottom of it she would surely explode.

With a determined grunt, she swung her feet off

the bed and instructed Anna to get her favourite peach morning gown ready. Once dressed, she marched to Sebastian's private study and knocked on the door. When she heard a voice telling her to come in, she pushed it open and strode inside.

'Sebastian, I must— Father?'

Arthur Mason sat behind Sebastian's desk, white brows furrowed as he read through some papers. Jacob, as usual, was behind him, looking over his shoulder.

'Yes, Kathryn?' her father said, without looking up.

'Father, what are you doing in here? Where is Sebastian?'

'Working,' he said matter-of-factly. 'And as for the Duke—he said he was leaving for London after breakfast.'

'London?'

He had never said anything to her about going to town. Her heart plummeted. Without another word, she whirled around and marched out through the door. It was early still, so maybe he was having breakfast.

'Kate?'

Jacob had followed her.

What now?

'I don't have time for this, Jacob.'

'One moment, please, Cousin.'

She slowed her steps but didn't stop. 'What do you want?' After no sleep the night before, she was irritable and exhausted.

'What has you so vexed this morning, Kate?' Jacob enquired. 'Are you and the Duke having a tiff? You didn't seem to know he was heading to London…and only a week before your wedding.'

As if she'd confide in him about such things. 'Everything is fine,' she said, mustering up as much confidence as she could. 'Is there anything else?'

'Nothing at all.'

'Good.' She curled her hands into fists. 'Now, unless you have something truly important to tell me, I must be off.'

Despite her exhaustion, she managed to race down the corridor and into the dining room. It was completely empty, so she dashed out into the receiving area, where the door was still open. She spied Sebastian's coach, pulling up outside on the drive.

'Sebastian!' she called when she saw his tall form standing in front of the coach, one foot on the steps. Not caring that Eames and the footmen were around, she picked up her skirts and ran out. 'Sebastian!'

He froze, his body stiffening. 'Kate.'

'You're...leaving?' she huffed between breaths.

His back remained to her. 'I have business to attend to.'

'Business? In London?'

He let out a breath and lowered his foot. Turning around, he finally faced her. 'Yes, business.'

'You're going without telling me?'

'I didn't realise I needed your permission.'

His cool, impersonal gaze told her that something was definitely amiss.

'Could we speak before you leave? It won't take too long.'

His expression darkened, but he nodded towards the carriage. She took the hand he offered and climbed in. Sebastian gave instructions to the driver to wait, and then followed her inside.

'What is this about, Kate?'

'I just... I just wanted to ask...' She bit her lip, not

really sure what to say. 'If you have changed your mind about the wedding.'

About me.

He didn't even flinch. 'Changed my mind? What in heaven's name are you talking about?'

His irritated tone clawed at her, making her lash out. 'You haven't been to my bed in days. And now you skulk off to London without so much as a by-your-leave. Not a word to me, your fiancée.'

Those obsidian eyes hardened into black steel. 'You're being ridiculous. I have business interests in London, and sometimes that requires me to travel into town at a moment's notice. Besides, the air in the country makes me weary at times, and I find myself needing…variety.'

The meaning in his words was clear. She knew what kind of 'variety' he needed in London.

'You don't mean that.'

'I beg your pardon?'

Her heart twisted in her chest, but she couldn't help it. 'Tell me this marriage is not just about our business arrangement. Tell me it is more than that—that you have other reasons why you want to marry me. That I mean something to you. Because you mean something to me.'

Please tell me.

All those nights together. The things he'd done to make her happy.

He must feel something for me.

'Kate,' he said in a warning tone. 'Don't—'

'I love you, Sebastian.'

She hadn't meant to say it, but the words had spilled out of her. No, they'd burst out—after a week of trying to break free.

'I can't help it. I do.'

There. She'd said it. Bared it all for him. She could

be sitting in front of him without her clothes on and she still wouldn't feel half as naked as she did now.

Silence hung in the air. He sat there, still as a rock, not saying a word. Finally, he spoke, after what seemed like for ever. 'You're mistaken,' he began in a low tone. 'We have agreed this is a business arrangement,' he reminded her. 'That's all.'

Kate couldn't move. Couldn't breathe. Knew that if she did she would shatter into a million pieces.

Sebastian felt nothing for her.

She had imagined that Sebastian breaking off their engagement and the destruction of her grandfather's legacy would be the worst scenario in the world.

Now she knew it was not.

She wanted to slink out of the carriage and escape back to her room. Bury herself under the bedcovers and not come out for days.

'But what good would that do?'

The words came to her in the form of Pap's voice.

'You've never been one to run away from your problems, my girl,' he continued. *'That's not how I taught you.'*

And so she dug her heels in. 'You are a coward.'

'I beg your pardon?' Sebastian replied in an ominous tone.

Her throat threatened to close, but she pushed on. 'You heard what I said. You're a coward, Sebastian.'

'How dare you—?'

'I am not done speaking.' Her palms slammed down on the plush upholstery seat. 'You're a coward—hiding behind your father's death and your mother's attempted suicide because you're afraid to face what's really scaring you. The fact that perhaps there's another reason you're obsessed with not becoming like your father.'

'I can't let the cycle—'

'That's not it.' The tic in his jaw told her she was getting close to the mark. 'All these years you've wasted, trying not to be that man... Sebastian, you are your own person. You could never turn into someone else. It's not inevitable, but something you choose. And right now you're choosing to let something out of your control hold you back.'

Once she'd started speaking it was like a tidal wave, and she couldn't stop.

'When you're truly honest with yourself, and address what's really wrong, then you can open up to the possibility that someone could love you and you could love them in return. Now, tell me, what are you really afraid of?'

'You don't know what you're talking about.' The air in the carriage had turned chilly. 'As I said, you're mistaken.'

So that was it. He had made his choice to live in the past instead of moving forward with her.

'Of course, Your Grace,' she managed to mutter, even though her heart cracked within her chest. 'Forgive me. Please, allow me to delay you no further.'

Tears blurred the edges of her vision, but she dared not let him see them. She reached for the carriage door and pushed it open. Ignoring the startled footman, she leapt off the steps and dashed into the manor.

She was halfway to her room when she stopped.

I can't go in there. There—the place where she had shared so many achingly beautiful moments with him.

She bolted in the opposite direction and made her way outside again, through the entrance that led to the gardens.

A walk should clear my head.

Yes, that was what she needed. Some fresh air and sun. Time in nature, to contemplate and determine what she should do.

She trudged through the gardens, but even out here all she could think about was Sebastian—especially when she glanced up at the orangery. So she ambled out to the meadows and fields surrounding the manor, wandering aimlessly until her feet ached. The pain felt good, and for now it was enough to make her forget the stinging soreness in her chest.

I'm a fool for telling him I love him.

Of course he did not love her back. He had made it clear from the beginning that love would have no place in their marriage. Their partnership was to be built on a solid foundation of mutual need, not something unsteady like love.

She knew that, and yet she'd done nothing to stop her heart from falling into danger. And now that runaway train had plunged straight down into the abyss.

It felt as if she'd been walking for days, but really it couldn't have been more than half an hour as the manor was still in her sights, although in the distance. With a deep sigh, she began the long trudge back. What was she going to do? Perhaps she would figure it out by the time she reached the manor.

'Kate! Kate!'

She turned around at the sound of the voice. A figure in the distance came running towards her, and as it drew closer she cursed silently.

'Cousin Jacob? What are you doing here?' Kate couldn't even pretend to be glad to see him.

Jacob's face was red with exertion. 'Kate…you must come with me. There's been an accident!'

'An accident?' She pressed a hand to her breast. 'Who? My father?'

He shook his head. 'No…it's the Duke.'

Sebastian! A different kind of emotion gripped her chest like a fist. 'What—? Where—? But he just left for London.'

'It was a carriage accident.' Jacob continued to gasp for air. 'He'd only travelled a few miles from the estate when the horses got spooked. A fox or something must have crossed the road.'

'And Sebastian? How is he?'

Oh, Lord, please let him be all right!

Jacob's face turned grave. 'He's alive…but trapped under the carriage. He's asking for you.'

'Of course. I'll head back to the manor—'

'No!' Jacob seized a fistful of her sleeve. 'They sent me here to fetch you. I've taken your father's carriage by the back road—it's just down there—and I'm to bring you to His Grace right away.'

'Let's go now.'

Kate followed Jacob across the field towards the carriage waiting on the side of the wide path. She climbed in first, and scooted towards the opposite end of the bench. The cab dipped as Jacob clambered in, then settled beside her.

As the carriage began to move her chest squeezed tight with fear as images of what state Sebastian might be in sprang into her mind.

Please don't die, Sebastian. She didn't care if he never loved her back. *Just let him be alive.*

She wrung her fingers together in her lap, keeping her focus outside. Worry loomed over her like a storm cloud, creating a contrast to the beautiful English countryside. Right now the sun filled the bare land with golden morning light, but soon this field would be filled with flowers. What a beautiful sight it would be, with the sun shining on them.

Her heart crashed into her ribcage when she realised where the sunlight was coming from.

The sun was behind them.

Which meant they were travelling west—not northeast towards London, where Sebastian had been headed. She glanced around, noticing how the carpeting on the floor of the carriage was threadbare and the seat cushions so worn she could feel the hard wooden bench underneath them. Arthur Mason would never have rented such a carriage.

'Have you figured it out, Cousin?'

Her head snapped to Jacob. 'There was no accident.'

The smug smirk he flashed her confirmed it. 'You always were too smart for your own good.'

Oh, Lord. Jacob was kidnapping her.

Instinctively, she lunged for the door, but he blocked her and pushed her back. Her head hit the side of the carriage with a loud thud and pain exploded in her temple.

'Don't even think about it.'

The sound of a revolver being cocked made her blood run cold. Raising her gaze, she spied the barrel of the gun pointing straight at her. 'What's…this about?' She moaned, kneading the growing lump on the side of her head. 'Where are you taking me?'

'Where else do secret lovers go to escape their families?' Jacob sneered. 'Scotland, of course.'

'Lovers?' What in the world was he talking about? 'Scotland?'

'Yes. Gretna Green, to be exact. The letter you've left on your bed explains it all. You and I have been lovers all this time. We want to marry, but your father is forcing you to marry the Duke, so we've decided to elope.'

Despite her throbbing head, she quickly grasped the gist of his scheme. 'You rotten scoundrel!' Jacob *did* want control of Mason R&L. 'Greedy...*bastard*!'

Jacob only laughed. 'Did you think I was going to let years and years of hard work, of licking your father's boots and deferring to him, go to waste? I was the one who did all his dirty work, kept his hands clean so that everyone would remember Arthur Mason as a benevolent industrialist instead of the ruthless businessman we both know him to be.'

Kate couldn't deny that. In fact, when Pap had been alive, he and Arthur had often clashed over things like wages and the cost of materials. Her father always looked at maximising profit, while Pap had refused to sacrifice quality and had fought for his men to get fair pay.

'England is where I was going to build *my* empire,' Jacob continued. 'And now he's just going to hand over the reins to that stupid duke.'

His eyes had widened so much that Kate could see the whites around them.

'I will never let that happen. I worked hard for this. I deserve this. Deserve you.'

'I'll never marry you!'

'You won't have a choice, dear Cousin.'

'Not even the blacksmiths at Gretna Green will officiate a marriage where one party is unwilling.'

The corner of his lips turned up into a smile. 'That's the beauty of this, Kate. We're not really going to Scotland and nor are we getting married—not right away. We're heading west, and not north, just in case your dear duke tries to chase after us. After spending tonight at a coaching inn we'll make our way back to London, then send for Arthur in the morning. By then everyone will know what we've done. Once the gossip has spread, do you think your precious duke will still marry you? Will anyone believe you're still a virgin by the time we come back?' He snorted. 'Of course not. And that's all I need. Once you're spoiled goods, you'll have no choice but to marry me.'

Lord, she hated those words. *Spoiled goods.* Once again she was being treated like an object, not a person.

Unfortunately, though, Jacob was right. Once it came out that she was ruined, her father would only care that she be married one way or another.

What would Sebastian think of her ? Would he believe her? Even if he did, he would break off their engagement if even a whisper of scandal touched his family again. And, heavens—the Dowager Duchess! She wouldn't be able to weather another scandal.

Feeling drained and hopeless, Kate slumped back in her seat.

'That's right...be a good girl. Don't bother fighting it.' Jacob grinned. 'Now, get some rest. It'll be a few more hours until we reach the coaching inn. Don't worry, sweetheart. I won't touch you in such a filthy place. No, we'll have a grand wedding in New York, and we'll have our first night together as man and wife in the finest suite at the Astor Hotel.'

The very thought of being in bed with Jacob made her insides revolt. Damn Jacob and his greed!

I can't lose hope.

Surely she could find a way to flee.

Think, Kate!

Even if Sebastian didn't want her, she would do everything in her power to escape this fate.

Chapter Twenty-Two

Regret filled Sebastian the moment the carriage door slammed shut. No, it had begun the moment he'd spoken all those lies that had brought pain to those beautiful cornflower-blue eyes. He couldn't have hurt her more if he'd struck her.

He sat inside his coach for what seemed like for ever, unable to move an inch. His stomach churned with bile as his mind played the events in his mind over and over, torturing him with a vision of Kate's face crumpling and how her eyes had shone with tears as he'd uttered those brutal words.

He'd had no choice. She couldn't possibly mean what she said. Did she have any idea how powerful those words were? How he could use them against her?

No, he hadn't had a choice. It was for her own good.

Well, he had wanted to push her away and he'd succeeded. Spectacularly.

'I love you, Sebastian.'

But those words weren't the only thing that bothered him. It was what she'd said after that unnerved him. Because if he was honest with himself, she was completely and utterly correct. He was a coward. But, worse than that, he was a failure.

I have to make things right.

And he knew where to start.

Flinging the carriage door open, he bolted out and dashed towards the door. Kate had probably gone back to her room. He would make it up to her and beg her for forgiveness, but he had one other stop to make first.

He didn't even bother knocking, and yanked open the door to the Dowager Duchess's private sitting room. 'Mother!'

'Sebastian?' His mother looked up at him from where she sat by the window. 'Has something happened?'

Sebastian remained quiet. How would he explain this to her?

Rising from her seat, she walked towards him. 'You look troubled. Darling, what's the matter?' She paused. 'Does it have something to do with Kate?'

How the devil had she figured that out?

His mother tsked. 'I thought there was something going on between the two of you.' Tucking her arm into his, she tugged at him. 'Now, come.'

'But I have to—'

She ignored his protests and dragged him out of the room, then led him to the front hall. The footman opened the door as they approached. 'Please have Eames fetch Miss Mason and bring her to the orangery,' she said, as they walked across the threshold.

The young man bowed low. 'Yes, Your Grace.'

Once the footman had left, the Dowager Duchess tightened her grip on his arm. 'Come and walk with me.'

Unsure of what was happening, Sebastian allowed his mother to drag him towards the gardens.

'Now,' she began, 'tell me what's the matter.'

What was it about his mother that he could not say no or lie to her? He let out a breath. 'I've made a muck of things. With Kate.'

And he told her everything—about Kate's plan, their arrangement, his mixed-up feelings about her and his subsequent reaction, along with what had happened in the carriage that morning.

When he'd finished, his mother didn't say a word, but the way her lips quirked and her brows drew together told Sebastian that she was thinking.

She spoke as soon as they entered the orangery. 'If you didn't feel the same way, you would have just told her. But you didn't. Instead you said terrible things to hurt her. Why would you so utterly reject her without thought?'

'I don't feel the same way.' That was his automatic response.

'Don't lie to me, Sebastian. I am not blind. I have watched you two these last few weeks. Now, tell me why you seem intent on driving her away when you clearly have feelings for each other?'

The answer was stuck in his throat, because he had kept the truth from her all these years. But perhaps his silence revealed too much, because her expression fell.

'It's because of what happened between your father and I, isn't it?'

'Mother—'

'No, there's no need to deny it. Not for my sake.' Untangling her arm from his, she walked ahead, stopping in front of a row of hanging orchids. 'Sebastian, I am sorry,' she said, her voice hitching. 'Please forgive me.'

'Forgive *you*?' He was beside her in an instant. 'Mother, no. You did nothing wrong.' His fingers curled into his palms. 'If he were alive, it should be that…that man who should be asking forgiveness.'

Calling that bastard 'Father' always left a bitter taste in his mouth.

His mother's eyes turned vacant, as if the life had been sucked out of them. He remembered that look. It was the same one from five years ago, after she had been revived.

'I think it's time I told you the truth,' she said. 'Years ago…before I met your father… I had an interest in mathematics.' She shook her head. 'No, it was more than an interest. One of my mentors—a distant uncle who'd taken an interest in teaching me—encouraged me to work on a paper to submit to the Académie des Sciences in France.'

He blinked at her. 'Truly?'

'You've always been good with numbers, Sebastian.' She smiled weakly at him. 'Did you think you'd got that from your father?'

'Not with his lack of accounting skills,' he said wryly.

If she had been working on something for the French academy of science, then she really had to have been exceptionally gifted.

'But what happened?'

'What else? I met your father.' Reaching her hand out, she touched one of the orchid buds. 'I was madly in love. And I'd like to think he loved me too.' The delicate bloom was perhaps too fragile, and it fell to the ground. 'When we married, I gave up my work so I could be Duchess, and then I had you… Oh, don't fret, darling. You were the best part of that bargain. And I was happy for a time. We all were. Then your father…' Her lips pressed together tightly. 'I was a fool. The signs were there but I ignored them. Then he died, and with the scandal... I couldn't hide from it any longer. In a moment of weakness, I thought to end it all. The regret. The pain. I—'

'Stop.' A pain sliced through his gut. 'Please. Say no more.'

'But—'

'You don't have to explain further. I understand, Mother. I truly do. And why you had to hide away from me all these years. You couldn't stand the reminder.'

Saying it aloud didn't make things better. It was like an open wound that wouldn't stop bleeding.

Colour drained from her beautiful face. 'You thought that was why I stayed away from you? Because you reminded me of your father and I feared you would eventually turn into him?'

It was more a statement than a question. He knew it to be true.

'But there's more, darling. Something else is bothering you. Tell me. Do not be scared.'

Kate's words haunted him. *'Now, tell me, what are you really afraid of?'*

'I'm your mother. I shan't judge you. Please, Sebastian.'

His mother's soothing words made the agony of years of repressing his own inner turmoil slowly lift. 'I couldn't protect you, Mother.' His throat tightened. 'I'd been so blinded by my love for Father that I ignored you all those years. I couldn't stop him from hurting you. From making you want to take your own life. *I couldn't save you.*'

And that was the truth. Kate had seen it before he had. That all these years he'd been blaming himself because he felt he'd failed his mother.

She enfolded him in her arms. 'There, there... It's not

your fault. It was not your role to protect me. I made my choices. Allowed despair to take over. And I didn't want that to touch you, so I stayed away. That's the real reason. I wanted you to be free of my melancholia, to live your life as you always had without me weighing you down like an anchor. But it seems I only made it worse.'

Sorrow marred her face.

'And that's why you must forgive me. It's because of me you've run yourself ragged these past five years. I'm the reason why you haven't let anyone love you and why you've rejected Kate. Your guilt has made you think yourself unworthy of love. You think you don't deserve her. That you don't deserve happiness.'

'It's true. She'll be better off with someone else,' he said bitterly. 'Someone who won't be a hindrance to her.' As his father had been to his mother.

'Oh, darling, can't you see?' His mother's fingers wrapped around his forearms. 'You are *nothing* like him.'

'You two are like two peas in a pod.' Those had been her very words when he was growing up.

'How do you know that?'

'Tell me this, Sebastian...' The Dowager Duchess pressed her lips together. 'Why do you want to marry Kate? And don't say it's because you've ruined her. There are many lords out there who would have over-looked her lack of virtue for her dowry. And why go into business with her father to build this factory? You don't need the money, or the problems that go along with such a huge venture.'

Sebastian couldn't find any logical explanation ex-cept for one. 'Because she wants it. Just as she wants to save her grandfather's legacy.'

'The fact that you care for her hopes and dreams already proves you aren't like your father. No one else can give her that. You deserve her, Sebastian. You deserve to be loved. Don't let the ghost of your father prevent you from pursuing what could be a happy life with the woman you love.'

The woman I love.

'Kate…'

Yes, Kate was the woman he loved.

Slowly, the Dowager Duchess's mouth spread into a smile. 'And you'll tell her, won't you? That you want to marry her because you love her.'

'I will.' His heart plummeted. 'That's assuming she still wants to speak to me and doesn't despise me after this morning.'

By God, he would do anything to make her forgive him. Beg on his knees if he had to. Buy her a hundred factories across England. Because she was the only woman for him from now on.

'Mother, what do I do?'

'Just say what's in your heart. You— Ah!' Her hands clasped together as the telltale *clink* of the door latch told them someone was coming in. 'She's here.'

The thought of seeing her again after this morning set his nerves on edge and built excitement in him at the same time. Clasping his hands behind him, Sebastian began to pace across the tiled floor.

'Your Grace!'

'Eames?'

Sebastian halted. From the grave expression on the butler's face, he knew there was something wrong.

'Where is Miss Mason, Eames?' the Dowager Duchess asked.

The butler wrung his hands together. 'I'm afraid we can't find her.'

'Can't find her?' Sebastian thundered. 'What do you mean, "can't find her"?'

'One of the maids said that she saw Miss Mason on her way to her room, but when Mrs Grover checked it was empty. A footman mentioned he saw her outside, but no one has seen her since.'

Cold, icy talons of fear pricked at Sebastian.

'Tell all the servants to start looking for her. Everywhere. Have Mrs Grover and Kate's maid search her room. I'm going to see her father.'

Sebastian made it to his private study in record time, his mother trailing behind him.

'Arthur!' he roared. 'Where is Kate?'

The old man peered up at him from where he sat behind the desk. 'Kate? How should I know where she is?'

Damn this man! If it didn't have monetary value, he didn't give a whit. 'She's missing.'

'Are you sure?' His mouth twitched underneath his snowy moustache. 'Perhaps she's just wandering about the estate.'

'Your Grace!' Mrs Grover rushed into the study and curtseyed. 'Begging your pardon, b-but…w-we…uh…'

'For heaven's sake, spit it out!' Sebastian snarled.

The housekeeper's lower lip trembled as she handed him a piece of paper. 'This—this was on her bed.'

Snatching the note from her, Sebastian held it up and read through it.

'What is it?' the Dowager Duchess asked.

His jaw tightened. 'Here.'

His mother's brows knitted as she began to read. *'"Cannot live with this lie…forced to marry…leaving to be with Jacob…"'* She gasped. 'Sebastian… I'm so sorry.'

'What does it say, Your Grace?' Arthur asked.

'That she has run away with Mr Malvery.' The Dowager Duchess paled. 'To Gretna Green.'

Sebastian gnashed his teeth. 'No.'

'No?' She tilted her head to the side. 'What do you mean, "no", darling?'

'I mean—' he snatched the paper from her '—Kate did not write this. And she did not run away with Malvery.'

'But how can you be sure?'

'The handwriting is atrocious, for one thing.'

The loops, whirls, and smudges on the page made the note barely legible. Kate was an engineer: that meant she had to have excellent, precise penmanship for drawing up plans and blueprints.

'And half the words are misspelled.'

And deep in his heart he knew that Kate would never betray him like this.

'She could have been in a hurry,' Arthur said.

'Kate hates Malvery,' Sebastian countered. 'Why do you think she chose to marry me? And they can't have been lovers all this time.'

Not when Kate had been a virgin when she'd came to his bed and had spent nearly every night in his arms.

'What do you think happened?' asked Arthur.

'I think Malvery took her.'

'J-Jacob?' Arthur spluttered. 'But why?'

'I don't know why, precisely,' Sebastian growled. 'But when I find him—' *when, not if* '—he will regret trying to take what's mine.'

Chapter Twenty-Three

Kate's hope drained away as the carriage continued its journey. The further they were from Highfield Park, the smaller were her chances of escaping. Even if she did manage to flee when they arrived at the coaching inn it might be too late. No one would believe she hadn't run away with Jacob—not if they read that letter.

Stop it!

If Pap were here, he'd tell her never to give up. *'There's always a solution,'* he'd always said. *'And if you can't find one then you aren't looking hard enough.'*

'What is going on?' Jacob snarled. 'Why are we slowing down?'

Kate had been so deep in her thoughts that she hadn't noticed that the carriage had reduced its speed.

Jacob drew the curtain back. 'Driver! What are you doing? Why are we stopping?'

'Gotta stop for a piss!' the disembodied voice of the driver shouted back.

'You're stopping to—? I demand you keep going! I didn't pay you to dawdle about.'

'Wot am I s'posed to do, then? Piss me pants? Cor, I got more piddle than these horses…might even dribble some into the cab. You don't wanna sit in my stink, do ya?'

'Fine,' Jacob grumbled. 'But be quick about it.'

Kate gathered her thoughts. This was it! Her chance. But what to do…?

'Jacob, I need to…uh…powder my nose as well.'

'What?'

She blew out an exasperated breath. 'I have to…do my business.'

'Hold it in,' he snapped.

'But I can't. Please, Jacob? Or do you want to be locked up in here for the next few hours in my…you know…'

'Oh, all right.' He retrieved the pistol from his coat pocket. 'Move. But stay close, you hear?'

She opened the door and alighted. Scanning the surroundings, she spied a tree just a few feet away. Thankfully the driver was nowhere in sight, so she trudged over, Jacob plodding behind her.

'Do you mind turning your back?' she asked through gritted teeth. 'I need some privacy.'

'No way in hell I'm leaving you out of my sight.' He motioned to the tree with the gun. 'Go.'

Gathering her skirts, she marched behind the tree, turned so her back was to him, and crouched down. *What to do now?* She could only see flat fields all around her. She supposed she could attempt to outrun Jacob, but her skirts would slow her down. If only—

She blinked at something on the ground. Was that…?

'Hurry up!'

'I'm trying!' Reaching down, she ran her hands over the grass until she felt the large, spiky round seeds.

Burrs!

They'd used to grow right outside their house in West

Virginia, where she'd played. The familiar prickles sent a rush of excitement through her. Carefully, she gathered as many of them as she could in her right hand, then stood up and brushed her skirts down.

'All done.'

They headed back to the carriage and as she passed by one of the horses she pretended to trip. 'Oh, dear!' She grasped the bellyband, apologised to the poor animal silently, then shoved the burrs underneath the leather strap.

'Stop stalling.' Jacob pressed the barrel of the gun to her back. 'Go inside!'

Scrambling into the carriage, she settled into her seat, her heart hammering like mad the entire time. *Be patient*, she told herself. *And be ready.*

'Where is that confounded man?' Jacob groused. 'Driver!'

'Right 'ere!' The carriage bounced as the driver returned to his seat. 'Hold yer britches—we'll be off, then.'

Kate heard the driver whistle and they began to move forward. For the first few minutes everything seemed normal as the carriage bounced along the dirt road. *Dear God, please...* If the burrs didn't do their job, then she didn't know what else to do.

The carriage stopped without warning, but since Kate had expected it, she'd held on to her seat the entire time. Jacob, however, lurched forward.

Now!

A buzz of energy propelled her towards Jacob, reaching out to grab the gun. She cried out in triumph when her hand grasped the weapon. Quickly, she aimed it at Jacob, who scrambled to get up on the seat across from her.

'Don't move an inch, Jacob,' she warned.

His little beady eyes grew to the size of silver dollars. 'Do you even know how to use that?'

She pulled back the hammer of the pistol. 'You forget, Jacob. I was raised in a West Virginia coal mining town. Now, put your hands up.'

He did, and the hate-filled expression on his face only made her triumph sweeter.

'Wot's going on 'ere, then?' The driver's outraged shout made Jacob flinch. 'No need for guns, gents! I'll give ya wot ya want.'

Jacob gulped. 'Bandits. We've been set upon by robbers!'

Oh, for heaven's sake! Would this day ever become better for her? 'If you say anything, Jacob, I swear to—'

'Kate! Kate are you in there?'

The familiar baritone nearly made her drop the pistol. 'Sebastian?' Was she dreaming? Hallucinating? 'Sebastian, I'm here!'

The door was flung open and Sebastian's large frame filled the tiny interior as he barrelled inside. He immediately grabbed Jacob by the collar. 'Blackguard!' he growled, then hauled him outside.

Kate un-cocked the gun and leapt out of the carriage, just in time to see Sebastian deliver a blow to Jacob's face. Her cousin's head popped back and he landed on his back, out cold.

'John!' he called out to Mr Lawrence, who stood a few feet behind him, brandishing a shotgun. 'Take care of this bastard.'

'Right away, Your Grace.'

Mr Lawrence put the gun down and walked over to her unconscious cousin. Kneeling, he removed the loop of rope hanging from his shoulder and used it to tie Jacob's wrists together.

Sebastian finally turned to her. 'Are you all right? Did he hurt you? Touch you?'

She was in such a state of shock she blurted out the first thing that came to mind. 'What are you doing here?'

'What am I *doing* here?' he asked incredulously. 'I'm rescuing you! Are you—?' He glanced down at the gun in her hand. 'What are you doing with that?'

'I'm…uh…rescuing myself.'

Their eyes locked, and the look of pure relief on his face nearly had her weeping. She dropped the weapon and careered towards him, just as he opened his arms.

'Kate… Kate…' he murmured into her hair as he held her tight. 'Oh, God. I thought I'd lost you. That I would never see you—'

'That wasn't my letter,' she sobbed. 'Please, believe me.'

'I know… Shh, love… I know you didn't write that note,' he soothed.

Blinking back her tears, she looked at him. 'You do?'

'Of course I do,' he scoffed, then smiled down at her as he cupped her jaw with his warm hands. 'You would know how to spell "elopement".'

She barked out a laugh and then rubbed her cheek against his palm.

'I'm sorry,' he began, his tone remorseful. 'For the way I've been acting. And for the words I said to you this morning. I didn't mean any of them.'

'Then why did you say them?'

'I didn't want you to love me. Because I was afraid, Kate.' He swallowed hard and she could sense the internal battle within him. 'You were right. I was scared—of the truth. I couldn't protect my mother and I've felt so guilty. I didn't see how she was deteriorating. All those years I did nothing. She's brilliant, and beautiful—like you—and all that was eroded over time because I was too blinded by my love for my father. And in the end it nearly destroyed her. Because I couldn't save her from him. I failed her. And that's the real reason I feared turning into my father. Closing myself off to love made me feel I was in control of the situation, and it was the one thing I *could* do since I couldn't go back and change the past. But now I know all that was false.'

'Sebastian…' Her chest squeezed and her throat thickened with emotion she couldn't verbalise.

'Our marriage was supposed to be a business arrangement. But even before you agreed to marry me I already knew then I couldn't let Seagrave or anyone else have you. I deluded myself into thinking it was only because you might be with child. Then I started feeling things I wasn't supposed to.'

'Sebastian…'

He took her hands into his. 'So I stayed away, tried to put a stop to my emotions. But it was like trying to make a waterfall flow upwards.' He let out a huff. 'I tried to push you away. I said those things to you because I didn't want to end up hurting you and destroying your dreams, like my father did to my mother.'

'You couldn't,' she said.

'I know that now. It was my mother who made me see it.' His hands squeezed tight around hers. 'But, Kate, know that I love you. Only you.'

A dizziness came over her. It took her a moment, but Kate eventually remembered to breathe. 'I thought you didn't care for me at all. The night of the engagement ball… I was so overwhelmed by my own emotions. I wanted to tell you, but I was afraid. Afraid that you would change your mind if you had an inkling of how I felt about you. But this morning it just came out, and you said—'

'Shh…' Bringing her hands to his lips, he kissed her knuckles. 'Those were all lies. But if I've hurt you so much that you don't feel the same way any more I understand. I will do anything to be deserving of your love again.'

'There's no need for that. I love you, Sebastian. Only you.'

Strong arms came around her and hauled her to him without reserve, then his mouth came down and laid siege to her lips, so that she had no choice but to surrender. This was not their first kiss, but to Kate it felt like the first of something. That her life from now on would be bigger and better than before she met him.

When he pulled away at last her body felt boneless, and she dared not attempt to stand on her own. Instead, she leaned against him and pressed her cheek to his chest, feeling the solidness of the muscle underneath. 'Can we go home now? Please?'

'Of course, love. You can ride with me.' He nodded at Thunder, who stood patiently by the side of the road. 'Thank you, John,' he called out to his companion.

John bowed his head. 'No trouble at all, Your Grace. I'll haul this bugger into the carriage and take 'im straight to the magistrate.'

'I'd appreciate that, John.'

'Thank you, Mr Lawrence,' she said.

'Very welcome, miss.'

As they walked towards Thunder, she asked, 'How did you know where to find me?'

'It was easy enough. Malvery isn't exactly a sophisticated criminal mastermind. When he saw you run off after we quarrelled he went into the village, looking to hire a coachman. There's really only one coachman for hire in town—Thomas Brown. John overheard them negotiating in the tavern. Later, when he got back to his farm, John saw Brown's carriage heading in this direction.'

She glanced back and smiled at the man, who waved at her as he tossed Jacob into the carriage. 'Thank goodness.'

'Not that you needed my help,' he said wryly. 'Looks like you were doing very well on your own.'

'I didn't exactly have a plan for what to do next.' She smiled sheepishly up at him. 'So I'm glad you came after me.'

Halting, he turned to her, midnight eyes filled with a new emotion she'd never seen before—love.

'I will always come after you, Kate. Just try and get away from me. To quote our favourite Bard, "I'll follow thee and make a heaven of hell, to die upon the love I know—"'

'Oh, bother.' Her eyes rolled heavenwards. 'Not that drivel again.'

Gathering her in his arms, he leaned down close to her ear. 'How about…?'

His description of all the scandalous things he was going to do to her that night and every night for the rest of their lives made her shiver in all the most delicious places.

When he'd finished, he pressed a fiery kiss to that spot below her ear, then asked, 'Well? Was that acceptable?'

Wrapping her arms around his neck, she flashed him a wicked smile. 'That, Your Grace, was pure poetry.'

Epilogue

A few months later...

Kate, Duchess of Mabury, still didn't understand men as well as she did steam engines—and even if she did, she highly doubted her life would be simpler.

Take her husband, for example.

'Sebastian, where exactly are we going?'

'I told you, love, it's a surprise.'

'But why must I be blindfolded?'

He let out a frustrated sound. 'The very nature of a surprise demands one party must be kept in the dark until said surprise is revealed.'

'And so you decided to take that definition in its most literal sense?'

'Just indulge me this once, please, love?'

Kate sank back into the plush seating of the coach. Sebastian had said they were going into London for a night, to attend to some business with his solicitor, but when he'd produced the blindfold halfway through the journey, she'd known something was up.

She crossed her arms over her chest. 'I'll be bored. If you take off my blindfold, I could at least work on my design,' she said, patting the reticule on her lap, which bulged with another half-filled notebook and pencils. Once she was done with that, she would add it to the growing pile in her office at Highfield Park. And soon all those plans would turn into reality, as she finally settled into married life.

The wedding had been pushed through as planned, with no more setbacks, and Jacob was currently sitting in a London prison after his attempted kidnap of Kate. Apparently, Arthur had grown displeased with his cousin's failure to move their expansion along in England, and once Kate had secured a proposal from Sebastian he'd told Jacob he should be heading back to America. Much to Kate's surprise, Arthur had actually shown some remorse that his actions had driven Jacob to desperation, and he'd refused to bail Jacob out and completely washed his hands of him. Thankfully, with Arthur's vast resources and Sebastian's influence, they had been able to keep things hushed.

With all that ugliness behind them, Sebastian had taken her on a six-week-long honeymoon on the continent, where they'd visited his villa in the South of France, and another in Italy he was considering purchasing. Kate had fallen so in love with the gorgeous villa on a lake that Sebastian had bought it on the spot, and they'd extended their honeymoon for another two weeks.

As soon as they'd got back, however, Sebastian had immediately gone to work—not at the estate, but in London, gathering support from other peers in order to obtain approval from Parliament to start acquiring the land they needed to lay down railway lines. At the same time plans to start the construction of the factory were underway, but first they had to find the right location.

'Bored, eh…?' In her mind's eye, she could see him

raise a dark eyebrow mischievously. 'Perhaps I can help, Your Grace.'

'What—? Oh!' She felt her skirts being lifted and a hand wrapping around her ankle. 'Sebastian! We're in a coach.'

'I know,' he said, in that smooth, low baritone that never failed to make her shiver.

'B-but…do we have time?'

'All the time we need, love.'

And thus, for the next hour or so, her husband did, indeed, find a way to alleviate her boredom.

Making love half-undressed while blindfolded proved to be Kate's favourite thing to do in a coach. There was something about the motion of the wheels under them, and the fact that she couldn't see anything—only feel, hear, smell, and taste—that added a thrill to their love-making.

'Can I remove this blasted blindfold now?' she asked, breathless, as she lay on top of a naked Sebastian.

'Not yet, love.' He pressed his lips to her temple. 'But we should set you to rights as we're almost there.'

Kate didn't know how he did it, but Sebastian managed to re-lace her stays, button up her dress, and even smooth her coiffure while she remained blindfolded. He finished just as the coach stopped. Finally, they had reached their destination. Wherever this place was.

'Careful,' he said, as he guided her down from the coach.

Her travelling boots hit solid ground, and she could smell and feel the humidity in the air and hear the shrieks of gulls above them. 'Sebastian, where are we?' She was dying from anticipation.

'One moment.' He guided her forward a few feet before halting. 'Ah, here we are.'

When the blindfold was lifted, the harsh light piercing through her eyelids made her pause before she even attempted to open her eyes. After blinking away the blurriness, she found her vision revealed that they were standing near water, on a large, empty piece of ground.

'Sebastian? What is this? Where are we?'

'We're on the Thames River, a few miles south of London,' he said matter-of-factly. 'But to be more specific we're standing on the site of the future Mason & Wakefield Railway Works.'

She gasped. 'All of this land is ours?'

'Yes—and we'll be ready to break ground as soon as you approve the plans. Do you like it?'

'Of course I do!' She flung herself in his arms. 'Thank you,' she murmured against the side of his neck.

'And a few miles up there—' he nodded upriver '—is where Cornelius will be establishing the DeVries Furnace and Iron Company in London. That way, all the necessary materials can be shipped down here via the Thames.'

'That's fantastic news.'

While Cornelius DeVries hadn't originally planned to open his own forge in England, somehow Arthur and Sebastian had used their combined powers of persuasion and convinced him it would be a wise move. Kate had been thrilled, as had Maddie, because it meant that the DeVrieses would be staying in London for a long time, whether or not the two sisters found English husbands.

'By the way,' Kate began, 'a letter from Mama—your Mama—arrived this morning. She'll soon be finished with packing up her Hertfordshire home and shall be fully moved into the dower house by week's end.'

Sebastian's face lit up. 'Wonderful.'

It was clear that the Dowager Duchess had finally

put the past behind her and found a new purpose in life. After everything had been settled, her new mother-in-law had confessed to Kate that when she'd initially read Miss Merton's letter she had been intrigued by her description of Kate and Maddie and their unusual interest in the sciences, and that was what had prompted her to invite them to Highfield Park. She'd said she saw herself in both the girls, and that was why she'd wanted to help them.

And Kate was confident that if she herself could find love, then Maddie, too, would find someone who truly deserved her. Speaking of which...

'You know what Mama living at Highfield Park means, though, don't you?' she said.

'What?'

'The Season will be here again soon.'

'And so?' Sebastian asked. 'What does that have to do with us?'

'Well...' Kate bit her lip, wondering how to broach the topic with her husband. 'Apparently, after her success in matching me, Mama has decided to continue with her project.'

'Project?'

'Yes. Finding girls like me and bringing them to Highfield Park to find them their own husbands.'

'Oh, dear Lord...' Sebastian massaged his temple. 'That means our peace shall be disturbed.'

Kate laughed. 'But it also means Maddie is coming back.'

'Good,' Sebastian said. 'I like her.'

'And Caroline, too, unfortunately.'

Her husband groaned. 'Why?'

'Sebastian!' Kate admonished. 'It would be unkind to

leave her out. Besides, Mama has explained that finding Caroline a husband will help keep her out of trouble.'

'As long as she stays away from us,' he grumbled. 'Now, come.' He gave her a quick kiss on the nose. 'Let's have a walk around.'

Kate could barely contain her excitement as she and Sebastian toured the site. Sure, it was mostly bare for now, but she could see the potential. When they paused near the edge of the water she closed her eyes and pictured her factory. Yes, *hers*.

It's really coming true, Pap.

And she knew that if her grandfather were here, he would be the first to celebrate with her.

'Lord, you're exquisite when you do that.'

She chuckled and turned to Sebastian. 'Do what, exactly?'

Those onyx eyes darkened with promise. 'When you stand there thinking. Dreaming. Breathing.'

Reaching out, he drew her closer, his arms wrapping around as he lowered his head, his mouth capturing hers in a kiss that left her breathless.

'You know,' he said as he pulled back, 'you never did answer my question.'

'I—I beg your pardon?' Her knees wobbled, and she had to brace herself against him or risk melting into a puddle. 'What question?'

The corner of his mouth inched up. 'Do you believe in love?'

'Of course I do, my Pyramus,' she answered without hesitation. Even though she couldn't open it up and take it apart, she knew love existed. The very evidence stood before her. 'And how about you?' she asked. 'Do you still think love is as unsteady as sand?'

Cupping her chin in his hand, he gazed down at her.

'Your love is anything but unsteady, my Thisbe. It is unwavering like stone. Constant as the sunrise…as the rain in the spring and snow in the winter.'

Moisture gathered at the corners of her eyes. 'I am your faithful love, until the end.'

'Until the end,' he agreed, his breath hitching. 'But let's not talk of the end, love.' Slipping an arm around her, he turned her to face the water and the bright blue sky above. 'Because this is just the beginning.'

* * * * *

GAME OF COURTSHIP
WITH THE EARL

To Jason, the best husband and dog dad ever.
Never stop nerding with me.
Mahal kita.

Chapter One

London, 1842

Extracting valuable materials from useless objects was a concept familiar to Miss Madeline DeVries of Pittsburgh, who had, since the age of five, learned the science of metallurgy from her father.

When heated to a high enough temperature, a hunk of ordinary ore lost its impurities and turned into something extraordinary.

If only I were like ore, Maddie thought. *And I could be rid of my flaws.* Then she, too, could be extraordinary, like iron, born from the smelting process, changing the world as she knew it.

At this moment, however, Maddie would settle for just being *ordinary,* if only so the other guests at the Worthington ball would stop staring and whispering as she walked by.

'Gads, they grow them big in the colonies, don't they?'

Maddie would have laughed, except she'd heard that insult before.

'What do you think feed them, do you think?'

Now that was a new one.

Her shoulders slumped. Really, she should have been used to it by now. After all, seven years had passed since that unfortunate summer when she'd grown a foot taller. From then on, she'd towered over all the women—and most men—her age and beyond.

Her father, Cornelius, pragmatic and calm as always, had merely patted her hand and assured her everything would be all right, then gone back to discussing the day's production numbers.

Her mother, Eliza, on the other hand, had declared it a complete and utter tragedy.

'Who will marry you now?' she had cried. 'Where will we find someone who won't have a neck ache each time they look up at your face? Your prospects in this town are meagre enough as it is.'

It was a silly statement, because Pittsburgh boasted a large population of eligible men, but what Mama really meant was the lack of men that were of their newly acquired social standing. With the seemingly unquenchable thirst for building and commerce and progress all over the United States, the DeVries Furnace and Iron Company's business had flourished. Their family grew rich, elevating them from their humble origins.

From then on, there was no stopping the tenacious Eliza DeVries from achieving her dream of taking her place at the top of the social ladder. Not the closely guarded societal borders protected by the old rich families—not even the borders of *America*. And that's why they'd travelled all the way to London—so that the DeVries family could gain a foothold on those elite drawing rooms by joining the families of England's nobility through the marriage of their two children.

Or at least, one of us.

Maddie's spirits sank even lower as she glanced at

her sister. As usual, a gaggle of beaux surrounded the prettier and daintier DeVries daughter, eager to catch her attention.

Caroline was not rock, nor ore, nor iron. No, to anyone with full capacity of their senses, the younger DeVries was like gold: glittering, shiny, and beautiful. In her light blue taffeta gown, her blond curls arranged artfully on her head, and her skin glowing under the candlelight, she shone like the precious pure metal, valuable by itself with no need for any external process to remove impurities.

Glancing down at her own attire made Maddie groan with woe. In an attempt to create a more delicate appearance, Eliza dressed her eldest daughter in the frilliest frocks in light pastel colours, which did nothing to mask Maddie's considerable height. Indeed, it only drew attention to her size, and she ended up looking like an over-decorated wedding cake.

Tonight's outfit was a particularly frothy concoction of pink tulle, white French lace, and lilac bows down the front of the skirt and sleeves. It was a dreadful combination, and Maddie could only wish she were a wallflower, unnoticed and unremarked upon. Instead, she had to endure the stares, the pointing, and the not-so-very-subtle jabs at her person.

The stirrings of a waltz distracted Maddie for a moment. Envy rose in her as she watched the delicate ladies take their place with their dashing, handsome partners. How she longed to twirl about the ballroom again in some gentleman's arms. The last and only ball she had danced at had been months ago. Sometimes, she wondered if it had been all real or just a dream.

When the dancing began, Maddie decided she had served enough time in the main ballroom enduring everyone's gibes. Surely she could find some relief from the gawking guests. She spied the doorway on the other side of the room where several ladies disappeared through.

That must be the retiring room.

She weaved through the throng of people but halted when she heard the familiar voice of her mother. Glancing around, she found Eliza DeVries in the company of a group of well-heeled matrons.

'...yes, indeed. My Caroline has been taught by the best tutors since she was a young child.' Her mama's nasal tone was unmistakable, and Maddie had to stop herself from rolling her eyes as her mother extolled the virtues of her younger daughter.

'Finest in the Americas, maybe,' came the snooty retort from the woman on her mother's left.

'I'm sure you have many excellent teachers back home, Mrs DeVries,' the crisp, polite tone of the Miranda, Dowager Duchess of Mabury, interrupted. 'And I find both DeVries girls to be lovely, in both disposition and their individual talents and characteristics.'

Maddie couldn't help but smile as she met the Dowager's knowing grin over the back of Mama's head as her mother held court with the other women.

The DeVries family couldn't have asked for a better sponsor for their season in London than the Dowager. Indeed, attempting to navigate it by themselves had been a disaster. When they'd arrived in London at the beginning of the year, they didn't receive many invitations. So, they had hired a guide to assist them, the Honourable Miss Harriet Merton, who in turn had managed to obtain the assistance of the Dowager Duchess in launching the young American misses. The Dowager had invited them to stay with her in Highfield Park in Surrey. There had been three of them in the beginning—Maddie, Caroline, and Kate Mason, daughter of New York industrialist Arthur Mason. However, Kate had married the Dowager's own son, Sebastian Wakefield, Duke of Mabury. After the wedding, Papa had decided that he wanted to see the rest of England—and perhaps take a rest from the tediousness of husband hunting as well—so he took the family on a tour of the countryside.

Maddie had thought they would be invited back to Highfield Park, where the Dowager would continue to host balls and parties for them. However, the Dowager had wanted to give the newly-weds some privacy. So, she'd taken up residence in London and asked the De-Vrieses to stay with her, which also allowed the two girls more opportunities to be out in society. They'd arrived a month ago, and they had attended some ball or soirée nearly every night since.

'Yes, indeed, Your Grace,' Mama tittered.

One of the ladies in their circle cleared her throat delicately. 'If you will excuse us, Your Grace, I promised Lady Neville I would say hello to her before the night is over.' The other women made their excuses as well and then bade them goodbye.

Now that her mother and the Dowager were no longer surrounded by those haughty ladies, Maddie began to make her way to them.

'I'm so grateful to you, Your Grace,' Mama began. 'And you do your best to include my Madeline in your compliments.'

'She is well accomplished,' the Dowager replied. 'You should be proud of her.'

'I am, truly. Maddie is a wonderful girl.'

The compliment made Maddie's steps falter. Her mother was proud of her? *That was a first.* It wasn't that she thought her mother to be a heartless harpy, but it was always evident that Mama favoured Caroline, even while growing up. Maddie didn't give a care because her father doted enough attention on her.

'But I must face reality,' her mother continued, seemingly unaware that Maddie was right behind her. 'Maddie is two and twenty—far too old to be making a spectacular match. Not to mention, her other…attributes…ward away any eligible gentlemen.'

The Dowager caught Maddie's gaze and panic crossed over her usually unflappable face. 'Um, perhaps you shouldn't discount Maddie quite so soon. She may yet surprise you.'

Mama waved a hand. 'You are very kind, Your Grace. I've done my best to mitigate her stature, but no gentleman would want such a physically imposing wife. He would be the laughing stock wherever he went.' She tsked. 'No, I've resigned myself to such a fate for her. And as long as Caroline marries a lord, Maddie can be a spinster. Cornelius has made our family wealthy enough that she need not worry when we meet our timely demise. She shall be well taken care of. And if I may say so, it might be nice to have a companion in my old age.'

And that minuscule hope that had been building inside Maddie shrivelled away. It was one thing to hear the words from others, but from her own mother, it hurt. Hunching her shoulders over, she hurried away to the first set of doors she came upon. The gust of fresh air she inhaled as soon as she exited told her she was in the Worthingtons' terrace gardens.

Thankfully, it was well lit, and a small group of ladies occupied the benches near the door, which meant it was safe for Maddie to be there. Miss Merton had warned her and Caroline many times about venturing off alone during balls lest they find themselves unchaperoned with a man. A scandal could ruin their prospects.

Not that anything scandalous would ever happen to me. Even if Maddie and some man were to be found alone in a darkened garden, no one would believe they were in a passionate embrace. *Everyone would think I was helping him pluck a fruit from a high branch.*

She nodded to the ladies, made her way to the edge of the terrace, and pretended to admire the various plants and shrubberies blooming and the flowers scenting the air with sweetness. Maddie was sure they were lovely, but she could hardly concentrate on them, not when her mother's words occupied her mind.

No gentleman would want such a physically imposing wife...

Laughing stock...

Spinster.

She had come out in society five years ago, and except for a few notorious fortune hunters, no one had made an offer for her hand. In truth, Maddie had resigned herself some time ago to a life of spinsterhood. She had her work at the furnace to occupy her, after all. While many men would have scoffed at the idea of a woman learning science, the eccentric Cornelius DeVries held no such prejudices, especially when it came to his eldest daughter. She'd been going to the forge with him ever since she could remember, and because he had no son, he passed his knowledge on to her.

Indeed, she had thought it wouldn't be so terrible, especially since Papa had made it clear the company could be hers someday, should she want it.

But that was before they'd come to England. Before she'd realised that it was possible to have everything one desired—a fulfilling life with one's passion *and* a husband and family—when her good friend Kate Mason married her duke and became the current Duchess of Mabury.

A few days before her wedding, Kate had confessed to Maddie that, though at first they had agreed on the betrothal as a business arrangement, she and the Duke had somehow fallen madly in love in the process. Not only that, but Mabury was building a train engine factory just for her so she could pursue her dreams of designing her own locomotive. And soon, Kate would undoubtedly also start producing a different kind of creation—an heir to the Mabury dukedom.

She truly was happy for her friend; Kate deserved it. But it only made Maddie want all that for herself, too. She'd been in denial because she never thought it possible, that she could only ever be tall, shy Maddie who hid behind her books and her work and never thought to ask or dream of more.

But perhaps she was fooling herself. Kate finding the love of her life who supported her in all her pursuits was a one-in-a-million chance.

And tonight was another reminder that it would be impossible for Maddie to have everything she wanted in life.

'Maddie?'

She spun around at the sound of the Dowager's voice. 'Your Grace.' Her cheeks warmed as the Duchess obviously knew Maddie had overheard her conversation with Eliza.

'I hope the fresh air has done you some good?'

'Yes,' she lied, not knowing what else to say.

'Excellent.' The older woman drew closer to her. 'I told your mother and father that I was feeling faint, so I'd like to retire early. I said I would require assistance and hoped you could accompany me back to Mabury

Hall. Would you be amenable to leaving now and skipping the rest of the ball?'

Would she be amenable to leaving this boring ball and avoiding all the gapes and whispers from the haughty guests as she passed by?

Was the sky blue?

'Yes,' she said. Realising she was too enthusiastic, she added, 'I mean, of course, Your Grace. If it pleases you, I would be happy to assist you.'

'Good. I've already bade goodbye to our host and hostess, and the carriage should be coming round any moment.'

Relief poured through her as she followed the Dowager back inside and then outside to the street at the front.

Soon, they were pulling up to Mabury Hall, the Wakefields' fashionable town house in Mayfair.

'By the way,' the Dowager began as they alighted from the carriage. 'I wanted to let you know that I'm expecting a guest tonight. The daughter of a dear friend who unfortunately passed away some time ago.'

'My condolences for your loss, Your Grace.'

'Thank you, dear.' She paused, smiling sadly. 'Her brother wrote to me, and I agreed to sponsor Lady Persephone for the season.'

'Lady Persephone?'

The Dowager chuckled. 'Yes. Elaine did have a wicked sense of humour. Anyway, Lady Persephone has travelled quite far—all the way from Scotland. Her journey will not have been easy, which is why I instructed her to make haste and arrive at any time. A letter came today telling me to expect her later this evening. I'll welcome her properly in the morning and will introduce her to everyone.'

'Will she need help when she arrives? I'm more than happy to assist her.'

'There's no need for you to wait up, Maddie,' the Dowager said as the butler opened the door for them. 'The household staff will have everything ready. I am going to retire to my room, but I wanted to be here just in case. You should head to bed and get some rest.'

Maddie stifled a yawn. 'Thank you, Your Grace. I believe I shall.'

Her maid, Betsy, was already waiting for her in her room by the time she entered, and she helped Maddie get undressed and washed up for bed. When she slipped between the silky covers, she nearly fell asleep, but the sound of neighing horses and the rolling wheels of a carriage jolted her awake.

That must be the Dowager's guest.

Curious about what a girl named Persephone would look like, Maddie hauled herself out of bed and strode to her window, which had a view of the street.

Sure enough, a coach piled high with luggage stopped just outside the townhouse. A footman opened the door, and as a boot landed on the step, the carriage dipped low.

Maddie let out an audible gasp as the passenger fully alighted. This definitely wasn't what she had been expecting when she'd run up to the window for a glance at Lady Persephone.

For one thing, the person who hopped out of the carriage was decidedly not female. For another? This male person was a giant.

Even from the second level of the house, she could tell that he was almost as tall as the carriage itself. His hulking shoulders were covered by a travelling cloak and his face obscured by a hat, so she couldn't quite be sure of the man's age. Perhaps he was Lady Persephone's father, who had accompanied her on this journey?

As if sensing her spying, the man turned his head

upward—right at Maddie. Her hand flew to her mouth, then she quickly shuttled backwards. She didn't know why, but her heart pounded like mad against her chest. Still, she wanted to peer outside again so she could see the stranger's face.

I can't risk it.

Surely he had seen her or, at the very least, seen someone spying from the window. It would be embarrassing if anyone had caught her like some peeping Tom. Perhaps tomorrow she'd be introduced to him and that would quell her curiosity.

Shaking all thoughts of the man from her head, she slipped back into bed.

Lord Cameron MacGregor, Earl of Balfour, couldn't help but feel like he was being watched. So, he glanced up at the lofty town house and spied a flash of a figure from a window. Said figure quickly disappeared from view, but at least now he knew he wasn't imagining it.

But this was London, after all. Crowded, hot, and full of eyes everywhere. With each visit, his impression of the city did not waver.

'My lord?' the footman asked with a delicate cough and a nod towards the inside of the carriage.

Right.

'Seph?' he called to his sister. 'We're here. Are you awake?'

A loud yawn sounded from the darkness, and after a quick shuffling of fabric and paper, a small, pretty face emerged from the carriage. Large, owlish eyes blinked sleepily from behind the lens of gold-rimmed glasses. 'Have we arrived in London, Cam?'

'Aye.'

A gloved hand darted out, grasping for the handle on

the side of the door but missing it completely. 'Careful, Seph.' Cam caught her hand before she fell out of the carriage.

'Sorry. I'm just so tired.'

'All right, easy there.' He guided her down the step. 'That's it.'

Persephone wavered as both feet landed on the ground. 'It's as if the world under me is still rocking to and fro.' She took a deep breath and steadied herself before looking up at the grand town house before them. 'Is this Mabury Hall?'

'I hope so,' he said with a chuckle. 'Otherwise, whichever fancy lord or lady we're disturbing in the middle of the night won't be happy to have a pair of Scots at their door.'

'Do you suppose—'

The front door opened and a tall, white-haired man in a dark suit appeared. 'Lord Balfour? Lady Persephone?' Despite his quiet, deferential tone, his accent was recognisably from London.

Cam answered with a quick nod. 'Aye.'

'Good evening, my lord, my lady.' His polished shoes clacked audibly on the stone steps as he hurried to them. 'Welcome to Mabury Hall. I am Eames, the butler. Her Grace, the Dowager Duchess of Mabury, asked me to welcome you and ensure you are settled in for the evening.' He motioned to the door. 'If you please.'

'Thank you, Eames.' Tucking Persephone's arm into his, Cam climbed up the front steps and into the house.

Eames slipped in behind them, then nodded to a woman dressed in a maid's black-and-white uniform who stood by the staircase. 'Your valet and Lady Persephone's maid should already be in your rooms unpacking. Allow us to lead you there.'

They trailed behind the butler as he climbed up the stairs. When they reached the top, he directed Persephone to follow the maid down the long hallway on the left. 'Lady Persephone will be staying next to the other young ladies in this wing, along with Mr and Mrs DeVries. Lord Balfour, I'll show you your room in the other wing.'

Persephone's eyebrows knitted together. 'Is that all right, Cam?'

''Tis fine, Seph.' He kissed her temple. 'Get some sleep. I'll see you in the morning.'

He watched as Persephone followed the maid down the hallway and disappear as they turned a corner, then Eames walked him in the opposite direction. They arrived in his rooms, where his valet, Murray, was already unpacking his trunks.

'If you need anything at all, my lord,' the butler said, 'just pull the bell and someone will be right up.'

'Thank you, Eames.'

'You're welcome, my lord.' With that, Eames bowed and left.

'Would you like a bath prepared, my lord?' Murray asked.

'It's much too late. I'm about ready to keel over.'

Murray pointed to the washstand. 'There's fresh water in the jug for ye to wash up, my lord. I'll prepare yer clothes.'

'Thank you, Murray.' Cam cleaned himself with the water and washcloth as best he could as Murray assisted him with his nightclothes.

He was looking forward to sleeping in a proper bed tonight. Exhaustion had him ready to collapse, as he hadn't had a decent night of rest in the last few days. He had to protect his sister, after all. They travelled with enough servants to watch over them, but there could never be enough eyes on her, not with her…peculiar nature.

Persephone tended to be clumsy and was near-blind without her spectacles, but more than that, she was absent-minded, especially when she was in deep thought, which was nearly all the time. She was so much like their mother in that way.

And that was the other reason Cam couldn't sleep.

I promise, Ma, he said silently. *I'll take good care of her. Just like you and Da woulda wanted.* He owed it to his departed parents.

Elaine MacGregor had died of a lingering illness seven years ago, and their father, Niall, a few months after. One day, his valet had found him in bed, unmoving, his body already cold. The doctor said Niall had had a heart condition and if he had been feeling unwell, he had kept it from them.

Fitting, really, that his father died of a broken heart. Though Niall had tried to remain strong for his children, he had confessed to Cam how much he missed his wife. *'She was the love of my life, my boy,'* he told him one night when he was in his cups. *'I can't tell you what that's like, but perhaps someday you'll understand.'*

Not likely, Cam snorted. He'd would never again allow anyone such power over him. Once was enough, thank you very much.

Besides, they didn't come all the way to England to find him a wife. They were here for Persephone and to fulfil the promise he, his brothers, and his father had made to his mother as she lay dying.

Persephone… I was so looking forward to her season in England. I would have ensured she would make a good match. I want her to have her choice of husbands, whoever and wherever that may be.

Elaine MacGregor was not wrong; while Niall's earldom should have been enough of an enticement for a
respectable match for Persephone, it had been obtained
purely by chance, from a distant relative who'd had no
sons of his own. Before that, they had been farmers, then
whisky distillers. The Glenbaire Whisky Distillery had
been in the MacGregor family for many generations, certainly longer than the earldom his father had inherited.

They were trapped between two worlds—too high for
the merchants and too low for the aristocrats. An English
season, however, would help signal that the MacGregors
were taking their place in society and Persephone would
be available to a wider range of potential suitors. Thus,
Elaine had been planning it ever since Persephone was
born.

I have no regrets, she had told her husband and sons.
*Being with you, my love, and raising our children has
been the best part of my life. But Persephone… I would
hold off Death if I could and make a bargain with the
Devil himself if I could be there for her a little longer. So
please, give her the season that I wished I could give her.*

Persephone had been so young when Ma died. *She's
still too young now,* he thought with a mental shake of
his head. Well, nineteen wasn't young for a lass to be
married, but Persephone was special. She was already
more sheltered than any of the debutantes on the marriage mart, and then there were peculiarities. Still, he
would do as his dear mother asked, which would also
help Persephone gain some exposure to polite society.
But if he were truly honest with himself, he would not be
broken-hearted if she didn't immediately find a match.

Murray's voice broke into his thoughts. 'My lord, if
there is anything else…'

He shook his head. 'Thank you, Murray. Get to bed.

I'll see you in the morning.' With that, Cam slipped into bed and fell asleep.

The following day, Cam woke up, if a little later than usual, feeling refreshed and clear-headed. When he arrived a few minutes after Cam rang for him, Murray informed him that it was already half past nine.

'Her Grace instructed us not to disturb you, my lord. I've brought you some food.' He set the tray down on the table next to the bed.

'And my sister?'

'I believe she woke up early and headed to breakfast, along with the other guests. They are likely in the parlour.'

Cam didn't like that Persephone was meeting other people without him. He had hoped to speak to the Dowager in private and explain a few things, mostly about Persephone. She had to understand, after all, what she was getting herself into when she offered to sponsor his sister. And if the Dowager thought the task was much too difficult, he would understand and find another way to fulfil his promise to his mother.

After he finished dressing and eating, Cam went downstairs to meet his hostess. Eames informed him that the Dowager was already expecting him and led him to her private sitting room. Cam took a deep breath and prepared himself for the meeting. English people could be quite fussy, after all, but he was well versed in dealing with them.

Once Cam had become of age, Niall had begun to bring Cam with him to his business trips in England, and now that he had taken over running the business, Cam came at least once a year to check in with his man of business, George Atwell, and visit their most profitable customers.

While many of the English looked down on the Scottish, most of them, especially the gentlemen, were happy enough to consume their fine whisky, a fact that the MacGregors had exploited since they'd started exporting their product to England.

His father had a natural charisma, something Cam was happy to have inherited and found useful when dealing with people. *'That's the ol' MacGregor charm,'* his father would always say. *'Works on anyone, especially females under the age of one hundred.'*

And thanks to his English mother's lessons on the proper graces and manner, Cam knew how to act around the higher classes. Indeed, on his trips to London, he would often get comments on his manners. 'You're so civilised!' some of these fops would say, thinking it was a compliment to a Scot like him. But he ignored such words and continued to fawn and flatter their customers on their excellent taste and tough negotiating skills, but privately, he laughed all the way back home with more profit with each trip.

'His Lordship the Earl of Balfour,' Eames announced.

The dark-haired woman sitting in the brightly lit sitting room placed her book down and rose from her chair. 'Welcome, Lord Balfour,' she greeted as she glided towards him. 'Oh, my.' She craned her neck up at him, her dark eyes widening in surprise. 'I didn't realise you'd be so tall.'

Cam was used to such reactions; after all, his height was unusual. 'Your Grace.' He bowed, which did not even put them at eye level. He was about to reply with a witty compliment, something along the lines of not expecting her to be as bonny as a spring day, but stopped short when he looked down to observe her face. The Dowager Duchess was much younger than Cam had imagined, though he should not have been surprised, as she was the same age as his mother would have been.

His chest constricted at another reminder of his ma. While he had managed the grief well, the small reminders of her absence did not fail to cause a reaction in him.

When the Dowager's eyes narrowed, he put those thoughts aside. Clearing his throat, he slipped on the mask he always used around the quality. 'Please forgive my lateness in arising this morning and not properly presenting myself and my sister.'

'There is nothing to forgive. You've had a long journey.' She gestured to the empty chair in front of her. 'Please, have a seat.'

He did as she bade and exchanged a few pleasantries with her, relying on the MacGregor charm to get through the necessary ritual the upper classes insisted on performing. His impatient nature, however, longed to get straight to the point of why they were here, but he allowed Her Grace to lead the conversation as she was his hostess.

'Lord Balfour, though I have expressed it in my letter to you, allow me to offer you my condolences for the loss of your mother and father,' the Dowager finally said.

'Thank you, ma'am.'

'I'm not sure if your mother ever spoke of me, but we were dear friends for many years.' A wistful smile touched her lips. 'She and I married the same year. We even discovered that we were with child at the same time. We wrote each other frequently those first few years. But as these things go, we both became busy with our lives and our letters waned. I only regret...' She sniffed and dabbed at the corner of her eye with a handkerchief.

'Thank you for answering my letters, even though I hadn't thought to write to her in years.'

'You're very welcome. And thank you for your generous offer to sponsor Persephone.'

Cam had been surprised to receive the very late letter of condolence to their family a few months ago. He had written back to thank Her Grace, then she'd written again asking about him and his brothers and sister. It was his youngest brother, Liam, who was the most intelligent of them all, who had given Cam the idea to ask the Dowager for help in giving their sister the season their mother would have wanted, since none of them had the faintest idea about balls and invitations and gowns.

To his surprise, the Duchess had agreed to sponsor Persephone in London. Since Cam was the Earl and he frequented London, he decided to accompany her. Besides, there was always Glenbaire business he could attend to and customers he could visit. In fact, he needed to meet with a potential customer, one of the largest gentlemen's clubs in the city.

Cam usually had his man of business in London, George Atwell, conduct all of the initial introductions and presentations when it came to deals in England. However, the owner himself insisted that he would consider stocking Glenbaire in his club only if Cam himself came to town. While other men would have been insulted, Cam was intrigued. Indeed, it was how Niall had done business himself before he'd become the Earl and he'd had to delegate such tasks.

'It seems you have something else on your mind, Lord Balfour.' The Dowager's dark eyes trained on him, the intelligence in them unmistakable. It rather reminded

Cam of his mother's when she'd tried to suss out secrets from him 'Why don't you tell me what it is?'

'Er… Yes, about that.' But how was he to explain about Persephone? 'You see, my sister—'

'I've met her this morning,' the Dowager interrupted. 'What a delightful young woman.'

Delightful? Had she really met Persephone? Most people would not use that word in describing his sister, unless they were mocking her. However, there was no hint of malice in the Dowager's tone of voice.

'She is already with another of my guests. I think they're getting along quite well, too,' she continued.

'Other guests?' Cam didn't realise there would be other people staying there as well.

'Yes. Along with Persephone, I'm also sponsoring two girls from America for the season. Anyway, you were saying, my—'

Before she could continue, the door to the sitting room burst open. 'Cam! Eames told me you were here.'

Cam groaned inwardly as his sister flounced into the sitting room. 'Forgive my sister, Your Grace. She is—'

'You must meet my new friend,' Persephone interrupted.

A friend?

The fact that Persephone would consider anyone a friend boggled Cam enough to forget propriety. He gave an apologetic glance to the Dowager, who only returned it with a cryptic smile.

'Come in, Maddie,' Persephone called, then reached beyond the doorway, pulling out first an arm, then a person attached to said arm. 'This is Miss Madeline DeVries.'

Cam was halfway to rising when he locked eyes with his sister's new friend.

Mother of Mercy.

It was as if he'd been punched in the gut, for he found himself unable to look away from mesmerising eyes the colour of the clear blue sky. The rest of her face was quite arresting, with her clear milky skin, high cheekbones, and those plump pink lips that begged to be kissed.

Sheer force of attraction walloped him, and his throat was too dry to say anything. However, as she came closer and he rose to full height, something else caught him off guard. He didn't have to bend low to meet her eyes. In fact, the top of her head came to just about the tip of his nose.

Cam wasn't sure if it was astonishment, or the instant attraction to the woman, or if he were still disoriented from the trip that scrambled his mind—or all three—but all he could do was stare at her.

'Cam?' Persephone's voice cut through the daze. 'Please forgive my brother. He's usually much more affable.' She turned to him. 'Well? Say something.'

A woman had never rendered him speechless before. But yes, he definitely should say something instead of just staring at her.

Turn on the ol' MacGregor charm, his pa would have said if he were here.

Cam wanted to tell her that she was a stunning, mighty goddess. Like Athena or Queen Hippolyte, from the Greek myths of old. However, his addled mind somehow came up with something else.

'Holy mackerel, you're a great big Amazon!'

The room turned silent as a tomb and realisation struck Cam like a bolt of lightning.

Hell's bells.

But before he could apologise, Miss DeVries's pretty

face scrunched up and she burst into tears, then dashed out of the room.

'Oh, for goodness' sake!' Persephone smacked him on the arm. 'What were you thinking, saying that to her?'

Cam could live to a hundred years and never know the answer.

Chapter Two

As soon as the Duchess had introduced them in the parlour that morning after breakfast, Maddie instantly liked Lady Persephone MacGregor. The pretty red-headed Scotswoman was vibrant and chatty and, much to Maddie's delight, interested in her work at the furnace. In fact, she mentioned that she herself took part in her family's business, but before Lady Persephone could elaborate, she'd stopped and slapped her hand on her forehead as if she'd just remembered something, then dragged Maddie out of the parlour before barging into the Dowager's private sitting room.

And then disaster had struck.

Maddie ran, not caring if it was discourteous to the Dowager, as long as she was far away from that—that *lout*. Besides, he had been rude to her first.

A great big Amazon, he'd called her.

Just when she thought she'd heard every insult possible, there were, apparently, more barbs and gibes out there in the world, waiting to be sprung on her.

But she'd never had them spoken so directly to her face, and not from such a handsome man.

So, the man she'd seen outside the window last night

was the Earl, but she should have guessed. When their gazes had met across the room, the strangest sensation had pooled in her belly. It had been warm, not like drinking a hot cup of tea on a chilly day but, rather, something much more intense.

Surprise and delight had filled her when, for once in her life, she had to look up at a gentleman. While insignificant to anyone else, to Maddie, it was as if everything was right in the world and her confidence had soared.

Then he'd said those hurtful words and shattered it again.

Tears blurred her vision, but she found her way to a place where she could seek solace. After staying at Mabury Hall before going to London, she already knew the house and made her way to the library. Slamming the door behind her, she strode to the wing-back chair by the window and plopped down.

'Er, Miss DeVries? Are you here?'

The lilting feminine tone told Maddie it was Lady Persephone.

'There you are,' the Scot said as she walked towards her. 'I'm so sorry my brother's a dimwit.'

Maddie flashed her a weak smile. 'It's not your fault.'

She sat down on the chair opposite her. 'Ma would be so disappointed in him. She taught us better than that.' Her eyes blinked behind her gold-rimmed spectacles. 'He's usually so pleasant, especially when around women.'

A twinge plucked at Maddie's chest at the mention of other women. Of course he would attract a lot of female attention; he was handsome, after all, and she'd noticed many ladies didn't seem to care what a gentleman said so long as they were rich and attractive.

'I'll make sure he apologises to you, Miss DeVries.'

The thought of seeing him again after the morning made Maddie's stomach churn. 'Oh, no. Please… I can't possibly…' She buried her face in her hands. 'It's so embarrassing.'

'Maybe he meant it as a…compliment?' Lady Persephone offered. 'You know, Amazon women are fierce warriors—'

'Who match men in their abilities,' Maddie finished. Oh, she knew exactly what he meant. 'There have been many insults about my height thrown at me, but none have every compared my stature to that of a man's.' And perhaps that's what had hurt the most. To have been so stripped of her femininity with just one sentence.

'I know my brother, and he didn't mean to insult you.'

'Can we speak of something else, please, Lady Persephone?' If she had to think about the Earl any more, she would surely expire from mortification.

'Of course. But please, do call me Persephone, at least when it's just us.'

'And you must call me Maddie,' she replied, then took a deep breath. 'Do you really consider me your friend? We just met this morning.'

'Does England have friendship rules that I didn't know about? I'm growing quite weary of them.'

'If there are, I wouldn't be aware of them.' The corner of Maddie's mouth quirked up. 'As you know, I'm American.'

'Then we can make up our own rules.' Persephone reached over and patted her hand. 'And if I say we're friends, then we're friends.'

'I'd very much like that.' It was too bad her brother was nothing like Persephone. Perhaps they weren't blood related. 'And seeing as we're friends, maybe you could continue what you were telling me earlier? About working with your family?'

'Ah yes.' Persephone's eyes lit up as she leaned forward and adjusted her spectacles. 'Do you know anything about whisky?'

Maddie spent the rest of the morning with Persephone, and for the first time in a while, she felt at ease. It had been so long since she'd had a genuine friend to talk to like this—not since before Kate had married.

Persephone was a breath of fresh air, and it was such a delight to be friends with another like-minded person. However, they were opposites in some ways. While Maddie was reserved and shy, Persephone never seemed to stop talking, especially about her scientific pursuits. Like Maddie, she'd been taught by her father everything about distilling whisky, though her interests spanned an array of subjects from Greek philosophy to astronomy. By the time they were called for luncheon, Maddie felt at ease around the Scotswoman.

Of course, Maddie's mother and sister weren't quite as welcoming. Both women had a lot to say when Maddie mentioned that she and Persephone had become friends.

'Friends?' Caroline sounded aghast. 'She is not a friend. She's a rival.'

The Dowager had left before the meal was over as she had a last-minute fitting at the modiste, while Lady Persephone had retired to her room as she still felt weary from their long journey. So, the three DeVries women finished dessert and coffee on their own.

'Not that she's much competition,' Mama added in a haughty tone. 'That red hair? Freckled complexion? How unfashionable.'

Caroline's eyes gleamed. 'I heard from my maid that she arrived with her young, handsome brother. An earl!'

Mama turned to Maddie. 'If this Lady Penelope—'

'Persephone,' she corrected.

Mama snorted impatiently. 'If this Lady Priscilla is your friend, then perhaps we can use your connection to her to our advantage.'

'*Persephone*,' she reiterated. 'And that's not what friendship is about.' For some reason, that twinge in her chest returned at the idea of the Earl with her sister. 'If you'll both excuse me, I must fetch some ink and paper from Eames so I can reply to Kate's letter.'

'Don't wander off now. We must get ready for the Gardiner ball tonight,' Mama called after her.

'Yes, Mama.' *Not another dreadful ball.* But at least Persephone would be there. It would be nice to have someone to talk to, although considering Persephone's beauty and delicate stature, Maddie predicted she would once again be alone for the evening. And of course, she assumed the Earl would be there to escort her.

Her stomach knotted at the thought of seeing him. Though Persephone had assured her numerous times her brother 'just wasn't like that,' Maddie did not want to ever encounter him again. Which was impossible if she wanted to remain friends with Persephone. That, and if Mama and Caroline had plans for him…

She shut those thoughts out of her head. Being a guest of the Dowager's, at some point she was going to cross paths with the Earl again. His barb was not the first she'd heard and certainly not the last she would ever hear. *You must toughen up, Maddie*, she told herself. Develop a thicker skin, as they say.

After obtaining the writing materials from Eames, Maddie went up to her room and finished her correspondences. By the time she was done, Betsy had arrived to help her bathe and prepare for the ball.

'Oh, heavens.' Maddie winced as she saw the gown Betsy was holding up. 'Yellow,' she moaned. If it wasn't pink, it was *yellow*. The lace cuffs and white satin rosettes down the full skirt did not do the dress any favours. It reminded her of a cake she had once seen in a baker's shop window. How did her mother manage to find the most hideous dresses in London?

With a deep sigh, she allowed Betsy to dress her in the monstrosity. When the maid showed her the curling tongs, she blew out a breath. Mama always wanted her hair in tight sausage curls, as if she were a child's doll. Everyone else at these balls had elegant waves piled on top of their heads, held together with sparkling hairpins and combs.

'All right,' she said, resigned. 'Let's get on with it.'

After what seemed like forever, she was done preparing for the evening. 'No, thank you.' She waved away Betsy's offer of a mirror to examine her work. It didn't matter anyway. After dismissing Betsy with a grateful nod, she gathered her reticule before leaving her room. As she made her way downstairs, Caroline's nasal voice reverberated up the stairwell.

'My lord, if you don't mind my saying, you are absolutely hilarious!'

My lord? As far as Maddie knew, there was only one person in residence who could be called that. *Maybe Caroline was talking to someone else*, she assured herself as she reached the bottom of the stairs.

'I don't mind at all you saying that, Miss DeVries. And if you don't mind my saying, you do look bonny tonight.'

Maddie's heart sank at the sound of the familiar voice. Was it too late to go back and hide in her room?

'Bonny?' Caroline giggled. 'You, my lord, are a flatterer.'

'Aye, but I only pay compliments where they're warranted.'

Her stomach churned, and Maddie gripped the banister, readying herself to turn back. Unfortunately, Persephone, who stood right beside her brother, spotted her.

'Maddie. Oh, thank goodness you're here.' Persephone hurried towards her, then dragged her to where Maddie's parents, Caroline, and the Earl were waiting. She sent a pointed look to her brother. 'Allow me to present Miss Madeline DeVries. Miss DeVries, this is my brother, the Earl of Balfour.'

The Earl's face betrayed nothing of what had happened that morning. 'Good evening, Miss DeVries.'

'My lord.' Though her head turned in his direction, she focused on the wood panelling behind him, not daring to look up into his eyes.

'His Lordship was just telling us a funny story about their journey here,' Caroline interjected.

'The most amusing tale,' Mama added. 'You are such a talented storyteller, my lord.'

Maddie pressed her lips together. But it should not surprise her that her mother and sister fawned over him. He was unmarried and possessed a title, after all.

'I'm more interested in his whisky,' Papa chuckled.

'I have a few bottles with me, and I'd be honoured to share some with you,' the Earl said. 'Her Grace has told me all about your ventures back in America and now here in London, Mr DeVries. I respect a self-made man.'

Maddie could only stare as her father preened at the Earl's compliments. Since he was a shrewd businessman, she thought he'd be immune to flattery.

'Tell me, my lord,' Papa began. 'How did an Earl become a whisky maker?'

'Da wasn't always an Earl.' It was Persephone who answered. 'He was a distiller first. In fact, the MacGregors have been distilling whisky since the seventeen-sixties. Of course, we started as an illegal—'

The Earl coughed. 'Perhaps it's not that much of a fascinating story. Oh, here comes the Dowager now.' He nodded towards the stairs. 'Your Grace.'

Everyone curtseyed or bowed as the Dowager made her way to them. 'Ah, I see we're all here. Now, we don't want to be late. Let's move along, shall we?'

Persephone and her brother took their own carriage, while Maddie and her family rode with the Dowager.

While Mama, Papa, and Caroline spoke of how pleasant the Earl was, Maddie fumed. Who was that man she'd just met? Where was this charming angel this morning, who said all the right things? Did the Earl have an evil twin lurking about, insulting women?

Thankfully, the ride wasn't too long, and soon they were being announced as they entered the Gardiner ballroom. As usual, Caroline's admirers flocked to her and were already lining up to write their names on her dance card. The Dowager made the rounds, introducing the Earl and Persephone to her friends, and as she always did, Maddie stood off to the sides, watching the dancers.

In the beginning, Maddie had attempted to hide from the other guests or blend in with the walls. Both had been impossible, given her height and garish dress. In any case, the barbs and gibes found her anyway, wherever she went. But, as she did at every ball and gathering, she ignored them and concentrated on watching the elegant couples twirling across the floor.

'Miss DeVries.'

Maddie froze at the sound of the Earl's voice. It took all her strength not to turn to him as he came up beside her. 'I find myself feeling faint.' She sidestepped away from him. 'If you'll excuse me, my lord—'

A hand came to rest on her upper arm, on the exposed skin just above her gloves. The touch made her snap her head up. A jolt struck her when she met his intense stare. Up close, she realised that his eyes were green, like bright twin emeralds.

'Miss DeVries, please don't leave.'

She ignored the warmth that spread through her despite the fact only his gloves separated their bare skin. 'My lord, this isn't proper.'

The guests around didn't seem to pay them any mind, but if just one person saw him touching her with such familiarity... Well, that would certainly send tongues wagging.

'Maddie. Here you are,' Persephone said as she came up to her from behind. 'I need you—' She took in a sharp intake of breath. 'Cam.' Her teeth chewed at her bottom lip, like a child caught stealing sweets.

'Seph?' He drew his hand away from Maddie's arm. 'Where have you been? I've been searching all over for you.'

'You have?' she said innocently.

'Ever since I saw you running from Lord Kinsley like the devil himself was on your heels.'

'Nonsense.' She forced out a laugh. 'Er, I just remembered... I had to powder my nose.'

His eyebrows knit together. 'He was about to add his name to your dance card, too.'

Colour drained from Persephone's pretty face. 'I—'

The butler announcing the next dance interrupted her. 'Miss DeVries would love to dance.'

'I beg your pardon?' Maddie cried as she felt a hand push her forward—straight towards the Earl.

'Go on, now,' Persephone said. 'The music's about to start.'

Maddie stiffened as the Earl's arms came around her. Before she could protest, he pulled her into the sea of dancers.

'M-my lord,' she stammered. 'Please release me.'

'Thanks to my sister, it's far too late for that.' The way he rolled his *R*s sent shivers across her skin. She gasped, heat creeping up her cheeks.

'Miss DeVries?'

'Y-yes?' She looked up at him. A terrible mistake, as those green eyes mesmerised her, making it impossible to turn away.

'Your hands?'

'W-what about them?'

The music played, and so he took her hands and placed one on his shoulder, then slipped the other into his. His other hand landed on her waist. Before she knew it, they were swaying to the music. A waltz.

She was dancing.

And floating, too, as her heart soared in happiness. She almost forgot who she was dancing with. *A handsome partner*, she told herself, without thinking about who he was and what he had said to her. All that mattered was that after weeks of watching the beautiful couples from the sidelines, she was one of them. Delight filled her as they twirled about, and just for that one dance, she could imagine herself a dainty and delicate lady.

Lost in the moment, she allowed herself to glance up at him. Her breath caught in her throat when those intense eyes stared back at her. There was something about the way he gazed at her that sent a pleasant thrill through her, starting from somewhere deep in her belly and spreading throughout her body. The sensation distracted her so much that she didn't notice that the music had stopped and they were no longer spinning around the ballroom. The dance was over, and so was the fantasy.

She curtseyed to him as he bowed, but as she made a motion to walk away, he quickly crowded her off to the side. She barely had time to resist. 'My lord? Wh-where are you taking me?'

'I'm not stealing you away. I just want to have a wee chat,' he chuckled. 'Now, don't you run off like a timid little rabbit again.'

Perhaps it was the months of being ridiculed and laughed at, or maybe it was the way he acted around her family, or that he had once again ruined a wonderful moment for her, but something snapped inside Maddie.

'Little rabbit?' she hissed. 'Are you mocking me, my lord?'

'That's not what I meant,' he sputtered.

'Am I an Amazon or timid rabbit?' she interrupted. 'Both cannot be true at the same time.'

He slapped a hand on his forehead. 'Why are you being contrary? Just let me apologise so I can be done with you.'

Be done with her?

Like she was an obligation?

'If you're attempting to apologise, I regret to inform you that you are doing a poor job of it.' Maddie gasped at the audaciousness of her words, and her heart drummed madly against her chest. But it was as if a spirit had taken over her body, and there was no stopping it, nor the outrage that had built up inside her and was now overflowing.

He let out a frustrated sound and ran his fingers

through his blond locks. 'What is it about you that I can't put two words together correctly? I was trying to compliment you this morning.'

'By implying that I was…was…' She grasped for the right word. 'Mannish?'

'Mannish?'

'Yes.' That was a word, right? 'Like a man.'

'Yes—er, no! I meant to say you were impressive as a…er… I mean, Ama—'

She put a hand up. 'Say no more, my lord. Lest you dig yourself into a deeper hole.' There were too many people around them, and most of them were beginning to stare. 'That was a lovely dance, my lord,' she said in a loud tone so they could hear her. 'Thank you, and I look forward to another one.'

In a hundred years, when I've turned into dust.

With a respectful nod, she walked away in the opposite direction. Pretending she knew where she was going, she smiled at the ladies and gentlemen she passed. She'd nearly circumnavigated the room when she spied Persephone next to some sculpted potted topiary.

Oh, thank heavens.

'Persephone,' she called to her friend. 'Shall we go—wait, are you hiding?'

The Scotswoman popped out from between the two shrubs and glanced around, eyes darting left and right. 'N-nay,' she denied, but shrank back behind the branches.

'You *are* hiding,' Maddie said firmly. 'From what?'

'Not what. Who.'

'And who are you hiding from?'

'Them.' She pointed out into the ballroom. 'The men.'

'Which man?'

'All of them,' she said, exasperated.

Maddie frowned. 'Why?'

'Because they will want to dance. And I… I can't dance,' she confessed.

'You've never been taught?' Maddie asked. 'You should have said something. I'm sure the Dowager—'

'I have been taught, but I just can't do it.' Her lower lip trembled. 'I'm very clumsy, and no matter what I do, I can't count correctly or remember the steps.' She sighed. 'I can tell you how many casks of whisky we'll be producing each year just by looking at the barley harvest, but for the life of me, I always forget which way to turn for the quadrille and what foot goes out first for the waltz. I'm hopeless.'

'I'm sure that's not true. Perhaps we can—'

Persephone let out a squeak and hid behind her. 'They've found me.'

'Found you—oh.' Persephone twisted her around. Sure enough, two gentlemen were approaching them. 'Lord Wembley. Mr Carter.' Maddie had been introduced to them a few weeks ago when they'd attended an event at Highfield Park, the Duke of Mabury's country home, and had spied them at a few events in town.

'Miss DeVries,' Lord Wembley greeted her. 'Good evening. I was, uh, wondering if perhaps you would like to dance?'

Maddie blinked. 'M-me?'

'Yes. I'm hoping your dance card is not full yet?'

'It is not.' In fact, it was woefully empty.

'In that case, I would like the dance after,' Mr Carter interjected.

A heartbeat passed as she stared at the two men. She wondered if someone was playing a trick on her.

'Miss DeVries?' Lord Wembley repeated, offering his hand. 'If you please?'

Maddie placed her hand in his and followed him to the

middle of the ballroom. Unease settled in as she felt eyes on them—after all, they must have made quite a comical couple, with Lord Wembley's eye level at her chin.

However, when the lively music began and the couples started the quadrille, Maddie launched into the dance without a care in the world. In fact, with the quick steps and whirling about, she hardly gave a thought to the difference in their stature. And when they finished, giddiness coursed through her as Lord Wembley flashed her a smile as he bowed. If people were staring at them, she was too overjoyed to notice.

As she promised, she joined Mr Carter for the gallop, and after that, another gentleman, Lord Porter, asked to partner with her for the cotillion. By the end of that third dance, however, Maddie was weary, and so after thanking Lord Porter, she shuffled off towards the retiring room.

'Psst!'

Maddie stopped and glanced around.

'Maddie!' came the disembodied voice.

Was that...? 'Persephone?'

'Aye.' Scooting out from behind a pillar, her friend let out a long breath. 'Thank goodness those gentlemen asked you to dance.'

'I'm glad, too.' She smiled at her weakly. 'I never usually dance so much at a ball.'

'And why not? You do it so well.'

'Because no man wants me,' she stated.

'They did tonight,' Persephone pointed out. 'In fact, three of them did.'

The turn of events still boggled Maddie. 'No one asks me to dance at balls because they're all intimidated by my height. I have no idea why those three gentlemen asked me tonight.'

'Curious.' She tapped her fingers on her chin. 'So, you've never danced before?'

'Well…there was this one time…' She relayed to Persephone what had happened during Kate's engagement ball, when the Duke of Mabury had danced with her and then more men came forward to ask her. But since then, at every ball they'd attended in London, Maddie had been relegated to the sidelines. 'Maybe it was because we were out in the country, and men are different here in town.'

'These silly Englishmen.' Persephone shook her head in disgust. 'But then again, they are not like they are back home. In fact—' She inhaled a sharp breath. 'Maddie, you said that after your dance with the Duke, more gentlemen came forward to ask you?'

'Why, yes.' She pursed her lips. 'Do you think those men were attempting to curry favour with him?'

'Perhaps, but let's examine the chain of events. You danced with the Duke, and right after, you were flooded with invitations to dance. And tonight, after you danced with Cam, three gentlemen approached you.' She snapped her fingers. 'Therefore, we can conclude that after a man of high rank shows interest in you, other gentlemen follow in his wake.'

'Shows interest in me?' That made her laugh. 'The Duke is like…like a brother to me.' And he was thoroughly in love with Kate.

'And what about my brother?'

She wasn't sure what the Earl was to her, but the emotions he brought out certainly were far from brotherly. 'Need I remind you, *you* pushed me into dancing with him.'

'But the results are the same, are they not?' Persephone smirked at her. 'Men love a challenge. They can't resist it. When they see another man pursuing something, then it becomes an object of desire, and so, they must triumph over their competition to win said object.' She patted Maddie on the arm before she could refute her statement. 'Trust me. I grew up with five older brothers.'

Maddie had never thought of it that way, but she supposed it was a logical conclusion. Not that it made her feel any better.

'What's wrong? We've just solved your dancing problem.'

'My dancing problem?'

'You obviously love it but never get a chance to do it. I've watched you looking so enviously at the dancing couples all evening. But now you know how to entice these gentlemen into asking you, and you can dance at every ball.'

'So in order to get invitations to dance, someone must first dance with me.' She shrugged. 'Oh, never mind. I'll never get to dance, which means no man will ever court me or ask me to marry them.'

Persephone frowned. 'Marriage is your end goal?'

'Isn't it yours? That's why the Dowager is sponsoring you, is it not?' It was then Maddie realised that while she had spent hours talking to Persephone that morning, they'd touched little about her family or why she had come to England.

Persephone's nose wrinkled. 'I suppose. But we're not talking about me. Maddie, you're brilliant and wealthy. You don't need a husband to provide or protect you. You have your father's business to run.'

'I know, but...' She sighed. 'I still... I still want a family. Why can't I have that and still pursue my interests?'

'Of course you can, if that's what you want.' Persephone's eyebrows furrowed together. 'I have an idea.'

'An idea?'

'Yes. A plan, if you will. So you can get everything you want. But first, you must stay here.'

Before she could ask further questions, Persephone darted away.

What on earth did she mean by *plan*? Maddie was tempted to leave, but Persephone's words intrigued her. A few minutes later, her friend returned, but she was not alone. No—she was dragging someone along with her. A very tall, familiar someone.

'Slow down, Seph, before you trip—' The Earl's mouth clamped shut when their gazes met.

Her heart leapt to her throat, and she forced herself to turn away from those emerald orbs. 'What is the meaning of this, Persephone?'

She motioned to her brother with her hands. 'My plan.'

He raised a blond eyebrow. 'And what have you two been cooking up, now?'

'I haven't been cooking anything,' Maddie retorted.

'Just listen to me, will you?' Persephone clucked her tongue. 'Cam, we need your help.'

'Do you, now?' He crossed his arms over his chest.

'Well, Maddie does.'

'What do you mean, I need help?' Maddie cried. 'And why him?'

'Remember what I said earlier? About men and competition?'

It took a moment for Persephone's words and what her friend had in mind to sink in. She couldn't possibly think that… 'Oh, no.'

Persephone waggled her eyebrows. 'Oh, yes.'

Maddie wanted nothing more than to evaporate off the face of the earth at that moment.

Cam blew out an exasperated breath. 'For goodness' sake, will one of you explain to me what's going on?'

'Cam, you have to dance with Maddie at the beginning of every ball,' Persephone declared.

'Have to dance? Why?'

'So that other men will dance with her, of course.'

His head swayed back and forth from Persephone to Maddie and back to Persephone again. 'Why do you need me to dance with her?'

'Because if you do, other men will want to as well. And that will bring her closer to her goal.'

'Which is?'

'Why, marriage, of course.'

Silence hung in the air for a heartbeat before the Earl spoke again.

'Absolutely not.'

Chapter Three

'Absolutely not.'

Cam knew there were very few absolutes in the world. But when Persephone said he needed to dance with Miss Madeline DeVries so she could find some milksop Englishman to marry her, he knew that was *absolutely* something he could not take part in.

'Whyever not?' Persephone asked.

A bitter taste crept into his mouth as he recalled watching Miss DeVries with those other men.

Cam couldn't do it—not if their first dance was any indication of what would happen each time he did. He thought the initial pull of attraction he felt upon meeting her was just a normal male reaction to a beautiful woman. He'd even tried to ignore her as she'd descended the stairs at Mabury Hall like some ethereal goddess earlier that evening, though his heart had thumped like mad. *Once the novelty of her wears off, I'll stop feeling this way*, he had assured himself.

But the moment he'd taken her in her arms for that waltz, he'd been enraptured by her. How could he not react to her, with the way her sky blue eyes sparkled and her skin glowed under the light of a hundred candles. Not even her hideous gown could detract from her beauty.

His attraction had intensified with every second he'd held her.

Which was why he'd done what he always did: defused the situation with humour.

He hadn't meant to offend her once again when he'd attempted to apologise. Persephone had berated him that afternoon over his appalling words and threatened to never speak to him again if he did not make things right with Miss DeVries. Of course, Cam wanted to apologise, if only to be done with her so he could stop this torture of being around her and not being able to have her.

Because he knew that pursuing her would only lead to disaster.

'Need I remind you, we are not here for me. I am not in search of a wife.'

'I'm not asking you to marry Maddie, only to help her. It's only one dance, Cam,' his sister pointed out when he didn't answer.

'At every ball?'

Persephone clapped her palms together. 'Exactly. Maddie, these gentlemen won't be able to ignore you any longer, and you'll be married soon enough.'

Cam chewed on his inner cheek. *If none of these English men want her, then they are damned fools.* Still, the very idea of having her in his arms again and then watching someone else dance with her after soured his gut, never mind the thought of her belonging to another…

'I said no,' he repeated. *Absolutely, definitely not.*

'Cam, it's just until she finds enough candidates to choose a husband from. It's just one dance.'

One dance? He had barely controlled himself during that first one. Sweat built up on his palms at the thought of being so close to her, touching her. No, he would never again act on his attraction to someone he wanted so badly.

And he wanted Miss Madeline DeVries so badly, he'd forget his own name.

'There is no need for you to trouble yourself, my lord,' Miss DeVries bristled. 'I am perfectly capable of finding my own suitors.'

'See, Seph? She doesn't want me.' That should have given him relief, but why did his chest tighten at the words? 'Now, if you ladies will excuse me.' With a nod, he turned on his heel and strode off. *I need air.* And he needed to think.

He made his way to one of the balconies and closed the door behind him. Leaning forward over the side, he took in a breath. The breeze helped, but it wasn't quite like it was back home, where scents of pine, peat, and malt tinged the fresh air.

He was eager to go back, to be far away from this place. But Niall, Cam, and the rest of his brothers had a promise to keep.

Nay. He was keen to go back home because he needed to get far, far away from *her*.

Miss Madeline DeVries.

'Maddie.' He would never allow himself to call her by her given name, so what was the harm in whispering it to the wind? Still, the name on his lips felt entirely intimate. But it would not be his to say. Someone else would call her that. Her husband. On their wedding night.

He released the balustrade, as his knuckles had gone white from gripping it too tightly. Would Scotland be far away enough for him to forget her? It would have to be, because he could not risk being a slave to his passions again.

It had cost too much the first time.

Cam had been an eager, randy lad of just nineteen

when he'd first laid eyes on Jenny Gordon in the village. He'd gone there with his best friend, Kirk, when he'd seen her walking to the tea shop. The attraction had been instant and intense, and she'd enchanted him with her beauty. At that moment, he'd vowed to make her his and set out to woo her, turning on the old MacGregor charm every chance he could. He'd been a man in love and he'd been obsessed with making her his.

His ma and da had warned him many times and tried to get him to temper his passion throughout the courtship. It wasn't that his parents had been against the match or had any objections against Jenny herself; but they'd said he was too young to settle down; or perhaps they had recognised that what Cam had felt was not love. But he'd been too captivated with Jenny to listen to their advice, and soon, he'd got his wish—they were betrothed.

As the wedding had drawn closer, however, he'd noticed Jenny acting strangely. She had become withdrawn from him and distant. He'd chalked that up to the wedding planning, as even he had been caught up in all the details.

However, the day before the ceremony, his entire world had shattered. Jenny and Kirk had come to him and told him she could not marry Cam—they had fallen in love with each other!

'You were so charming and persistent, I was flattered with the attention,' she had confessed. *'My ma and da begged me to accept your proposal even though I hardly knew you. And then everyone around me was expecting so much of me because I was to be a countess. I thought it was what I wanted. The wedding, the balls, the parties—it was too much. I—I had my doubts. I asked Kirk for advice, and eventually he guessed I was having sec-*

ond thoughts. He was wonderful and patient with me and I couldn't help myself.'

'But you said you love me,' he had accused.

'I—I thought I did, Cam. I really thought I did. I just needed more.'

'I love her, Cam,' Kirk had said sheepishly. *'And I'm sorry.'*

'You would make someone a wonderful husband, Cam,' Jenny had added, as if that would soothe his broken heart. *'Just not mine.'*

Cam had wanted to lash out at them but just couldn't bring himself to do it. Kirk had been his best friend since they were in short pants, and he was one of the finest men he knew, tempering Cam's impulsive nature with his mature, calm presence. Indeed, Cam had got into only half the scraps he had because Kirk had been there to cool him down. He was the opposite of Cam—strong, intelligent, patient, and kind—and it was no wonder Jenny had fallen in love with him.

She'd needed more. More than what Cam could give her. His good looks, charm, and title were not enough for her.

They'd left that same day and eloped, then moved away, perhaps to spare Cam the humiliation. That had been nearly a decade ago, and though Jenny's face had nearly faded from his memory, the lesson from that time had not. He vowed to never be swept away by passion and attraction ever again.

Of course, he'd discreetly bedded many an eager lass since that time, but never more than once, and while most of them had been beautiful, he swore to never allow his feelings to grow for a woman. While he knew his duty as the Earl of Balfour meant he needed to produce an heir, there was time enough for that. Perhaps in the future he might find some comely, respectable lass to marry, one who wouldn't inspire such an obsession in him. If not, he had three younger brothers who could step into the role. As such, women and marriage were far from his mind at the moment.

Well, he'd thought that they were far from his mind, but then again, he hadn't met another woman who sparked such an instant, fervent attraction.

Until Miss Madeline DeVries.

'Bollocks,' he bit out. After tonight, he needn't worry about her, not after he'd mucked things up, as it was obvious she did not want him. He would do everything in his power to stop this instant attraction before it transformed into something deeper.

Ignoring the tightening in his chest, he headed back inside the ballroom. These events usually had a card room set up for the gentlemen, so he decided to seek it out. He was also in town for business, after all, and perhaps he could make some connections there. As he waded through the sea of people, a snippet of conversation caught his attention.

'…must be useful. I bet her family doesn't even need any ladders in their home. They simply ask her to pluck things off top shelves!'

He normally wasn't one for gossip, but he knew who they were referring to.

'And she can predict the weather before everyone else!' quipped another.

A barrage of sniggers and sneers met the jests—all of them women.

Damned foolish people.

He was about to walk away when he heard something that made him halt.

'I do feel sorry your mother and father have to be burdened so, Miss DeVries.'

'Thank you, Lady Gertrude,' Caroline DeVries sighed. 'My mother does fret about her finding a match. But I think the spinster life will suit Maddie. Perhaps she's even looking forward to it. I mean, can you imagine her, a lady of a household? She is not only ungainly, but also so terribly shy and awkward. How would she entertain? It's no wonder she doesn't have any suitors.'

'But then, why did Lord Porter dance with her?' someone asked.

'And Mr Carter and Lord Wembley,' another voice added.

Caroline harrumphed. 'Who knows? Perhaps the gentlemen had some kind of bet.' She chuckled. 'Which of them could survive dancing with my sister?'

A peal of laughter from the group. 'You are so right, Miss DeVries.'

Cam gritted his teeth as anger rose in him. How could her own sister talk of Maddie in such a manner? She sounded like she even encouraged it.

When he had met the younger Miss DeVries earlier, he'd thought her pretty enough, if a little flighty, but that was much expected from girls her age. But now, he had an inkling of what she was really like. He guessed that if Maddie was indeed 'shy and awkward,' her sister had had a hand in making her so.

Hands balled into fists at his sides, Cam marched away from the group, his eyes scanning the room. Once he found his target, he strode towards her, the crowd of people between them parting like the Red Sea.

'Miss DeVries.'

'Cam?' Persephone, who stood right next to Maddie, asked, her head cocking to the side.

Ignoring his sister, he said to Maddie, 'May I have this next dance?'

Maddie's head turned towards him, her eyes widening like an animal trapped by its prey. 'M-my lord?'

'A dance,' he repeated, then leaned closer to her ear. 'If you still want to continue this plan, this is your last chance.'

Her nose wrinkled. 'I told you, it is not my plan.'

'Just go,' Persephone urged. 'Do it.'

Though she hesitated, Maddie took his offered hand. 'I would love to, my lord.'

Their second was a livelier dance, though Maddie managed it well. Cam, too, found himself enjoying it, if only because he saw how happy it made her. The dance was over much too soon for Cam's liking, and once they stopped, he could feel all the eyes on them.

'Why are they staring?' Maddie asked.

'Looks like you've got your wish.' He nodded to the gentlemen on their right, who stood there like predators ready to pounce the moment Cam let go.

He'd never wanted to punch strangers so badly in his life.

'My wish?'

'To have more suitors.' The very words left a bitter taste in his mouth, and Cam knew he had to do something. So, he deposited her back at Persephone's side. 'There. I hope that was satisfactory?'

'Aye. And my plan is working.' His sister nodded behind him, and when he craned his neck back, he saw a handsome, dark-haired man approach them.

'Lord Balfour,' he greeted. 'Have you been enjoying your evening so far?'

Cam searched his memory for the man's name. 'Mr Baine.' Edward Baine was the son of a viscount, if he recalled. They'd been introduced earlier in the evening by their host and hostess. 'And yes, I have.'

Baine turned to the women. 'Lady Persephone. And Miss DeVries. I haven't seen you since the Chatsworth ball.'

Maddie blinked. 'That was months ago, my lord.'

'Was it? If so, then it has been remiss of me not to have furthered our acquaintance sooner.' He grinned sheepishly at her. 'I was wondering if I could have your next dance? Unless you are already spoken for.'

'Not at all,' she replied and took his offered hand.

When Maddie and Baine were out of earshot, Persephone nudged him. 'See? I told you this would work. I'm a genius,' she tittered. 'Now, all we have to do is repeat it at the next few balls, and soon Maddie will have her pick of suitors.' Her face lit up like an excited child's. 'Thank you for agreeing to do this, Cam.'

'You're welcome.' Cam blew out a breath. He just hoped he wouldn't regret it.

Chapter Four

Maddie told herself she was not disappointed when the Earl did not show up for breakfast that morning. The Dowager had said he had urgent matters to attend to with his man of business in London, who had arrived earlier that day. However, she was thankful he wasn't there, as her mother and Caroline were especially insufferable this morning.

'Oh, did you see that dashing Mr Baine?' Mama tittered as the footman refilled her teacup. 'The two of you looked wonderful on the ballroom floor.'

'I agree,' Papa said. 'Although I don't know much about dancing.'

'And he was only two inches shorter than you,' Caroline added with a sneer.

Maddie took a sip of her tea. 'He danced well.'

'I'm so happy to hear this, Maddie,' said Miss Merton, who sat across from Maddie at the breakfast table. Originally, the Honourable Harriet Merton had been hired as a chaperone for Maddie, Caroline, and Kate Mason to help the American misses navigate the perilous London season. However, it had been her idea to ask the Dowager for help and act as sponsor for the girls. Many weeks ago, before they'd headed to London, her sister had taken ill, and so she'd gone to stay with her in Bath until she recovered. She had arrived late last night and thus was able to see them only this morning.

'Of course, the Earl danced with you twice,' Mama pointed out, as if Maddie couldn't remember it herself. 'Is twice too much? Cornelius, should you be having a word with His Lordship—'

'Mama.' She sent a pleading look to her father.

Cornelius cleared his throat. 'Eliza, dear, perhaps you should—'

'Oh!' Mama's eyes sparkled. 'An earl...'

'Your Grace, may I be excused? I must prepare for my gentlemen callers.' Caroline's gaze flitted towards Maddie. 'It's so tedious, but I can't turn away any of them lest I be accused of favouritism. Be glad you don't have that problem, Maddie.'

The jab hit its mark, like an arrow straight into Maddie's chest. While dancing was an enjoyable form of entertainment at balls, it was not an indication of a gentleman's interests in a young lady. Gifts and calls the following day were the real test, proof that they were willing to go beyond the ballroom dance-floor in their pursuit. While Caroline had entertained regularly these last few weeks, Maddie still had not received even one caller.

'Of course, Caroline,' the Dowager said.

Caroline gave Maddie one last smirk before she got up and walked out of the breakfast room. Maddie sighed with relief as the atmosphere became much lighter without her sister, with the conversation topics focusing less on Caroline.

After breakfast, Persephone took her aside. 'If you're not busy, let's head to the library.'

'I'm never busy,' she sighed. 'But I'm so glad I have you now, at least.'

Persephone smiled at her. 'Me, too.' Arm in arm, they walked towards the other wing of the town house. 'I've never had sisters before. Or close female friends. My ma died a few years ago. She was probably the closest thing I've had to any feminine influence.'

'I'm so sorry, Persephone.' Although Eliza could be vexing most of the time, Maddie knew she was lucky to have her mother.

'Well, here we are—oh, no.' She ran her hands down her dress and into the pockets. 'I've lost my spectacles!'

'You're wearing them,' Maddie pointed out.

'I know that.' The Scotswoman straightened the glasses perched on her nose. 'I mean my spare ones.'

'Spare ones?'

'Yes. You never know what can happen. Sometimes they'll just fly off my face for no reason, so I always carry a spare.' Her lips twisted. 'I must have dropped them somewhere between my room and the breakfast room. I should retrace my steps.'

'Do you need help?'

'Don't be silly.' She waved Maddie away. 'Stay here. I'll be right back.' Whirling around, she left the library.

Maddie entered the library by herself and headed to the row of shelves near the back of the room. She had finished the last book she'd borrowed, so she decided to search for the next volume in the series.

'Hmm.' As she glanced at the titles and volumes, it seemed that they were not in order and a few were missing, including the one right after the book she had just finished. She checked the lower shelves first, then craned her neck back. A dark brown book caught her eye, and she squinted at the spine.

'Volume three. There you are.' But why in the world was it all the way up there? She would have to stretch all the way up to reach it. *Perhaps I can find a ladder.* Seemed like such a bother for just one book.

Shrugging, she got on her tiptoes and extended her arm all the way over her head. 'Come on...' Her fingers barely brushed the leather-bound book.

'What the devil are you doing?'

The lilting burr made her heart leap into her throat and she lost her balance, sending her falling back. 'Oh!' Her body crashed into the opposite bookcase, which was mercifully sturdy, though the impact left her breathless.

'Maddie!' The Earl was beside her in an instant, hauling her to her feet. 'Are you all right, darlin'? Are you hurt?'

His strong, warm hand wrapped around her upper arm sent a strange zing straight down to her belly. 'I... I'm fine, my lord. Just a little shaken.'

'Should I call a doctor?'

'A doctor?' She shook her head. 'I told you, I'm fine.'

Emerald eyes searched her face. 'Did you hit your head?'

Having him so completely focused on her frazzled her nerves, sending her heart hammering. 'N-no, my lord.' She glanced down at his hand, which was still clutching her.

He quickly dropped his arm to his side. 'What were you doing, anyway?'

'Just trying to reach for a book.' She forced out a laugh, trying to cover up the drumming of her heartbeat. 'I'm afraid I'm not used to having things out of my reach.'

Frowning, he glanced up at the shelf. 'Which one?'

'I beg your pardon?'

'Which one did you want?'

'Th-that one. Volume three.'

He reached up and plucked it off with little effort. 'That's quite heavy reading.'

'I assure you, I can understand it perfectly well,' she rebutted. But then again, she didn't know any other young lady who would have chosen to read *Principles of Geology Volume III*.

'I mean, it's a weighty tome.' He bounced it up and down in his hand. 'You could have been hurt if it fell on your head.'

She pressed her lips together. 'I would have used a ladder, but I didn't see one.'

'Well, it's a good thing I was here then, isn't it?' He flashed her a smile.

Good Lord in heaven, her knees wobbled and she nearly fell back once more. 'Thank you.' She took the book from his hand and held it to her chest like a shield, though what she was protecting herself from, she wasn't sure. Perhaps his imposing presence, which seemed to fill the narrow space, making it difficult to breathe. 'If you'll excuse me...'

Maddie sidestepped to the left to pass him; however, he did the same, which meant he blocked her. When she moved right, so did he, and they ended up doing an awkward dance with neither of them getting past the other.

'Stop.'

She did, right in the middle of the aisle. Still, he was so wide that he didn't have any space on either side of him to let her through. This close, he loomed over her, and she couldn't help but stare up into those eyes, which were twinkling with amusement.

'If only there was music. We could probably coordinate our steps better.'

Heat crept up her cheeks at the reminder of their

dances last night. The awkwardness in the air was swiftly becoming unbearable. She wished she were somewhere other than this place. 'I should really leave, my lord. It's not proper for us to be here without a chaperone.'

'Aye,' he began. 'But then again, considering the plan you cooked up, aren't we past propriety at this point?'

Her face warmed even more, but not because of embarrassment. 'I told you, I didn't cook up anything. It was Persephone's idea.' She squared her shoulders. 'And you don't have to dance with me, my lord. Not anymore.'

'Ah, the suitors have been lining up outside, have they? Banging on the door?'

Now he was just plain insulting her. 'I would rather remain a wallflower than receive another pity dance from you. Now if you'll excuse me—' She once again attempted to move past him, but an arm shot out to block her way.

'Miss DeVries, wait. I swear to you, on my mother's soul, that I've not been raised in a barn. I don't know why...' He scrubbed a hand down his face. 'I can't seem to stop saying the wrong thing these days, but that has absolutely nothing to do with you. The fault is all mine. I am sorry for inadvertently insulting you. Forgive me for my thoughtlessness.'

The apology rendered her speechless. There was no excuse, no justification of his actions, just a sincere expression of regret for hurting her. 'I suppose...that you have had a long journey from Scotland. I know when we came from America, I was out of sorts for a few days and not myself.' Yes, maybe that was why he had insulted her that first time.

'Perhaps, but it is not an excuse. Therefore, I would appreciate your forgiveness.'

'You have it, my lord.' She could not help but see the sincerity in his face.

'Thank you.'

'But you are not incorrect.'

'I beg your pardon?'

Sighing, she turned to the shelf on her left and ran her fingers across the spines of the books. 'Despite our "efforts" last night, no gentleman has come knocking on the door, no gifts have been sent, or even requests for calls.' Her arm dropped to her side. 'My sister, meanwhile, never has an empty dance card and has more suitors than she knows what to do with. So, perhaps dancing with me is a waste of your time and I am simply not a desirable candidate for a wife.'

He muttered something under his breath, but exactly what, she couldn't comprehend.

'I beg your pardon, my lord?'

He spoke up. 'I think we should make a plan.'

'A plan?'

'Aye.' He crossed his arms over his chest. 'We can't just charge in and hope for the best. That's what my da always said.'

'I never thought of it that way.' Her father was the same, especially when it came to their furnace. They didn't exactly just mix rocks together and fire them up. No, they had to measure and weigh the minerals, then they went through the smelting process step by step. 'But what else must I do?'

He paused for a moment. 'I think there is more to it than simply dancing.'

'There is? But what else could there be, aside from the fact that I am simply not as desirable as Car—'

'There is more,' he interrupted through gritted teeth.

'The dancing is just part of it. For this plan to work, we must do more.'

'More?' she echoed. 'What more could we possibly do?'

'It's simple, isn't? When I dance with you, other men want to dance with you as well. Therefore, if you want gentlemen to come courting, I must court you as well.'

For a brief moment, Maddie wondered if *Principles of Geology Volume III* had indeed dropped on her head and she was in a dream conjured in a comatose state.

'It would be pretend, of course,' he added quickly.

'Pretend.' Still, heat gathered around the suddenly constricting neck of her collar. What did she think he meant, anyway? That he would court her for real?

'So, what do you say, Miss DeVries? Do we have an agreement?'

Part of her wanted to say yes—it would not be a real courtship. But a different part of her told her to proceed with caution. 'You can't possibly be serious.' She shook her head. 'Dancing is one thing, but to pretend to court me—it's simply...*mad.*'

'What's mad?'

Maddie nearly jumped out of her skin, then let out a breath of relief when she realised it was Persephone.

The Earl clasped his hands behind his back. 'Ah, here you are, Seph. Glad you're here and you can be a witness to our agreement.'

The Scotswoman placed her hands on her hips. 'What agreement?'

'Your little plan,' he said.

'But I thought you already agreed to dance with Maddie at every ball?'

'Yes, but we decided it's not enough. For Miss DeVries

to receive any kind of male attention beyond the ballroom floor, I must also pretend to court her.'

Maddie looked at Persephone sheepishly, who blinked back at her, then looked at her brother, and then back at Maddie, owlish eyes growing wide. *Oh, Lord. Even she thinks it's a stupid idea.*

'It's brilliant, absolutely brilliant.' She clasped her hands together. 'I'd been thinking about it all morning, actually.'

'You have?' Maddie asked.

'Yes, when Caroline mentioned all her suitors. Oh, you were so brave putting on that front whenever she needled you, Maddie. But I knew her words wounded you.'

'Wounded you?' the Earl repeated. 'What exactly did she say?'

'That Maddie should be glad she didn't have any suitors—'

'She didn't mean it that way.' Maddie's cheeks puffed out in defence. Oh, Lord, how much more embarrassment could she take this morning? Persephone didn't do it on purpose, of course, but to have her shortcomings laid out in front of the Earl was too much.

Persephone wasn't derailed and forged on. 'Cam, this idea of yours… It might actually work. If you court Maddie, then other men will follow in your wake.'

'Pretend to court her,' he qualified.

'Yes, yes.' Persephone rolled her eyes. 'But oh, this is exciting, indeed.'

'This can't be proper,' Maddie protested. 'What if our deceit was exposed?'

'By whom?' Persephone clucked her tongue. 'As long as this stays between the three of us, no one will know. Besides, once other men begin courting you and you choose a suitor other than Cam, it will not matter. It happens all the time.'

She supposed Persephone was right. A young woman could choose only one, and it wasn't like the Earl's reputation would suffer from a rejection from an American heiress with no title. *And it's a pretend courtship.* She couldn't hurt his feelings, because he had none for her in the first place. The thought sent something wilting inside of her, but she ignored it.

'How exciting,' Persephone tittered. 'I can't wait to see this all unfold.'

'But let's not forget why you are here in England, Seph.' The Earl raised a blond eyebrow at her. 'Ma wanted you to have this season. You should at least dance once tonight. I've actually been approached by at least two young men asking for an introduction.'

'Oh, dear, I've lost my spectacles,' Persephone burst out.

'They're on your face, lass,' the Earl pointed out.

'I mean my spare ones.'

Maddie frowned. 'I thought you already went to look for them?'

'I d-dropped them again…somewhere.' She backed away. 'I'll see you later then, Cam. Maddie.' She turned tail and hurried away from them.

The Earl's lips pressed together and a line appeared between his eyebrows. 'I should go speak with her. But before that, do we have an agreement, Miss DeVries?'

Doubt still crept in her mind, so she shot him back a question. 'Why would you do this?'

He seemed taken aback but quickly recovered. 'I have made a promise to my sister to help you in this endeavour, and I'm afraid I cannot back out on my promise,' he countered. 'She has very few friends—nay, she has no friends at all. But she has obviously taken a liking to you. Coming to England has not been easy for her. I appreciate that you have made her feel less alone in such a strange place, in what must be a confusing time for her. So please, allow me to do this one thing to thank you. For her.'

Maddie could only stare at him, stunned. It was not at all the reason she'd expected. 'I... Yes.'

Oh, Lord, she was really doing this.

He was really doing this.

Cam stared down into those beautiful sky blue eyes, wondering what in God's name he was thinking.

What was it about Madeline DeVries that he just could not resist? She'd already given him a way out of that silly plan, and he should have taken that gift she'd offered. But no, he'd had to entangle himself further, suggesting this ridiculous pretend courtship that would surely lead to disaster.

Dancing with her was one thing, but courting her was another. That would involve spending more time together.

I should have left well enough alone.

Still, seeing her so forlorn had sparked something in him—not to mention, that brat of a sister of hers had only fuelled his outrage. Why anyone would think Maddie was inferior to Caroline—including Maddie herself— was a mystery to him.

I cannot do this.

He reminded himself of the last time he'd acted on his impulses, envisioning Jenny and Kirk that morning they'd come to tell him the news.

Never again.

He would have to stop this madness before he completely lost himself. But how?

An idea sprang up in his mind: have her married as fast as possible, ensuring that she was out of his reach before this attraction turned into an obsession.

Aye, that was the answer.

This was a ruse, a ploy, and nothing more. Though he still needed to take precautions.

Clearing his throat, he began, 'Now that we are in agreement, perhaps we can lay down some rules.'

Her expression turned serious. 'Rules?'

'Yes. If we are to achieve your goal, then we must do so methodically. We must have a strategy, along with some rules. To protect all parties.' *Mainly, myself.*

She seemed to mull his words over. 'All right, my lord. And what are these rules?'

Cam blurted out the first thing he could think of. 'We must only dance once per ball.'

'Once?' She sounded disappointed. 'But we've already danced twice in the same evening.'

And Cam would never forget it. How she'd felt in his arms and the way her face had lit up with excitement both times. Maddie simply standing and doing nothing was enough of a temptation, but when she was dancing, she was like a living goddess. He wouldn't be able to resist her if he had to do that more than once a night.

'Two dances with the same partner is usually accept-able at any event,' he began. 'But if you show me too much favour, other gentlemen might infer that your mind is already made up, and they may decide it is not worth the effort to court you.'

'That makes sense,' she relented. 'What else?'

He thought back to his time with Jenny and how he'd wooed her. She'd often loved getting presents from him and he had given her plenty. 'I'll not shower you with gifts,' he stated in the coolest manner he could muster.

'I must decline them anyway,' she pointed out. 'Miss Merton says young ladies can only accept gifts from their fiancé.'

'Fair enough.' There would be no trouble there, then. 'Next, we spend minimal time together.' When he was trying to win Jenny, he'd often found ways to run into her in the village or show up at her father's home. No, he could not be around Maddie constantly. She was far too tempting.

'What do you mean by minimal?'

'I do not actually need to court you but, rather, put on an illusion of it.'

'And how would you do that, my lord?'

'Tonight, after our dance, I will ask your father for permission to call on you.' Even though they were staying in the same house, he would still have to do things properly. 'I will do this in front of other guests, and hopefully let the gossips of the ton do their work, and I won't need to actually pay you a call. We need not spend any more time together outside balls or during mealtimes at the Dowager's home.' And he planned to miss as many of those as possible without offending their host. 'And we will especially never find ourselves alone. That's our fourth rule.'

Her brows wrinkled. 'Whyever would we need to be alone? And it's not like we would have a chance.'

'*Ahem.*' He gestured around them with his hands.

'Oh. Right.' Her cheeks pinked. 'But what should I do about other suitors?'

'I'm sure your mama will know how to handle them.' He ignored the tightening in his chest. 'That's the fifth rule, by the way. I won't meddle in your affairs.'

'Y-you won't?'

'Of course not. It's your decision, after all.'

'Ah, of c-course,' she stammered. 'I did not mean to imply that I would need your assistance on such matters. Any more rules I should know about?'

'I shall let you know if I think of anything else to-night.' He bowed his head, then turned on his heel.

As he left the library, he blew out a breath, hoping to ease the tightening in his chest. He could not take any chances. He needed to keep her at arm's length, and these ground rules would ensure he would never make the same mistake again.

Chapter Five

Cam surveyed the Earl of Hartnell's ballroom, where the elite of London's society gathered, and laughed, and revelled as if all was well and normal.

But nothing about Cam's life seemed normal—at least not since he'd met Miss Madeline DeVries. His instinct to stay as far away as possible from her was the correct reaction.

And yet, now he was in much deeper, and it was all his doing.

It wasn't too late yet. He could tell her he'd changed his mind. Maybe he could leave now and he wouldn't have to dance with her.

'Cam, we're here,' Persephone said, seemingly popping out of nowhere. His sister had insisted they go to the Hartnell ball earlier than the Dowager and the De-Vrieses. 'It will allow Maddie to have a more dramatic entrance, as she'll always be announced after us,' she had explained.

However, when it was time to go, Persephone had conveniently torn her dress and then bade him to head to the ball in their carriage first and that she would ride to the ball with the Dowager.

'Glad to see you've arrived.' Persephone had been acting oddly since they'd arrived in London—well, odd even for her, he supposed. 'Disaster was averted with your dress, I presume?'

'My what—oh, yes.' She fiddled with a bit of lace on her dress. 'Anyway, we're here. You should ask Maddie to dance now.' She nodded towards the other end of the room, where Maddie, her sister, and her parents were walking towards the refreshment table. They barely had time to accept the glasses of lemonade offered by the footman when two gentlemen came swooping in.

'Perhaps Miss DeVries doesn't need my assistance after all.' Cam gnashed his teeth.

'Maybe.' Persephone's lips puckered like she'd eaten a lemon when both men wrote their names on Caroline's card but completely ignored Maddie. 'Just look at how sad she is.'

Though fleeting, Cam clearly saw the disappointment on Maddie's pretty face. Irrational anger bubbled through him. Even dressed in that ridiculous ruffled green-orange gown that washed out her complexion, Maddie was still far lovelier than her insipid sister.

'Now's your chance to help poor Maddie so she can find a husband and have the family she's always wanted.'

His chest tightened at Persephone's words. Yet, he himself had reached that conclusion this morning. Pretending to court Maddie now might be the only way to ensure her marriage. Then he would not be able to act on his obsession.

'Well?' Persephone demanded. 'What are you going to do? They just announced the next dance.'

Cam didn't reply to Persephone but instead snatched a flute of champagne from a passing waiter, then downed it in one gulp and handed the empty glass to his sister before marching across the room.

Maddie must have felt his eyes on her, as she turned her head to face him. Her plump lips parted as their gazes met, and that attraction once again tugged at his gut. She quickly turned away, and a thought surfaced in his mind: Did Maddie even feel anything at all towards him? Perhaps the real reason she'd tried to dissuade him from this pretend courtship was that she was repulsed by him.

It was, however, too late to back out now, because as soon as Maddie's mother saw him approach, she nodded and waved at him. Ignoring her now would amount to a cut.

'My lord,' Eliza DeVries greeted him breathlessly, her excitement barely contained. 'How lovely to see you. We were told you had gone ahead of us.'

'Mrs DeVries,' he murmured, then turned to Maddie's father. 'Mr DeVries. I was wondering if I may have the honour of dancing with your daughter?' When Caroline smiled at him and took a step forward, he added, 'Miss Madeline.'

Eliza let out a squeak and covered her mouth with her hand, while Caroline's jaw dropped.

'Of course, my lord,' Cornelius replied with a chuckle. 'Though you should really be asking my daughter.'

He offered his hand to her, ignoring the viperous stare from Caroline. 'Miss DeVries? May I have this dance?'

'My lord.' She took it, and he whisked her away. When they arrived at their position, she glanced around. 'People are staring at us again.'

'Good,' he bit out.

This was why they were doing this, after all.

An uncomfortable sensation settled in his stomach,

but he ignored it. He placed his hand on her waist while taking her other hand, then the music began to play.

Once again, Maddie's face brightened as they danced. She seemed transformed—much lighter, happier, and less nervous. She even smiled at him, a gesture that made his heart leap. He would never forget that moment or her pretty face, and so he filed it away, and perhaps one day, when he was old and grey, he could look back on this with fondness, knowing he'd done the right thing for her.

'You truly love to dance, don't you?' he observed.

'I do.'

'Why?'

She didn't have time to answer right away as they changed direction. Once she was back in his arms, she said, 'During my very first lesson, my dance master would constantly shout insults at me when I made mistakes.'

He ground his teeth together. 'And what insults would he hurl at you?'

'Nothing I could understand. He was Italian.' The slightest smile appeared on her lips. 'But, after that, I vowed to study hard and learn how to dance. And during those afternoon dance lessons, I concentrated so hard on getting the steps right that I couldn't think of anything else. It was as if my mind was so preoccupied with thoughts of turning the right way or holding my body up straight that I could forget everything outside that ballroom. And forget that I'm not as—' Her lips clamped shut and her eyes lowered.

'Not as what?'

'It— It's nothing, my lord.'

Cam suspected what she wanted to say. That she was not as pretty as her sister. *Bollocks*. 'And what happened after all that practice?'

That smile returned. 'Eventually the dance master told me that I was better than Caroline.'

'Maybe it was your handsome Italian dance master that inspired you,' he teased.

She laughed, throwing her head back and exposing her long, elegant neck. 'Signor Cavallini was nearly seventy years old and had ten children and six grandchildren.'

'He sounds quite energetic.'

'He was a dance master.'

Her cheeks puffed from exertion, giving them the prettiest blush, and once again he could not tear his eyes away from her. More than that, he could not help but admire her tenacity. Instead of whining or running away in tears, she'd faced the challenge and striven to become better.

Cam did not believe that women were weaker than or inferior to men. His own mother had proved that, and he had learned never to underestimate her. Elaine Mac-Gregor had had an inner strength that was understated. It had been unnoticeable, just beneath the surface, but it had been there.

Growing up, he'd wondered how an English lady like her had found her home in the Highlands. One day, when he was about sixteen, while they were taking a walk in the woods, he'd asked and she had answered, *'I fell in love with your father at first sight, and so how could I not love the place where he came from? And while life here is so different and much rougher than where I grew up, I had to learn to adapt. Look at the reeds in the river.'* She had pointed to tall, skinny stalks on the water. *'When the water rushes past them, do they break off? No, they bend and curve, and in doing so, they remain intact.'*

'My lord?' Maddie's words broke into his reverie. 'Are you all right?'

His heart stuttered in his chest as those luminous blue eyes stared up at him. 'Aye.'

Thankfully, the dance was nearly over. As soon as the music stopped and the dance finished, he escorted her back to her parents' side. Sure enough, three gentlemen were fast approaching them.

Cam fought the urge to scare them off. However, he had to play his part, if only to further their grand scheme so Maddie could be wed and out of his reach.

'Mr DeVries,' he began, loud enough for the other men to hear as they wrote their names on Maddie's dance card. 'I would like your permission to call upon Miss Madeline.' From the corner of his vision, he saw Maddie stiffen.

'Call upon her?' Mr DeVries chuckled. 'We are all staying at the Dowager's town house. You can see her anytime.'

His wife let out a squeak and gripped his arm. 'That's not what he means, Cornelius.' Her eyes sparkled as she choked out, 'My husband grants his permission. We will see you in the parlour at half past three tomorrow. Myself and Miss Merton will be there.'

Maddie looked at him helplessly, her hands writhing together. 'T-tomorrow? I mean… His Lordship did not s-specify when… He should really send you a card first—'

'Maddie, don't be silly,' Eliza hissed. 'Like your father said, we are all staying in the same house. A card would be a waste of good paper.' She let out a chuckle. 'We will see you tomorrow.'

'I look forward to it.' He glanced over at Maddie. 'Miss DeVries, thank you for the lovely dance.' His gaze flickered to the gentlemen, who all regarded him with the same expression. Cam recognised it, of course—any man would have. They were eyeing him, assessing him and his competitive position.

Stupid fops, he thought as he turned and walked away. They saw Maddie's value only because he wanted her, not for what she could offer. That she could be a good wife, a partner in life.

Hell.

He halted in his tracks and massaged his temple with his thumb and forefinger. How did he get manipulated into actually paying Maddie a call? This was against their rules.

I have to stop this now. This obsession was heading into dangerous territory. It seemed he needed to add one last rule.

Do not fall in love.

Chapter Six

Maddie could not believe it. *She was dancing! At a ball!*

She should be happy. No—ecstatic. And part of her truly was elated that she was no longer a wallflower, wilting in the background while she watched others in their merriment.

Yet, the dancing left her wanting for more. Or rather, it wasn't the dancing but her partners. Or most of them, anyway. Her current partner included.

Lord Andrew Annesley was the second son of a marquess. Mama could hardly contain herself when he strode over to ask for her next dance. He was handsome and of a good pedigree. Why, he was even taller than most of the other men she partnered with, reaching nearly to her eye level.

However, there was just something about him that was...lacking.

'And so... I said, "Sir, I am no fool. That is...not a peacock...feather,"' Lord Annesley huffed as they returned to each other when it was their turn to perform the steps in the middle. When they'd begun the dance, he had been telling her a story about his trip to the milliner that afternoon. 'And I demanded...my money back.'

'How, er, tenacious of you, my lord.' Oh, heavens, the man never stopped talking. And maybe that was what bothered Maddie. Lord Annesley chattered on and on about everything and nothing at the same time.

In fact, that seemed to be the commonality among her dance partners tonight. They spoke only about themselves or gossiped among the ton or other inconsequential subjects. None of them even asked Maddie about her interests and thoughts. Well, none, except one.

You truly love to dance, don't you?

And as she did with each of her dance partners tonight, she kept comparing Lord Annesley to the Earl. Instead of talking about himself, the Earl had asked her why she loved to dance and even let her ramble on without interrupting. Dear Lord, and *how* she had rambled on about Signor Cavallini and her silly dance lessons! She winced with embarrassment at the memory.

'Miss DeVries?' Lord Annesley frowned at her disapprovingly. 'Are you listening—'

Maddie twirled around and skipped away from him to return to the opposite corner, blowing out a breath of relief. Why did quadrilles take so long? She glanced at the musicians, willing them to pick up the tempo. However, as she turned her head, she saw a glimpse of the Earl chatting casually with a small group of people. The fluttering in her stomach made her miss a step, but thankfully, no one noticed. What was it about him that made her so flustered? And why did her mind keep circling back to him?

It had been better when she'd thought him to be a boorish lout who insulted her. But in the span of one day, he'd managed to turn her opinion of him, first by apologising, then by showing how much he truly cared about Persephone. Her heart stirred at his thoughtfulness. Maddie knew most men would not care about their younger sister's feelings, but he clearly did.

He's pretending to court you because of Persephone, she reminded herself. *As thanks for being her friend.*

It was hard to not be disappointed by their first rule that they could only dance once per ball. But she understood that showing him more favour than her other suitors—well, potential suitors, at this point—would not bode well for their plan. She wanted to attract men, not scare them off.

'I thoroughly enjoyed our dance, Miss DeVries.'

Maddie secretly sighed in relief as she curtseyed. 'Thank you, my lord.'

'If you are not otherwise engaged,' he began as he led her back to her parents and sister, 'I would like to call on you this week.'

'I am not— I mean, of course.' One other dance partner—Mr James Davenport—had implied that he might pay her a call in the next day or so.

'Wonderful.'

She returned his smile, as it seemed like the right thing to do.

This was what she wanted, right?

'Oh, Maddie.' Her mother gripped her arm in excitement once Lord Annesley was halfway across the room. 'It looks like your fortunes have taken a turn. Lord Annesley's father has one of the oldest titles in England, I'm told.'

Maddie didn't even wonder where her mother had got that information, considering neither of them had even been introduced to Lord Annesley before this evening.

'We only spoke for a few minutes when we were introduced earlier,' Papa said. 'He was very, uh, enthusiastic and passionate with his words.'

Especially when it came to fashion, Maddie added silently.

'What else did you talk about?' Mama asked.

'He says he would like to pay me a call this week,' Maddie informed them.

'Oh, a call from a lord!' Mama flicked her fan open and waved it frantically. 'It must be your new gown. The seamstress fought me on the sunset and chartreuse, but I knew it was the right combination to draw attention to your features and away from your height. We must order new gowns in these colours for you immediately.'

Maddie groaned inwardly. 'I still have at least three gowns I haven't worn. I'm sure they're perfectly fine.'

'Nonsense. You will have *every* gown in that colour.'

'You seem overly excited, my dear,' Papa said gently. 'Caro, perhaps you could escort your mother to the retiring room? Be a dear and sit with her for a moment.'

Mama's fanning turned even more brisk. 'Excellent idea, Cornelius.'

'You can use the time to plan your shopping trip together.' Papa gave Caroline an encouraging nudge towards Mama. 'And you can visit that glove store you've been talking about all evening.'

'Oh, yes, a wonderful idea.' Caroline took their mother's elbow and guided her away. 'Come now, Mama. You need rest. I think I will need those kid gloves in....'

'Thank you, Papa,' Maddie said to her father once they were alone.

'Mr DeVries, Miss DeVries. Good evening.'

Maddie turned towards the gentleman who had approached them. 'Mr Wadsworth,' she greeted in return. Their hostess had introduced Mr George Wadsworth earlier in the evening, and he had immediately asked to write his name on her dance card.

'I would like to claim my dance,' he said, then added, 'If Mr DeVries wouldn't mind.'

'Of course not.' Papa gestured to her. 'Have a lovely time.' He winked at her.

'Thank you, Papa.' She allowed Mr Wadsworth to lead her away. However, even as she took her position on the ballroom floor, she could not help but search the room for the Earl's familiar, tall frame. It was usually easily easy to spot him, but it seemed as if he had all but disappeared.

Why am I looking for him, anyway?

All that mattered was that her dance card was filled, and perhaps, if their ploy worked, she would soon have at least one or two suitors to choose from. At the very least, if she did not have any suitors, she could still enjoy the dancing.

The next morning, as Maddie headed down to breakfast, she ran into Persephone at the top of the staircase.

'How was the rest of ball?' Persephone asked. 'From the smudges under your eyes, I can tell you were up all night. Tell me,' she tugged at Maddie's sleeve. 'Did you receive any proposals?'

Maddie chuckled. 'No proposals, but there were a few gentlemen who said they would pay me a call this week. But where did you go? I didn't see you all evening.'

'Where else?' Persephone puffed out a breath. 'Hiding in all the anterooms, which is why I didn't have a chance to watch you. The Countess of Hartnell should consider redecorating her home, as it is severely lacking in foliage or objects large enough to conceal oneself.'

'Oh, dear.' *Poor Persephone.* 'What can I do to help?'

Persephone linked their arms together as they descended the stairs. 'I'm afraid no one can help me. Besides, we need to concentrate on you.' She lowered her voice. 'And I cannot wait to see if this plan of yours will work. A pretend courtship. Why didn't I think of it?'

'We don't know yet if it will work.' Caroline's words from last night came back to her—telling her they would pay her a call was different from actually doing it.

'I'm sure it will,' Persephone assured her as they reached the bottom of the steps and made their way to the breakfast room.

Breakfast at Mabury Hall was an informal affair, where everyone came and went as they pleased. The Dowager, Miss Merton, Maddie's parents, and Caroline had already started, so the two girls took their places at the table. Once again, the Earl was not present, and Maddie bit her tongue to keep from asking where he was. Perhaps he was once again meeting with his man of business.

'Kate and Sebastian want to visit soon,' the Dowager had been telling them. 'I received a letter from her this morning, and she mentioned that they're nearly ready to break ground on the railway—'

'Your Grace,' Eames greeted as he entered the breakfast room.

'Good morning, Eames.' The Dowager eyed the two stacks of letters and cards on the silver tray the butler carried. 'We're quite popular this morning, aren't we?'

'Indeed, Your Grace.' He handed her the larger pile, then gave the rest to Maddie's parents.

Papa opened the card on top of the pile. 'Hmm.'

'Ooh, that card looks expensive.' Mama leaned over. 'Who is it from?'

'Lord Andrew Annesely,' Papa read aloud, then the next one. 'And this one's from a Mr Davenport.'

'That one says Sir Alfred Kensington!' Mama sputtered, pointing to the last card.

Caroline's delicate blond eyebrows drew together. 'I don't recognise those names.'

'They're all gentlemen Maddie danced with,' Mama announced.

Maddie couldn't move or say anything. She actually had callers after a ball. A soft nudge at her feet startled her, and she turned to Persephone, who smirked at her and mouthed, *See?*

'Are there any more?' Caroline enquired, her lips pursed together.

'A few,' Papa mumbled as he went through the stack. 'Mostly business acquaintances—ah!' He handed one to his wife. 'I don't recognise this one.'

'Mr Garrison,' she read. 'Didn't you dance with him last night, Caroline?'

'One? That's it?' Caroline fumed. 'I only received one measly card?'

'Isn't your afternoon schedule for the rest of the week already full?' Miss Merton enquired. 'Why, if you had got more than one, you wouldn't have been able to meet them all.'

Caroline stood up so fast, the chair scraped loudly on the hardwood floor. 'Please excuse me, Your Grace. I've lost my appetite.' The Dowager barely had time to nod before she stomped out.

Mama didn't seem perturbed by Caroline's dramatic exit. 'Maddie, three gentlemen want to call on you. I can hardly believe it!'

She couldn't either.

And all because the Earl danced with her and asked permission from her father to call on her. Why, only two of the gentlemen had heard him, yet news of it had travelled quickly to the other men in the room. Kate often jested that if the ton's gossips could be harnessed into a form of communication device on the tracks, they could revolutionise the railroad industry.

'We must be ready for when they come calling,' Mama continued. 'Oh, we will head straight to the dress shop today. I only hope Mrs Ellesmore has more of the same fabrics from your gown last night.'

Maddie stifled the urge to scream and looked around helplessly, searching for someone—anyone—to save her from her mother's horrendous fashion sense.

'Eliza,' the Dowager began with a delicate clearing of her throat. 'I believe Miss Merton requires your assistance today.'

'I do?' Miss Merton asked. When the Dowager sent her a meaningful look, she quickly added, 'Yes, I do. For, er—'

'Sorting out and replying to our invitations,' the Dowager provided. 'I'm afraid I'm entirely too busy today.' She gestured to the stack of envelopes in front of her. 'I trust no one else but Miss Merton to sift through the pile and accept ones from the most prominent hostesses and exclusive events in London your daughters must attend.'

Miss Merton's head bobbed up and down. 'We must choose only the best balls and parties, after all. But I cannot do it alone.'

Mama gripped the edge of the table. 'That is important work, indeed. But what about Maddie's gowns?'

'I told you, Mama. I don't need any new gowns.'

'Nonsense. You must have them.'

'But—'

'I shall take her,' the Dowager suggested. 'That's one of my errands today, anyway. She may as well come with me.'

'It's not—'

'I *insist*,' she said with a cryptic smile.

'Don't be rude, Madeline,' Mama warned. 'She shall accompany you, Your Grace.'

'It's settled, then. Persephone, why don't you come along? We would love the company.'

'I'd be happy to.' However, Persephone's expression told Maddie she would rather do anything but that.

'You must be back as soon as possible, as the Earl will be paying you a call today.' Mama practically shook with excitement. 'Lady Persephone, where is your brother, by the way?'

'He's in a meeting, Mrs DeVries,' she replied. 'And asked not to be disturbed.'

'How unfortunate.' Mama tsked, then glanced down at Maddie's gown. 'But then again, perhaps it's better he wasn't at breakfast, seeing as you're in such a drab outfit.'

'If you'll excuse me.' The Dowager rose, and so did everyone. 'And we must move along. Ladies, I will see you in the hall at half past nine. Have a good day.'

Miss Merton picked up the stacks of cards the Dowager left behind. 'We should start on these right away, Mrs DeVries. If we do not answer them within the appropriate amount of time, the hostesses might think we are snubbing them.'

'We cannot have that,' Mama agreed.

'Let's head to the Dowager's sitting room then.' With that, the two women left.

'I shall begin my day as well,' Papa announced. 'By the way, Maddie, the architect said they'll be sending over the plans for the new forge on the Thames today.'

Though the DeVrieses had originally planned this sojourn to London to find husbands for Maddie and Caroline, somehow Cornelius had been convinced to open a London branch of his iron furnace to service the joint English railway venture between the owner of Mason

R&L, Arthur Mason, and his new son-in-law, the Duke of Mabury. 'I'll need you to help me look them over.'

'Of course, Papa.'

He nodded his goodbye to both of them before leaving.

'I detest going to the modiste,' Persephone sighed. 'I wish I were looking over plans for a forge, too.'

She smiled at her friend. 'Me, too. But I suppose we must endure this one morning at the dressmaker's. Besides, without Mama there, I might be able to persuade the Dowager that I don't need new gowns.' And certainly not in those dreadful colours.

'Before we go, we should tell Cam what a success his plan is,' Persephone suggested.

'W-what?' The idea of seeing the Earl this morning both thrilled and alarmed her. 'I don't—'

'Come on.' She hooked her hand into the crook of Maddie's elbow and dragged her along. 'I know he's not actually having a meeting. He's in the smoking room, having his morning coffee and reading the paper.' Her mouth twisted. 'He usually loves eating a hearty breakfast. I'm not sure why he'd skip it today to have coffee by himself.'

Maddie knew why, of course.

Their third rule.

He was avoiding her. 'Maybe it's not a good idea to disturb him.'

'Nonsense. He should know all about your suitors. After all, he came up with the plan.' Persephone's grip was surprisingly strong, and soon they were outside the smoking room. 'He's in there,' she said, pulling the door open. 'Go on.'

'What if he's—' She found herself staggering through the doorway, then heard the door slam shut behind her.

She spun around. 'Persephone?' *Did she just toss me in here and then leave?*

'What are you doing here?'

The Earl's familiar voice made her jump. 'Persephone... She said you were in here.' When she turned to face him, emerald-green eyes pinned her to the spot and made it hard to breathe.

'I asked her to meet me here after breakfast. Why are you here? And didn't we discuss this?' He prowled towards her, his long strides making quick work of the distance between them. 'Fourth rule. We cannot be alone.' He stopped halfway as his entire body tensed and his arms stiffened at his sides.

'I know, my lord. But she thought I should come see you first.'

Drat! What was Persephone thinking, running off like that?

'And why is that?'

'To tell you our plan is turning out well.'

'Is it now?' He cocked his head to the side.

'Y-yes.' Why was she acting like a scared mouse? She should be thankful to him. 'It seems I've at least three gentlemen coming to call this week. And it's all thanks to you.'

The Earl's expression remained impassive. 'Congratulations, then.'

'That may be premature,' she said with a forced laugh. 'They're only coming for fifteen minutes of boring conversation in front of a room full of chaperones.'

'Is that what you think this afternoon will be like when I come to pay my call to you, then?'

Oh, dear, had she forgotten her mother had strongarmed him into that? 'I'm so sorry for that, my lord. My mother can be tenacious. A-and we don't have to have our call today. I'm sure if you explain you were busy, she wouldn't mind delaying it.'

'Perhaps I will.'

The way he said it so casually made her chest tighten. 'We're agreed, then.'

'I can ask Persephone to relay the message of regret to your mama.'

'That would be wise.' Mama would have a conniption, but they had no choice.

'Then I will see you at our next dance.'

The words made her stomach—and other regions below that—flutter. 'I, uh, I should… I will definitely…' Flustered, she didn't bother completing the sentence and spun around, pushing on the door before scurrying out. She was so occupied with trying to get away from him that she didn't realise there was someone else coming down the opposite way.

'Maddie?'

Maddie jumped back before she crashed into the Dowager. 'Y-Your Grace.'

'Are you quite all right?' Knowing dark eyes peered at her. 'You look flushed.'

'I am fine, ma'am. If you'll excuse me, I need to dress for our outing.' After a quick curtsey, she slid past her and raced up to her room, then rang for her maid.

As Betsy helped her change, Maddie tried to focus on anything except the Earl. But of course, her mind kept wandering to him as it always did.

I will see you at our next dance.

Her heart hammered and her insides turned to the consistency of molten iron fresh from the furnace. But why did he affect her so?

This whole thing was a farce. A sham. A trick they

were playing on the aristocracy. He did not actually want to dance with her.

None of it was real.

'Miss? You're all ready.'

'Thank you, Betsy.'

Creeping out of her room, Maddie proceeded downstairs, praying that she wouldn't encounter the Earl. Lord, how was she to face him after this morning? *I shouldn't have run away.* She should have nodded coolly, then turned and left with her head held high. Or she could have laughed and said something witty.

By the time she reached the foyer, Persephone and the Dowager were already waiting for her. Her Grace's gaze narrowed at her, but she didn't say anything and nodded to Eames, who held the door open for them.

The Dowager's carriage took them to Bond Street to Mrs Helena Ellesmore's dress shop. She was the best dressmaker in London, and all the mamas and debutantes of the season clamoured to get an appointment with her and thus booked weeks in advance—except for the Dowager Duchess of Mabury, of course. The modiste had made Kate's wedding gown and trousseau when she'd married the Dowager's son, for which she'd not only charged an exorbitant amount because it had all had to be done in a month, but also received increased fame among the ton. It was no wonder that she would clear her schedule for her most important client.

'Welcome, Your Grace.' Mrs Ellesmore curtseyed low as they alighted from the carriage. 'Miss DeVries. How lovely to see you again.'

'Good morning, Mrs Ellesmore,' the Dowager began. 'This is Lady Persephone MacGregor.'

'An honour to meet you, my lady.' She eyed Persephone, perhaps assessing if she was to be another client she could add to her roster.

The Dowager gestured towards the shop. 'Let's go inside, shall we?'

'Now,' the seamstress asked as she led them into her shop. 'I've cancelled my appointments for the next few hours as per your request, Your Grace. How can I help you?'

'It's not me you can help.' She turned to Maddie. 'But, rather, Miss DeVries. She needs some new gowns.'

'Please, Your Grace, Mrs Ellesmore, if I may be, er, frank, I don't really need any new gowns. My mother insisted, but I do have a fair number I have yet to wear.'

'None that you would want to wear,' Persephone interjected. 'You hate those gowns. I can see how miserable you are when you wear them.'

'I— I don't… I mean, I wasn't…' She sent Mrs Ellesmore an apologetic look. 'I'm so sorry. They are very well made.' Too well made, in fact, as no matter how hard she tried, she couldn't tear or rip any of them as an excuse not to wear them.

To Maddie's surprise, the seamstress let out a chuckle. 'Oh, my dear, I'm glad I'm not the only one who thinks they are awful. Why, I often wonder why your mother chose those ghastly bright colours, as they don't become you.'

Maddie let out a breath of relief. Thank goodness Mrs Ellesmore was not offended. 'But why do you continue to make them for me?'

'Because she and the Dowager are my best clients, and I do what my clients tell me.' She tsked. 'Poor dear. I always felt so sorry for you, especially when she let your sister pick out her own fabrics and gowns.' She looked Maddie up and down. 'I've so many ideas for you. The

things I could come up with, especially with your co-
louring and height. No man would be able to turn away
from you.'

'Mrs Ellesmore, now's your chance,' the Dowager declared with a beaming smile. 'Mrs DeVries is occupied
for the day, so you may do as you wish.'

'Do as you wish?' Maddie echoed.

The Dowager continued, 'If Mrs DeVries complains,
I shall tell her everything was my idea and you may send
me the bill instead.'

Mrs Ellesmore clapped her hands together. 'Wonderful.' She dragged Maddie to the dais in the corner of the
room before she could protest. 'My mind is swirling with
ideas... Blue will suit you because of your eyes. With the
right shade, we can even make them appear violet. And
your neckline! Low, to expose your décolletage and long
neck. You will look graceful as a swan.' She rounded the
dais, muttering to herself. 'Four—no, five gowns. And
one ball gown, at least.'

'Is there any way we can have at least one ready for
tomorrow?' the Dowager asked. 'The Countess of Houghton is hosting her garden party in the afternoon.'

'Hmm, I might have something that would suit her that
is ready. Thank goodness I haven't cut the hem yet. But
Your Grace, Lady Danville will be most disappointed...'

'I'm sure you can find a way to appease her. Why
not give her a discount on her next gown, and whatever
the difference, consider it a rush fee for Miss DeVries's
dresses?'

'A generous and kind offer. I'll fetch the dress and
have Miss DeVries try it on immediately.' She hurried
away into the other room.

Maddie fiddled her fingers together. 'Your Grace, it's
not that I'm not grateful... But you don't have to do this

for me. And even if Mama does complain, I'm sure I can convince Papa to pay for the dress.'

'Maddie, please allow me to do this.' The Dowager smiled weakly at her. 'I must confess, I share Mrs Ellesmore's opinion, but I did not want to say anything to your mother for fear of offending her.'

She doubted her Grace could offend Mama; if the Dowager told her to dance the jig in the middle of Covent Garden, Eliza would do it to keep their sponsor happy if only to keep their family circulating within the upper social circles of the ton.

'But then, I thought perhaps if I could...remove her influence for a few hours, I could help your wardrobe. The colours and styles she chooses do you no favour.'

'She thinks those colours and styles give me a more "delicate" look.' Maddie's shoulders slumped. 'And distract from my flaws.'

Persephone guffawed. 'That is one way to state it.'

'Flaws?' The Dowager shook her head. 'My dear, your height and figure are nothing to hide. I believe with the right gown you will be stunning.'

'You are too kind, Your Grace.'

'One more thing.' The Dowager glanced around, looking over at Persephone, who was occupied with examining a dress form on the other side of the room. 'I do not mean to pry, but you should know that after I ran into you in the hallway, I saw the Earl leaving the smoking room.'

Oh, Lord.

Her heart thudded in her chest. Maddie was, unfortunately, a terrible liar. Besides, how could she lie to this woman who'd opened up her home to them and so obviously cared for her well-being? 'Nothing happened, Your Grace.'

'The Earl is the son of my good friend, and knowing Elaine, she raised her children properly. But I'm not blind, nor will I turn a blind eye if he's somehow taking advantage of you.'

It took all of Maddie's might to suppress the urge to laugh at the ludicrous notion. The Earl taking advantage of her? If anything, she was the one exploiting him.

'He has not said or done anything to offend you?'

'I assure you, Your Grace, he's been a perfect gentleman.'

'Here we are.' Mrs Ellesmore returned, followed by a young woman who carried a pale peach gown. 'Gertie, please help Miss DeVries into the dress.' Gertie walked over to Maddie, then drew the curtain around them so she could undress her and assist her. Once she was laced up, Gertie pulled the curtain away.

'How lovely you look,' the Dowager exclaimed.

'Now, that suits you much better than chartreuse,' Persephone added.

Turning to face the mirror behind, Maddie couldn't help but gasp when she saw her reflection. The understated colours were muted further with a layer of delicate lace on top, and the only adornment on the dress was the cluster of white and peach roses on the neckline, which exposed her neck and upper chest.

'See?' Mrs Ellesmore said smugly. 'The right colour and cut only enhances your beauty and height. You are like a towering goddess from Mount Olympus.'

An anxious thought surfaced in her mind. 'Mama would never let me wear this to the garden party, would she?'

The Dowager clucked her tongue. 'Do not worry about your mama, dear. I will take care of her.'

'And I will not breathe a word, either,' Mrs Ellesmore promised. 'Now, how about—' She covered her mouth with her hands. 'Wait here. I have something special I've been saving in the other room. Gertie, please retrieve the new fabric that was delivered this morning.'

The young woman scurried off, then returned, carrying a bolt of fabric. It was an unusual shade of blue that shimmered under the light.

'Isn't it beautiful?' Mrs Ellesmore caught the loose end of the fabric and waved it with a flourish. 'And see how light it is? It will make you look as if you are flying when you dance the waltz.'

The Dowager's dark eyes widened. 'Mrs Ellesmore, you truly are a genius. That colour would look absolutely striking on her.'

Mama would never approve of it, Maddie thought. The fabric was too rich and bold. If Caroline were here, she would insist on buying the entire bolt to prevent anyone else from having it. *But neither of them were here now.*

'I must make you a gown with it. I insist,' Mrs Ellesmore said firmly. 'When is your next ball?'

'In three days' time. The Baybrook ball,' the Dowager answered. 'Can you have it ready by then?'

'For you? Of course, Your Grace.'

Maddie inhaled a sharp breath, her gaze still fixed on the beautiful fabric. Was this really happening? It was as if she was in some fairy tale and she had not one but two magical godmothers. 'How can I ever thank you?'

Mrs Ellesmore laughed. 'There is one thing you could do—never wear those awful gowns again.'

Chapter Seven

'My lord?' George Atwell cleared his throat. 'Should I repeat those figures for you?'

Cam gripped the arms of the leather chair tightly. Ever since their encounter this morning, he could scarcely think of anything else but Maddie. He'd been caught by surprise when she'd come to him, and even more by her news.

Our plan is turning out well.

Bloody hell.

'Er, yes. Or, better yet, just write them down and I shall examine them later.'

Since Cam was also in London for Glenbaire business, the Dowager was kind enough to offer the smoking room in Mabury Hall as his temporary office. Cam was glad for the distraction of his work and that Atwell had arrived soon after Maddie had run off, which prevented him from doing something foolish.

Like chasing after her.

'There's one more thing we need to discuss before I go, my lord. The gentlemen's club whose owner insisted on meeting you.'

'Ah, yes. The Underworld.' Actually, the club's name

was legally Hale's, but everyone called it The Underworld. 'Do we have a place and time for this meeting?'

'No, but a boy from the club came to my office and gave me this.' Atwell retrieved a black calling card from the breast pocket of his vest. 'He said to put it directly in your hands.'

Cam took it and held it up to the light. There was no writing on the card, except for an embossed gold stamp of what appeared to be a coin. *Charon's Obol.* 'I'm guessing this is payment for the ferryman.'

'I beg your pardon, my lord?'

'It's nothing.' He tucked the card into his pocket. 'I'll take care of it.'

'If that is all, my lord, I must be off.' Atwell began to put away the papers and envelopes strewn about on the desk into his leather satchel. 'I'll be sure to post these letters for you right away. I shall see myself out.'

'Thank you, Atwell.'

Alone once again, the silence inside the room deafened Cam's ears. The door that led outside and connected to the rest of the house seemed far away. Or perhaps he was just too much of a coward to go out there where he could run into Maddie again.

I am a grown man, he scoffed to himself. *And she is just a silly girl.*

Yes, that's what Maddie was.

Just a silly girl, who wanted to fulfil her dream of finding a husband and raising a passel of children.

Nothing more.

Bolting from the chair, Cam marched out of the smoking room with a determined stride. It was half past two, and the house was unusually quiet. According to Murray, Persephone had left to accompany the Dowager and Maddie on an errand sometime after breakfast.

He puffed out an exasperated breath. *Persephone*. She was really the only female he should be worrying about. Maddie had distracted him from his real purpose in coming to London.

Once Persephone returns from her outing, I'll sit her down to talk and get to the bottom of her disappearing acts.

While he would never push her to choose a husband, she still needed to mingle among society so she could gain some maturity and lose some of her awkwardness.

Cam had been so distracted by his thoughts of the past that he must have taken a wrong turn. He'd meant to go back to his rooms but was now outside the library instead. The last time he'd been there, he'd wanted to borrow a book but had got distracted by Maddie.

Perhaps this time he could peruse the shelves in peace. However, when he heard muffled voices coming from the inside, he halted. Carefully, he opened the door a crack.

'I do like how they've expanded this west-facing wall. I wasn't satisfied with the first version and....'

Cam recognised the speaker as Cornelius DeVries, so he entered, thinking it was safe.

How wrong he was.

'But what about the space between the two furnaces and the stove?'

His heart jumped at the sound of Maddie's soft voice. *I should get out of here.*

But as always, when she was around, he was like a moth to a flame, and his feet would not move.

'What about them?' Cornelius asked.

'The furnaces are too far from the stove, which means we'll have to make the pipes longer,' she continued. 'We'll lose heat, especially since London has cooler temperatures throughout the year than Pennsylvania.'

'What—oh, yes, yes. Thank you, dear. I didn't think of that.'

What in the world was going on?

Curious, Cam crept closer. A bust of Aristotle sitting on top of a column blocked his view of her, so he peered around the marble figure.

Cornelius and Maddie were bent over one of the large tables in the middle of the room, poring over large sheets of paper spread out on the surface. Wanting to see what they were examining, he inched closer, gripping Aristotle's head for support. Unfortunately, the great philosopher wasn't affixed to the column as firmly as he'd thought, and it slipped from the pedestal, the weighty effigy crashing to the ground and rolling across the floor.

Hellfire!

Mercifully, the bust remained intact, but now two sets of sky blue eyes fixed on him as father and daughter lifted their heads towards him.

'Er…good afternoon, Mr DeVries.' Colour heightened Maddie's complexion in the most adorable way. 'Miss DeVries.'

'Lord Balfour, how nice to see you.' Cornelius glanced at the clock. 'Mercy me, you're supposed to call on my daughter this afternoon. Did I get the time wrong?'

Cam cursed silently. He was supposed to ask Persephone to relay his regrets to Mrs DeVries, but he wasn't sure if she'd arrived.

'The Earl decided to cancel,' Maddie explained. 'Persephone told me and I was just about to tell Mama after we finished here. He had, uh, a prior appointment at half past three.'

'An urgent business matter, I'm afraid,' Cam added. 'My sincerest apologies to you and your wife.'

'Oh, dear, your mother will be disappointed.' Cornelius's brows drew together. 'Well…do you have fifteen minutes now? You could join us.' He gestured to the other side of the table.

Maddie shook her head. 'Papa, this isn't how it's done.'

'Isn't it? Fifteen minutes of conversation in a room with a chaperone? I'm your father. I don't think there is a more appropriate guardian for your virtue than me,' he said with a chuckle. 'My lord? What do you say?'

What could he say? 'If you approve, then I have no objections.'

Cam already knew this was a mistake, but as was the case when it involved Miss Madeline DeVries, he might as well toss that mistake over his shoulder and add it to the growing pile behind him. Besides, his curiosity was already stoked given what he'd overheard. Clasping his hands behind him, he strode over to them.

'What would you like to discuss, my lord? The weather?'

'It seems I was interrupting you, Mr DeVries.' He nodded at the papers on the table. 'Perhaps you should finish your discussion with Miss DeVries first? Again, my apologies for the intrusion.'

Or, rather, being caught spying on you and your daughter.

'Not at all, my lord. Actually, it's a good thing you did arrive, as Maddie and I often get caught up whenever we discuss business and end up losing track of time.'

'Business?' He couldn't help but glance over at Maddie, who was staring at the floor as if she suddenly found her shoes interesting. 'You discuss your business with Miss DeVries?'

'Of course,' he said matter-of-factly. 'She's been by my side at the furnace since she was in pigtails. I've taught her everything she knows. One day she may even take over for me.'

Take over?

'Anyway, my dear,' Cornelius said, turning back to Maddie. 'You were pointing to the river before His Lordship arrived. Did you have a problem with the site?'

Maddie hesitated. 'Perhaps now is not the time—'

'Please.' Cam waved a hand. 'Do not mind me. I can wait.' And, only the heavens knew why, he wanted to hear Maddie talk more about furnaces and stoves.

She pursed her plump pink lips. 'They're building too close to the edge of the river.' A finger tapped on the drawing—which looked like building plans—on the table. 'We must consider soil erosion in the next few decades, or else our furnace may someday end up in the Thames.'

'Doesn't erosion take millions of years?' Cam interrupted. 'It doesn't sound like that's something you have to worry about now.'

'Normally, yes.' Maddie traced her fingers along the wavy line that was meant to represent the riverbank. 'However, any type of waterway that has a large volume of traffic will likely erode faster. We have three rivers back in Pittsburgh, and though we cannot see the effects of commerce and increased traffic yet, I cannot help but think this progress has a price.'

'We must be ready.' Cornelius's voice took on a serious tone. 'As I always say, if you fail to prepare—'

'—then prepare to fail,' Maddie finished with a grin.

Cornelius beamed at his daughter, the pride in his eyes evident.

And Cam didn't blame him, because right now, he, too, felt all sorts of emotions for the woman standing before him. Most of them he couldn't say in polite company.

Maddie didn't seem to notice the change in Cam's

countenance or how his entire body tensed as she continued on. They seemingly spoke an entirely different language as they launched into some kind of debate. Words Cam had never heard before were thrown about, like *ash content* and *carbon oxide*. As he watched her, one thought popped into his head.

Yes, please. Tell me more about carbon and coke.

He wanted to hear what she had to say about erosion and piping.

Perhaps while he was unrolling one of her silk stockings and—

'You look like you're lost in thought,' Cornelius said. 'Or are we boring you to death? What's on your mind, my lord?'

Cam nearly choked at the thought of revealing to the man what was currently occupying his thoughts. 'I… uh… No, please. I am not bored at all. I'm quite fascinated by your spirited discussion. In fact, it reminds me of the time when my father was alive and my brothers and I would talk business.'

'Ah, your whisky business.' Cornelius stroked his chin. 'I'm afraid I don't know anything about whisky. You and your brothers must know everything about production, then, if you learned from your father.'

'From growing the crops all the way to bottling,' he said proudly. 'Learned everything from Da, and he learned it from his father. The knowledge has been passed on from father to son for generations.'

'Isn't Lady Persephone part of the business too?' Maddie piped in.

Now Cornelius looked intrigued. 'Tell us more.'

'There isn't much to tell, really,' he said with a shrug. 'When Ma and Da died, we all felt…lost. Most of the responsibilities of the distillery and the tenants and lands of the Earldom had fallen on my shoulders. My younger brothers, therefore, took on the rest, including raising Persephone, who was only thirteen at the time. Lachlan, Finley, and Liam, bless their hearts, had stepped up in caring for her.' He chewed on his lip. 'Though looking back, I'm not sure that was good idea.'

'And why not?' Cornelius asked.

'Lachlan and Finley had been working on the production side of Glenbaire, while Liam was a genius when it came to developing and refining distilling techniques, as well as blending and growing crops. Thus, Persephone had practically grown up in the distillery, following us around and soaking up every bit of knowledge she could. By the time she was fifteen, she could change a faulty discharge line and regulate a pot still's temperature by looking at the foam through the sight glass.' She had obviously inherited her intelligence from their mother, who Cam suspected had been somewhat of a bluestocking. *Your ma's the smart one, boy*, Da had always said.

'Why, that's wonderful!' Cornelius exclaimed. Maddie, meanwhile, gave him the oddest look.

'But now, I wonder if I'd done Persephone a disservice by letting her run wild in the distillery.' He winced. 'She is…very different from what a lady should be, and my ma might not be happy with me for how she turned out.'

Cornelius harrumphed. 'Nonsense. It's in her blood as much as it is in yours. Just like my Mad—'

Bong! Bong! Bong!

'Oh, dear!' Cornelius exclaimed as the clock struck the hour. 'My lord, it looks like we've wasted your allotted fifteen minutes. Forgive me.'

'Do not trouble yourself, Mr DeVries. I'll pay Miss DeVries a call at another time.'

What was a good day to arouse himself so thoroughly to the point of pain, Wednesday or Friday?

'I'll tell Mrs DeVries. She'll be thrilled.'

'If you excuse me, I'm late for my appointment.' He gave Maddie a quick glance—any more and he might embarrass himself. Thank God Murray had selected a long frock coat for him to wear this morning that covered his nether regions.

Swiftly, he turned around and marched out of the library, counting each step until he was safely outside. He expelled the breath he'd been holding with a loud huff.

Silly girl, my arse.

Who was that woman in there? How had he not known this side of Maddie existed? He'd been so spellbound by his initial attraction to her that he'd never bothered to find out more about her. She was not only so damned beautiful, but now he'd discovered her to be brilliant as well.

And since when had he ever found intellect arousing?

He groaned. As if he wasn't already captivated by her, he now also had to deal with full-blown lust.

This was precisely the reason why he tried to stay away from her and build up sky-high walls around himself to keep her out.

Focus on her flaws, he urged himself.

What flaws?

Not even her hideous outfits could deter her appeal. That particular shade of green she'd worn last night reminded him of the regurgitated contents of his stomach after a night of drinking back when he was younger and couldn't hold his liquor. Then there were those ridiculous hairstyles that made her look like a child's porcelain doll.

Yes, think of that. Vomit and children's toys. If he could focus on those aspects, perhaps he'd finally succeed in ridding himself of this infernal obsession with Miss Madeline DeVries.

Chapter Eight

Maddie wrung her hands together as Betsy put on the final touches on her hair. 'Are you sure it looks all right?'

The maid grinned at her. 'You look beautiful, Miss Maddie.'

Instead of the usual torture with the curling tongs, to-night Betsy had pinned up her locks into elaborate curls around her head. Then, she'd added small pins decorated with silk roses to match the ones on her dress.

'Thank you so much, Betsy. I know you're disobeying Mama's orders and risking your job over a silly hairstyle.'

'Think nothing of it, Miss.' Betsy's face turned sour. 'If I may speak frankly, I always hated those outdated styles Mrs DeVries had me do for you. Your hair's so beautiful, and I've been wantin' to do something more to yer likin' but I've been afraid of yer ma. But Her Grace said if I got in trouble, she'd hire me or find me a position somewhere else.'

It seemed the Dowager had thought of everything. Indeed, she'd even come up with a plan to ensure Mama didn't see her until it was too late. Right before their set time to leave for the Houghton garden party, the Dowager would make an excuse to delay her departure, and

Persephone—who had heartily agreed to participate—would invite Mama, Papa, and Caroline to ride in their carriage. Meanwhile, Maddie and Miss Merton would offer to stay behind to accompany the Dowager. Once Mama was safely out of the house, Maddie would change into her new gown.

'Are you ready, miss?'

'I suppose.' Maddie accepted the matching reticule Betsy handed her and offered her thanks once again before heading downstairs.

'Madeline, I hardly recognised you!' Miss Merton exclaimed when she saw Maddie coming down the stairs. 'That dress is gorgeous—and so are you.'

'Thank you, Miss Merton.' She turned to the Dowager, who beamed at her. 'Do I look all right?'

'I concur with Miss Merton—you do, indeed, look gorgeous. Now, let's run along.'

The Earl and Countess of Houghton lived in a grand home in Hanover Square. The butler welcomed them inside, and then they were ushered out to the magnificent gardens. There was no doubt that Houghton House had one of the largest and most beautiful gardens in London, a fact that the Earl never made anyone forget. It had a wide array of plants and flowers, but its crowning glory was the white marble fountain in the middle. Guests were scattered about, admiring the garden's lovely flora or chatting and socialising in small groups as liveried footmen roamed about, offering tasty morsels of food and glasses of champagne.

Maddie glanced around nervously, wondering where her mother was as the Dowager led them towards their hostess.

'Lady Houghton, thank you for the invitation.'

The Countess of Houghton curtseyed. 'Welcome to

Houghton House, Your Grace. I'm so thrilled you are here. I have not seen you since the Duke's wedding.'

'I wouldn't miss it for the world, Lady Houghton. The gardens are looking especially lovely this year. You must be so proud.'

'Oh, I am, Your Grace.'

'You remember my guests?'

'Why, yes, of course.' The Countess nodded at Miss Merton in greeting. 'Miss Merton.' She turned to Maddie, head craning back. 'And… Miss…?'

'DeVries, Your Ladyship. Madeline DeVries.'

'W-why, you're… I didn't…' she spluttered. 'Why, I hardly recognised you, Miss Madeline.'

Probably because you didn't spot me from a mile away in my hideous dress, Maddie thought wryly.

'It's wondrous how a new gown can truly transform a woman, isn't it?' the Dowager commented. 'Mrs Ellesmore is a genius when it comes to cuts and selection of fabrics.'

'She's as pretty as a peach.'

'Indeed,' Miss Merton agreed. 'If you don't mind my saying, Lady Houghton, your roses have fierce competition this afternoon.'

'Your Grace, you've arrived!'

Oh, no.

Mama.

Her mood plummeted like a rock kicked over the side of a cliff. Sure enough, Mama was fast approaching, Papa and Caroline trailing closely behind.

'Have you seen Maddie?' Mama asked.

'Eliza, dear.' Papa struggled to keep a straight face. 'Maddie is right here.'

'What?' Mama placed a hand on her heart as pure

shock registered on her face. 'Madeline, what are you wearing?'

Maddie opened her mouth, but the Dowager managed to speak first. 'I'm afraid it's all my fault, Mrs DeVries. I spilled some ink on poor Maddie's dress and there was nothing clean for her to change into. Thankfully, I had this old dress in the closet. We only had to let out the hem a few inches. My deepest apologies for ruining Maddie's gown with my carelessness, Mrs DeVries. But I think she looks beautiful in this one,' the Dowager said. 'Don't you agree? Like a spring goddess.'

'You're too kind, Your Grace.' Mama's cheeks puffed up. 'And do not fret over the ink. Accidents happen, right?'

'Yes. Happy accidents.' The Dowager flashed Maddie a grin.

'If you'll excuse me,' Caroline interjected with a sneer. 'I'm feeling rather faint. I think I shall take a rest in the retiring rooms.' She marched off without another word.

The Dowager cleared her throat delicately. 'Now, Lady Houghton, I don't want to monopolise all your time, especially with so many guests here. Would you excuse us? I would like to introduce the DeVrieses to a few more acquaintances.'

'By all means, Your Grace.'

'I think we may have a new sensation of the season,' Miss Merton stage-whispered to Maddie as they followed behind the Dowager. 'They say a late-blooming flower is the prettiest.'

'Whatever do you mean, Miss Merton?'

A twinkle appeared in her companion's eye. 'You, my dear.' She gripped Maddie's hand. 'Everyone is looking at you. I predict you're going to be a sensation for the rest of the season.'

Despite feeling the stares on her, Maddie didn't want to raise her hopes. 'I think you overestimate this dress, Miss Merton.'

'We'll see.'

'Your Grace, Miss Merton,' the older gentleman who approached them greeted them as he bowed low. 'Pardon the intrusion, but I had to come over and pay my respects.'

'Sir Allendale,' the Dowager greeted. 'How lovely to see you in town. How is your son, Walter?'

'He's doing well, thank you. Just finished his last year at Eton. In fact that's why I came over.' Lord Allendale signalled to someone behind them. 'Here he is. My pride and joy, Walter.'

A young man, tall and reed-thin with a mop of unruly blond hair, hurried over. 'Y-Your Grace.'

Sir Allendale touched his shoulder. 'He begged me to be introduced to you and your, uh, lovely guests.'

'*Father.*' Walter's face was completely scarlet as he glanced down at the ground, but not before his eyes flickered to Maddie.

'I would be glad to make the introductions,' the Dowager said. 'Sir Allendale, Mr Allendale, you already know Miss Merton, but this is Mr Cornelius DeVries, Mrs DeVries and their daughter, Miss Madeline DeVries. This is Sir Wilbur Allendale and his son, Mr Walter Allendale.'

'A pleasure,' Sir Allendale greeted them, then nudged his son forward with an encouraging pat on the back.

'Honoured—' Walter cleared his throat as the word came out like a squeak. 'Honoured to make your acquaintance, Mr and Mrs DeVries. Miss M-Madeline.' He turned even redder.

They exchanged a few more pleasantries for a few

minutes—except for Walter, who remained mute—until the Dowager declared she *had* to say hello to another friend over by the buffet table.

'We hope to see you again, Your Grace.' Sir Allendale bowed. 'And your guests.'

'That would be lovely.'

As they walked away, Maddie's ear caught the older Allendale scoff at his son, '…you wanted the introduction. Why did you just stare at her like a ninny?'

'I tried, Papa, but my tongue would not untangle itself, and then I forgot to breathe…'

'This is the masquerade ball over again,' the old man moaned.

Miss Merton, who obviously heard the exchange as well, let out a giggle. 'Poor boy. He's painfully shy, you know. Lost his mother at a young age, and so his father dotes on him.' She tsked. 'He's a bit young, but he's a good prospect.'

'Prospect for what?' Maddie asked.

'For marriage.' Her companion chuckled. 'I think the lad's halfway in love with you.'

'M-me? But he hardly spoke a word. Couldn't even look at me.'

'Last year, it was rumoured he was deeply enamoured with Miss Georgina Miller. He was so nervous, he passed out while dancing with her at the Earl of Crainbourne's masquerade ball.' Miss Merton's eyes narrowed thoughtfully. 'On second thought, you wouldn't want a fiancé who keeled over each time he saw you. I think Mr Allendale is like young wine—he could do with a few more years of maturing.' That twinkle in her eyes returned as she smiled wryly at Maddie. 'But I suspect you may soon have your choice of vintage.'

Maddie was sceptical of Miss Merton's words—except that they had yet to reach their destination and already two acquaintances of the Dowager's had requested an introduction to them.

'See?' Miss Merton said. 'I told you.'

'Lord Lambert is old enough to be my father,' Maddie pointed out. 'Perhaps he merely wanted to make his acquaintance with Papa since there are few gentlemen of his age here.'

'Pish-posh, dear. Just enjoy the attention.' Miss Merton handed her a glass of chilled lemonade as they had finally reached the refreshment table.

'Your Grace. Mr DeVries. Mrs DeVries.' It was Lady Houghton once again, but this time, she was not alone. She came with a young gentleman in tow. 'Forgive the intrusion.'

'Not at all,' Papa said. 'We are always happy to see our generous hostess. You honour us with your attention.'

The countess smiled. 'Excellent. I was making the rounds when I realised I was remiss in not making an introduction. Your Grace, may I present my nephew, Desmond, Viscount Palmer, who also happens to be co-hosting this party with me since the Earl is indisposed at our Hampshire estate.'

The young man stepped forward and bowed deeply. 'Your Grace.'

'And this is Miss Harriet Merton, Mr and Mrs Cornelius DeVries, and their daughter, Miss Madeline, from America.'

'Lovely to meet you,' Viscount Palmer said, his cool blue eyes regarding everyone.

'You have such a dashing nephew,' Mama commented. 'Why have we never seen you until now? Your aunt has been to most of the events of the season, and we were here for her ball a few months ago.'

'I'm afraid my father has been ill, and I've been watching over him,' Palmer replied. 'The Earl has been languishing for some time, so I haven't been to town at all.'

'I'm so dreadfully sorry to hear that,' the Dowager said. 'Please relay my regards next time you see him, and I wish him well.'

'What a wonderful son you are,' Mama exclaimed. 'Does your Viscountess not mind being in the country during the season?'

'I'm afraid I've not been blessed with a wife, Mrs DeVries.'

Mama looked to Maddie conspiratorially. 'Interesting.'

Maddie kept her lips pressed tight but groaned inwardly.

'I do hope we see more of you,' Mama continued. 'Will you be at the Baybrook ball?'

'I plan to be, unless I am called back to Chester Manor.'

'So will we. With Maddie, of course.'

Cool blue eyes turned to Maddie. 'Perhaps Miss Madeline can save space on her dance card for me.'

'She will,' Mama answered.

'I look forward to it. If you'll excuse me,' the Viscount began. 'I believe I see some old friends arriving. I should welcome them. Your Grace.' He bowed to the Dowager and nodded to the rest of them before striding away.

Miss Merton sent her a knowing grin and mouthed, *See?*

Maddie smiled back. Viscount Palmer initially seemed cold, but she had to admit there was something about his aloofness that piqued her curiosity.

Perhaps this dress had some kind of magic.

Because for the first time in her life, Maddie felt like

she was being seen. Not stared or gawked or gaped at. But people were truly looking at her with interest.

'I shall see to my guests as well. Do enjoy yourselves. We have games out on the lawn, if you are so inclined, and other amusements inside the house, including a quartet playing in the music room.' She curtseyed to the Dowager before she, too, headed off.

'Oh, Maddie.' Mama looked ready to burst, her cheeks pink and puffy. 'I wasn't keen on garden parties—after all, who would want to stand under the sun all afternoon? But I have a very good feeling you may meet more eligible lords here. If only there were dancing, then it would be acceptable for them to call on you. Oh, and that Viscount Palmer! He's so handsome, and the heir to an Earldom.'

Maddie's eyes slid heavenwards. Mama was probably already planning what to wear to the old Earl's funeral.

'Aren't you glad I convinced you to come, dear?' Papa said to Mama, and Maddie gave him a smile of thanks for changing the subject.

'Yes, and I almost forgive you for leaving me out of the Earl's call to Maddie yesterday.'

Blood rushed to Maddie's ears at the reminder. She'd been so caught up in the plan to conceal her new gown from Mama that she'd nearly forgotten about the Earl. She took a generous sip of the lemonade, though it did nothing to cool the embarrassment rising up her neck. Oh, why did he even come into the library yesterday?

Though Maddie had heard some of the story from Persephone, she didn't know Cam's perspective. *Oh, Cam.* He had to shoulder all that responsibility, not to mention take care of his brothers and sister. How could he even think he did Persephone a disservice when she'd obviously grown up to be an intelligent and kind person, worth ten times any other debutante she'd met? She couldn't help but admire him.

Oh, stop!

They were supposed to pretend to court, but somehow they'd once again broken one of the rules of their scheme.

The Earl was being polite, she reasoned. And it was her father who had asked him to stay.

Besides, it had been an excellent way to maintain their deception, though her stomach soured at the thought that her father had to be involved in their deceit, even if it was unwittingly so. But then the Earl had left so abruptly, as if he could not stand to be with her another minute.

Do not think about him.

But it was no use. He was like a tune or an idea buried in her head. The moment she started thinking of him, she could not stop.

Think of something else. Anything. Something completely unrelated to the Earl.

So, she began reciting Steno's principles to herself.

The Principle of Superposition. Principle of Initial Horizontality. Principle of Strata Continuity. Law of Constancy of Interfacial Angles.

The Earl's handsome face and all its angles came to her mind. Would he like this dress she was wearing?

Drat.

Maybe thinking of Steno was too ambitious. Maybe she needed something more Earl-adjacent.

How about Persephone?

Maddie frowned. Her friend was nowhere in sight. *Again.* But where could she be hiding? And why? There was no dancing here, after all. 'Has anyone seen Lady Persephone?'

Mama shrugged. 'She hurried off as soon as we arrived. Who knows where she could be by now?'

Handing her empty glass to a waiting footman, she announced, 'I'll go search for her, then. She might have got lost.' Unfortunately, with the Houghton gardens being so extensive and having a vast array of greenery and statues to hide behind, locating her friend might be an impossible task.

I'll begin with the hedges.

She headed towards the east side of the garden, entering the first row. Finding it empty, she turned a corner and continue to zigzag her way through the rest of the hedges.

Oh, dear. This will take far too long.

She had to move faster if she wanted to find her friend soon. With a determined snort, she straightened her shoulders and dashed out from the hedges—only to bump into someone walking along the path.

'I beg your pardon!' she exclaimed and staggered back. A pair of strong hands encircled her upper arms, preventing her from completely falling over. 'I—'

'Maddie?'

The low burr never failed to make heat coil in her belly. 'You— I mean, my lord.' *Do not look up. Whatever you do. Do. Not. Look—*

Too late. Maddie found herself mesmerised by emerald-green eyes. 'W-why are you here?'

'I was invited,' he said. 'I came with Persephone and your parents, but it seems my sister has once again disappeared. Have you—' He sucked in a breath. 'What the devil are you wearing?'

'A gown?'

His gaze dropped low, and his eyes reminded Maddie of molten iron. 'That is not green.'

'I beg your pardon?'

'Your gown. What happened to the green one?'

'I don't know.' Perhaps Betsy was burning it in the hearth as they spoke. 'And it was not green, it was chartreuse.' This was a ridiculous conversation—not to mention, they were alone and he was holding her with a familiarity that was unseemly.

Well, it would be unseemly if someone else were around....

Oh, heaven help me.

'My lord, please release me.'

His hands immediately dropped to his sides. 'I was only holding you to prevent you from falling over. And may I remind you, you were the one who jumped out from behind that bush into me.'

She dusted her hands on the delicate lace of her skirts. 'How was I supposed to see you coming around the corner?'

'Does your father know you're wearing that?'

What was with him and the blasted gown? *He probably hates it.* 'Yes, my father does know, thank you very much.'

He gnashed his teeth so hard Maddie could hear them scraping together. 'Well, never wear it again.'

Now, that was taking his hatred of the gown much too far. 'This was a gift from the Dowager, and I will wear it when I please.'

'Not if you want all of London staring at you,' he retorted with another scrutinising look at her neckline.

Shock at his words made her entire body go rigid.

How dare he?

But she would not cry. Not in this dress that made her feel like she was worthy of attention. And certainly not because this boorish oaf implied she was displaying her wares like a seaside doxy. And so, she channelled her emotions elsewhere and allowed anger to rise in her until she was ready to explode. 'You—'

'Miss DeVries, are you lost?' came a cool voice from behind her.

Turning around, she saw Viscount Palmer standing a few feet away from them.

'The gardens have many winding paths.' The Viscount closed the distance between them easily. 'So it's easy to find oneself—' he turned to the Earl '—led astray.'

The Earl's nostrils flared. 'Why, you young pup—'

'My lord,' Maddie interrupted. 'Thank you for finding me. I did get lost.'

'Lord Balfour,' the Viscount acknowledged. 'May I show you the way back to the party, as well?'

'No, thank you,' the Earl said brusquely. 'I'll be finding my own way.'

'As you wish.' Palmer offered her his arm. 'Miss DeVries?'

Maddie didn't dare sneak a glance at the Earl, no matter how much she was tempted. 'Thank you, my lord.' Gingerly, she placed a hand on his arm and allowed him to lead her away, which Maddie was immensely grateful for, because her thoughts were scattered like marbles spilled across the floor. If she'd attempted to walk away on her own, she probably would have wound up in the Thames.

'Here you are.' The Viscount lowered his arm, so Maddie dropped her hand to her side. 'I have delivered you safely back to you parents.'

'Maddie?' Mama's eyes widened.

'My dear, you look flushed.' Papa's brows knitted together. 'Did you find Lady Persephone?'

'I did not.' She forced out a chuckle. 'I got lost instead. But the Viscount found me.'

'Oh, we owe you a great debt,' Mama said dramatically. 'Who knows where she could have ended up?'

'Calm yourself, dear.' Papa patted her hand. 'But thank you, my lord, for assisting my daughter.'

'My pleasure.' He tipped his hat. 'If you'll excuse me, I must return to my duties as host.'

Mama looked ready to faint from happiness. 'I… I…'

'What a polite young man, that Viscount Palmer,' Papa remarked.

Caroline—Maddie had failed to notice she had returned—sniggered. 'He's only a viscount?'

'And an heir to an earldom,' Miss Merton said.

Her sister's lips pulled back tight. 'Aren't you lucky? And this one isn't nose-to-bosom with you.'

The remark about her bosom reminded Maddie of the Earl's words.

The neckline isn't even that low.

Indeed, it was appropriate, especially for a warm day like today. Why he had such a conniption about it, she didn't know.

'He's looking back at you,' Miss Merton whispered.

Maddie tilted her head up, and sure enough, from across the garden, the Viscount caught her gaze. He cocked his head to the side before turning away and continuing to speak with another guest.

'How did the Viscount find you?' Miss Merton enquired. 'I thought you were searching for Lady Persephone?'

'Looking for me? Why?'

Maddie's heart leapt out of her chest as the lady in question appeared from nowhere. 'Dear Lord, you scared me.'

'Scared you?' Persephone tilted her head to the side. 'How did I do that?'

'I thought you were hi—never mind.' *Why didn't you tell me your brother was here?* But Maddie supposed she should have guessed. He always accompanied Persephone to parties. 'So, where have you been?' she asked in a low whisper.

'Hiding where no man would dare come near.' She nodded to the tables and chairs set under a canopy, where a few older women were drinking tea and eating cakes. 'In plain sight, by the ton's most notorious gossips.'

She laughed, her spirits lifting. Despite her close connection to a certain *Man-Who-Must-Not-Be-Thought-Of*, Maddie hoped she and Persephone would remain friends.

Chapter Nine

Cam wondered what the consequences of punching an English viscount in the face would be.

Because whatever they were, it was probably worth it. Especially the face that belonged to that smug, meddling Palmer.

I should not have come here.

As he watched the Viscount disappear around the corner with Maddie, Cam's fury grew. He had thought he'd be safe from his growing lust for Maddie at this garden party; after all, there would be no dancing here. Besides, Persephone had been eager to come, and Cam was happy to indulge his sister. He didn't even mind that the De-Vrieses had ridden with them, as he always found Cornelius's company amiable enough that he could tolerate his wife and younger daughter.

Though arriving together, they'd gone their separate ways as Cornelius had been pulled away by some acquaintances, and Cam had struck up a conversation with the Earl of Kerrigan, whom he had met on his last trip to London. At some point, however, Persephone had slipped away so Cam went in search of her.

Why was it that each time he went in search of his wayward sister, he managed to find Maddie instead?

Mother of mercy, she looked magnificent today. The dress enhanced all her best features—not to mention, the silk flowers on the neckline drew attention to her creamy, rosy skin and elegant neck. All he wanted to do was fix his lips on the spot where her shoulder met her neck, then move lower and lick his tongue under the silky fabric.

Which was why he'd lashed out at her, hoping to push her away.

Maybe I overreacted.

Where the hell was the old MacGregor charm? Once again, not only had he succeeded in insulting her, but this time, he had managed to anger her as well. She'd looked ready to unleash the fires of hell on him.

But more than that, he'd seen something else in her face that had made him feel like the worst cad in existence—hurt. He'd actually wounded her. Now all he wanted to do was get down on his knees and beg for forgiveness. He almost had, until Palmer had interrupted them.

Damned prick.

Earlier, he and Kerrigan had been introduced to Palmer by another mutual acquaintance, as he was apparently taking the place of Houghton as host today. Cam wasn't sure why, but he disliked Palmer from the beginning. He did not miss the Viscount's thinly veiled animosity directed towards them. Was it due to the fact that Cam was Scottish and Kerrigan was Irish?

Watching him walk away with Maddie certainly did not help endear him to Cam. More than that, an uneasy sensation pricked at his gut because he'd pegged Palmer for what he was—rich, titled, connected, and raised in this society that seemed determined to keep upstarts like him and Kerrigan out. A lump grew in his throat as he admitted to himself that Palmer was exactly the kind of husband Maddie was looking for.

Hands clenched into fists at his sides, he marched back towards the middle of the gardens, where the guests were gathered. His eyes searched among the throng and found Persephone with Miss Merton…and Maddie. Even from afar, her loveliness arrested him, making his chest ache fiercely with wanting.

At least that damned Palmer wasn't sniffing about like a dog looking for its next meal.

Cam knew he should go over there and attempt to apologise. But as he saw Maddie laugh at something Persephone said, he froze. He did not want to further cause her pain, so instead, he shoved his hands in his pockets and trudged towards the house. The Houghtons' butler stopped him as he was about to exit.

'Shall I send for your carriage, my lord?'

He shook his head. 'No. But please relay the message to my coachman that he should wait for my sister, Lady Persephone, instead.'

'Of course, my lord.' He frowned. 'Did you want me to call a hackney cab?'

'No, I shall walk.'

Cam didn't wait for the bewildered butler to object as he made a hasty exit out into the stylish streets of Hanover Square. Without a destination in mind, he picked a direction and walked as he attempted to distract himself from further thoughts of a certain maddening American miss. However, all he could think about was the pain he'd caused Maddie. In the previous instance that he'd inadvertently insulted her, she'd forgiven him, but he doubted she would be so easily swayed this time. No, he would have to find another way to tell her how sorry he was.

He continued strolling along the neighbourhood, past the elegant town houses, until he found himself on a busy shopping street. *A gift.* He would find her a gift to mend the rift between them.

An apology gift, he clarified firmly. It would not be a courting gift and, therefore, would not violate any of their rules.

His mind made up, he strolled down the street, searching the various window displays of the shops he passed by.

Milliner. Glove shop. Tailor. Confectioner. Perfumery.

He shook his head mentally. Maddie would not be swayed by such trinkets.

As he continued down the street, his prospects for an apology gift for Maddie dwindled as he reached the less fashionable area of the neighbourhood, with only businesses like grocers and tatters and cobblers. He was about to retreat when the display window of the last establishment he passed by caught his eye. It featured an array of old knick-knacks and bric-a-brac, from raggedy dolls to rusted instruments to old clocks. The faded sign above the window read Carson's Curiosities.

Having no more prospects for a present, Cam pushed the door open, a bell jangling overhead as he entered the threshold.

'Good day, sir,' the white-haired man behind the counter greeted. 'How may I assist you?'

'I'm just browsing.'

'Of course. Please feel free to look around. I'll be here if you need me.'

'Thank you.'

A stuffed falcon on Cam's left watched him with its eerie glass eyes as he walked by, while on his other side, a stack of old books occupied a marble table. He paused to look at the books, thinking of Maddie, but upon further inspection he saw they were in some kind of language he didn't understand, so he moved on, proceeding deeper into the shop.

In the corner, he spied a display case with various objects protected behind the glass. He drew closer to the cabinet, peering through the window at the jumble of items inside. There seemed to be no rhyme or reason to the collection—a pair of scissors, a figurine of a cat, a miniature portrait of a boy and girl—though most of the things he could not even identify. The middle shelf held medical instruments, perhaps, as he saw some ominous-looking tongs that were about the length of his arm, pincers, a file, and a hammer.

'I believe those are blacksmiths' tools.'

Cam's head whipped back to the old man, who had seemingly appeared from nowhere to pop up behind him.

'Pardon me, sir. I didn't want you to get lost back here.' The old man grinned. 'Are you interested in antique tools?'

'I thought they were medical tools. Or torture devices.'

The old man laughed. 'I have some of those, too, from the medieval period. But these—' he gestured to the blacksmith tools '—are only about…oh, two hundred years old. We don't rely on blacksmiths nearly as much today, with those humungous furnaces that produce iron by the ton.'

The mention of furnaces had him thinking of Maddie immediately. 'May I see them please, Mr…?'

'Carson.' He retrieved a key from his pocket, opened the case, then stepped back.

Cam leaned forward and examined the iron tongs, not really sure why he wanted to see them. They were inappropriate gifts for any occasion. He was about to pick up the hammer but paused when he saw the small object next to it.

'Huh.'

It was brass pipe of some sort, about the size of a small spoon but tapered at the end. 'What was this for?'

Carson took the object from the shelf and examined it up close. 'Hmm... It looks to be a blacksmith's blow-pipe, but it's much too small to be part of this set. So, I can't be certain what it is.'

'I may know someone who does.' The pipe was small enough that he could easily conceal it. That, and no one would ever mistake it for a courting gift. 'I'll take it.'

If Mr Carson thought it was strange Cam wanted to buy a spoon, he didn't show it. Instead he happily wrapped up the item and took Cam's money.

Leaving the shop, Cam found himself strolling back up the street, towards Hanover Square, the package wrapped in brown paper in his inner coat pocket. He wasn't certain when he would give it her. Or if he would even get the chance to approach her, given her fury this afternoon. He would stay clear of her for now and pray that the distance would soften her anger.

Avoiding Maddie had been excruciating, but it had to be done. It was especially hard, as she'd had a few gentlemen callers the next day. Cam feared she wouldn't even dance with him now that she had men clamouring for her attention.

'Do you need anything else, milord?' Murray asked as he brushed some lint from Cam's coat.

'No, thank you, Murray.' He nodded at the valet to dismiss him. When he was out the door, Cam retrieved the package wrapped in brown paper from his trunk and slipped it into his coat pocket. He wasn't sure when he'd get a chance to give it to Maddie, but he'd been carrying it around with him, the weight soothing against his chest.

Hurrying downstairs, he cursed softly as he saw everyone was already in the foyer.

'Apologies, everyone, I—'

Good God in Heaven.

Everyone in the room—hell, the room itself—melted away, and his focus pinpointed to Maddie. She was like a shimmering star in her blue dress, eclipsing all other heavenly beings. Silver diamond pins winked in her golden hair, and the low neckline of the dress showed off even more of her rosy complexion, as well as the swell of her generous breasts.

'Cam? Cam!' Persephone tapped him on the shoulder, bringing him out of his reverie. 'We are already late. We should run along.'

He cleared his throat. 'Er, right.' Coming to his senses, he led Persephone outside to their waiting carriage.

'You know what you have to do, right?' Persephone said once they were alone.

'What?'

His sister tsked. 'The first dance. With Maddie.'

How could he forget? 'Of course. I shall whisk her away the moment we arrive.' *Assuming she doesn't cut me directly for implying she was a strumpet.*

'I'm so very glad you're doing this for her, Cam.' She sighed. 'Maddie has such a good heart. She deserves someone who can appreciate what she has to offer. I think she just lacked confidence—and having that dreadful woman for a sister didn't help. Maddie thinks she's lesser and doesn't deserve to be cherished because she doesn't fit the mould of what society dictates is a proper young woman.' Her nose wrinkled. 'But I've seen her slowly gaining that self-confidence, especially after you danced with her. So, thank you for agreeing to dance with her.'

The package wrapped in brown paper weighed heavily against his chest. 'My pleasure,' he bit out.

The rest of the short ride continued in silence, and soon they were alighting out of the carriage and being announced as they entered the Duke of Baybrook's sumptuous town house on Upper Brook Street.

'Cameron, Earl of Balfour! Lady Persephone Mac-Gregor!'

Persephone tugged at his arm and they made their way across the room to where the DeVrieses were sitting. She sat on the empty chair next to Maddie, who was so deep in conversation with Miss Merton that she didn't notice them approach.

'Maddie!' she hissed, and then jabbed her in the back.

Maddie yelped and shot to her feet. 'What in heaven's— Persephone?'

His sister nudged him with her foot, then cocked her head to Maddie.

'Miss Madeline,' he began. 'May I have this dance?'

Unfortunately—or fortunately for Cam—everyone in the immediate vicinity had their attention on them. Though Maddie hesitated, she eventually acknowledged Cam. 'I would love to, my lord.'

Cam took the hand she offered and led her to the middle of the ballroom floor. He could scarcely breathe with her so close. 'You look lovely, Miss DeVries.'

She nodded politely but did not look him straight in the eye. In fact, throughout the dance, it was as if she did everything she could to look everywhere except at him. Though her head tilted to him, her eyes focused behind him, or on his forehead. The cool politeness she exuded made his gut twist. He almost preferred the rage she'd nearly shown at the Houghton garden party.

When the dance ended, Maddie rushed through her curtsey, her pretty lips twisting impatiently. Cam was tempted to delay her, but seeing as the other dancers were leaving the floor, he dutifully escorted her back to Miss Merton. Sure enough, there was already a gentleman waiting for Maddie.

'Miss DeVries, may I have this dance?' the man asked, his gaze drifting down to her chest briefly.

Maddie smiled at him. 'Of course, Mr Davenport.'

Damn it all to hell.

Cam's throat tightened as if he'd swallowed nails as he watched Maddie being led away by another man. But what was he supposed to do? Their one dance of the evening was done, a rule he'd insisted on.

He was about to turn away when he felt something bump against him.

'Oh!' came the feminine cry.

Being so tall, Cam was used to not seeing other people run into him, so his instinct and reflex made him reach out and grab the first thing he could—which turned out to be Miss Caroline DeVries.

Double damn.

'Forgive me, my lord. I'm so very clumsy.' She attempted to make her voice breathy and low, but it grated on Cam's nerves. 'Oh, my dance card is empty at the moment.' Grabbing his hand in hers, she pushed closer to him. 'I would love to dance.'

Her audacity was incredible. Cam wanted to push her away, but there was at least one group of matrons behind Miss DeVries that was already looking at them expectantly. He harrumphed and guided her towards the ballroom floor.

This was going to be a long and painful dance.

'My lord, it's such a sin we have never danced before.' Caroline curtseyed low—much lower than deemed appropriate, her bosom nearly spilling out of her daring low-cut pink gown.

'Indeed.' He averted his eyes as he bowed to her.

Cam was wrong. Dancing with Miss Caroline DeVries was not painful. It was excruciating. The polka was a lively dance which required the male to keep his partner close as they spun around, but she seemed to be taking liberties with the definition of 'close.' With every twist and turn, her torso pushed nearer and nearer until she was brushing against his chest.

Irritation got the best of him, and so he sent her a warning glare, to which she responded by batting her eyes at him as her left arm squeezed his shoulder tightly.

Fighting the urge to leave her, he instead looked over her head. Unfortunately, at that exact moment, Maddie and her partner sailed right across his line of sight, and Cam faltered when she threw her head back and laughed as Davenport whirled her around.

'My lord,' she hissed. 'You stepped on my foot.'

'Did I? Forgive me,' he said through gritted teeth, his gaze following Maddie like a hawk.

His patience grew thin as the dance progressed, and somehow, he managed to complete the dance without further incident or crushing his partner's toes. He bowed to Miss DeVries quickly. In that brief moment he took his eyes off her, Maddie disappeared.

Where was she?

One by one, he scanned each and every couple, but none of them were Maddie and Davenport. They had simply disappeared. A terrible feeling buried itself in his chest as he hurriedly escorted Miss DeVries back to her companion.

'My lord,' she said coquettishly. 'That was—'

'Have you seen Maddie—er, Miss Madeline?' he asked Miss Merton.

'She was dancing with Mr Davenport,' the companion replied. 'Are they on the other side of the room?'

'No, I didn't see them among the dancers.' He took a deep breath, trying to compose himself.

'I'm sure Maddie's all right.' Caroline laughed. 'Silly girl. She may have got lost again.'

Miss Merton rose to her feet. 'True, but her dance partner should have guided her back here to me.' Her shoulders straightened, and her expression turned serious.

Cam had never seen the normally cheerful Miss Merton looking so dour. She reminded him of a female hound watching protectively over her pups, ready to bare her teeth should any danger come to her young.

'I shall go search for her,' Miss Merton said.

'And I will assist you.' He barely spared Miss Caroline a glance as he hurried after Miss Merton. 'Where do you think they are?'

Miss Merton paused, her delicate eyebrows gathering together. 'Music room.'

'Music room? How do you know—' But Cam didn't finish his sentence as she darted off with the speed of a woman half her age. He rushed after her, catching up to her just outside the ballroom as she hurried towards what he assumed was the music room. Sure enough, he saw two figures making their way down the hallway.

'...and are these paintings special, Mr Davenport?' Maddie asked.

'Very special indeed, Miss DeVries.' Davenport's hand

gripped her elbow and continued to lead her away. 'I promise, you will find them amusing.'

Cam's blood boiled, and he flew after the couple. 'And just where do you think you're taking her?'

Maddie, too, stood still, her eyes flashing. 'You—'

Davenport froze, then dropped his hand to his side. 'I beg your pardon, sir?'

'It's Lord Balfour to you,' he corrected. 'And answer my question.'

To his credit, Davenport remained calm. 'I was merely assisting Miss DeVries.'

'Assisting in her ruination, maybe. You know better than to abscond a young miss away from her chaperone.' He gestured to Miss Merton, who had caught up to him.

'What is the meaning of this, Mr Davenport?' she demanded. 'Maddie, are you all right?'

'Yes, Miss Merton,' she assured the companion. 'I was dizzy and the ballroom was too stuffy. Mr Davenport said we should go to the music room where I could sit down and look at some paintings.'

'By yourselves?' Cam bit out.

'He said there would be other guests there and that Lord and Lady Baybrook always left the music room open for anyone to enjoy.' She looked at him meaningfully. 'Isn't that right, Mr Davenport?'

Davenport swallowed audibly. 'Uh…'

Miss Merton let out an indignant cry. 'Why, I never… Mr Davenport, I have been attending the Baybrook ball for years and they have never allowed guests in there. However, I do know that it is a popular room for couples to conduct trysts.'

All the colour drained from Maddie's face as the truth of what Davenport had planned for her sank in. 'Mr Davenport, is this true?'

He forced out a chuckle and scratched at his collar. 'This is all just a misunderstanding. We're all gentlemen and ladies here.'

'I can see only one gentleman here, Mr Davenport.' Miss Merton's eyes flashed with fury. 'And a good thing, too, that Lord Balfour was vigilant in watching over Miss DeVries and noticed she was gone.'

Davenport's expression turned unpleasant. 'She's such an awkward, naive fool,' he spat out. 'How you could possibly want her—'

Rage filled him as he reached down and grabbed Davenport by the collar. He pulled a fist back.

'Lord Balfour, no!' Miss Merton cried.

'What?' He blew out a breath. 'You know what he was planning to do. This blackguard doesn't deserve any mercy. I ought to beat him within an inch of his life.'

'My lord, think of the scandal,' she implored. 'Think of Maddie.'

He was thinking of Maddie. Didn't she see that?

'P-please, my lord.' It was Maddie who spoke this time. 'There's no need for violence.'

Reluctantly, he lowered his hand and released Davenport.

'Filthy scum,' Davenport sneered back. 'Just you wait! I will tell everyone what a violent beast you are. You best go back where you came from. And that little tart? She knew what she was doing! She wanted it.'

Anger reignited within Cam, and he lunged at the bastard again, but a hand on his arm stopped him.

'My lord, a moment,' Miss Merton began, giving him a gentle squeeze then stepping in front of him.

'Are you hiding behind an old lady now?' Davenport scoffed. 'Coward.'

'Young man, do you have any idea who I am?' Miss

Merton's spine turned rigid as her tone took on a firm yet refined quality. 'I've been moving in the upper echelons of the ton when you were but a mere child in the cradle. I've seen so many seasons and debutantes and fops like you. Do you not think I knew exactly what you were up to? Do you truly believe you are the first so-called gentleman to abscond with a young lady in her first season at this very ball?' Her gaze could have melted the flesh off Davenport's face. 'Leave and never speak of this again nor come near Miss Madeline. I don't want to see hide nor hair of you. If I do, I will spread rumours that will have ladies reaching for their smelling salts. Do you understand me?'

'Y-yes, ma'am,' Davenport sputtered.

'Go!'

Turning tail, Davenport scarpered out the door.

Cam stared at Miss Merton, slack-jawed. 'That was... incredible.'

Miss Merton's smile turned sweet, as if all was well and nothing had happened. 'We play to our strengths. Now,' she turned back to Maddie. 'Are you all right, my dear?'

'Y-yes.'

'There, there.' Miss Merton smoothed back a curl that had come loose from her coiffure. 'Everything will be all right.'

'I was just... We were dancing, and I felt dizzy. He said we could escape the stuffiness in the music room and there would be other guests there.' She worried at her lip. 'Mr Davenport was right. I am a fool.'

'No, you are not a fool, Maddie.' Miss Merton gripped her firmly by the shoulders. 'An innocent, but not a fool. You couldn't have known what Davenport had planned.

I'm just very glad for Lord Balfour's keen observation skills.'

Maddie's head whipped towards him, and she took in a quick breath. 'My lord, th-thank you. Who knows what could have happened had you not interfered.'

'This was not your fault, darling,' he responded. Miss Merton's eyebrow went all the way up to her hairline, but he continued on. 'Davenport's a despicable scoundrel. You've done nothing wrong.'

Maddie didn't look convinced, her shoulders sagging as her head lowered.

'Oh, dear me.' Miss Merton sighed. 'Maddie, would you like to go home? I'm sure we could leave quietly without anyone noticing. Perhaps a cup of tea and bed is what you need.'

'No, Maddie.' Cam gently touched her chin and tipped her face up. 'Do not run away. Not now.' He could see her confidence—the one she'd worked so hard on these past few days—seeping away. He would not let that happen.

'Dance with me, Maddie.'

Chapter Ten

'D-dance with you?' Maddie thought she'd heard him wrong.

'Yes.' His tone was deadly serious.

'But, my lord,' she breathed. 'The rules. I thought we agreed on one—'

'Forgot the damned rules,' he muttered.

'A dance might help you calm your nerves,' Miss Merton suggested.

She winced inwardly, thinking of what a fool she was. Mr Davenport had paid her a call just yesterday. He'd been witty and charming, but also polite and well mannered. He'd done all the right things, spoken all the right words. Mama had been thrilled by his visit and she'd promised him a dance at the ball. Maddie had immediately decided that she no longer needed to dance with the Earl, but unfortunately, she had forgotten to inform Persephone that, and then it was too late.

After that awkward dance, she wanted to forget him, so she had been glad Mr Davenport was waiting for her. However, when she'd seen Caroline and the Earl dancing, a spark of an unknown emotion had lit inside her.

She didn't want to see him with his arms around another woman, and certainly not her sister.

Perhaps some part of her did know what Mr Davenport was up to but didn't care because she'd been so overcome by the sight of her sister and the Earl dancing.

'Maddie?' Miss Merton's soothing voice jolted her back to the present.

She looked up at the Earl. 'I'm not sure—'

'Please, Maddie.' Emerald eyes bore right into her. 'Just one more dance.'

A breath lodged in her throat. 'All right.'

He gently took her hand into his. From then on, everything was like a dream. She allowed him to lead her to the ballroom floor. Music played, his arms came around her, and once again, she lost herself in the dance. This time, though, she focused on him. Her feet knew the steps and her body moved to the rhythm, but her mind fixed on the man who held her close.

For a moment, it all felt real.

'Thank you for the dance, Miss DeVries.'

And then it was over. 'Thank you, my lord.'

He escorted her back to Miss Merton's side. 'Good evening, Miss Merton, Miss DeVries.' With a curt nod, he left.

Air rushed out of her, leaving Maddie feeling breathless as she watched his tall form walking away.

Miss Merton sidled up to her. 'Are you sure you would like to stay? I could feign a headache so you could escort me home.'

Maddie was sorely tempted; however, she saw Mama marching excitedly towards them and knew there was no escape.

'Maddie, did I see you dancing with the Earl again?' Her entire body practically vibrated with excitement.

'What did you talk about? Did he say anything about paying you another call?'

'Mama,' she said gently. 'It was just a dance.'

'A second dance,' she corrected. 'But I suppose you're right. Until he has asked to court you, you must keep your options open. Miss Merton, are you quite sure there aren't any other eligible dukes in the room?'

'I'm afraid not,' the companion replied.

Mama inhaled deeply. 'What rotten luck that the Duke of Mabury had to fall in love with Kate Mason.' She harrumphed. 'Do not worry my dear. With your newfound popularity, we'll find you someone.'

Maddie danced with a few more gentlemen, and while she did enjoy herself, she could not help but compare them all to the Earl.

I should be thankful he offered a second dance, considering how rude I was to him during the first.

Miss Merton had been right—the dance did calm her down after her encounter with Mr Davenport, but more than that, the self-doubts that had been building in her— wondering if she'd done anything wrong or if it was her fault she was nearly ruined—all but disappeared. Any other man would have coddled her or tucked her away like a fragile doll. But the Earl did the opposite.

'I am so glad you are finally meeting some eligible gentlemen,' Miss Merton remarked after her last partner escorted her back. 'You are such a graceful dancer.'

'Thank you, Miss Merton.' She sat down next to the companion. 'But dancing is far different from courting, is it not?'

'Be patient, dear.' She patted Maddie's hand. 'Your time will come too.'

Maddie glanced across the room where Caroline was surrounded by her usual gaggle of beaux. At some point, most of those men would pay her a call and eventually court her. Of course, her sister had no plan to actually accept any proposals from her current crop of suitors. She was waiting for a larger catch—no man lower than an earl or, if possible, a duke. She would relish the chance to have everyone curtseying to her and calling her 'Your Grace.'

'Do not compare yourself to your sister,' Miss Merton admonished, seemingly reading her mind. 'You are two different women, and—do not repeat this to your mother, but—some women are just born flirts.'

'I wish I knew how to flirt,' she murmured under her breath so Miss Merton could not hear her. It seemed to her that flirting was a necessity in navigating the season. She observed the other women in the room who were also surrounded by men, the way they would laugh at whatever the men said or bat their eyes coquettishly. She would look foolish if she tried that, especially as she would have to crane her neck down for them to even see her eyes. Could such things even be learned? Or, as Miss Merton said, did one have to be born with it?

Though she attempted to put the question out of her mind, it continued to plague her throughout the evening and even until she went home and was in bed. It was early morning when she came to the conclusion that while dancing was an excellent way to meet gentlemen, flirting could help her keep them interested in her and possibly receive a proposal.

If flirting can be learned, how does one do it?

Were there tutors for that? Or books? Whom would she practise with? What if she was terrible at it?

Betsy's arrival to wake her up and dress for the day was a welcome reprieve from her thoughts. She was glad to see Persephone at breakfast, because once again, she had been missing the entire evening of the ball.

'And where were you hiding this time?' she teased her friend. 'Behind those Italian sculptures Lady Baybrook seems to love displaying in every corner? That one of Achilles in the drawing room was quite wide and would have kept you well concealed.'

'Ah, why didn't I think of that?' Persephone tsked. 'As it was, I crept behind Venus at first, but all the men kept staring at her, so I had to duck behind Athena.'

'A wise choice,' Maddie quipped.

'But how was your evening?' Persephone asked. 'No, wait. Tell me about it after breakfast so we can speak privately. We can go to the garden.'

Mabury Hall's garden was not as grand as the Houghton's, but it was still sizeable enough. Maddie quite enjoyed taking a stroll on the meandering paths through the lavender, foxgloves, wisteria, and hollyhocks.

'So,' Persephone began. 'Tell me all about the ball. Did you have gentlemen clamouring after you? How many times did you dance?'

Maddie paused, unsure what to tell her friend. 'Something…happened.' And so she told her about the incident with Mr Davenport and intervention from the Earl and Miss Merton.

'I had no idea Miss Merton could be so fierce,' Persephone exclaimed. 'When I first met her a few days ago, I thought her to be a sweet and shy spinster.'

'You're thinking of me,' Maddie joked, though it wasn't quite funny to her. 'I don't know if this plan is going to work. Perhaps I'm only going to attract the wrong kind of attention. Maybe Mr Davenport was right.'

'No, no.' Persephone halted and faced her. 'Don't say that. You've had three callers this week.'

'I'm still so shy and I never know what to say around

gentlemen except for discussions on weather. I'm hope-less.'

'No, you are not.'

'I've been thinking,' Maddie began. 'About...flirting.'

'With whom?'

'No, I mean I've been thinking of it. That perhaps I need to learn how to do it.' She told Persephone of her observations of the night before.

'Hmm.' Persephone's mouth pursed. 'I suppose you are not wrong. But how are you to learn? Are there books on the subject?'

'If there are, I've yet to come across them.'

'Perhaps all you need— Cam, how lovely to see you outside.'

A small flutter tickled Maddie's belly at the Earl's name. As he came closer and she locked eyes with him, that flutter turned frantic as a bee's wings. The morning sunshine glinted off his golden hair and the light hit his face at all the right angles to show off his handsome features.

'Good morning, Seph. Miss DeVries.'

'My lord, good morning,' she greeted, glad that her voice did not shake.

'Glad to see you aren't hiding in your office,' Persephone laughed.

'Aye, I thought I'd enjoy the fresh air.' He smoothed a hand down the left side of his chest. 'Seph, I'd like to speak to Miss DeVries for a moment. Would you mind giving us a few minutes of privacy?'

'Of course,' she said cheerfully. 'I shall...go and smell some of the hydrangeas.'

Maddie nearly grabbed Persephone's sleeve to stop her from leaving, but her friend was too quick and scampered away. Swallowing hard, she turned to the Earl. 'What can I do for you, my lord?'

'How are you this morning, Miss DeVries?'

'I'm quite well, thank you for asking.' Oh, Lord, she really was awkward.

'I trust last night has not soured your taste for balls and dancing?'

Did he have to bring that up? 'No, of course not.' She bit her lip. 'And once again, thank you for your assistance.'

'Think nothing of it.' He paused, once again patting a hand over his heart. 'I meant what I said, earlier,' he said in a low voice. 'You did nothing to deserve that. He acted of his own accord, and that has nothing to do with you or what you were wearing.'

'What I'm wearing? Why—oh.' He was speaking of the last words he'd said to her at the Houghton garden party.

'What I said to you was entirely out of line. It seems I'm forever asking for your forgiveness for the things I say,' he said sheepishly. 'But I hope you could find it in your heart to forgive me. Again.'

She'd been fuming mad in the garden—had it only been three days since? It seemed like forever ago. 'You prevented my ruination. Of course I can forgive you.'

He let out a breath. 'Thank you.'

'Is there anything else, my lord?'

'I—' He cleared his throat as his hand reached inside his coat pocket and pulled something out. 'I wanted to give you something.'

'Give me something?'

'Aye.' He handed her a package wrapped in wrinkled brown paper.

She tested its weight, trying to guess its contents. 'What is it?'

'Open it.'

Carefully, she unwrapped the package, revealing an object that looked like a pipe. Maddie immediately recognised it. 'Hmm.' Lifting it high, she turned it in her hand.

'I thought maybe you would appreciate it,' he said. 'I was told it's part of a blacksmith's set of tools.'

'Not quite. It's much too small, and blacksmiths' tools are made of a heartier material than brass.'

'Then what is it?'

He didn't know? Why did he buy it, then? 'It's an assayer's blowpipe.' When he gave her a blank look, she continued, 'While it is very similar to the blacksmith's blowpipe, it's much smaller because it's only used to test the proportions of precious metals in ores.'

He leaned over. 'How does it work?'

'The assayer mixes a sample of the ore, along with some other chemicals. Then, he lights a flame using a lamp or candle, then uses the pipe to direct the flame and increase its temperature.' To demonstrate, she placed her lips on the mouthpiece and blew out. 'See?'

The Earl's eyes widened to the size of saucers. 'I, uh…' he sputtered then coughed.

'Are you all right, my lord?'

'Er…yes—yes.' He raked his fingers through his hair.

Maddie frowned. Why would he give her such an object? And more importantly, why did her give her anything at all?

'It's not a courting gift,' he said quickly.

'Of course not.' Maddie would never mistake it for such, anyway. 'And thank you.'

'You're welcome. Now, if you'll excuse me, I must take my leave. Good day, Miss DeVries.'

Maddie watched him as he strode away from her, still

confused by the gift, the brass warm in her palm. More questions assaulted her mind. Why did he choose this not-courting gift for her? If he were truly sorry, then he might have picked something that most, if not all, females might expect, like flowers or ribbons or other such trivial trinkets. Instead, the Earl had found something he thought she would like, based on her interests.

I didn't even realise he'd been listening to Papa and I going on about the furnace.

He'd actually paid attention to what she was saying and acknowledged it with this gift.

It made her stomach flutter.

Wrapping her fingers around the blowpipe, she called to him, 'Wait, my lord.'

He halted, body going stiff. 'Aye?'

Scrounging up all her courage, she sauntered after him and sidestepping his large frame so they were face to face. 'My lord, I was wondering if you could…assist me further?'

'Assist you?' A blond eyebrow rose up. 'In what way? Are you in trouble, lass?'

'No, no. Not at all. I need further help with our plan.'

'Did you want me to dance more with you?' He tsked. 'I can only dance with you so much—you know that.'

'It's not that. See…your attentions have been effective so far,' she began. 'But there is one other thing you could help me with.'

'Of course, what is it?'

'Well…uh…' How did one ask this question? She supposed one just *asked*. 'I was wondering…if you could teach me how to flirt?'

'I beg your pardon?' Cam wondered if arousal from Maddie's earlier demonstration with the blowpipe had truly addled his brain. 'Teach you to flirt?'

'Yes. I don't know how, you see.' Her fingers played with the blowpipe in her hand, and Cam wished to God he'd never set eyes on the damned thing. 'It seems to me that flirting is a necessary part of the courtship ritual.' A furrow appeared between her eyebrows. 'No wonder Mr Davenport thought me to be a naive fool.'

'Never say his name again.' Cam's mood darkened at the sound of it. 'Don't believe anything he said about you, Maddie. You're not a fool.'

'But I am naive,' she pointed out. 'I have no experience with men. Oh, how could I even think I could be like her?'

'Like who?'

'Caroline. She has so many prospects, and I'm still middling about.'

Cam's anger rose further. How he hated it when she compared herself to her sister. 'I'm sure the right gentleman will come along and sweep you off your feet.' His stomach soured at the thought, but he continued on. 'And why would you think I would be a suitable tutor for such a venture?'

'You're a man.'

'Aye.' The insistent twitch in his cock confirmed it.

'And you have had…experience with women?'

'Aye,' he answered again, but did not like where this line of questioning was going.

'Which means you know how men and women flirt with each other. I don't know who else to ask. Please? There is no one else to teach me. I doubt my parents or Miss Merton would assist me. And I certainly can't ask my sister. Or yours.'

Cam's gaze drifted towards Persephone, who stood on the opposite end of the hedges, bent over a geranium bush. An idea came to him. 'If I agree, you must do me a favour as well.'

'Anything.'

'At the next ball, you must ensure Persephone does not disappear again.'

'Whatever do you mean, my lord?'

Though he admired her loyalty to his sister, he would not let them play him for a fool. 'Do not act innocent with me now, Miss DeVries. You know about my sister's antics.' The sheepish smile on her face confirmed as much. 'At the next ball, you will take Persephone in hand so that I may at least introduce her to a few gentlemen.'

She paused, as if weighing her options. 'I... All right. We have a deal, my lord.'

'One more thing.' He lifted a finger in the air. 'If we are to proceed with such an undertaking, then I insist you call me by my given name.'

'Your name, my lord?'

'Aye.'

'Why?'

Cam's mind blanked for a moment. Why did he say that? 'Because...because in order to flirt effectively, you must be at ease. All this *my lord* and *Your Lordship* will only hinder the learning process.'

'All right.' She paused. 'Does this mean you must call me by my name, as well?'

'Aye. But this is only when no one else is around.'

'No one else is around?' she echoed.

'Of course. How else am I to teach you? In the parlour with Miss Merton and your mother looking on?'

'I thought perhaps you could give me instructions and I could test them out on other gentlemen.'

The thought of her 'testing' anything out on any other man made him want to punch something.

'But I suppose you are correct,' she added. 'It would make sense if you teach me how to flirt and then I could practise with you first. I would not want to embarrass myself in public.'

'It's only practical.' God in heaven, what was he saying? Had he really offered to teach her to flirt and then have her try it out on him?

'And I promise, I shall not let Persephone run away,' she said with a determined nod. 'You have my word.'

'Excellent.'

'When shall we have our first lesson, my lo— Cam?'

His heart gave a little jolt at the way she said his name. Cam couldn't recall how many times he'd wondered how it would sound like from her lips. It was much better than he'd imagined. 'How about now? Meet me in the smoking room.'

'Right here? What if we are caught alone?'

'I shall inform Eames that I am headed to Mr Atwell's office, then send my coach off. But I will slip back inside the house and meet you there in—' he checked his pocket watch '—half an hour.'

'I understand,' she said. 'I shall see you there then.'

His throat had gone dry, so he managed only a nod.

This was preposterous. Ludicrous. All-out crazy. But he just could not say no to her. Besides, who knows what other scheme she or his sister might come up with? Better that he keep watch on her and stay close, or they might find someone else to rope into their plans.

You're doing this for Persephone, he told himself. He was determined to give her the season Ma had wanted for her. And she would get it, if only she would stay still and let him.

But now, he was once again caught up further into this scheme with Maddie. Teach her to flirt? He did not know the first thing about how to teach a lady to flirt. He knew *how*, of course, but it came naturally to him, with the old MacGregor charm. How could he instruct someone else—a woman, at that—on such matters?

Or maybe he didn't have to teach her.

Not exactly.

As he gathered his thoughts, he did exactly what he told Maddie he would do with Eames and his coachman. To his surprise, Maddie was already in the smoking room when he arrived, sitting on the leather chair opposite the one he usually occupied.

'Papa left for a business meeting and Mama and Caroline went for a stroll in the park,' she said. 'I thought it best to slip away as soon as possible while there was no one around.'

'And Persephone?'

'With the Dowager and Miss Merton. I told them I had a headache and was upstairs in my room.' Blue eyes stared up at him expectantly. 'Shall we begin, my lord?'

'Of course.' He strode over to her and sat down. 'First, we—what is that?'

Maddie had retrieved something from her skirts and placed it on her lap. 'A notebook and pencil,' she said matter-of-factly. 'I'm taking down notes. It's the best way to remember things and ideas.'

'Right. Now…' He smoothed his hands down his thighs. 'What is flirting?' Maddie's pencil *scritch-scratched* across the page of her notebook, and Cam found himself transported back to his days in the schoolroom. 'Flirting is the act of signalling one's interest to attract a potential mate.'

Scritch-scratch.

'Many species of animal, for example, engage in a type of flirting. It varies from species to species….' Cam had never been a studious boy, but by sheer force of will he was able to make his mind recall those lessons his schoolmaster had ingrained in him.

Scritch-scratch. Scritch-scratch. Scritch-scratch.

Dear God in heaven, this would not do. Maddie looking studious as he droned on only served to distract him. That little furrow between her eyebrows was utterly arousing. Then there was the way her pink tongue stuck out from the corner of her mouth and she concentrated on taking notes… It made him want to lick at it. He had to think of the least arousing thing on earth.

'Mating toads,' he croaked out.

Scritch—

'I beg your pardon?'

'Mating toads signal their interest by producing sounds at loud volumes,' he continued. 'Their vocal sacs can amplify….'

Cam had nearly exhausted his knowledge of the mating rituals of frogs and toads when a delicate cough interrupted him.

'*Ahem.*'

'Yes?'

Maddie regarded him. 'It's not that I'm complaining…'

'But?'

'As much as I am impressed by your knowledge of the animal kingdom, I thought we would be engaging in more…practical lessons.' She put her notebook aside. 'Is learning all about animal husbandry necessary?'

His first plan to distract her with useless facts hadn't fooled her, it seemed. So perhaps he had to switch tactics. First, he needed to assess what she did know about flirting. 'Tell me, then. What do you think these lessons should be about?'

'Well.' She stood up, and by instinct he did as well.

'How exactly do I begin flirting? According to Miss Merton, there is a very limited amount of subjects I can discuss with a gentleman. The weather, music, art, general events, the items in a room… But how do those lead to flirting?'

'They do not,' he replied. 'Flirting isn't just talking. Yes, that's a big part of it, but it's not just about what you say, but what you do not say.'

She looked up at him, big eyes eager and earnest. 'How so?'

'The way you look at a man, for example, could be an indication of your interest. When a man is speaking, you should look into his eyes. You must appear that you are eager to hear anything he has to say.'

'Anything?'

Cam smiled to himself. The vexed expression on her face gave him an idea on exactly how to proceed.

He continued. 'Aye. I know these English fops can drone on and on about the silliest thing, but you'll have to endure.' He wondered how long Maddie could keep that up. *She would surely hate it.* And perhaps if he made it sound as terrible as possible, she would give up on this idea of flirting.

'And what else?'

'Well…' He thought for a moment. 'The way you speak with your body is another factor.'

'A body can speak?'

'Aye. Think of it as a kind of language, like French or Italian. Your body language.' It took all of Cam's effort not to stare down at said body. 'It says a lot about you. For example, when you face a gentleman you want to flirt with, try leaning your head towards him.'

'Like this?' She leaned her head forward and came

close enough that Cam swore he could smell her flowery perfume.

He gulped. 'Er, yes.'

'Seems silly.' She shrugged. 'What else?'

'The next step is letting the gentleman know you have been listening to him. So, you must say things like, *Oh, yes, my lord* or *I agree, my lord.*'

'But what if I don't agree?'

'It doesn't matter,' he stated. 'You must agree. With absolutely everything.'

She sighed. 'All right. Is there anything else I must do?'

'Laugh, too, at their jokes. Even if you do not find them funny.'

'Laugh—' Her lips pressed together. 'Fine. I'll do it.'

Fine? Cam let out a huff. He expected her to complain. Or give up and realise it was not worth flirting with these milksop aristocrats. He would have to find a different tactic to sway her from this ridiculous notion. 'All right, our lesson is over for now.'

'So soon?' She sounded almost disappointed.

'Why? Is there anything else?'

'Well, there is one more question I had.'

Cam supposed he might as well get all her questions out of the way. 'Tell me, then.' She didn't answer, but instead, her face turned bright red. 'What is it?'

She licked her lips. 'It's about…kissing.'

Cam's entire being froze. This did not bode well.

He should ignore her question and send her packing. 'What about kissing?'

Cameron MacGregor, you utter and complete fool.

'H-how do I know if a man wants to kiss me?'

Think, think! Cam wasn't sure how to answer that, exactly, as all sense seemed to be leaving his head and going…much lower. 'So you may prevent it, correct? Because as you know, kissing is something reserved for husbands and wives.'

She didn't look convinced but said, 'Of course.'

'Of course. Has anyone ever tried to kiss you?'

She nodded. 'Back in Pittsburgh. He was one of my father's apprentices, and his name was—'

'I don't need details,' he interrupted. 'Did he succeed?'

'No.'

His tightening in his chest eased. 'Good.'

'He was too short,' Maddie continued. 'He couldn't reach my lips.'

'Truly?'

'Yes. He asked me to wait so he could fetch a box!' She burst into laughter. 'Then I left. It—it was really the f-first time I was glad I'm so tall.' She wiped the corners of her eyes with her fingers. 'I didn't even know he wanted to kiss me. We were just alone and he tried it.'

'Well, that's your first mistake,' he said. 'Being alone with a man.'

Something sparked in her eyes—something dangerous. 'Is it?'

Retreat! his instinct screamed. But other parts of him said, *Full speed ahead!*

'Definitely.'

'And what other mistakes should I avoid?'

Cam's heart hammered in his chest. 'You let him get close enough.'

She took a step forward. 'Like this?'

'Aye. And then he may assess your interest in your gaze.' Her brilliant blue eyes bore right into him. 'And then he will lean down.' He bent his head closer. *This was a practical lesson, after all.* 'And you must not encourage him.'

'How do I do that?'

'By not touching him.' Surely, she wouldn't dare—

A hand landed over his heart. 'Like this?'

Oh, Lord God above, he was going to do it. He was going to kiss her.

And Cam couldn't quite bring himself to stop.

Chapter Eleven

Oh, heavens, what was she thinking?

Well, perhaps for the first time in her life, Maddie was not thinking. No. This time, she let her instinct take over. Not just that—she let it run wild.

The first brush of his lips was shockingly gentle. She wasn't sure exactly what she was expecting, but it was not…that. They moved over hers in a light caress, as if testing her reaction. So, she slid her hand up to his shoulder, giving it an encouraging squeeze. She sighed against him and sidled closer.

'Maddie,' he groaned against her mouth before his fingers cupped her jaw, thumb stroking her chin. To her shock, he tugged at the corner of her mouth as he slipped his tongue over her parted lips. The intimate touch caused a shock in her, down low to the crevice between her legs. To her surprise, Maddie found herself opening to him further, his tongue sliding across hers, tasting her as if she were delicious treat.

A hand landed on her waist, moving to her bottom, cupping her through her layers of skirts. He pulled her close, their bodies pressing together tight in a motion that made Maddie's knees weak. A knee somehow slid between her legs, pushing up against her, and when she slid down, the most delicious shudder went through her.

'Hello? How are the lessons going?'

Cam's strong hands released her and Maddie leapt away from him. 'Persephone!' she cried as her friend entered the smoking room.

'What are you doing here, Seph?' Cam combed his fingers through his dishevelled hair.

Oh, dear, did she do that? She did remember feeling how soft it was. For some reason, she thought it would be rough and wiry. Not silky like a babe's downy hair.

'I wanted to see you how you were progressing with the flirting lessons,' she replied matter-of-factly.

'You told her?'

'Of—of course I did.' Knees still weak, Maddie staggered backwards but stopped herself before she fell any further.

'Even the part about where she cannot disappear at the next ball?'

Persephone nodded. 'I would do anything to help Maddie.'

'She's my friend. I can't lie to her.' Indeed, that had been Maddie's first instinct because of the bargain she had struck with Cam. But it wasn't right, exchanging Persephone for her personal gain. To her surprise, Persephone agreed.

'I even helped keep the Dowager and Miss Merton occupied so she may attend these lessons with you.' Persephone ambled over to them. 'So? How did it go?'

Maddie couldn't look him in the eye. Her mind was still all a-jumble from that kiss. 'It—it went well.'

'Indeed.' Cam tugged at his coat lapels with his hands. 'I was going through some practical lessons with Maddie.'

'What kind of practical lessons?' Persephone asked eagerly. 'Will they help her find a husband?'

Maddie nearly choked trying to stop the gasp from escaping her mouth.

'I've been teaching her what to do,' he said, a cool mask slipping over his face. 'And what not to do.'

Oh, dear.

She'd made a misstep.

He didn't want to kiss me.

Despite the bizarre start, she'd enjoyed his lesson. Talking to Cam was refreshing. Except for her father, men didn't generally talk to her so candidly, so she was disappointed when he'd ended their lesson so abruptly. She hadn't wanted them to end so soon, and so she'd asked about kissing. She'd been staring at his lips, wondering...

What happened could never happen again. She was the one who'd encouraged it—no, she'd practically mauled him. Mortification made her entire body grow hot.

'Thank you, m-my lord,' she stammered. 'It's been enlightening, to say the least. If you'll excuse me, I must run along.'

Maddie could not have left the room fast enough. She ran up to her rooms and closed the door behind her, bracing against the heavy wood as if she could keep the embarrassment from getting inside and catching up to her like an invader trying to storm a castle.

Cam's lips on hers.

His strong shoulders.

His hands on her bottom.

Heat coiled low in her belly. She was not ignorant of what happened between a man and a woman. Her mother had explained to her, in a roundabout way, about where children come from. Plus, she'd heard a conversation or two between the men at the furnace to fill in the gaps. However, aside from that, she had no experience at all and had never even been kissed.

Until now.

Her first kiss.

It hadn't even affected him, and why should it have? He was an experienced man. Perhaps he kissed women every day.

The thought of it made her cross and ate at her, like when she'd seen him dancing with Caroline. Though this was worse, because she was imagining him kissing another woman and not just waltzing.

I must remain unaffected.

'Yes,' she said aloud with a firm resolve. 'It didn't even affect him.' It was part of the lesson she'd practically begged him for. If he could manage to act like nothing had happened, then so could she.

Maddie was relieved that the next event was a dinner party the following day and it was to be at Mabury Hall. There would be no dancing here, and perhaps if she were lucky, no Cam, either. As was the case since he'd arrived, he hardly joined them for meals.

'Don't you look bonny,' Persephone remarked as they met in the hallway. 'Mrs Ellesmore is a genius.'

'Thank you.' Maddie normally hated the sight of a yellow gown, but when this one had arrived earlier that day, she had gasped aloud. The fabric was not the usual bright yellow her mother picked but a champagne gold that matched her hair. The ruffles were minimal, only on the bottom, and the dress had a fitted bodice and an open neckline that tapered to a V down her chest.

'Are you disappointed not to be dancing tonight?'

'Not at all. I'm glad to rest my feet.'

'Good, because I'm glad we won't be at a ball for a good while. That means I won't have to dance with anyone Cam introduces me to.'

Maddie's step nearly faltered at the name. 'Y-yes, I'm glad for you.' And for herself, because after yesterday's mortifying events, she didn't know how she could even look Cam in the eye. It was one thing for her to resolve to act like nothing had happened, but quite another in reality.

The thoughts of the kiss plagued her mind. She relived it in her mind over and over, unable to forget his lips and his hands and that delicious tingle between her legs. But she would get to the end of the memory and how they had been interrupted. Embarrassment flooded her once more, as if it had just happened.

'Where is your brother, by the way?' Maddie made her tone appear as casual as possible.

'Since he's the highest-ranking male in the house, he'll be escorting the Dowager to dinner,' Persephone said.

Maddie ignored that minuscule stab in her chest. 'Ah, of course.'

'Silly, isn't it?' Persephone blew out a breath. 'Just because some distant uncle on my father's side keeled over without any sons, my brother gets to walk ahead into the dining room ahead of us.'

Maddie chuckled. 'According to Miss Merton, the rest of the dinner won't be as formal, as they're seating us more casually in order to encourage conversation.'

The Dowager and Miss Merton had set up tonight's dinner party to further both Maddie's and Caroline's prospects with their most promising gentlemen callers. It would give them an opportunity to become more acquainted outside dancing at balls and the rigid morning-call ritual.

They'd narrowed the guest list down to two gentlemen each. For Maddie, they had invited Sir Alfred Kensington and Lord Andrew Annesley, and for Caroline, Lord George Butler and Jasper, Viscount Moseby. They had also planned to invite two other couples, but Miss Merton didn't disclose their names.

'We should make haste. Dinner's about to start,' Maddie said to Persephone.

The two girls made their way downstairs to the hall just outside the dining room, arriving just in time as the butler announced dinner. Persephone bade her a quick goodbye and dashed up front. Maddie was all the way in the rear with her parents and Caroline, and so she didn't get a chance to see the other guests.

The doors to the dining room opened, and they all filed in. Except for the part that she had to be in the same room with Cam, she was looking forward to this, as she wanted to put her flirting skills to test. At least she could put to use what she had learned from that disastrous day.

The moment she entered, however, her eyes immediately went to Cam. He was seated at one end of the table, opposite the Dowager. Maddie's heart did a funny little flip at the sight of him looking so impeccably handsome in his formal evening attire, his jaw freshly shaven and golden hair tamed back. The snowy white of his shirt contrasted with his golden skin, and Maddie once again found her gaze glued to those lips.

Mercifully, she had to turn the other way to reach her seat on the other side of the table. She said a little prayer asking the Good Lord that he hadn't caught her staring at him.

When she took her place, she saw Lord Annesely to her right and, to her surprise, Viscount Palmer on her left.

'My lord,' she greeted as they took their seats. 'I did not realise you'd been invited.'

'Miss DeVries,' he acknowledged. 'I'm afraid I am only a last-minute addition. My aunt and uncle asked me to come along.' He nodded to Lord and Lady Houghton, who were seated at the other end of the table on the Dowager's side, next to Mama and Papa and one other couple. 'Apparently, Sir Alfred Kensington was thrown off his horse this afternoon and so has taken abed.'

Maddie covered her mouth with her hand. 'Oh, heavens. I do hope he's all right.'

'It wasn't serious, at least from what my aunt heard.' He took the glass of wine one of the footmen had filled for him. 'Anyway, the Dowager asked her if I was still in town, and if so, could I possibly attend her dinner party tonight so we do not have an imbalance of guests.' He smiled warmly at her as he took a sip from his glass. 'I must admit, I've never been happier to fill an empty seat.'

Was he flirting with her? Maddie wasn't certain. When they'd first met, he'd been quite aloof, though by the end, after he'd returned her to her parents, she'd thought they'd made a connection—she couldn't have imagined that look they had exchanged. However, when he hadn't turned up at the Baybrook ball, she'd written him off.

'How fortuitous,' she replied, taking a sip from her own glass.

'Indeed. I was disappointed that I could not make it to the Baybrook ball for that dance you promised me. The Earl had taken a turn for the worse, and so I had to make haste back to Hampshire.'

'Is your father—'

'Fine.' He put the glass down. 'After getting him settled, I came back to town early today.'

'I'm so glad your father's condition did not worsen, my lord. And that—'

Their conversation was interrupted as the doors opened and the liveried footmen arrived to serve the first course. Meals at Mabury Hall and Highfield Park were always sumptuous affairs even on normal days, but on special occasions they were spectacular, thanks to the household's talented French chef, Monsieur Faucher. Tonight's first course was a delicious consommé of fresh vegetables. Maddie had been served the dish before, but it was never the same each time because Faucher used only the vegetables that were in season. Maddie's spoon was halfway to her mouth when she felt a prickle on the back of her neck. Immediately, her gaze lifted towards the head of the table, and sure enough, Cam was staring right at her.

He quickly turned away as Persephone, who sat to his right, spoke to him. Maddie returned to her food.

After that kiss, there was no way she could ever be near him again.

But then, she would miss talking with him and spending time with him. His candour, his wit, the way he talked to her as if she weren't just some silly little girl. Whenever she spoke, he had his full attention on her, like he actually cared about what she said. It showed, especially in his actions, like the not-gift that was currently hidden underneath her pillow.

'Delicious, isn't it, Miss DeVries?' Lord Annesely remarked.

'I—yes.' She swallowed her spoonful and then wiped her mouth with her napkin. Remembering he was here because of her, she decided to begin putting yesterday's lessons into practice.

It's not just about what you say, but what you don't say. When a man is speaking, you should look into his eyes.

Placing her spoon down, she turned her head towards Annesely, hoping to catch his gaze. 'My lord, have you, um…' What were his interests? 'Seen any new fashions recently?' Oh, heavens, that sounded utterly vapid.

You must appear that you are eager to hear anything they have to say.

His eyes lit up and he put his spoon down. 'I'm glad you asked, Miss DeVries.' Sitting up straight, he parted his coat and gestured to his waistcoat. 'Isn't it divine? It's the latest fashion from Paris.'

'It's, uh…' She didn't know how to describe the shiny pink-and-green-striped monstrosity wrapped around his torso. Ugly? Eyesore? Blinding?

You must agree. With absolutely everything.

'Absolutely divine, my lord.'

Lord Annesely beamed at her. 'I'm glad you think so. You know, I've always thought French fashion was much more refined than English…'

Maddie kept her smile frozen on her face as she let Lord Annesely continue on his oral treatise of French versus English fashion, throwing in a 'yes, my lord' and 'how right you are, my lord' a few times for good measure. Her mind, however, drifted off, once again thinking back to that kiss yesterday.

Cam's soft lips.

His strong hands, cupping her bottom.

'Miss DeVries? What do you think?'

Lord Annesely's question jolted her back. 'Um, yes, my lord?'

'I knew you would understand my passion for cravats,' he said excitedly.

'Of course.' Mercifully, the footmen stepped forward to clear their plates, and Maddie was thankful for the reprieve.

'The French truly are a marvel,' Lord Annesely continued as they were served a delicious-smelling terrine. 'They just have that… I don't know what.' He barked out a laugh. 'Right? Because that's what the direct translation of *je ne sais quoi* is!'

A second ticked by before Maddie realised it was a joke. 'Oh, of course it is.' She let out a forced laugh. 'How clever you are, my lord.' Inside, however, Maddie was dying a slow death. *Only eight more courses to go.*

Course after course came, and Maddie continued to flirt with Lord Annesely, agreeing with everything he said and laughing at his terrible jokes, all the while trying to maintain eye contact. Frankly, it was exhausting, and when they finished dessert, she nearly wept in happiness.

'I quite enjoyed Lord Annesely's tirade against double-breasted coats,' Viscount Palmer quipped from her left. 'If he could speak with the same passion in Parliament, he could get a lot of laws passed.'

Maddie couldn't suppress the laugh bubbling inside her. 'My lord, you are incorrigible,' she whispered.

'Don't tell me you weren't swayed by his arguments for the abolition of top hats?' He winked at her.

'Did you say top hats?' Lord Annesely interrupted, his brows slashing down. 'I—'

'If everyone is finished,' the Dowager announced, 'let us head to the parlour.'

They all stood up and followed the Dowager over to the adjacent room, where the footmen served sherry for the ladies and brandy for the gentlemen.

'Miss DeVries, this was such an enjoyable dinner,' Lord Annesely began. 'I'm afraid I cannot stay for too long as I'm heading to our estate in the morning. But, I was wondering if you'd like to go on a carriage ride with me next week?'

Maddie couldn't believe what she was hearing. A carriage ride? 'That sounds lovely, my lord.'

'I shall be back in town Monday, so how about Tuesday?'

'I will tell my mother and Miss Merton to keep the afternoon free.'

'Excellent. If you'll excuse me, I must bid goodbye to the Dowager. Pleasant evening, Miss DeVries.'

'A pleasant evening to you, too, my lord.' As she watched him walk away, a single thought appeared in Maddie's mind.

It worked.

She had doubted Cam's lessons and methods, but they produced results. Her first instinct was to run to him and tell him about her success, but then the reminder of their kiss yesterday came flooding back. Once again, the memory made her hot with embarrassment.

'Miss DeVries, I saw you had an empty hand.' Viscount Palmer offered her a glass of sherry.

'Thank you, my lord.' She accepted it and took a sip, the liquid calming her frayed nerves.

'Now that Lord Annesely has departed,' he began, 'I was hoping to catch your attention.'

'Why would you need my attention, my lord?'

'I thought it would be obvious by now. I wish to know more about you.'

'For what—oh.'

'I regret not going to the Baybrook ball and writing my name on your dance card,' he continued. 'Then, it would have been acceptable for me to pay you a call this week.'

'Well, my lord, you are here now. You could get to know more about me.' Did she just…flirt back with him?

Yes, I did.

'How right you are, Miss DeVries.'

Confidence surged through Maddie as the handsome Viscount smiled at her. Perhaps those lessons from Cam were worth it. She only had to put those thoughts of that awful kiss out of her mind.

Well, the kiss wasn't awful. No—in fact, it had been wonderful.

At least, up until the end.

Unable to help herself, she looked back across the room at Cam, who was standing by the mantel with Lord and Lady Houghton, the firelight caught in his golden locks. Had they always had a red glint to them? How come she'd never noticed?

Oh, heavens.

She had to get that kiss—and Cam—out of her mind. The carriage ride with Annesely would be a good distraction, plus Palmer was right here beside her. Still, why did she wish that it was Cam she'd be out and about with? And Cam right beside her now instead of Viscount Palmer?

'Miss DeVries?' the Viscount asked. 'Would you like another sherry?'

'Er…yes, my lord.' She had to put those thoughts away for now. Of the kiss and of Cam. There was no use thinking of him, as their courtship was all a game. A play they were putting on. She should remember that and instead look forward to her own future—one that didn't include him.

Chapter Twelve

Cam eased his grip on his brandy glass and unclenched his jaw, fearing both might break if he did not relax.

But how could he relax when he had been forced to watch Maddie flirt with that dandy throughout the entire dinner?

And now, she was deep in conversation with Viscount Palmer.

He wanted to throw the brandy. At Palmer's face. Preferably after filling the glass with hot nails.

Cam was quite relieved that they didn't have to go to another ball this evening. Miss Merton had explained the purpose of this dinner party, which was to invite the gentlemen who were likely to match with the DeVries sisters. He'd even told himself that he was pleased, because this meant Maddie would find a husband soon enough and be out of his reach.

That's why he'd agreed to this fake courtship plan, after all.

Of course, when he'd seen Palmer arrive, he'd been incensed. 'What is he doing here?' he had asked Miss Merton.

'Oh, it's a tragedy, my lord. Sir Alfred was thrown off

his horse,' the companion had cried, then explained that Palmer was not Maddie's potential suitor and only filling an empty seat for the injured Sir Alfred Kensington. While he would never wish anyone harm, Cam couldn't help but feel relieved the man was not here.

One less suitor for Maddie.

Downing the rest of the golden liquid, he handed the glass to a footman. 'If you excuse me, Your Grace, Lord Houghton, Lady Houghton, I must refresh myself.' After a nod from the Dowager, he made his way out of the parlour.

Had he not been a guest at Mabury Hall, Cam would have left the dinner party. However, he was the Dowager's escort tonight, so politeness and good manners dictated he stay by her side until the last guest had left. A few minutes of reprieve from having to watch Maddie and the Viscount should help him get through the rest of the evening. Not that leaving the room would be of help, as she didn't even need to breathe the same air for him to think of her. This last day, his thoughts had been consumed by nothing but her and that kiss they'd shared.

Half of him was glad that Persephone had interrupted him. And the other half? Well, that part continued to torture him with the memory of her sweet lips and eager body, as well as images of what could have been. He could have continued to let her slide on his thigh until she shuddered with pleasure. Then he could have pressed her against the wall, lifted up her skirt, and touched her in all the soft and sweet places on her body. Or pulled down the bodice of her gown so he could find out what her breasts looked like.

'My lord, where are you going?'

Cam halted and turned. 'I'm just—Miss DeVries?'

Sure enough, Caroline DeVries stood at the other end

of the hallway, her expression akin to a cat who had trapped a mouse in a corner. 'Are you off to have a secret tryst with someone? With my sister, perhaps?'

'I beg your pardon?'

'Of course, she's occupied at the moment. With Viscount Palmer.'

His fingernails dug hard into his palms. 'If you'll excuse me, Miss DeVries, I should get back to my duties as our hostess's escort.' He attempted to walk past her, but she blocked his way. 'I suggest you move aside, Miss DeVries. Besides, we should not be alone together.'

'*Pfft*. It's just a hallway.' She sauntered closer to him. 'And you've done far worse with other women, I imagine.'

His patience was beginning to wear thin. 'Miss DeVries, this is a completely inappropriate conversation.'

'Do you have these conversations with Maddie?'

'I don't know what you're talking about.'

'What do you have planned for my sister?' Her eyes narrowed into slits. 'You dance with her at every ball, sometimes twice. You've paid a call to her with my father present. And then there was that tryst.'

'Tryst?' He swallowed hard.

'In the garden.'

'Garden?' Relief poured through him as he realised she wasn't speaking of the smoking room. 'My sister was but a few feet away and your mother and Miss Merton could have looked outside the window and seen us.'

Her eyes flashed. 'Do you plan to court Maddie or not? Will you be proposing soon?'

'That is none of your business. Besides, why are you playing the concerned sister now? You do nothing but put Maddie down and belittle her every chance you get.'

'I have not,' she sputtered. 'I am only concerned for

her. Maddie will not be suited to the life of a countess. She's too shy and awkward. She'll only embarrass herself. And you.'

So, that was what this was about. Who did this lass think she was? 'Really now? Tell me, then. Who should be my countess?'

A seductive smile curled up her lips. 'Someone sophisticated. Beautiful. Delicate.' She drew closer. 'You're an earl, my lord. Surely there is someone else you're attracted to? Someone more to your taste?'

'You don't know me at all.' Cam laughed aloud. 'Lass, the last thing I want is to marry someone I'm attracted to.' Never again. Not since Jenny. 'Now—' He towered over her. 'Run along, and do not ever approach me alone again, you *ken*?'

Sidestepping her, he marched away, feeling her hating stare burn a hole into his back.

She could go jump in the Thames, for all I care.

How dare she even suggest that she would be a better match for him than Maddie.

As he walked away, he cursed silently as he realised that his only escape from this narrow hallway was blocked by that witch behind him. Now he had no choice but to go back to the parlour and continue to watch Maddie and Palmer converse so closely all night. He couldn't help but wish he was the one in deep conversation with her; he could listen to her ideas and thoughts about anything and everything under the sun all night long. All these boring and tedious parties would be so much more tolerable if he could spend them by her side. He could already imagine the little smiles and looks she would flash him, or perhaps she'd have some witty remark she would whisper to him. Lord, she was so pretty when she acted all awkward and shy.

He supposed there was one bright side to this, and that was that after tonight, maybe he would never have to look at that odious viscount ever again.

After running some morning errands, Cam returned to Mabury Hall in the afternoon and asked Eames where his sister was.

'In the library, my lord,' the butler informed him. 'But please do take the entrance through the dining room, as the sitting room is currently occupied by Miss Madeline and Viscount Palmer.'

'Viscount—' Cam couldn't even finish as he marched off in the direction of the sitting room. He flung the door open. Sure enough, there he was—Viscount Odious, seated across from Maddie. Her blue eyes went wide as saucers, while the Viscount's mouth turned down into a disapproving frown.

'My lord!' Miss Merton exclaimed. 'Did Eames not inform you that this room is occupied?'

'I'm afraid I didn't see him,' he lied. 'What's this, now?'

'The Viscount is paying my daughter a call,' Mrs DeVries informed him in an irritated tone.

'Really, now? How much time d'you have left?'

'Five minutes,' the Viscount replied in an irritated tone.

'I see. Excuse me, then.' He shut the door, then spun around, planting his feet firmly on the ground, then took his watch out of his pocket. He watched the second hand like a hawk, tracking its movement until it completed exactly five journeys around the face. Once it was done, he flung the door once again.

'Your call is done,' he announced, much to the shock of Miss Merton and Mrs DeVries.

Viscount—Odi… Palmer got to his feet. 'I had a lovely time, Miss DeVries. Thank you.'

'Thank you, my lord.' She sneaked a glance at him, her expression confused.

Cam glared at the Viscount as he passed by, and to his irritation, the damned man didn't react at all. In fact, he behaved as if Cam weren't even there.

'This is highly unusual, my lord,' Miss Merton began. 'What was the purpose of your interruption?'

Three pairs of eyes stared at him, waiting for an explanation. 'I required…some…' He glanced around and picked up the first thing he could grab—an embroidered cushion. 'This. I needed this.' He waved it around.

'A cushion?' Miss Merton raised a brow.

'Yes. I needed to show my valet the excellent needlework on it.' He tutted. 'The man's been slipping, you know. His stitches have not been up to standard. Now, if you'll excuse me, I must see my sister.'

He stifled the desire to run and somehow managed a dignified stride into the library. Letting out a breath, he called, 'Persephone?'

No answer, but from the way the door that led to the dining room was left ajar, he guessed she had already left.

'My lord?'

His entire body reacted to the sound of Maddie's voice. Slowly, he turned around. 'Miss DeVries?'

She stood by the entrance, looking so lovely in a light blue gown that emphasised the colour of her eyes, the sun shining behind her, lighting her up like an angel. 'Miss Merton and Mama have gone upstairs.'

'And?'

'And I stayed behind because I said I needed to speak with Persephone.'

'She's not here.'

She looked visibly relieved. 'Thank goodness. I was hoping to have a moment of your time.' Stepping inside, she closed the door behind her.

'How may I be of assistance?'

'It's not you. I mean, I—' Her teeth sank into her lip. 'I'm afraid it's my turn to apologise.'

The words had him agog, and for a moment his mind ceased all function. 'Apologise? What for?'

'F-for taking advantage of your kindness.'

He stared at her, still unable to process the words coming out of her mouth.

She sighed and then leaned closer. 'The other day. In the smoking room. Our lessons.'

'You...were taking advantage of me?'

'Our—my kissing you,' she whispered, her entire face turning scarlet.

Oh. 'The kiss.'

'Yes. It was just... It was just a lesson after all, correct? And I may have taken it too far and c-coerced that kiss from you. I would just like to say I apologise and I promise it will never happen again.' She wrung her hands together. 'And I would understand if you feel uncomfortable around me and wish to end our fake courtship agreement.'

Cam couldn't quite believe what he was hearing. She thought she had been the one who had wronged him by 'coercing' him?

Somehow, his life had turned into some kind of comedic play.

But he wasn't quite ready to close the curtains.

'I don't think it would be wise.'

'You don't?'

'No. Not at this stage, anyway. I've already paid a call on you, then danced with you several times, sometimes twice. Maddie, if we give up now, then you'll be humiliated. Your other suitors might drop you, wondering why I, an eligible young peer, would suddenly lose interest in you.'

'Oh.'

'Don't you see? It's much too late to quit now. We must see this to the end.' Yes, that was it. They'd done all this hard work, and to bow out now would guarantee defeat. 'So, we must continue on, but you must also allow me to help you. To…sooner achieve your goals.'

'My goals?'

'To marry. I can't be running around pretending to court you forever, after all. Hopefully you'll find a suitable match before my hair turns grey.'

She laughed. 'I hope it does not come to that.'

'I hope so, too. But don't just marry the first man who comes in that door,' he warned. 'You must avoid scoundrels who may take advantage of you.'

'Oh. Like Mr Davenport.'

'Exactly.' He despised hearing that name from her, but in this instance he was the only example Cam could think of. 'As I mentioned, what he attempted with you is not your fault, but you must be vigilant. I'm not worried about what you might do, but rather, I am concerned about other men.' He was one himself, after all, and knew how their minds worked.

'Oh, you should definitely help me, then.' Her voice lowered once more. 'Please, Cam?'

'Help you? With what?'

'Help me avoid these scoundrels. You seem to have a good instinct.'

'Well—'

'You already do it for Persephone, correct? You meet

other gentlemen, examine their prospects, and select which ones would be suitable to introduce to her?'

'It's not quite the same—'

'Then you could do it for me.' She clapped her hands together. 'I mean, you could warn me which gentlemen are scoundrels. You could be like my elder brother, too.'

The mere thought of it made Cam want to retch up his breakfast.

'Yes, that's it. I've always wanted an older brother.'

If she says brother one more time, I'm going to hang myself.

'Very well, Maddie.' He cleared his throat. 'Once the time comes and you have a list of gentlemen coming to call, I can help you assess their suitability.'

'Thank you so much, Cam. That truly is very kind of you. If you'll excuse me, I must head upstairs before Mama comes down to find me.'

Cam watched her walk away, his mind still reeling from what had just occurred. He wasn't just deep into this scheme, but rather, he had jumped right into it, head first.

Glancing down and seeing that he held the cushion with a death grip, he tossed the damned thing to the floor.

Chapter Thirteen

Maddie wasn't certain exactly what had happened this week, but she was flooded with cards, and more gentlemen came to call on her, even those with whom she'd danced but who hadn't shown further interest previously. They hadn't even attended any balls, but she had been introduced to more gentlemen at various events, including at the opera, at one charity art show, and during a stroll in Hyde Park. She had also gone on that carriage ride with Lord Annesely, and despite the first disastrous visit, Viscount Palmer had called once more this week, and they had also spent some time conversing at the art exhibit. He planned to join them at the ballet tomorrow night.

'See, I was right all along,' Persephone had told her. 'It's all about competition. I think news of Cam, Lord Annesely, and Viscount Palmer's interest in you has spread through London, and now all these men are calling around, wondering what the delightful Miss Maddie DeVries has to offer.'

Maddie still wasn't sure how to feel about that. On one hand, she was getting what she wanted, but on the other, all those gentlemen showed interest only because other men wanted her. And not because of her.

'How wonderful,' Mama exclaimed as she went through the various cards that arrived that morning. The DeVrieses, Miss Merton, and Persephone were having breakfast by themselves that morning as the Dowager had an early appointment. 'Both my girls are a success this season.'

'Maybe there won't be a need for a second one,' Papa added, taking a sip of his tea. 'And we can go home.'

Caroline, on the other hand, pouted. 'Ugh. All these gentlemen have nothing to offer. Mama, I cannot go home without a titled husband. I'll be a laughing stock.'

'Caroline, dear, don't you think it's time you made a decision?' Miss Merton said diplomatically. 'At the very least, you should let some of these gentlemen down instead of continuing to receive them week after week. Some might say you are much too picky.'

Caroline's nostrils flared as she shot to her feet. 'Then perhaps you need to find me better prospects!'

'Caroline!'

Maddie jolted in surprise. Papa never raised his voice to them.

'You will apologise to Miss Merton.' His voice lowered in volume but did not soften. 'She is not your servant, but rather, she is doing this family a great favour.'

Caroline's eyes filled with tears. 'I—I apologise, Miss Merton.' She sniffed.

'It's quite all right, dear,' Miss Merton assured her. 'We all lose our tempers.'

'May I be excused?' Caroline jutted her chin defiantly. As soon as Papa nodded, she fled the room. Papa tsked and Mama placed a hand over his in a comforting gesture.

The rest of the breakfast continued in muted conversation, and finally, Papa and Mama excused themselves as

well as Miss Merton, so Persephone and Maddie found
themselves alone.

'That sister of yours sure has a temper.'

'Caroline's not that terrible,' Maddie found herself
saying. 'She was a sweet child.'

'Sweet?' Persephone stuck out her tongue. 'I can't
imagine her being sweet, even as a wee child. She's
spoiled rotten.'

Maddie had never truly thought about how or when
Caroline had become who she was. 'We weren't always
rich, you know. But then the furnace became successful
and Papa and I worked together all the time, so he made
up for it with Mama and Caroline by giving them everything they wanted.' She remembered what Caroline was
like as a child and how they used to play together. Seeing her in tears now made her heart clench.

'What time are your callers arriving this afternoon?'
Persephone asked. 'Are you having any more of your lessons with Cam?'

'I… I'm not sure, really.' She chewed on her lip. Cam
had all but disappeared this week. *And right when I
needed him, too.* He'd promised her he would help her
weed out the scoundrels from her callers, but now he was
nowhere in sight.

'Why don't we go to the library?' Persephone suggested. 'Unless you're much too busy for me now.'

Maddie chuckled. 'For you—never.'

The two women left the breakfast room, and as they
passed through the hall, Maddie saw Eames opening
the front door, and a familiar dark-haired female figure
strolled in. 'Kate?'

'Good morning, Eames— Maddie!' she cried, then
rushed over to her. 'You don't know how happy I am to

see you.' Kate drew her in for a fierce hug. 'I've missed you so.'

'So have I!' Happiness filled her as she drew back and looked at her friend. 'You're looking so well. But what are you doing here? I mean, I know you can come and go as you please.' This was Kate's home, after all, as she was the current Duchess of Mabury. 'But why didn't you send word of your arrival?'

'I had a meeting with the architects that ended early and wanted to surprise Mama and everyone.' She looked over at Eames. 'Is the Dowager in her sitting room?'

'I'm afraid not, Your Grace,' the butler replied. 'She left early and is not expected back until luncheon.'

'Oh, no.' She tsked. 'But this means I'll be able to spend time with you, Maddie.'

'Wonderful. Will you be staying until tomorrow?'

'I'll have to leave after luncheon, I'm afraid. I promised Sebastian I'd be home in Highfield Park tonight.' From the glow on her face, it was obvious that Kate was very much in love with her husband. 'But—oh, are you Lady Persephone? Mama has told me all about you in her letters.'

'Oh, how rude of me,' Maddie exclaimed. 'Allow me to introduce you. Your Grace, this is Lady Persephone MacGregor. Lady Persephone, this is Her Grace Kathryn, the Duchess of Mabury.'

Persephone curtsied. 'I'm honoured to meet you, Your Grace.'

A mysterious smile touched Kate's lips. 'The honour is mine, Lady Persephone. I've been eager to meet you.'

She blinked. 'Y-you have?'

'Yes. But why don't we sit down for tea in the library.' She nodded to Eames, who immediately set off. 'Come.'

They headed off in the direction of the library and

settled in the wing-back chairs and sofa by the window. 'I hope you can visit us in Highfield Park at some point,' Kate began. 'When I heard Mama had another guest arriving, I thought she might bring you, Lady Persephone, to visit us there to ease you into the season.'

Persephone looked confused, so Maddie began to explain, 'When the Dowager agreed to become our sponsor, we stayed in Highfield Park at first. We weren't quite ready yet for a London season, and she asked us to stay there at first, if only to stop us from floundering.' Maddie sent Kate a smile. 'That's also where Kate met and fell in love with the Duke of Mabury, the Dowager's son.'

'That's the short version of events, anyway,' Kate laughed. 'But let's not talk about me—it's boring. Tell me all about what's been happening with you. You haven't had much time to write letters.' She feigned a pout. 'But I forgive you, because from what I've heard, you've been busy with all your suitors who are lining up outside the door?'

Maddie couldn't help but smile. 'Not quite. A few callers, and two prospects who are serious.'

'Three,' Persephone said. 'Don't forget my brother, now.'

How could she forget?

'Your brother?'

'Yes, Your Grace. Cameron, Earl of Balfour. He's quite mad about Maddie here,' Persephone offered cheerfully.

'Really, now?' Kate's dark eyebrows lifted in question.

Maddie wanted to tell her friend about their plan and how Cam was assisting her rather than trying to marry her, but the less people knew, the better. Besides, if she told Kate, she would have to tell the Duke, because they shared everything, and she didn't want Kate to have to lie to her husband.

'And he's taller than her,' Persephone added.

'Then he must be tall indeed.' Kate grinned at her.

'You'll see for yourself soon enough. But, Your Grace,' Persephone began. 'I have heard so much about you from Maddie. Is it true you are a railway engineer?'

Kate's expression changed. 'Yes, I'm designing my own locomotive now, but I helped my grandfather design the Andersen steam engine. It's one of the fastest and most efficient locomotives today.'

Persephone's eyes grew wide. 'But you are working on an engine of your own design now?'

'Persephone's very much interested in mechanics,' Maddie explained. 'Her family runs a whisky distillery.'

'Truly?' Kate leaned forward. 'You must tell me all about it.'

Maddie was glad that Kate was distracted by talk of engineering, and truth be told, she had missed her friend and missed this type of conversation. Though she was not as passionate about the furnace as Kate was about her engines, her work had made her feel useful and productive. There was progress being made in the world, and she couldn't help but feel that someday her own small contributions would somehow make a big difference.

Eames eventually came with some tea, and they continued talking until luncheon. The Dowager arrived just before lunch, and she was thrilled to see Kate. Luncheon was a lively affair, with everyone welcoming the new Duchess back, though Caroline remained muted throughout the meal.

'I hate to leave so soon,' Kate said as she and the Dowager walked to her waiting carriage. 'I promise you, Mama, Sebastian and I will come to stay. Then we can all go to Highfield Park together.'

'I look forward to it, dear.' She kissed Kate on the

cheek. 'I shall head inside so you may have a few minutes of privacy.'

Kate turned to Maddie. 'So, is there anything you need to tell me? About your suitors, maybe?'

'They are all quite agreeable,' she said.

'I'm sure they are, but is there anyone you truly fancy?' Kate leaned forward, her gaze narrowing. 'There is, isn't there? Is it the Earl?'

'What? Uh…' What was she supposed to say? 'I wish we had more time. Then I could tell you everything.' Perhaps by then she would have enough suitors and she could tell Kate the truth. For now, she would delay telling her friend, which would not exactly be lying.

Kate embraced her. 'All right. I'll let you keep your own counsel for now. Just promise me you'll follow your heart, all right? Do not let your mother pressure you into making a decision you might regret later.'

'I won't.' Her throat burned, and she could see Kate's eyes water as well. 'Come now. I'm still going to see you, Your Grace,' she teased.

'Of course.' Kate chuckled as the footman assisted her into the carriage. 'See you soon, Maddie.'

'You too.'

Maddie waved as the carriage pulled away, her friend's words lingering in her mind. She never resented Kate for what she had, but as was the case for anyone with privilege, she sometimes failed to see that not everyone's circumstances were the same. Not all women had the luck of falling in love with the first man they met, and it was even harder for people like Maddie who did not fit society's standards of what a woman should look like.

At the same time, however, she pondered Miss Merton's words about not being too picky. With two potential suitors, Maddie was luckier than most, and she did not even want a title, just a husband who could give her a family she could love and care for.

Cam's face appeared in her mind, but she quickly shook it away. But, just as luck would have it, a familiar carriage was quickly pulling up in front of the house. She froze, unsure what to do. If she were to flee now, he would see her running away from him. But if she were to stay, she would have to acknowledge his presence. Seeing as there was no alternative, she chose the latter.

Why am I hiding from him, anyway? He promised her he would help her once the time came that she had potential suitors.

And that time was now.

'My lord, good day,' she greeted him.

Cam had just stepped down the step when their eyes met. His expression faltered for a moment, as he obviously did not expect to see her there. 'Miss DeVries. What a lovely surprise. What are you doing out here by yourself?'

'I was seeing a friend off.'

His lips pulled back. 'I see. You have been popular lately.'

'About that.' She lowered her voice. 'May I walk inside with you?'

'Of course.'

'Now,' she continued as they meandered back into the house. 'I was wondering if you are able to assist me now. In our—' she glanced around surreptitiously '—project.'

'Project?'

'You know. The project.' She leaned closer and whispered, 'To sift out the scoundrels from my list of suitors.'

'I see.' He paused thoughtfully. 'And did you have this list?'

'List?'

'Yes. A list. One that we can go over.'

'I didn't realise I needed an actual paper list.'

'That's what I said, right?' he reminded her. 'Once you have a list, I shall help you. I will need time to learn about these fellows, of course. I do not know every gentleman in London, after all.'

'Oh.'

'I shall see you later, then, Miss DeVries.' He tipped his hat to her, then handed it to Eames along with his coat before striding off in the direction of the smoking room.

'Huh.'

All right, then. If it's a list Cam wants, then it's a list he will have.

Marching up to her room, she opened her notebook and wrote down names of all the gentlemen who had shown some interest in courting her. No one had asked her papa's permission yet, but a few had made overtures.

When she finished her list, she hurried down to the smoking room and knocked. When she heard Cam call out, 'Come in,' she opened the door and peeked inside.

'Murray, just put it on the— Maddie?'

'Cam,' she greeted from the doorway. 'I have it.'

'Have what?'

She waved a piece of paper in her hand. 'My list.'

'List—oh. You have it already?'

'Of course.' As she crossed the threshold, he held up a hand. 'What is it?'

'You shouldn't have come here by yourself. Anyone could come in,' he pointed out. 'And find us alone.'

'How was I supposed to give you my list? I couldn't very well ask Eames to deliver it to you.' Before he could protest, she handed him the list. 'Here you go.'

He plucked the list from her fingers, eyes scanning through the list. 'All of these men want to court you?'

'They've implied their interest,' she said.

'How so?'

'Well, everyone on that list has at least paid a call on me at least once,' she said. 'But we've all had a second point of contact. I didn't know how many names you would have time to look into, so I've narrowed it down to a list of five based on a set of criteria.'

'Criteria?'

'Yes. Either they've paid me a second call or we've done an activity, like go for a ride or stroll in the park. Or some I've made plans with.'

'How organised of you,' he commented. 'All right. I will ask around and find out what I can.'

'Thank you, Cam. I'll see myself out.'

Cam knew this time would come.

He just didn't think it would be this soon.

He thought he would at least have two weeks, maybe a month, before Maddie made any progress, especially since they had yet to attend more balls. But apparently it had taken only a matter of days for news of her popularity to spread.

Cam sank deeper into the leather chair, wishing it would swallow him up. He had delayed as much as he could by avoiding Maddie, but he could say no to only so many engagements, as he still had to escort his sister around.

And so, for the next two weeks, he went to the opera with Persephone and attended teas and other socials. All the while, he watched Maddie with other men. Palmer—who was on her list—even joined them in the Dowager's private box at the ballet.

He did, however, make good use of his social activities by enquiring about the men on Maddie's list. Actually, it didn't take much to find useful information—London's gentlemen were as terrible as the ladies when it came to gossip, especially when there were no women around. There were still two more names on the list he could not dig up dirt on, but perhaps he could hire a private investigator.

Cam decided he would ask George Atwell when he arrived for their meeting. And speaking of which, he was due to arrive soon, so he made his way to the smoking room. He barely had time to settle into his usual chair when he heard a knock on the door.

That was probably Atwell now. 'Come in,' he called. When he saw Maddie enter, he groaned inwardly. 'You're not Atwell.'

Her lips were pressed tight together as she strode in. 'I don't mean to be impatient or ungrateful, Cam. But it has been two weeks. I don't suppose you have any information for me?'

'Information about…?' he asked, feigning innocence.

'The list,' she said. 'About the gentlemen.'

'Ah, yes. Actually, I have.' He gestured to the seat opposite him and retrieved the wrinkled sheet of paper from his pocket. 'Baron James Clifton,' he read aloud, then clucked his tongue.

'What's wrong with him?'

'Notorious gambler. He will obliterate your dowry within a year.'

She frowned. 'You do not know how big my dowry is.'

'And you do not know how terrible Clifton is at cards.'

'My father hates gamblers, anyway.' She blew out a breath. 'Who else?'

He looked at the next name on the list. 'Lord Andrew Annesley.' He shook his head.

'What about him? He was at the dinner party the Dowager hosted. You didn't seem to object to his presence.'

'Yes, well, he's a nice fellow. But rumour is, his mother's got him under her thumb,' Cam explained. 'A bit of a harridan, that one. She controls everything he does, from what he eats for breakfast to what articles he reads in the paper. You wouldn't want to live with a mother-in-law who controlled every aspect of your life, would you?'

'I suppose not.' Her shoulders slumped over. 'Who else?'

'Lord Thomas Harver.' He touched his fingers together and placed his forefingers on his chin while drawing his eyebrows together for dramatic effect. 'I do not know how to explain this one, Maddie.'

'Why?' She scooted to the edge of her seat. 'What have you heard?'

'Harver's a widow three times over.' Actually, Cam had heard different versions—some said only twice, and other said four times, so he'd picked the number between them. 'And all his wives died in mysterious circumstances. The last one was found by the butler at the bottom of the staircase.'

She shuddered. 'I always thought there was something strange about him. Who else?'

Cam paused. He didn't need to read the last two names on the list, because he already knew what information he had on them: absolutely nothing. 'Sir Alfred Kensington—he's a little old for you, isn't he? His hair is completely white.'

'Old? It's not like he's decrepit,' she pointed out. 'He's probably only a few years younger than my father.'

'I heard that fall from his horse wasn't that terrible, and he only suffered a sprained ankle.' He tsked. 'But you know, when you get to his age, every little trip and fall brings you closer to your deathbed.'

'Cam!' she admonished. 'You cannot say such things. Besides, I saw him yesterday at Hyde Park. He seemed fit as a fiddle.'

'Did you now?' Damn.

'Well, you know…uh…he…' *Think of something!* He wouldn't lie to Maddie, but he had to say something about Kensington. 'He…he…smells like soup.'

'Smells like—are you jesting with me, Cam?'

'No, I'm not. I swear to you.' He held a hand to his chest. 'Go ahead and take a whiff next time he's around. He's definitely got that aroma of lobster bisque.'

Maddie's face turned green as she covered her hand with her mouth. 'All right. How about Viscount Palmer?'

Double damn.

It had been even harder to find any dirt on Palmer. 'Yes, well… I noticed you have never danced with him. Are you sure he knows how to?'

'No, we have yet to dance, but we have had the most pleasant conversation at the ballet, and he has requested to dance with me first at the Hayfield ball next week.'

Over my dead body would he dance with Maddie first. 'But he's quite a bit shorter than you, isn't he?'

'Cam, all the men on the list are shorter than me.' She sighed.

Except me.

Cam's stomach flipped at the thought, and the one that came after that.

Me, Maddie. Put me on your list. Pick me.

Triple damn.

He curled his hands into fists. No, he had to stop his thoughts from wandering in that direction. This little exercise was meant to help Maddie find a suitable husband

and not expose his own growing need. He only had to think of Jenny to know where this would lead.

'I wish I were shorter.' Her head drooped low, her gaze falling to the floor. 'If I could make myself smaller, I would.'

'No,' he protested. Sliding forward, he got to his knees in front of her and reached over to her so he could tip her chin up. 'Never make yourself small, Maddie. Not for anyone.'

Luminous blue eyes stared up at him, and her plump pink lips parted. 'Cam…'

Slowly, he leaned closer, and she, too, moved her head forward. Time slowed down, and their lips were mere inches away when a knock on the door had him reeling back. He slammed back into the chair but managed to quickly scramble to his feet. 'One moment, Atwell!' he called out. 'Maddie—'

'I… Sorry… I shouldn't,' Maddie stammered as she shot up from the chair. 'Thank you for the information. It was definitely helpful.' She dashed towards the door and flung it open, then ran past a very confused-looking Murray.

Cam stared at the door, unsure what to do.

'My lord?' Murray asked. 'Your coffee?'

'No.'

'No?'

'I don't want any coffee,' he bit out.

'What do you want then, my lord?'

Her.

I want her. 'I want to go out. To the fencing club. Please have my clothing ready. And when Mr. Atwell arrives, tell him I had an emergency.'

'Right away, my lord.'

Chapter Fourteen

Cam had been a member of the Beaumont Fencing Club for the last few years, ever since he'd started taking regular trips to London. Like many men his age, Cam enjoyed sport, and when most people first laid eyes on him, they immediately thought he preferred boxing. While he could always go a round or two in the ring, Cam actually liked fencing, which required a different kind of grace, skill, and strength from pugilism. He was glad that his mother had insisted he learn the gentlemanly sport, as Cam found he excelled at it. Most of his opponents thought he would be slow and lumbering due to his size, but he quickly proved to be the opposite—fast as lightning, with a deadly reach and accurate aim.

Usually, an afternoon of physical activity was enough to calm him on a stressful day, but it seemed nothing could put him at ease. He'd already obliterated two opponents, and no, his agitation had not abated. Not even imagining Kensington's and Palmer's faces over their helmets could soothe him; in fact, he probably would have seriously injured his sparring partners if it were not for the protective gear they wore.

'Thank you, gentlemen, but I must be on my way,' he

murmured to the other members. He could practically hear all of them sighing with relief as he walked away.

Cam entered the changing rooms, then headed to the first set of benches. He sat down, removed his helmet, and buried his face in his hands.

They'd almost kissed. Again. He was supposed to be helping her find a husband, not lusting after her. Not wanting to kiss those luscious lips or feel her body against his. The only other time he'd been this out of control was with Jenny.

I cannot do this again.

'…so, you're really banned from The Underworld for life? Why did Ransom have you tossed out on the street?'

The voices he was overhearing were difficult to ignore as they reverberated round the small room. Rising to his feet, Cam began to undress so he could leave before it got too crowded.

'I was having a bit of fun with one of the whores in the back room. Bitch went running to him, said I roughed her up.'

Cam had the canvas jacket halfway off when he went rigid. He recognised that voice. Viscount Odious.

'When he confronted me, I said, "That's what they're here for, right?"' He spat. 'Then he personally escorted me out and told me never to come back. Stupid whore. And damn that Ransom.'

'He's a ruthless bastard, that one,' someone said.

'Bastard is right,' Palmer scoffed. 'In any case, soon I'll have so much money, all the clubs in London will be begging me to be a member.'

'Your father's nearly at death's door, right?'

'Unfortunately, no. The twisted old git's hanging on for dear life, if only to spite me. No, I've a much better plan.'

'Is it that chit you were with at the ballet? The giantess?'
Maddie. They were definitely talking about Maddie.

'She's American, correct?' Another voice piped in. 'Heard her father's richer than sin. But why not go for the sister? She's much more pleasant to look at.'

'I thought I would take a gander at her, seeing as she'd look better on my arm and I wouldn't have to hurt my neck each time I tried to kiss her.' Palmer laughed. 'But word around town is that she's a little tease. Keeps men hanging on with her favours here and there, but ultimately won't let go—of her dowry, at least. No, no. With my father beating off Death at every turn, I cannot wait that long.'

'You almost have her, then?'

'Nearly there. I'll ask her father's permission to court her, and we'll be engaged soon enough.'

'What if she wants a long engagement? Or what if her father says no?'

'Well, there are other ways to speed along a wedding, are there not?'

'Pleasurable ways,' someone quipped.

Laughter rang throughout the room, the sound only making Cam's fury rise.

Palmer continued. 'See, chaps, that's the advantage of homely misses and undesirable wallflowers. They're so grateful for the attention, you'll have them following you around like a bitch in heat in no time. I'll marry her, have a bit of fun, get her with child, and pack her off to the country. Then I can spend her dowry in peace and live to a standard I'd like to get accustomed to.'

'You are a genius, Palmer.'

'Aren't I?'

It took every ounce of strength Cam could muster not to march over there and beat the Viscount senseless. *Or skewer him*, he thought, glancing at his sabre. Unfortunately, he'd dealt with enough Englishmen to know they would never take anyone else's side against their own, especially not a Scotsman. He knew he'd have to rein in his fury—a scandal could ruin Persephone's chances at a successful London season.

Bottling his rage, Cam didn't bother to change out of his fencing clothes and raced out of the club. 'Mabury Hall,' he told his driver as he got in the carriage. 'As fast as you can.'

The drive did nothing to soothe his fury. All he could think of was that bastard Palmer and all the ways he could make him hurt. But first, he had to ensure Maddie never saw him again.

His first instinct was to speak with Mr DeVries and tell him what he'd learned. Unfortunately, Eames had told him that Mr DeVries was not at home.

He had no choice, then. He would have to go directly to Maddie and make her see reason. He had only one guess as to where she could be, so he stormed into the library.

'Maddie?' he called out, shutting the door behind him. 'Maddie?'

'I— Cam?' She rounded the corner from behind one of the shelves. 'Cam, what's the—what are you wearing?'

'It doesn't matter.' He crossed the distance between them. 'You cannot marry Palmer. In fact, you are never to see him again.' He could only guess what kind of 'fun' Palmer had in mind, and he would kill the Viscount first before he touched Maddie.

'What?' She replaced the book in her hand onto the nearest shelf. 'Cam, what happened? You look as if you've run a mile.'

'Are you listening to me, Maddie?' He wanted to shake

her until she agreed but settled to speaking slowly. 'You. Cannot. See. Him. Ever.'

'I don't understand. Where is this coming from? Just a few hours ago, you couldn't find any objectively good reason I shouldn't consider Viscount Palmer. And now I'm to stay away from him?'

'He's a bas—he wants you for your money.'

'They all want me for my money,' she said matter-of-factly. 'That is why women have dowries.'

How could she be so glib? 'You can't marry him, Maddie. He's a foul miscreant. He means to get you with child and forget about you while he spends your dowry. He called you a…'

'A what?'

Homely. Undesirable. Bitch in heat.

No, he would not repeat Palmer's awful words to her. Not when she'd worked so hard to build her confidence. And while he didn't want Maddie to marry that bastard, he did not want to destroy her, either.

'Tell me,' she said gently. 'What is this really about?'

He swallowed the lump in his throat as she took a step closer to him.

'What has made you so worked up?'

You, he wanted to rail at her. *You have me riled up and twisted me about so I cannot think straight.* But as the air thickened and tension stretched taut between them, neither of them spoke.

Her lips parted, and she let out a breathy, 'Cam?'

His teeth ground together in frustration. 'Tell me, Maddie, do you even like him? Could you even see yourself spending the next twenty or forty years next to him?' Her plump lips parted, and he couldn't help but stare at them. 'Would you even want to kiss him?'

'Not as much as I want to kiss you.'

The last string that held his control together broke. Maddie closed the distance between them and reached up to him, but Cam was faster and caught her face in his hands as he slanted his mouth over hers. Maddie grabbed onto his shoulders and clung to him, opening her lips to his kiss.

He swept his tongue into her mouth and he swore he could taste sweetness. He deepened the kiss, nearly devouring her as she moaned aloud and moved up against him, breasts crushing into his chest. He'd been dreaming about them, wondering what they looked like, how they tasted, and what her colour her nipples were.

As if she'd read his mind, she grabbed his hand and pressed it against her breasts. Needing no further invitation, he delved into the neckline and popped one delectable globe out, then trailed his lips down to her neck so he could look down at her exposed breast.

Holy hell. Her nipples were the loveliest shade of brown, dark and taut, while the large areola was a pretty pink. Dragging his mouth away from her neck, he licked at the stiff peak.

'Cam!' Fingers dug into his hair and the scraping of her nails on his scalp made his cock instantly harden.

He suckled and laved her breast, giving it the attention it deserved. Maddie sighed and moaned, and he wondered if she was even aware of how her hips thrust at him invitingly. Sliding a hand down her back, he cupped her bottom and pulled her to him, allowing her to rub herself against him.

Cam teased and tortured her nipple some more, and while he could do this for hours, he wanted to give Maddie the relief she needed. She let out a protesting cry when he released her breast.

'Lord, Maddie… You're too much… You're driving

me wild.' He looked at her, those sky blue eyes fixed on him. 'I could give you so much more…' But he couldn't go on further. In fact, they'd gone on far enough. He loosened his hold on her and took a step back but found himself unable to move as Maddie's arm slipped around his waist, holding him in place.

'Then give it to me, Cam,' she said without hesitation. 'Please. I want it and everything else you can give me.' A hand boldly slipped down to his buttocks and pulled him forward.

Dear God in heaven, she was truly an Amazon goddess. She didn't ask. She *took* what was rightfully hers.

He caught her mouth in a kiss before she could speak further, then walked her backwards against the bookshelf behind her. His hand slipped further down, then bent her leg to plant her foot on the lowest shelf. He grabbed her skirt and lifted the frothy fabric over her knee so he could reach underneath. The first touch of his hand on her warm thigh made her jolt.

His fingers trailed a path up her soft skin, up to the downy triangle left exposed by the slit in her drawers. When she didn't protest, he gently stroked the lips, which were now damp with her desire. His cock swelled, straining against his tight fencing breeches. He parted her and pressed a finger into her, until the first knuckle.

Dear God, she was tight.

'More,' she pleaded against his mouth. 'Oh, please, Cam.'

And so he pushed further, until his finger was fully in her, wrapped in her heat and slick. If this is what she felt like with his finger, he would surely die once he was inside her.

Slowly, he moved his hand, sliding his finger gently along her slick passage. Apparently, this was not enough for Maddie, and her hips undulated at a much faster pace than his hand.

Patience, he urged silently. Withdrawing his finger, he twisted his hand so he could find that button just above her entrance that he knew would drive her wild. When he brushed his thumb over it, Maddie fell against him, head leaning on his shoulder and fingers digging into his arms.

She panted, her breath hot on his neck, as he continued to stroke her. She grew slicker by the second, so he managed to slip a finger inside her, and then another. 'Cam!' Her hips moved in time with his fingers as he thrust them into her. When her grip on his arms tightened and her spine stiffened, he knew her peak was close.

'That's it, lass,' he encouraged. 'Let go. Let it happen.'

She whimpered loudly as her body shuddered. His cock twitched painfully as she brushed against his hips. He bit the inside of his cheek to stop himself from spending like an untried lad. When it was over, she slumped back against the bookshelves, eyes closed as she breathed hard.

'We must stop now, darling.' Could she even hear his whispered groan? 'We can't be found like this. I'll not have you compromised like this.' She deserved much better than a rut against a shelf.

A loud gasp rang in his ear, and while he was lost in passion, he was still mindful enough to recognise that was not a gasp of pleasure, nor had it come from Maddie. He froze in place.

What in the world—?

'You Goddamned bastard, get off her!' A hand grabbed at the straps of his fencing coat and hauled him off Maddie. He barely had time to recover before a powerful fist connected with his jaw, sending pain across his face.

Cam staggered back and miraculously he didn't lose his balance. There were shouts and cries around him, but he was too stunned to make sense of what was happening. When the stars disappeared from his vision, a man appeared before him—dark-haired, dark-eyed, and very, very displeased.

'You bastard,' he raged. 'How dare you do this to Miss DeVries?'

'Do this—who the hell are you, anyway?'

'Sebastian, Duke of Mabury.' Dark eyes flashed with fury. 'Your host and owner of this house.'

'Oh.' *Hell.* 'Your Grace,' he said with a bow.

Mabury lunged forward, and this time, Cam was prepared and ducked away from him.

'Don't, Your Grace!' Maddie shouted as her mother rushed in, sobbed, and wrapped her arms around her.

'Oh, Maddie.' Mrs DeVries was frantically trying to put her hair to rights. 'My poor, poor Maddie.'

Mabury gnashed his teeth. 'What were you doing to her?'

'I was trying to stop her from making a big mistake,' Cam explained.

'By ruining her?' Mabury roared.

'Sebastian!' A petite brunette Cam had never seen before put herself between them. This must be Mabury's wife. 'Calm yourself.'

'Calm myself?' Mabury said in an incredulous tone. 'Did we all not see the same thing? This…this beast rutting on Madeline?' His face was scarlet with wrath, hulking shoulders heaving. 'If I could, I would ensure him a long, slow death, then bring him back to life so I could do it all over again.'

'So would I, darling, but I need to see to Maddie first.' The Duchess sent Cam a seething glare before heading over to Maddie's side. 'Are you all right, Maddie? Are you hurt?'

Maddie shook her head. 'Please, Kate. I don't want any more violence. This is a simple misunderstanding.'

Mrs DeVries pointed an accusing finger at Cam. 'That...fiend has stolen your virtue!'

'Mama, compose yourself. Nothing happened.'

Cam bit the urge to say, *It was not nothing*, except it was obvious whatever he said or excuses he made would not help in this scenario. Indeed, by all accounts, he was the villain here. Maddie was an innocent virgin, and he shouldn't have let passion overtake him. 'I'm so sorry,' he said to no one in particular.

'You should be sorry,' Mabury growled. 'And so you must marry her.'

'Of course, I will marry Maddie.' They had been found *in flagrante delicto* by her mother and the Duke and Duchess, and the Dowager was there in the doorway, too. The only way this could be worse was if Mr DeVries had witnessed this. 'We will get it done as soon as I can procure a special licence.'

Mrs DeVries moaned. 'The scandal. Think of the scandal.'

'Everyone, please.' Maddie disentangled herself from her mother. 'There's no need to overreact.' She sent him a sideways glance. 'If no one says anything, then there's no need to fuss. We do not have to marry.'

'What are you saying, Madeline?' Mrs DeVries planted her hands on her waist. 'I cannot lie to your father.'

'Maddie, think about this—'

'Don't give him a way out—'

Despite the din around him, Cam could not make out what everyone was saying because the only thing he could think of was that Maddie had said she didn't want to marry him.

The truth hit him straight in the chest like an axe.

Of course she didn't want him.

But what she wanted didn't matter. After what they'd done and with all the witnesses here, they would have no choice. Her father would expect that.

'Stop!' Maddie shouted. 'You're not listening to me.'

'Maddie, you must—'

'This bastard—'

A delicate clearing of a throat made the noise cease. The Dowager glided into the room, calm as a millpond. 'Emotions are running rather high at the moment, so I suggest we all take a breath and think about what we need to do. Kate, please escort Mrs DeVries to Miss Merton. I normally wouldn't have the heart to wake her during her afternoon nap, but I'm sure she won't mind, given the circumstances. Explain to her what happened, then come back down here.'

'Yes, Mama.' The Duchess placed an arm around Mrs DeVries. 'Come now, Eliza.'

'B-but what about Maddie? Shouldn't she come with me?' Eliza asked.

'I'm going to arrange a cup of tea for Maddie. Before you go up to Miss Merton, send word to your husband and ask him to return to Mabury Hall at once.'

'Of course, Your Grace.' Mollified, she allowed the Duchess to take her away.

The Dowager went over to Maddie. 'I'll take care of everything, dear.' Looking over her shoulder, she said to her son, 'Sebastian, take the Earl away, please, but do not let him out of your sight. I will send for him after I've spoken to Miss DeVries.'

'Gladly,' Mabury said, glaring at Cam.

Cam evaded the Duke's grasp when he attempted to grab his arm. 'I'll come, Your Grace. No need to shackle me. I'll not run away.' He sent one last glance at Maddie, but she would not look him in the eye. How he wished he could speak to her.

He'd offered marriage, and she'd turned him down. They'd been stopped just in time, and Maddie remained a virgin. *I should never have touched her.* His lust and desire had been overwhelming, and the thought that she wanted him—and that she wanted to kiss him—had been too much of a temptation. *And I didn't want to marry, anyway.*

But then, why did her rejection bring that twisting, painful sensation in his chest instead of gratitude and relief?

He followed Mabury out of the library, down the hall into what he assumed was the Duke's private office. Mabury said not a word, so Cam studied the man.

The Duke was tall, but still a good half a foot shorter than him. He was wide, though, his shoulders straining against his tailored coat, and his skin was sun-kissed, as if he spent a lot of time outdoors. As he strode over to the mantel to pour some brandy from a decanter into a glass, Cam couldn't help but notice that his hands were not pale and soft but, rather, rough and calloused. It reminded him a lot of his own father's hands.

When Mabury turned back to face him, he began with, 'Your Grace, please allow me to apologise for—' Another blow struck him on the cheek, though not as hard as before, as it only sent his head knocking back. 'I suppose I deserve that.' He was definitely going to have a black eye in the morning.

'I needed to do that. For Maddie,' the Duke explained,

his tone curiously polite. Then he handed the glass of amber liquid to Cam.

'And what's this for?'

The Duke shook his head. 'For having your proposal rejected.'

Cam would have smiled, except it hurt to do so. 'Thank you.' The Duke had sounded sympathetic, as if he knew what that particular experience was like.

Mabury folded his arms over his chest. 'Why?'

Such a simple question.

One word.

Three letters.

Yet, Cam couldn't explain it himself.

He downed the contents of the glass in one gulp, the alcohol sliding smoothly down his throat and warming his belly. 'As I said, it began because I was trying to stop her from making a mistake.' With a deep breath, he told Mabury about Viscount Palmer and what he'd overheard at the club.

'Bloody bastard. I always hated that snivelling fool.' The Duke's dark brows slashed together. 'Still, that doesn't excuse why you mauled her against my complete set of Shakespeare's works.'

'You're right.' He pulled at the collar of his fencing coat. 'I wasn't... I didn't think...'

'You'd get caught,' the Duke finished.

Cam placed the glass back on the mantel. 'I was caught up in the passion,' he explained. 'I wanted her.'

'She's an innocent.'

'She is, and that's why I'm not making any excuses.' Maddie could have stopped him at any time, but he was the more experienced between the two of them. 'I should have known better. But I plan to make things right.'

'Oh, you will marry,' he declared.

'Why do you care, anyway?'

'She's my wife's dearest friend and like a sister to me. I'll kill anyone who upsets my wife.' He sounded deadly serious. 'Was she willing?'

'Aye. I would never force myself on a woman.'

The Duke's stare softened. 'Why didn't you say so?'

'And humiliate her in front of her mother, your wife, and the Dowager by implying she's a wanton woman who asked for it? Nay, I'll not do that to her.' Besides, what they had shared was beautiful. He didn't want to cheapen that.

Mabury turned pensive. 'Cornelius won't force her to marry you. You'll have to find a way to convince her.'

Cam was tempted to reach for the entire decanter and pour the entire contents down his gullet. Maddie's rejection had stung more than he'd thought. 'Why did she turn me down?' When the Duke did not answer, he came up with the explanation himself: because she didn't want to marry him.

Plain and simple.

This was like Jenny all over again, but worse. It wasn't that she was in love with Palmer or she would have said so.

She just didn't want *him*.

He wasn't enough for her, either. And why would he be? She was so intelligent and lovely and kind, and he was unworthy of her. He was not smart, certainly not like his mother had been or how Persephone or Liam were. He had the MacGregor charm, yes, but that was it. All charm, but no substance.

'Here, have another.' The Duke offered him another glass. 'You look like you need it.'

'Aye, I do.' He took a sip.

'Even if there are no consequences, you still need to marry her,' the Duke said. 'Her mother—'

'I know. She will force my hand somehow.' He knew Eliza DeVries well enough. She would do anything so her daughters could marry well, even if it meant a scandal. Eliza would go public with Cam's deeds, and if they didn't marry, Maddie would have to either live as an outcast or leave England. He could not let that happen to her.

'It just occurred to me, Balfour, that you simply told her that you were marrying. And if there's something I've learned the past few months as a married man is that women definitely do not like being told what to do. At least, the ones worth having.'

'So, I will ask her again to marry me properly.' *Even if she doesn't want me. Even if I'm not worthy.*

'She still has to accept your proposal.'

'Aye, that she does.' He could only hope he could somehow make her say yes.

Chapter Fifteen

Everything had happened so fast, it was as if Maddie's mind remained two steps behind her body. One moment, Cam was on her, pinning her against the bookshelf, and the next…chaos.

Oh, heavens. What was to happen now?

'Have some tea, dear,' the Dowager said. 'It will calm you down.'

Maddie blinked, surprised to find herself sitting in the wing-back chair by the window, a shawl wrapped around her and a cup of hot tea in her hand. She did as the Dowager bade and took a sip. The hot liquid was, indeed, soothing. 'Thank you, Your Grace.' She put the teacup down.

'Do not thank me yet, dear.' She sent Maddie a comforting smile. 'But I promise you, we will get everything sorted out.'

'I have taken care of Mrs DeVries, Mama,' Kate said as she entered the library. 'Oh, Maddie.' She dashed to her side and wrapped an arm around her shoulders. 'I'm so sorry. Will you tell us what happened? Did he…force himself on you?'

'No, he did not.' Maddie would have laughed, but the entire situation was already absurd. Cam, force himself on her? Why, she had been a willing participant, from beginning to end.

The pleasure was unlike anything she'd felt before. She wanted it. If anything, she wanted more, and even now, she still throbbed and ached, the dampness between her thighs evidence that the encounter had really happened. His fingers…his mouth…

'*Ahem*.' The Dowager's lips were pressed together, but the amusement in her eyes was clear. 'It's all right Maddie. You know you can trust us. You are safe here.'

'I know.' She smiled warmly at Kate. That's why the Dowager had sent Mama away. She knew the only way Maddie would tell the truth was if her mother were not around. 'I—we—kissed, willingly. It just went a bit too far. But we didn't mean to.' They'd been swept away by the passion, and now that they had been caught, they were trapped.

'But why don't you want to marry him?' the Dowager asked. 'I thought he was interested in courting you. You danced with him at every ball, sometimes twice. He paid you a call. I heard he even interrupted your time with Viscount Palmer. Your mother was practically preening at his jealous rage. I thought for sure you would welcome a proposal from him.'

'Is there someone else?' Kate enquired. 'Perhaps you've recently met another gentleman you prefer more than the Earl?'

Maddie swallowed hard. *Now I know how a trapped fox feels.* Their lies and deception had finally caught up with them.

'It's not what you think.' Having no other choice, she confessed to Kate and the Dowager about the fake courtship plot. The entire time, neither woman said anything, but they looked at each other every so often. '...so, you see, the Earl doesn't really want to marry me.'

'Yet, he ravished you in the library,' Kate said drolly. 'Men always say one thing and mean another. Change their mind at a whim. And they say we are the unpredictable sex.'

The Dowager tilted her head to the side. 'So, the Earl did all of that for you? Pretend to court you so that you may find a husband?'

'Persephone practically had to beg him on my behalf.' She sighed. 'Besides, our plan was working. There were several gentlemen who were ready to ask my father's permission to court me. Why did Cam have to go muck that all up by storming into the library, demanding I not marry Viscount Palmer?'

'You didn't say anything about that,' Kate said.

'Did I not?' She bit her lip. 'I was in the library, and then he came all in a rage. We'd just had a nice conversation about my list earlier in the day.'

'What list?' Kate's eyebrow rose high.

'My list of—' Oh, dear, she kept going backwards. 'Let me start again.' So she explained this time, about her list of eligible men that Cam was helping her with. 'Later, he came into the library, demanding that I not marry the Viscount. He wouldn't tell me why, only that I should never see him again. I asked him what was going on, and then... Then, things just got out of hand.'

Kate and Dowager once again exchanged knowing glances.

'I know what we did was not proper,' she continued. 'But I swear to you, I'm still a virgin, and there's no chance I could be...in the family way, so there's no need for us to marry. Besides, I do not want a pity proposal.'

'Maddie,' the Dowager began. 'I agree that you do

not deserve a pity proposal, but I'm not sure you have a choice.'

Maddie wrung her hands together, feeling the walls closing in on her.

'Your father will not force you, but your mother will be apoplectic,' the Dowager began. 'If you do not marry the Earl, she may well find another way to force his hand.'

Unfortunately, she could not put it past her mother to do something drastic, if it meant Maddie would be a countess. 'So I must marry him now to prevent a scandal or my mother will cause a scandal so he is forced to marry me?'

'You could go back to America,' Kate pointed out. 'Or you could come live with me at Highfield Park. You could focus on the London furnace as you've always wanted. You could run it and we can work together. You won't even have a husband to answer to. You'd be free.'

'Thank you, Kate. You are a dear friend.' But she wouldn't be able to have the family she wanted. No husband, no children. She would be a ruined woman no man would touch.

The Dowager's dark gaze bore into her. 'Tell me, Maddie. Why don't you want to marry him now? You could do worse than a rich Earl.'

Maddie avoided her gaze. 'I told you, I don't want a pity proposal.'

'But if he had got down on one knee, would you have accepted?'

'He does not want to marry me. He has made that clear from the beginning.' That's why they had all those rules. He didn't want her. This was all fake. 'If he's forced to marry me, he'll be miserable.'

The room grew quiet for a moment, then the Duchess said, 'I think it's time you and the Earl have a private chat.'

'Oh, please, no.' How could she possibly face him after all that had happened?

'But you must dear. Explain to Balfour why you do not want to marry him.'

'But Mama and Papa…' Oh, heavens, her father would be home any minute. She could not face him, either, not when she knew how disappointed he'd be with her.

'I'll take care of them. Kate, dear, would you please send for the Earl?'

Kate squeezed her shoulder, then headed out the door.

'What do I say to him?'

'Be honest. Tell him what you told me, and I'm sure he will do the right thing.'

'You think he'll withdraw his proposal?'

The Duchess didn't answer. 'I'll be right outside and ensure no one but Balfour enters.'

Once she was alone, Maddie shot to her feet and began to pace. She practised what she would say to him in her head.

Obviously, we cannot be forced to marry. My mother can spread all the rumours she wants, but Kate, the Duke, and the Dowager won't corroborate their story. We'll be free and never have to see each other again after today.

The very thought of never seeing Cam made her heart clench tight. But it would be better that way. Cam would agree, and he'd take it upon himself to go back to Scotland.

The loud creaking sound made her jump, and as she watched the door open, her heart pounded like a drum.

Cam walked through, still dressed in his fencing gear, his hair mussed. Slowly, he approached her. 'For what it's worth, I am sorry,' he said, head bowed low.

'I'm sorry, as well.' She took a deep breath. 'For trapping you in an impossible situation. But don't worry. My father will not force me, and none of those who witnessed what happened will breathe a word to anyone. W-we can still avoid a scandal.'

'You misunderstand me.' His chin lifted and emerald eyes caught her gaze. 'I meant to say that I'm sorry for the terrible proposal and that now you have an even more terrible prospect for a husband in me.'

'You're not terrible, Cam,' she quickly said. Indignation rose in her, hearing him say those words. 'Don't say that, please.'

'I understand why you would say no.' He clasped his hands behind him. 'I'm not intelligent like you. I wouldn't be able to talk about philosophy or geology. I can be impulsive and brash. While I'm indeed an earl, I'm only one generation away from being a tradesman.'

'So am I,' she reminded him. 'But that's not why we shouldn't marry.'

A furrow appeared between his eyebrows. 'What is it then, Maddie?'

'B-because…because y-you don't want to marry me.' She hated it that she stammered and her throat burned with tears as she said it. Even more, she hated that she had to admit it.

'What—is that all? Maddie, no.' He was in front of her in an instant. 'Do not think that. Of course, I want you. How could you not believe it, after what happened between us?' A gentle hand cupped her chin, forcing her to look up into his bright green gaze.

'It—it was fake. All pretend.'

'The courting, yes, but not everything else. I want you, Maddie.'

She forgot to breathe for a moment. 'You do?'

'Aye.' A smile curled up the corner of his lips. 'And you want me, too.'

A hot flush spread all over her, reminding her of his kisses and his touch. 'Yes,' she admitted.

'Did you enjoy it?'

She shut her eyes tight but nodded.

'Did you want more?'

Slowly, she opened her eyes. 'Yes.'

A fire burned in his gaze. 'Then you shall have it.'

She tipped her head back as he kissed her, softly at first. Just a brush of his lips. So she angled her head and opened up to him, and to her surprise he groaned into her mouth. Her body ignited once more, the memory of the pleasure he'd given her coming alive and making her want it again. Her arms encircled his neck, drawing him deeper. She wasn't sure how long they were kissing, but eventually, he broke it off.

'I want you, and that's the truth, Maddie. And I hope that's enough of a reason for you to say yes.'

Maddie saw something in his expression that made her pause. It was fleeting, but she was sure it had been there. *Doubt.* Like a chink in his self-assured, brash armour. As if he wanted to tell her more, but exactly what, she didn't know. But she was desperate to find out.

'Yes.' The word came to her without thought.

'Yes?' He seemed surprised, as if he were anticipating the opposite.

'Yes. I will marry you, Cam.'

Before she could gauge his expression, he captured her mouth. She had so many more questions for him, more things she wanted to know, but they all promptly flew out of her mind. All she could think of was Cam's warm, soft lips on hers. Her hands reached up to tug at the hair on his nape as he seemed to enjoy that quite a bit, especially when she scratched at his skull.

'Maddie,' he moaned. 'I—'

The sound of hinges squeaking made them pull apart. 'Is everything all right?' the Dowager asked as she entered. 'I thought I heard…silence,' she said with a wry smile.

Maddie smoothed her hand down her skirt. 'Yes, Your Grace.'

Cam took her hand into his. 'You'll be happy to know, Your Grace, that Maddie has accepted my proposal.'

'Splendid news!' The Dowager hurried over, then kissed Maddie on both cheeks. 'Congratulations, my dear.'

'Thank you, Your Grace.'

'We must tell everyone,' she continued. 'And tonight we will celebrate.'

'You're too kind, Your Grace.'

As Cam's grip tightened around hers, Maddie sneaked a glance at him.

He's going to be my husband.

The thought sent a giddy feeling through her. However, there was a nagging feeling in the back of her mind, and her earlier questions came flooding back.

He wants to marry you, that logical voice in her mind said. *He said so. He showed you.*

Yes, but was that enough?

Oh, bother.

What more did she want? Cam would be a fine husband, despite his own objections. He would give her the family she wanted. She couldn't possibly hope for more than that.

Chapter Sixteen

'Oh, think of it. My daughter, a countess!' Eliza DeVries's attitude had completely reversed once the Dowager had announced to everyone that Cam and Maddie would be married. 'I knew she would make a good match. We are so happy we will have you as our son-in-law, my lord.'

Less than an hour ago, you called me a fiend.

But Cam bit his tongue and said, 'Thank you, Mrs DeVries.'

Cornelius DeVries on the other hand, was strangely calm for a man who'd received news that his daughter had been ruined.

'You have my blessing, of course,' he said. 'But all that matters is that Maddie has fully accepted your proposal.'

'Yes, Papa.' Maddie looked up at Cam. 'I fully accepted.'

'Oh, Cam,' Persephone exclaimed as she embraced him. 'I'm ecstatic for you both, but—' She lowered her voice. 'I thought this was all pretend? What happened?'

Cam wasn't exactly sure how to explain it to his sister.

Well, Seph, I ruined your friend in front of her family and our hosts. So now we must marry or her mother will ensure there will be a scandal.

'I'll explain later,' Maddie whispered. 'I promise.'

'Congratulations, my lord, Maddie.' Miss Merton was next to offer her felicitations. 'Oh, my, another wedding to plan. How lovely.'

'I can help,' Kate said. 'I'm a veteran of speedy wedding preparations.' She looked up wryly at her husband.

'I'm telling you, Balfour, there's no need to wait,' Mabury said. 'You'll thank me for it.' For a man who had been ready to kill him, the Duke was now awfully chummy.

'We have only been engaged for a few minutes,' Cam pointed out. However, marrying sooner than later definitely appealed to him. Then he could have Maddie in his bed for the rest of his life.

How Maddie could think he didn't want her, he didn't know. Lord, he wanted her so much, he would expire from it. He could not wait to give her endless pleasure, night after night, until it made both of them mindless.

He'd thought he wouldn't be enough for Maddie, but then she'd admitted that she wanted him only on a physical level.

Yes, she said when he asked her if she wanted more.

Now, that, he could live with.

Things couldn't have turned out better, he thought smugly. The physical side of their relationship would keep their marriage strong, much better than any other kind of entanglement. Their marriage would have a sturdy foundation on mutual desire, and nothing more.

He'd broken every rule he'd set from the beginning of their fake courtship plot, but not the very last one he'd added for himself.

He would not fall in love. Not with anyone, and certainly not with Maddie.

'Surely you would want to be wed in Scotland, Balfour,' the Duchess said. 'So you could be surrounded by your family?'

'I only have my brothers and Seph, I'm afraid, as my father did not have any siblings,' he said. 'On my mother's side, we have an uncle and some cousins, but they're all here in England. I would be just as happy to wed here.' *As long as the wedding takes place.* 'Besides, Maddie will be living in Scotland soon enough.'

'And travelling back to England with you regularly, I hope?' Cornelius asked. 'I could use her talents and advice once the furnace is up and running.'

'You know, you could build a furnace in Scotland, too,' the Duke said.

'Industry isn't only booming in England and America,' Cam added.

'Really?' Her face was all aglow. 'Is that possible, Cam?'

'Aye.' If it weren't, he would make it so. Cam knew Maddie would be happy if she had her work to occupy her. And Maddie happy would make him happy.

'Let us have a toast to Maddie and Balfour,' the Dowager said as Eames and a footman arrived with a chilled bottle of champagne and a tray of flutes.

Everyone was surprisingly cheerful, considering what had happened earlier. Almost everyone, anyway, as Caroline was conspicuously missing. Cam couldn't help but remember their encounter a few weeks ago. Lord, she was going to be his sister-in-law. He had a feeling this marriage would stoke her ire and she would lash out at Maddie even more. *I will have to keep an eye on that one.*

'To Maddie and Balfour.' The Dowager raised her glass and everyone followed suit.

'To Maddie and Balfour,' everyone cheered as they clinked glasses.

As Cam sipped his champagne, he couldn't help but think of the time he had announced to his parents that Jenny had accepted his proposal. Their reaction had been quite different from everyone's tonight and there certainly had been no champagne.

No, don't think of that, he chided himself. He would not have memories of Jenny sully tonight. He already had the perfect arrangement in place with Maddie. A mutually beneficial physical arrangement in private, and on the outside, they would be a respectable couple. And that's all there ever would be between them.

'I am utterly exhausted,' Maddie said as she, Persephone, and Kate settled into the carriage and a footman closed the door. 'How did you manage to survive your engagement?'

'I'm exhausted, too,' Persephone chimed. 'And I'm not even the one getting married.'

Kate laughed. 'You must learn to pace yourself and keep your strength up.'

Once news of the engagement had spread, the invitations to various events flooded in. Of course, while Cam and Maddie were not a sought-after couple, their connection to the Mabury title still held weight. The last few days had been occupied with balls, trips to the opera and plays, tea parties, and other such events. Just now, they had just left Lady Farrington's tea party, a long and boring soirée that was attended by many matrons and mamas, all of whom wanted to hear all about Maddie's engagement.

'I don't know how long I can do this,' Maddie said.

'You haven't even started with preparing for the wedding,' Kate reminded her. 'There's the trousseau to think about, the guest list, the engagement ball, the church, the breakfast. I'm just so glad Sebastian insisted on a short engagement and we married within a month.'

'Why so soon?' Persephone asked. 'Did you not want to wait and become better acquainted with your fiancé?'

'My Sebastian is an impatient man,' she replied with a smile. 'And he could not be swayed.'

Persephone sank back into the plush seating of the coach and crossed her arms over her chest. 'I should like a long engagement. Six months, at least. Maddie, how long do you plan to be engaged to my brother?'

'I…' Maddie frowned. 'Actually, we haven't discussed details yet.' In fact, they hadn't discussed anything at all, as they had not had a moment to themselves. They had attended several parties and balls, but they had never been alone. They hadn't even set a wedding date or decided exactly where they were getting married.

'As long as you come live with us back in Scotland, I'll be happy.' Persephone hooked her arm into Maddie's. 'I've always wanted a sister.'

She leaned against Persephone. 'I'm so glad you approve.'

'Aye, of course. I just wish you two had told me that in the midst of that fake courtship plan, you two were already falling in love.'

Maddie's mouth pulled back into a tight smile. She didn't want to disillusion Persephone, so she didn't deny it. *But love?* Could it even be possible?

Kate was in love with her Duke, and he was obviously besotted with her. But again, a love match was not very common among the British aristocracy. In fact, she'd seen how they almost frowned upon it. To them, marriage was about preserving wealth and titles. Perhaps in time, she and Cam would grow to love one another, in a respectable way.

Of course, there was nothing respectable about how their courtship had begun. Not with the way he'd kissed and touched her. How she'd missed being alone with him, but he'd been the perfect gentlemen the entire time. He didn't even dare touch any part of her body except her gloved hand.

'*Ahem.*' Kate sent her a knowing glance, then turned to Persephone. 'Lady Persephone, how are you enjoying your season so far?'

Persephone slumped in her seat further. 'I'm afraid, Your Grace, I am not enjoying it at all.'

Oh, dear. Maddie had been so caught up in her fake courtship with Cam, she had been ignoring her friend. 'I'm sure it will get better.'

'I'm not sure. And… I don't even know if I want a husband.' She sighed.

'Then why come to London?'

She worried at her lip. 'Because of a promise.' And so, she told them about her mother's dying wish for her to have a London season. 'She'd been planning it even before I was born. While she had no regrets marrying my Scottish father, she did worry that it would decrease my chances of making a good match. A season in London was to make me a more desirable wife. And Cam wanted to carry out this wish for her.'

Maddie clutched a hand to her chest. *Poor Cam.* The loss of his mother must have been devastating. 'It sounds like he loved your mother so much,' she managed to say through the tightness building in her throat. But how could she even doubt that? From the beginning, she had seen how devoted he was to Persephone.

'I'm just glad all this wedding planning is distracting Cam and he's not been bothering with making me dance at balls.'

Kate chuckled. 'Well—' The coach slowed to a stop, indicating they had arrived back at Mabury Hall. 'Oh, we're home. Thank goodness. I need a nap before to-night's dinner.' The Dowager had invited a few close friends over tonight to welcome Kate and Sebastian back into town.

'I could sleep right through until morning,' Perse-phone declared.

'A nap sounds heavenly,' Maddie agreed.

Once they were inside Mabury Hall, they all went to their separate rooms. Maddie was about to ring for Betsy when she heard a knock on the door. *Who could that be?* When she opened the door, she was surprised by the sight of her sister.

'Caro. How, uh, lovely to see you.'

Caroline had all but disappeared the last few days. On the day Maddie got engaged, Mama had said she was taken to bed with a cold. Maddie suspected that had been a lie. Knowing her sister, news of her engagement to Cam had probably stung, so Maddie had not verbal-ised her suspicions. However, Caroline hadn't emerged from her room until now.

'Hello, Maddie. May I come in?' She didn't bother to wait for an answer as she barged right inside.

'How is your cold?' she asked politely. 'You look healthy and lovely.' As always, her sister was impecca-bly dressed in a striped blue-and-white gown, a match-ing jacket, and a feathered hat atop her artfully arranged locks.

'Much better, thank you.' Caroline made it to the mid-dle of the room before spinning around to face her. 'It seems congratulations are in order.'

'Thank you.'

'Hmm.' Her eyes turned to slits. 'I don't see it.'

'See what?'

'What Cameron sees in you.'

Caroline could be incredibly cruel with her barbs, but never quite so direct. 'I beg your pardon?' *And why did you call him by his first name?*

'You know, we were speaking the other day.' She glanced down casually at her nails before lifting her chin up to meet her gaze. 'He told me the most curious thing.'

A knot formed in her chest. 'Caroline, I think you should leave—'

'He told me he would only marry someone he *didn't find attractive*,' she drawled.

Now that was a lie.

Wasn't it?

That split second of doubt was all Caroline needed and she took the opening for her next jab. 'His exact words were said, "Lass, the last thing I want is to marry someone I'm attracted to."'

Maddie wanted to kick herself. 'I don't believe you. Cam said he wants me. He even proved it,' Maddie added for good measure, though admitting it to her sister made her wince.

'So I've heard.' Caroline covered her mouth with her hand in feigned surprise. 'I didn't think you'd have the guts to actually throw yourself at the man. I thought it was all made up, but Mama was inconsolable, so I knew it had to be true.'

'Which disproves your point.'

'Ha!' Caroline crossed her arms over her chest. 'That's different. When it comes to screwing, a man's not picky. Any body will do.'

Her sister's language sent an uncomfortable shock through her. Where did she learn such words? 'That doesn't change the fact that we are engaged.'

'Really? Tell me, when is the wedding? Are you having it here or Scotland? Will his family be coming?'

'W-we haven't decided yet,' she said. 'We've been much too busy.'

'Or is he simply stalling? Think about it.' Caroline's smug smile made that knot in Maddie's chest grow tighter. 'Can't you see, Maddie? He doesn't want to cause a scandal, and you know Mama will do anything to force him to marry you. He's stringing you along to keep Mama quiet.'

'Why would he do that?'

'To prevent a scandal from besmirching his sister.'

The breath left Maddie's body. *Persephone.* 'Y-you know about that? About his promise to his mother?'

'Of course I do,' she said confidently.

Cam must have told her. How else would Caroline know? And what else could they possibly have talked about? Or done. The image of Cam and Caroline together made her want to retch.

'He's probably on his best behaviour, too.'

Now, that made her flinch. Cam had been the perfect gentleman since their engagement. He hadn't even tried to kiss her.

'He won't risk Mama's wrath or give cause to hasten your wedding,' Caroline continued. 'Once he's married his sister safely off, he won't need you any longer.'

Maddie bit the inside of her cheek. 'I think you should leave, Caroline.'

'I'm only looking out for you—'

'Leave,' she repeated. 'Now.'

Caroline sent her a withering look before she turned to leave.

Once Maddie was alone, she staggered backwards to her bed, her thighs hitting the mattress before she sat down.

It couldn't be. Caroline was lying.

I want you, Maddie.

Had he been lying about that? But then again, she knew Caroline was right; men were often not very picky with their bed partners. He could want her in that way—just not in any other way.

He didn't find her attractive at all. Why would she even think he did? He'd called her an Amazon the first time they'd met.

He finds me repulsive.

A tear ran down her cheek. Good enough to…to screw, but not to marry. Then his hand had been forced, and he didn't want to hurt Persephone's chances of making a good match.

She fell on her back on top of the mattress, then curled up into a ball. Cam had made her feel wanted and beautiful. But reality sank in. At the end of the day, she was still plain, shy, and awkward Maddie. Nothing could change that.

Chapter Seventeen

Cam didn't want to attend another boring dinner party, but he had his obligations to his host and hostesses. Now that the Duke and Duchess were in residence, it seemed their social activities had only doubled, and he was getting damned tired of it.

The only bright spot of his evenings was Maddie. Now that they were engaged, they could be seen together in public, and so he escorted her to all the social events. He could be by her side, in front of all the ton, and no one would question it. He could look at her all he wanted and soak in her beauty without having to worry about who was watching. Just being with her, around her, made his evenings enjoyable.

How he wished he could be alone with her. Even for just for one minute. He would make every second count. But he swore he would be on his best behaviour as he would not take any chances with her reputation.

And once they were wed—which he would ensure would happen as soon as possible—she would be all his.

'Where is your lovely fiancée?' Lady Bestwick, whom he had been introduced to earlier that evening, asked.

Everyone was gathered in the foyer for aperitifs before dinner.

Cam frowned. 'Perhaps she is still getting ready.'

'I was so looking forward to meeting her.'

'Dinner is served,' Eames announced to the guests.

As Cam took his place, he glanced around. Where was Maddie?

The doors to the dining room opened, and the Duke and Duchess strode in first, yet Maddie was nowhere to be found.

'Apologies, my lord.'

The murmur made him start, then he let out a relieved sigh when Maddie appeared by his side. 'There you are.' She looked incredibly lovely in a pale green silk gown. As he took her hand into his arm, he leaned down and whispered, 'That is not chartreuse, is it?'

Maddie stiffened and did not smile or laugh.

A feeling stirred in his gut at her reaction. *Perhaps she's just tired*, he told himself. Even he was being worn thin by their nightly events.

All the guests took their seats and dinner began. As usual, the guests *oohed* and *ahhed* over Monsieur Faucher's delectable creations. Seasonal roasted vegetables, braised meats falling off the bone, succulent fresh fish, lobsters with butter—a magnificent feast by all accounts. However, Maddie hardly touched anything and instead only pushed her food around. Not to mention, she responded with only single syllables whenever someone asked her a question, which was also the only time she participated in conversation.

'Are you enjoying your dessert, Maddie?' he asked.

'Yes, my lord.' But she only stabbed at the *pain à la duchesse* and did not take a morsel into her mouth.

When dinner was over and the men and women went

their separate ways for cigars and brandy with the Duke and tea and sherry with the Duchess, Maddie did not even acknowledge him. Then, there was the fact that Caroline, whom he had not seen in days, was strutting around like she'd been crowned Queen of England.

Something was very wrong.

And Cam intended to find out what.

For the rest of the evening, he went through the motions and pleasantries with the other guests and their host. However, he was already forming a plan in the back of his mind.

When the evening was over and the guests had dispersed, Cam rushed up to his room. He dismissed Murray even before he'd had a chance to finish undressing him, so he was left in only his shirt, trousers, and bare feet. Checking his valise, he found the flask of Glenbaire whisky he kept there and then took a swig. He hauled a chair to the door and sat there, listening for all the sounds outside. When it grew silent and no more light seeped through the tiny gap between the floor and door, he grabbed his candle and headed outside.

According to Persephone, Maddie had the room directly across from hers. So, he made his way to the other wing and found Persephone's door, then turned to the one opposite. Hopefully, he'd heard Persephone correctly and he wasn't about to barge into an empty room, or worse, any of his future in-laws'. He extinguished his candle before putting it in his pocket.

'Betsy?' came Maddie's voice.

Relieved that he was in the correct chamber, Cam ventured further in. The room was dimly lit, with only a single candle in the corner by the plush reading chair where Maddie sat, book propped on her crossed legs. The candlelight set her creamy skin and golden hair aglow, and with her chin resting on her palm and one shoulder bared, she looked like a Botticelli painting. He nearly forgot himself—that is, until her head lifted and her eyes went wide as dinner plates.

'Cam—'

He crossed the room in seconds, kneeling in front of her to cover her mouth with his hand. 'Shh… Or we'll be caught.' When her eyes blinked in understanding, he put his hand down.

'What are you doing here?' she hissed low. 'Did anyone see you?'

'Of course not,' he said.

She pushed at him, then uncrossed her legs. 'You shouldn't be here.' Planting her feet on the ground, she made a motion to get up but quickly toppled over. 'Oh!'

Cam quickly caught her, then hauled her up to him. 'What's wrong?'

'Foot…pins and needles…' She huffed against his chest. 'My lord, please leave before anyone discovers you here.'

'No.'

'No?'

Cam slid his hands down to her waist and pulled her even closer. While he was taking advantage of her temporary lameness, he didn't give a whit. He didn't risk coming here only to leave without answers. 'What's wrong with you tonight, Maddie?'

'W-wrong?' She turned her head away from him. 'I don't know what you're talking about.'

He sighed. 'You were quiet and morose all evening. You didn't say a word. Didn't even laugh at my fashion joke.'

She huffed but said nothing.

'I know something's the matter, darling.' He moved a hand down to her buttocks, cupping her through the thin fabric of her night-rail. That elicited a gasp, and Cam counted that as a small success. 'Tell me what's wrong. Tell me how I can make it better.'

'I…'

'Yes?'

'My lord… Cam.'

He played with a ringlet of her golden hair. It was like gold silk. 'Hmm?'

'I think we should reconsider the engagement.'

'I beg your pardon?'

The shock of her words was enough to make him loosen his grip, and she wiggled away from him. 'I said we should reconsider the—'

'I bloody well heard what you said,' he shouted. 'I want to know why you're saying it.'

'Shush!' She put a finger to her lips. 'Or someone will hear you.'

'I don't care if the Queen herself hears me.' Confusion, indignation, and hurt swirled inside his chest. 'Now, tell me what the hell this is about. Did Palmer get to you? Did he convince you to say these things?'

'No, my lord. I—I just feel perhaps we've rushed into this and we should think—'

'Who, then? If it wasn't Palmer, who?' He curled his hands into tight fists to stop himself from grabbing her shoulders and shaking some sense into her. 'Tell me why, Maddie. You owe me at least that.'

'You don't really want to marry me.'

'This again?' He let out an exasperated sigh. 'Woman, how can I get it into your head that I want you?' *And you want me.*

'You're only doing this for Persephone.'

'What?' He scratched at his chain. 'Now I am truly confused. Start again, please.'

She sank back down into the reading chair. 'If you do not marry me, my mama will cause a scandal. And that would ruin Persephone's chances this season.' She swallowed. 'And you couldn't fulfil your promise to your mother.'

Cam's spine went rigid and his voice turned hoarse. 'How did you...'

'Persephone told me just today. And Caroline, too.'

Caroline? *Of course.* Just as he suspected, it was that damned sister of hers. 'Whatever it was she told you, it's a lie.'

'That's what I thought, but how did she know about your promise to your mother?'

'I don't know.' He threw his hands up. 'She could have been bluffing. Did she say the exact words to you, about my mother's promise? Or did you?' Maddie didn't speak, but he saw the doubt cross her face, so he continued. 'Your mother probably told her or she overheard of her plan of starting a scandal about us, hoping it would force my hand to marry you. Then you mentioned my promise to my ma, and she ran with it.'

Lord, he was so glad he would be away from Eliza and Caroline once he and Maddie married and moved to Scotland. If there was truly a merciful God, the rest of the DeVries family would leave and go back to America. Still, he wasn't sure if an entire ocean was far away enough. 'I swear to you, Maddie, I spoke to her one time and that's it. A few sentences in the hallway.'

'A-and what else did you say to her?'

'I don't know.' He shrugged. 'But she was insisting that you could never be happy as my countess. That I should instead find someone else who I was attracted to who would be more suitable.' What a joke. 'And then—'

He halted, his jaw snapping shut as he saw the tears pooling in Maddie's eyes.

'And then you told her you would never marry someone you found attractive.'

Double damn.

'And so you decided to marry me.'

Without explanation, the words did sound dreadful. He had to explain. To give context. But to do that, he would have to tell her about Jenny. To open those wounds that had been sealed for so long.

'Maddie.' The ache in his chest made it difficult to breathe, but he would get through this. 'Maddie, please…' He bent down and folded his legs underneath him, sitting by her feet so he could look up at her. 'Let me explain.'

She did not say yes, but neither did she turn away. So with a deep breath, he began to speak. 'Nearing ten years ago, I had been engaged to a lass in our village. Jenny. The moment I laid eyes on her, I was smitten. The attraction was overwhelming. She was like a siren who enchanted me.' The corner of her mouth twitched. 'I pursued her. Wooed her. Showered her with gifts. Followed her like a lovesick fool. Miraculously, she agreed to marry me. Ma and Da did not approve, but I continued with my pursuit, and eventually she said yes when I proposed. Looking back, I should have heeded my parents.'

Bitterness and regret rushed back through him, as it did each time he remembered. 'But I was too lovesick, unable to see her unhappiness. She'd had her doubts from the beginning, but her parents wanted her to be a countess, so she accepted my proposal anyway. Then she'd been caught up in the wedding planning and felt like she couldn't back out. But then… Well, she fell in love. With my best friend. They told me the day before the wedding, on their way to Gretna Green.'

A small gasp escaped from Maddie's lips.

Cam did not want to see the pity in her eyes, so he bowed his head. 'They loved each other. True love. Their relationship was much deeper than mine and hers. Of course she would prefer Kirk. He was everything I was not. I was just a charming rogue, with nothing to offer but my good looks and a title I didn't even earn. Fool's gold—all glitter but no value. And since then, well, I told myself I would never marry someone I was that attracted to. I would never be blinded that way again nor allow myself to forge on with only obsession keeping me going.'

'I'm so sorry, Cam,' she said. 'They betrayed you and scarred you so deep. And I want you to know... It's all right if you don't find me attractive.'

'Maddie, I was so attracted to you that day you walked into the Duchess' private sitting room that I got tongue-tied.'

'So you are attracted to me?'

'Yes.'

'Yet you still want to marry me?'

'Of course. I want you, and you want me. That should be enough, right? What we shared in the library is more than what most married couples have. You don't know how glad I am that you felt that way too. We are physically compatible in every way.'

She seemed to ponder his words. 'Cam... I don't want to break our engagement.'

Relief washed over him, loosening all the knots and tension in his body. 'Thank God.' He got to his knees and scooted forward, wrapping his arms around her. 'I want you. You are one of the most attractive women I've ever laid eyes on. Let me show you. I promise you will never doubt me again. And you won't regret wanting to marry me.'

'I... Yes.'

His heart leapt into his throat. 'Are you sure? You understand what I'm trying to say?'

Her pupils blew out. 'Yes, Cam. Please, make love to me.'

Cam needed no further invitation. Nudging her knees apart, he knelt between and lifted the hem of her shift slowly up her legs and soft thighs, torturing himself by revealing her skin slowly, then finally, the soft curls that hid her sex.

'Beautiful,' he declared. Maddie's face was all flush, her eyes shut tight, her breathing heavy. He wished she would look at him, but seeing as this was her first time, he had to be more patient and understanding.

'You must relax for me, Maddie. You'll want to close your legs, but fight the urge as much as you can. All right?'

She nodded wordlessly.

Placing a hand on her knee, he skimmed his fingers upwards over her inner thighs until he reached the downy triangle between them. When he touched the curls, her body twitched, but her knees remained spread.

'This will feel good. You remember, right?' He interpreted her quick intake of a breath as a yes, so he probed her soft nether lips, stroking them up and down until she was slick, her hips squirming invitingly. He pushed one finger in.

'Oh!' Her hands gripped the sides of the chair. 'Oh, Cam.'

'I love hearing my name on your lips.' He pushed the finger deeper still, moving it around. She was sopping wet but still so tight. He would have to make sure she was prepared for him.

'Maddie, darlin', I'm going to kiss you...'

Her eyes flew open.

'Down here,' he continued, then leaned forward before she could protest. He touched his lips to her sex, moving over them in a soft caress. Her entire body went rigid, and she let out a soft cry. But he did not stop and instead licked at her, tasting her sweetness and lapping up her juices while inhaling her womanly scent. His cock twitched inside his pants, and so to relieve the pressure, he reached down to unbutton his falls and stroked himself while he continued to devour her.

'Cam!'

Fingers dug into his hair, scraping at his scalp. Cam slowed down his strokes, lest he spill without warning. He swirled his tongue around her entrance, then probed her with it. Releasing his cock, he moved his hand up to search for the little bud hidden above her folds. When he found it, he stroked it gently with his thumb at first, teasing the bud back and forth until she was moving her hips against him, seeking more friction. She moaned in disappointment when he released it, but then he quickly switched around so his mouth latched onto the bud and his finger entered her again, thrusting in and out, stretching her to capacity.

Her pants came at a faster pace and her hips rose to meet his tongue and fingers. He increased his pace incrementally, tuning his rhythm with hers, and when her body shuddered, he pressed on, letting her ride her wave of pleasure before she went all limp.

With a deep sigh, he laid his cheek on her thighs, enjoying the sight of her damp sex and the scent of her permeating the air. Feeling her hips shift, he rocked back on his knees so he could look at her, looking so satisfied and soft and sleepy as she lay back on the chair, head thrown back and eyes closed, one shoulder still bared.

'You were magnificent, Maddie.' Rising to his feet, he caught her hand and pulled her up. He undid the ribbon at the neckline of the night-rail, then tugged it down to her waist, revealing her breasts and those delectable brown nipples. He cupped one breast in his hand, testing its weight, and gave it a gentle squeeze.

Her mouth parted slightly. Unable to resist, he slanted his mouth over hers. She opened up to him, leaning back and allowing his tongue to enter her mouth. When his thumb brushed over her nipple, she let out a little gasp.

Cam didn't want to let go of her lips or breast, but he knew that he could not take long as he had to leave while the house was asleep. Reluctantly, he pulled back. 'Maddie, are you ready?'

Sky blue eyes stared up at him, luminous in the candlelight. 'Yes.'

Yes.

How she could ever say no to this man, Maddie didn't know. But with her body coiled with anticipation, she knew she wanted him.

He kissed her again, softly, then led her away from her reading chair and towards the bed. He guided her on top of the mattress and broke their kiss. Wordlessly, he began to strip away his clothing, starting with his shirt, then trousers. She couldn't help but gasp at the sight of his body—long and muscled all over, with hair on his chest and lower arms. Her gaze continued lower to his trim waist, to the erection jutting out of his body. Her heart pounded in her chest as he approached her, raising a knee up on the mattress to join her on the bed. They lay down on their sides, facing each other.

'Do you want to touch me?' he asked, voice low and husky.

There was only one answer she could give him, but it was stuck in her throat at the sight of him, so she nodded instead. Taking her hand in his, he guided it to his taut, muscled belly and pushed it lower. Her fingers moved past the wiry dark mat of hair before reaching the rigid length of his erection. He moved her hands up and down slowly. His skin was silky, yet the flesh underneath was hard as iron. Even as he removed his hand, she continued to stroke him, fascinated by the length and feel of him, starting when she felt the bead of wetness at the tip.

'Maddie, I'm not sure I'm going to last if you keep that up.'

She withdrew her hand.

'Are you ready?'

'Yes, Cam.' Oh, yes.

He wrapped an arm around her, then rolled himself over her, murmuring sweet words in that soft burr of his.

Maddie found herself spreading her thighs so he could settle between them.

'This will hurt a bit. I'm sorry.' Lifting his head, he stared down at her. Though she couldn't see his emerald eyes, she imagined them, blazing hot with desire.

A pressure pushed at her entrance and the tip of him probed her slowly, dipping in and easing forward. He filled her, and Maddie found it wasn't painful—at least, until it was. She winced as the pressure turned into a stinging ache.

'Maddie,' he groaned. His hand reached down between them to where they were joined, then spread her nether lips. He rocked back and forth, getting halfway into her. His fingers once again found the bud at the crest of her sex and teased it slowly, sending little shocks of pleasure through her body.

'Yes,' he moaned. 'That's it.' He pushed further in.

The fullness was a strange sensation, yet her body seemed to crave it. Her hips pushed up at him, drawing him deeper. When she once again reached that peak, he drove into her, drowning her mixed cry of pain and pleasure with his mouth.

Her body fully accepted him, his driving thrusts pushing her to new heights. The length of him stroked places she'd never been touched before as his fingers continued to play with her with the skill of a virtuoso, plucking and tugging and pressing like she was an instrument bound to his whims. Maddie didn't care—all she wanted was that feeling to never end.

Cam's breathing came in uneven spurts as her body gripped him. He pushed at her, riding her hard until that wave arrived, moving from the tips of her toes and washing over the rest of her, smothering her in pleasure. When it was over, Cam let out a strangled growl and rocked his hips hard. She felt the strangest pulse inside her as he gave one last push before going completely still.

With a deep sigh, he withdrew from her, then rolled to his side before gathering her close. Seconds passed. Or it could have been longer—Maddie couldn't really tell, as her senses had ceased to function.

'You must marry me now, darling.' He kissed her soft skin, then slid a hand over her belly. 'You might be carrying my bairn at this moment. We will be married as soon as possible.'

She hummed in contentment. That didn't sound too bad at all.

Sleep came and went, but the awareness of him in her bed never left her. A cycle of sleep had settled over her when once again she awoke, this time from the sleep-roughened voice in her ear.

'Maddie.' Arms held her tight and the hard male body

behind her pressed closer. Lips caressed her ear before Cam released her. 'Your maid will be by any moment.'

Unfortunately, he was right. 'You must leave.'

'For now.'

The mattress shifted as he left her bed. The rustling of fabric told her he was getting dressed, and she turned to face him.

'You were amazing, Maddie,' he said as he buttoned his shirt and leaned down to kiss her temple. 'As I knew you would be.' A hand cupped her cheek and she nuzzled at his palm, the calluses tickling her skin. 'We are making the right decision, you know.'

She paused. 'We are?'

'Mmm-hmm. I knew we would be physically compatible in every way, and our marriage will be a success. I thought with Je— I thought I wanted more in a marriage when I was first engaged. Like what my parents had. But this, between us, is much better.' He rose up. 'I will see you later.'

Maddie could only watch his shadow move in the darkness. When he was gone, she lay on her back, looking up at the blackness above her.

Hearing about his former fiancé had sparked jealousy in her. The emotion was ridiculous; he was a man, and of course he had a past. But to know that there had been a woman before her that Cam wanted to marry made her chest ache. Then he'd told her his story and the pain had deepened—for him.

Oh, Cam.

All the parts were coming together, like assembling a piece of machinery. He hid behind that brash and charming façade so no one would see the hurt. He'd made that vow to never marry anyone he was attracted to because he was afraid it would turn into obsession. And she didn't blame him, because he had been burned so badly.

Still, Maddie couldn't help but feel there was still more. Cam might think he's a man with no substance; yet, she'd been peeling back layers only to find more.

But would she ever get to the core of him?

Chapter Eighteen

After the night they'd made love, plans for the wedding quickly took shape. Cam wanted a firm wedding date and he wanted it as soon as possible. He was ready to obtain a special licence—hell, he would have eloped with her to Gretna Green, but Cornelius would not allow it. And since he was the only other DeVries Cam respected, he did not insist on it.

And so he settled for six weeks, which would be enough time to have the banns read and for his brothers to settle business at the distillery before they travelled to England. He agreed to have the wedding in London, as it would be inconvenient to have everyone travel back to Scotland, which would only delay the wedding. Besides, after what Maddie had endured in London, he wanted the ton to see that she was a desirable bride and make every man and woman who laughed or jeered at her regret their words.

'Must we attend another ball?' Cam asked as he and Maddie waited for everyone in the foyer.

'I'm afraid we must.'

'Why?'

'So I can show off my new gown.' She twirled around,

sending violet tulle fluttering around her like a cloud. 'And my fiancé.'

'You are beautiful in that gown. But—' he leaned down '—it would look much better on the floor.'

'My lord,' she admonished, a pretty blush creeping up her bare shoulders and neck. 'We are not alone.'

'Later, we will be.'

Cam had been visiting her room every night since the first time. The first few nights, he still believed he could resist her siren call, but after wearing the carpet in his rooms down with his pacing, he would eventually give in, anyway. He came to her after everyone was asleep and left before dawn. Their time together was much too short, but they made the most of it. Maddie was eager to please him, and in return, he brought her to peak after peak of pleasure. He was surprised either of them managed to stay awake the rest of the day.

'Oh, here we are,' Eliza announced as she, Cornelius, and Caroline descended the stairs. 'My lord, don't you look handsome tonight.'

'Thank you, Mrs DeVries.'

'You know, if it's just us, you may call me Mama.'

Maddie groaned loudly.

'What?' Eliza snapped her fan open. 'In six weeks, he will be my son-in-law.' Her eyes gleamed. 'And you will be Madeline, Countess of Balfour.' She waved her fan. 'Your Ladyship.'

Maddie looked to her father pleadingly. 'Come now, dear,' Papa began. 'No need to be so dramatic. Right, Caro?' Caroline merely sniffed and didn't say a word.

Good, Cam thought. Had Caroline been a man, he would have called her out for pistols at dawn for trying to get between him and Maddie. Hopefully, this was the last of her antics, as even he had limits on his control.

Once the Duke, Duchess, Dowager, Miss Merton, and Persephone came downstairs, they all left for the Devonshire ball. As his betrothed, Maddie was permitted to ride in his carriage and he to escort her to events. So he, Maddie, and Persephone all rode together to the Duke of Devonshire's grand home on Park Lane.

'Cameron, Lord Balfour! Lady Persephone Mac-Gregor! Miss Madeline DeVries!'

They descended the steps, all eyes were on them, and in particular, on Maddie. Cam himself couldn't take his eyes off her, and from the way she blushed, she enjoyed the attention. *Who's the awkward giantess now?* he wanted to shout at these silly Englishmen and women.

'Come,' he said. 'Let us greet our host and hostess.'

One more advantage of having Maddie on his arm at these events was that Persephone no longer disappeared. As long as Maddie was there, she stayed by his side and allowed him to introduce her to eligible gentlemen. Cam was pleased that his sister and fiancée got along, as they were the two most important women in his life.

As he did at every ball, he danced the first dance with Maddie. He held her close, much closer than permitted, which raised a few eyebrows from some eagle-eyed matrons, but Cam didn't care. How he enjoyed feeling her body next to his—whether they were making love or dancing—and he would not let anyone shame him into stopping. Besides, only Maddie's opinion mattered to him. She had only to turn those sky blue eyes at him and the feelings of doubt disappeared.

Once they were finished dancing, they joined Persephone, who stood by the sidelines with Miss Merton.

'Maddie,' Persephone began. 'Would you mind coming with me so I may freshen up?'

'I shall join you, as well,' Miss Merton said.

'Cam?'

He nodded. 'I'll come find you later.' When the three women left, Cam glanced around the room, hoping to find Mabury or the Dowager, but before he could locate them, he felt a tap on his arm.

'Oh, here's my daughter's fiancé.'

Cam winced at the sound of Eliza's voice. 'Mrs DeVries,' he greeted.

'My lord, I have brought over some friends who would like to make your acquaintance.' She nodded to the couple next to her. 'I told them, you simply must meet my future son-in-law, the Earl of Balfour. My lord, this is Viscount and Viscountess Shelby. My lord, my lady, this is Cameron, Earl of Balfour.'

Irritation pricked at him, but he politely said, 'How do you do?'

He chatted with the Viscount and Viscountess for a few minutes before excusing himself. 'I see an acquaintance whom I promised to introduce to my sister. I must find her.' Scanning the room, he saw the Duchess, Maddie, and Persephone speaking to a gentleman he'd never seen before. However, before he could reach them, the gentleman took Maddie's hand and led her to the ballroom floor.

'Who was that?' he asked the two women when he did arrive at their side.

'She's just dancing, Balfour,' the Duchess informed him. 'Not eloping with him.'

But he kept his eyes on her the entire time—and his hands.

One wrong move, he swore, *and I will rip those hands away from his wrists.*

After what seemed like an excruciatingly long dance,

Maddie and her partner returned. 'Thank you, Mr Thomson. I enjoyed the dance.'

'As did I, Miss DeVries.'

'I— Cam, you're here.' Her face lit up. 'I was just dancing with Mr Thomson. Kate—Her Grace—introduced us.'

'How nice,' he said through gritted teeth.

She quickly introduced them. 'The Earl is my fiancé,' she added. 'And Lady Persephone is his sister.'

'Pleased to make your acquaintance,' he said.

Cam merely nodded.

'Mr Thomson.' The Duchess began to lead him away. 'I believe I see Sir and Lady Walker talking to my husband and his mother. I'd like to introduce you.'

'Who was that?' Cam asked once the Duchess and Mr Thomson were out of earshot.

'A friend of Kate's.' Maddie slipped her hand into his arm. 'I'm parched. Shall we go get some lemonade?'

'I'd like some, too,' Persephone said.

Cam put Thomson out of his mind for now. This was a ball, after all, and Maddie loved to dance. She was allowed to dance with anyone she wanted. Several more times throughout the evening, gentlemen came and asked Maddie to dance, and etiquette dictated she accept their invitations, since she had already danced with Cam and Mr Thomson. Still, he did not have to like it and showed his displeasure by scowling the entire time Maddie was with another.

'You could ask any lady to dance,' Persephone pointed out.

'Why would I?' he bit out.

'Oh, how romantic,' his sister sighed.

He stared at his sister. 'Romantic?'

'Yes. Your jealousy. You really are in love.'

In love? Was she mad? No, he definitely was not in love with Maddie. He was going to marry her. He wanted her. Hell, he admitted he was attracted to her. There was no way, however, that he would fall in love with her.

But he would not stand another minute of watching her dance with other men. 'Persephone, will you please find Miss Merton or the Dowager? There is something I must attend to.'

Cam made his way out of the ballroom and away from the crush of guests, not really caring where he was going, just following one random hallway after another.

'Cam! Wait!'

He halted in his tracks and spun on his heel. 'Maddie?'

Sure enough, there was Maddie, running towards him. 'Lord, you're fast,' she said, huffing and puffing as she stopped and braced herself against his chest. 'Where were you going?'

'Nowhere,' he said. 'The ballroom was getting much too stuffy.'

'There was hardly any room for dancing.' She wrinkled her nose.

'You seemed to be enjoying yourself with all your partners.' That came out harsher than he wanted it to. Jealousy was a big, green-eyed monster that demanded retribution. Stepping forward, he caught her arm. 'Come with me.'

'Where?'

'Anywhere.' Tugging at her arm, she followed him as he led her down the darkened hallway to the first room they reached. Darkness concealed what type of room it was, exactly, but all he needed to know was that it was empty.

'Cam,' she gasped when he backed her up against a wall. 'What are you doing?'

'I want you.' He nipped at her lips. 'Now.'

'But we're not in my bed,' she protested. 'How can we—'

'I'll show you.' It was too dark to see her face, but that was part of the thrill. 'If you let me.'

'Show me.'

His mouth was upon her, devouring her. She let out a squeak as he lifted her skirts up over her waist and pressed two fingers into the slit in her drawers. There was no time to make her come first, unfortunately, so he stroked her until she was more than sufficiently wet and grinding into his palm.

'That's it,' he growled against her mouth.

One arm hooked under her knee, while the other unfastened the falls of his trousers, releasing his cock. After a few tugs with his hand he was completely erect and he slid into her in one smooth motion.

He smothered her cry with his lips, his tongue pushing in to her mouth with the same motion of his hips. Jealousy rode him hard, urging him to mark her. Make her his. Only his. When she clasped around him and her body vibrated, he let go, spilling inside her. His pleasure came in a quick fury, sweeping over him until he was drained.

'That was…' Maddie slumped against him.

'…phenomenal,' he finished. Withdrawing from her, he helped her with her gown, smoothing down as much of the wrinkles as he could. When he looked up at her face, all he could see was pure satisfaction.

'You enjoyed that,' he said.

A lazy smiled curled up her lips. 'Of course. I didn't think it would be possible…anywhere except on a bed. Where else can we do it?'

Ideas flooded into his mind. 'I'll show you. Don't worry.' He brushed away an errant curl stuck to her cheek. 'Now, if you head back into the ball first, I'll follow in a few moments.'

She nodded, then dashed off.

Cam righted himself, then leaned an arm against the wall, taking a deep breath. Nothing like a hard tupping to prove that all that was between them was physical. He would not allow any more than that. Not after Jenny.

Had he forgotten her and how she had left him a broken man when she and Kirk had eloped? He'd barely survived that first time; he wasn't sure he could do it again. Not with Maddie.

With the wedding now fast approaching, Maddie's days were a flurry of fittings, shopping, and appointments. As if that weren't enough, there were also other social obligations expected of the bride, such as going to teas and paying calls to the ton's most important members.

'Why must we attend all these events?' Maddie asked Miss Merton as they were on their way to the Viscountess of Lattimer's home for afternoon tea. 'I am already so busy with planning for the wedding.'

'I completely understand, dear. All this must be taking its toll on you.' Miss Merton patted her hand. 'But, as a future countess, you must make the right impression and connections. You shall be the Earl's most important social asset. He will be judged by how you act and conduct yourself, as will his family.'

'His family, too?'

The companion nodded. 'Most definitely. You will essentially be the matriarch, after all.'

Maddie had never thought of it that way. She had to do better.

No—she had to be perfect.

Just like with her dancing lessons, Maddie would not buckle under the pressure. She would work hard. She owed it to Cam and Persephone. If she were a success as Countess of Balfour, then Persephone's chances for a good match would increase.

And Cam would fulfil his promise to their mother.

That was the only thing she wanted.

Well, not the only thing.

Maddie could not help but notice the nagging feeling that something in Cam had shifted. Or maybe there had always been something different with him. His confession that night they'd first made love clarified some things for her, but there were still pieces missing.

Hate was a strong word, but she could categorically say she hated his former fiancé. With her actions, that woman had left deep scars in Cam, which may have healed but nevertheless had left their mark. That was what she had seen on his face the day he'd proposed; it was no chink in his armour, but rather, Cam had wrapped himself in this protective gear to stop anyone from getting too close and hurting him.

Maddie had hoped that a physical relationship would be enough. It should have been, but now she was wanting more. There was potential there—she just knew it. But Cam's emotional scars were preventing that from happening.

'We are here,' Miss Merton announced as the carriage slowed to stop. 'Come.'

Despite the fact that she was exhausted, Maddie put a smile on her face and did her best to charm all the important ladies of the ton. She drank her watered-down tea, pretended to be interested in conversations about shopping and fashion, plus feigned interest in the juicy gossip about whichever lord and lady were having an affair this week.

She hated every moment of it, but endured, for Persephone and Cam. Once they were on their way home, she breathed a big sigh of relief.

'You should have a nap, dear,' Miss Merton suggested when they arrived at Mabury Hall. 'Tonight's dinner is very important. The Dowager Duchess of Durham is a powerful figure in society, and the fact that she's hosting a dinner in honour of your engagement is monumental. Everyone's eyes will be on you tonight.'

'I understand.' Maddie was nervous just thinking about it. 'I will be the perfect future countess.' However, that nap would have to wait. She had one more important task.

'Hello, dear,' Papa greeted as she entered the library. 'Glad to see you're not too busy for your father.'

'Never.' Bouncing over to him, she kissed him on the cheek.

'I'm glad. Though I'm afraid I don't have anything as fun as wedding dresses and cakes to show you today.'

'Oh, please. After this wedding, I never wish to see anything white ever again.' Maddie could not say yes fast enough when her father had asked her to meet at the library when she returned from Viscountess Lattimer's tea party to look at the furnace design plans. 'Now, where are those drawings?'

For the next few hours, Maddie forgot all about wedding planning as she poured over the sketches with her father. They still weren't quite right, and while she was frustrated the designers did not listen to her suggestions, she was still glad for the distraction.

'This is good practice for you, Maddie,' Papa said. 'I've been thinking about building a furnace in Scotland.'

Maddie held her breath. 'And?'

'It might be an excellent idea, a few years down the line. We need to get the furnace here up and running, but once that's proven to be a success, we can start planning for this next venture. Perhaps by then you'll have a child or two, and they'll be old enough that you can put more time into the business.'

'Really, Papa?' Excitement made it difficult to breathe.

'Yes. Your future husband has such a way with words that it makes it difficult to say no,' he said with a chuckle.

'Cam convinced you to start a forge in Scotland?'

'He has convinced me something I already know— that with you at the helm, it will be a success.'

Maddie had no words to say after that. Cam had that much faith in her? He had never even seen her near a furnace.

'But first,' Papa continued, 'let's get this one off the ground, shall we?' He shook his head as he rolled up the plans and put them aside. 'I don't know how I'm going to do this without you, Maddie. But parents cannot hold onto their children. We must eventually let go, especially if that means our child's happiness.'

Tears stung the back of her throat. 'Thank you, Papa.'

'Are you, Maddie?'

'What, Papa?'

'Happy.' He qualified that with, 'Truly happy?'

Puzzled, she asked, 'What do you mean?'

'I know you, dear.' He walked over to her, guided her to a settee, then sat down. 'And I see you. You always put aside your own wants to make others happy.'

'That's not true.'

'Oh? Did you really want to come here and find a husband in the first place? Or did you do it because Caroline and your mother wanted to?'

'I—'

'And what about when you wear the dresses your mama chooses? And go to these events she plans? Do you do them for yourself or to please her?'

'She's my mother. Of course I want to please her.'

'But what about yourself? What about what you want?'

Maddie didn't know how to answer that.

'You've always been so selfless, Maddie. Even with Caroline. When you were younger, you would give her everything she wanted, even your prized clothes and toys.' He tsked. 'Anyway, I hope you think about what I said, Maddie.' He kissed her cheek. 'Because you deserve all the happiness in the world.'

'Thank you, Papa.' She embraced him, then got to her feet. 'I'm afraid I must be going. Mrs Ellesmore is coming over and I'll be poked and prodded with needles and pins all afternoon.'

He laughed. 'Good luck, dear.'

Maddie made her way out, but as she opened the door and crossed the threshold into the silence of the hallway, her father's words came back to her. Was she happy? And did she think she deserved happiness? But what would make her happy in the first place?

In the beginning, she'd thought all she wanted was a husband and a family. Now that she was to marry Cam, she would get her wish, and even more than that—fulfilling work to fill her days once her children were old enough.

But why did it feel like there should be more?

Chapter Nineteen

'Which dinner are we attending again tonight, Balfour?' Mabury asked as he handed Cam the glass of whisky.

'Damned if I know. They're all the same, aren't they?' He nodded his thanks and accepted the glass. The Duke had been kind enough to invite Cam to his private study for cigars before they left for tonight's activities, and so he'd brought a bottle of Glenbaire single malt to share.

'Do not let my mother and Miss Merton hear you. Cheers.' The Duke clinked his glass to Cam's and took a sip. 'Now, that's damned fine whisky.'

'Thank you, Your Grace.' The familiar taste of the buttery, malty liquid was a comfort; it made him think of home. A sudden pang of homesickness hit him. *I can't wait for all this to be over.* All he wanted to do right now was to take Maddie back to Scotland and be away from London. To have her to himself, day and night, instead of sneaking in a few hours with her from midnight to dawn. To make love to her every evening and then sit next to her at breakfast the next day.

'From the look on your face, I can guess you cannot wait for all this wedding madness to be over,' the Duke said.

'You guessed right.' He downed the rest of the whisky. 'If I had my way, we'd be on our way to Gretna Green now.'

'There's still time.' The corner of Mabury's mouth quirked up. 'But, once things settle down, you'll look back on all of this with fondness.'

'Liar,' Cam said with a chuckle.

'I was trying to cheer you up, old chap.'

'I appreciate it.'

Despite having been punched by him twice and his threatening to kill Cam, he quite liked the Duke. He could definitely see them becoming good friends over the years, which was a real possibility since the Duchess and Maddie were as close as sisters.

'I promise you, Balfour, it will all be worth it.' Mabury put his glass back down on the mantel, then looked at the clock. 'We should get going or we'll be late.' They left the study and made their way to the hall where everyone was waiting for them.

As ever, the others faded in the background as Cam's gaze sought out Maddie. Tonight, she wore a delicate, light pink silk gown that only enhanced her natural beauty, while her golden hair shone like a halo around her. She smiled shyly at him as he came to her. Why was it that she only had to glance his way and everything seemed right in the world? All those fears and doubts— thoughts he hadn't realised had been plaguing his mind— would all but disappear when she was around.

'Good evening, my lord,' she greeted.

'Good evening, Miss DeVries.' Taking her gloved hand, he kissed it. 'You look beautiful tonight.'

'Thank you,' she said, her skin turning nearly the same shade of pink as her gown.

'I hope you never stop blushing for me,' he said in a low voice, ensuring only she could hear it.

'Everyone.' Miss Merton clapped her hands to get their attention. 'We must make haste.'

As usual, Maddie and Persephone rode with Cam, though when they sat down, he made Persephone switch places with him so he could sit beside Maddie. He reached over and took her hand in his.

She cocked her head to the side. 'Is everything all right, Cam?'

'Yes.' No, it wasn't. He didn't want to be here. All he wanted was to go back to her rooms and be alone. 'I just want to hold your hand, that's all.'

'Of course, but—oh!' She scooted a few inches away from him. 'Please mind my dress. Silk easily wrinkles.'

He chuckled. 'Forgive me. I'm afraid I'm not well versed in the properties of fabrics, except maybe for their tensile strength.' Or lack thereof, as demonstrated last night when, in his impatience, he'd rent her night-rail down the middle. Maddie apparently had picked up his meaning, and once again a pretty blush coloured her cheeks.

'Why would you know that, Cam?' Persephone asked, blinking owlishly behind her spectacles.

'Never you mind, Seph.' But Maddie's blush deepened. 'By the way, where are we going again?'

'You don't know?' Maddie asked in an exasperated tone.

He shrugged. 'All these dinners, parties, balls... They're all melding together and I can't keep my head straight.'

She sighed. 'The Dowager Duchess of Durham is throwing a dinner in honour of our engagement.'

'Wait, we're the guests of honour?' First he'd heard of it.

'Yes.' Reaching over, Maddie brushed a stray lock of hair from his temple. 'It's very important. *She* is very important, and we must make a good impression on her.'

Cam frowned. Important? Since when did Maddie care about all these so-called doyens of the ton?

'Cam, how old is this tail-coat?' She clucked her tongue as she plucked a stray thread from the lapel. 'You must get some new ones made. Would you like me to speak with Murray?'

'I'll speak with him,' he muttered, then snatched the thread from her fingers.

'Everything must be perfect.' Maddie wrung her hands together. 'We cannot make a mistake.'

Irritation rose in Cam. 'What's the matter with you, Maddie? You're acting very strange.'

'Strange?' Her head snapped towards him, her eyebrows slashing downwards. 'I'm fine. Just tired from all the wedding planning.' The carriage halted and her body went rigid. 'We're here. Come or we'll be late.'

Cam had sensed the vexation in her tone, which was unusual for her. But perhaps all this madness was affecting her more than he thought, and now she was on the verge of breaking. *I shouldn't have insisted on having the wedding so soon.*

He wanted to apologise to her, but as soon as they entered the Dowager Duchess of Durham's home, they were swept up in a flurry of introductions, good wishes, and congratulations from people he hardly knew and, to be honest, likely never wanted to know. Cam was relieved when they finally sat down to dinner, as at least he had to endure conversations from only the Dowager Duchess and a few of her close companions. That, and Maddie was by his side.

'Lord Balfour, is it true you've decided to hold your nuptials in England?' came a question from the well-dressed man on the Dowager's right.

Cam searched his memory for his name. *Forsythe.* They'd been introduced as soon as they arrived and he claimed to be the Dowager's dearest friend. 'Aye, Mr Forsythe, it's true.'

'How lovely. And why not back in Scotland?'

'It seemed simpler,' he replied. 'If we held it back home, we'd have to prepare at least three households for travel. My sister is already here and so it would only be my three brothers making the journey, which makes a wedding in London much simpler.'

'Ah, yes. Preparing a trousseau and then having to travel for a few days would indeed be taxing,' Forsythe said. 'Not to mention, a grand wedding in London is nothing less than what your lovely fiancée deserves.'

'Aye, for sure.'

Maddie had never expressed her desire for a grand wedding, but he supposed that it would have to be a large gathering since it would be in town. 'And really, once my brothers have settled business at the distillery, they can make the journey anytime.'

'D-distillery?' The Dowager's hawk-like stare narrowed at him. 'What do you mean, distillery?'

'My family business, Your Grace,' he said proudly. 'Glenbaire Whisky Distillery.'

'Whisky? Business?' she echoed.

'It's been in my family for generations,' Persephone piped up. 'Even before it was legal—'

'Mr Forsythe,' Maddie interrupted. 'Her Grace tells

me you have the most divine collection of rare French paintings. How did you come to have an interest in art?'

'I'm glad you asked, Miss DeVries. You see, I was but a young lad when....'

Cam tuned out Forsythe and instead, for the second time that evening, was searching for an explanation for Maddie's odd behaviour. Persephone could sometimes launch into inappropriate discussions, but Maddie acted as if she would send the ladies in the room for their smelling salts if she spoke about the distillery.

At first he thought it might have been a fluke, except that as the dessert plates were being cleared, the Dowager's sycophants had launched into a discussion about the latest scandal in the gossip columns.

'So, who do you think is this Mr R caught by Lord M in bed with his lady wife?' Forsythe asked.

'Who else?' the woman on his right—Lady Christine or Cassandra—said. 'The writer describes this Mr R as a "dark god."'

'God of The Underworld, then?' Forsythe waggled his eyebrows knowingly. 'Have you read the column, Miss DeVries?'

Cam almost laughed, imagining Maddie poring over those sordid anonymous gossip columns.

Maddie put her napkin down on her lap. 'I'm afraid not. But I heard the most interesting tidbit at the Viscountess Lattimer's tea today.'

'Well? Tell us,' the Dowager pressed her.

'Apparently, a certain Viscount G and Lady Q have started their affair again.'

Forsythe gasped. 'No.' The rest of the flunkies let out gasps of disbelief.

Maddie smiled. 'Oh, yes, according to some reliable sources.'

Cam could only stare at Maddie. But before he could say anything, the Dowager spoke. 'Dear guests, thank you for coming tonight, especially our honoured guests.' She nodded at Cam and Maddie. 'Now, the evening is not over yet. As a surprise for the happy couple, I have invited Signora Carmina Giuselli, the London opera's prima donna, to sing a few songs for us in the music room.' The guests *oohed* and *aahed* in delight. 'But while we wait for her, there will be coffee, tea, and digestifs in the parlour. Please do join me.'

Everyone stood up and followed the Dowager out of the room. Cam fell behind as their hostess and her friends surrounded Maddie, ushering her along. He trailed after them to the parlour, which was now filled with the other guests. With Maddie occupied, he decided to seek out some friendlier company, scanning the room for Mabury until he found the Duke with his wife and Persephone speaking to a few other guests. *Thank God.*

As he crossed the room towards them, he halted when he heard his name.

'Why, yes, my future son-in-law is the Earl of Balfour.' *Oh, hell.*

Eliza DeVries continued, 'I'm so lucky, aren't I? And this is Maddie's first season, too. I just knew she would succeed. Just think, in a few weeks, we'll all be calling her *my lady.*'

Irritation grew in him. This night was turning into some sort of farce, and he just wanted to leave. Turning on his heel, Cam changed direction and marched towards his fiancée holding court at the other end of the room.

'Maddie.'

'So he told—Cam?' A smile lit up her face. 'Where were you? I thought you were just behind us?'

He was surprised she'd noticed he was gone. 'Might I have a word? In private?'

'Now?'

'Yes, now.'

She hesitated, glancing at her new friends. 'Of course, my lord. Would you excuse us?' Her flock parted to let her through, and she took the hand he offered. 'Cam, what is it?'

Cam ground his teeth together as he pulled her along, away from the guests and out into the hall.

'Cam? Where are we going?' She tugged her hand from his. 'Cam, what's the matter?'

He spun around to face her, unable to tell her the words that were really on his mind. 'Come away with me, Maddie,' he said, his voice hoarse.

'Away? What do you mean? And where?'

'Back to your room. Or to Scotland. We can go to Gretna Green and be married in days.' On impulse he wrapped his arms around her and crushed her to him. 'I don't care, as long as it's not here.'

'Cam!' she admonished, wiggling away from him. 'What are you doing?' she hissed, anger flashing in her eyes. 'We cannot do this here. Someone might see us.'

'Who cares what these silly fops and matrons think?' His chest tightened.

'You should care,' she said. When he made a motion to take her in his arms again, she raised her hands. 'And I told you, this gown wrinkles easily.'

'I don't give a damn about your infernal gown.'

'Cam, language.' She placed her hands on her hips. 'Can't you see? We have to be on our best behaviour. We must be *perfect* tonight.'

'Perfect? For these fops and fools?'

'Cam, shush. They might hear you.' She glanced

around. 'Please. Can't you just be on your best behaviour tonight? I've worked so hard. I don't want to give up now. I just need a little help from you...just need a bit more.'

She needed more.

That's all he had to hear.

Something inside Cam shrank and contracted and a cold wave washed over him. 'Of course, Maddie. What was I thinking? Forgive me.'

Maddie's shoulders sank. 'You don't have to apologise, Cam. Truly.'

'You should go back inside. Before they miss you.'

She bit her lower lip. 'I—Yes, you're right. I shall see you later, then, my lord.'

Cam watched her go, his chest tightening. When he tried to go after her, he found that his feet would not move. He hated that room and didn't want to go back, so he walked off in the opposite direction. Seeking solace, he found the glass doors that led to the garden. He inhaled, but the cool night air did nothing to soothe him.

Maddie needed more.

'All alone, my lord?'

Caroline DeVries.

He had no patience for her tonight. 'Miss DeVries, we are soon to be family, so I will get straight to the point. Your malicious attempts to drive Maddie and I apart will never work. So please, stop.'

She laughed mockingly. 'Yet here you are, all by yourself.'

He curled his fingers into his palm. 'Goodnight, Miss DeVries.'

'I can see why Mama likes you,' she began. 'You're like a shiny bauble she can show off. Perhaps that's why Maddie accepted your proposal. She's always wanted Mama's approval because I'm her favourite.'

'I do not see the point of this conversation, so I shall bid you goodnight.' Without another word, he walked past her and back into the house.

Caroline's maliciousness had nearly cost him Maddie, and Cam knew better than to listen to her. However, her words buried themselves in his mind, and considering Maddie's behaviour tonight, they somehow made sense. And it wasn't as if Caroline was lying; she was merely giving her observations.

Observations that were somehow in tune with his and explained why Maddie was suddenly acting strangely.

A shiny bauble, he thought bitterly. That was all he was.

Chapter Twenty

Maddie's jaw ached from smiling for hours, but she endured it, as well as the mindless conversation and the spiteful and venomous people around her.

It will be worth it, she convinced herself.

When she was small, Papa had worked long hours at the furnace, and sometimes they wouldn't see him for days. But his persistence and tenacity had paid off, and now the DeVries Furnace and Iron Company was one of the most successful furnaces in America and they would soon be making their mark in England, as well.

Her small sacrifice now would pay off later.

For Cam and Persephone and their dear mama.

Once she and Cam were married, she would take Persephone under her wing, and between Kate, the Dowager, and herself, no one would dare laugh at or mock her friend. Maybe she might even stop hiding behind foliage and statues and find someone who could cherish her and love her for who she was, quirks and all. Someone who would give her the same sense of self-worth Cam gave Maddie.

Maddie's heart slammed in her chest and urgency and dread rose in her, like she had just realised something important, but she couldn't name it. Maybe it was Cam's strange behaviour when they spoke earlier outside.

Come away with me, Maddie.

In the moment he had said it, it had sounded preposterous. Mad, even. Leave the party—their party—and run home to make love? Or elope to Scotland? Was he crazy? The ton would have eaten up that gossip, and then her work would have been for naught. All she needed was for him to put in the least bit of effort. Just a little more, she'd asked.

But now, part of her wished she had said yes to his proposal to run away. Not just yes, but *oh, yes!*

'Miss DeVries, did you hear what I said?'

Mr Forsythe's question yanked her back from her thoughts. 'What? I—I'm sorry. I must go.'

Maddie ignored their protests as she walked away. She needed to find Cam. Right now. But where was he? A pit in her stomach formed, and so she headed off in search of him. A quick scan of the room told her he wasn't in the parlour, but she did spot Kate and the Duke.

'There you are,' Kate said as Maddie approached them. 'Are you enjoying yourself?'

She wrung her hands together. 'Have you seen Cam?'

'I haven't. Sebastian?'

The Duke shook his head. 'I thought he was by your side?'

'He...left,' she replied, her voice trembling. 'Excuse me.'

'Maddie, wait—'

Whirling around, she sped off, heading out of the parlour to where she had last seen Cam. 'Cam!' she called, but the hall was empty.

'Maddie!'

Kate? She hadn't even noticed her friend was right behind her, face filled with concern. 'What's the matter?'

Maddie sniffed. 'Oh, Kate, I can't help but think... I think I've done something wrong. Everything is spinning out of control.' Defeat weighed down on her. 'I can't do this anymore.'

Kate's arms came around her in an embrace. 'Maddie,' she soothed. 'It's all right. Tell me what's wrong.'

Gathering her thoughts, Maddie told her what had happened with Cam. 'I just have this feeling, you know... I was a bit short with him, because I've been exhausted and I just wanted everything to be perfect tonight.'

'Perfect? Why would it matter if tonight were not perfect?'

'Because they're counting on me.'

'Who?'

'Cam and Persephone. And their mother. Don't you remember what Persephone said in the carriage? About Cam's promise to their mother? If I make the right impression, then Persephone will surely have a successful season. In the ton's eyes, I must be *perfect*.' Like gold. Precious and with no impurities.

'That's preposterous,' Kate huffed.

'But it's true. Cam and Persephone will be judged according to my actions.'

'First of all,' Kate began, 'who cares about what these biddies think? And second, that all shouldn't be on your shoulders. Yes, Cam promised his dying mother, but why on earth is that your responsibility? Did he ask you to do all this?'

'No.' In fact, Cam hadn't even asked her to help Persephone. 'I just wanted to do it for him.'

Kate smiled sadly. 'You've always been so sweet and unselfish, so of course you would do this for Balfour, no matter what the cost to you. But if he's the man that deserves you, then that shouldn't matter to him. All he would want is for you to be happy. Maddie, dear, are you happy?'

Happy.

This was the second time today anyone had asked about Maddie's happiness. She thought she was, but then that feeling came back from earlier today. That feeling that she wanted more.

I love him.

Oh, Lord, why hadn't she realised it before? She wanted more, wanted Cam—all of him. She wanted to have a true marriage with him. Not just the physical part, but on every level. But that armour he wore kept him from opening up to her. He didn't want to leave his heart open because it had cost him too much the first time.

'I think I know where he is—or where he's going. Thank you, Kate.' She quickly embraced her friend, then raced out the door. Sure enough, Cam was there, about to get into his coach, one foot on the step.

'Cam!' she called, chasing after him. 'Stop, please.'

He froze, but kept his back to her. 'What do you want, Maddie?'

The iciness in his voice did not escape her. 'I'm so sorry I was acting strange this evening.'

His shoulders slumped, then he turned to face her. 'It's all right. I understand now.'

'You do?'

'Yes.' A smile that did not reach his eyes formed on his lips. 'I'm sorry, too. That I cannot give you what you want. That I cannot give you *more*.'

Oh, that damned word. Why had she said it? 'Oh, no, Cam. It's not what you think—'

'Perhaps you should find someone else, someone worthy of you. Someone more your equal and not just a shiny, charming object with nothing else to offer.'

She stepped forward and gripped his arms. 'But I want you. All of you.' For the first time in her life, she wanted to be selfish, to take what she wanted. And she wanted all of him.

'I know you do. I told you we were compatible in that way.' Wrapping his hands around her wrists, he put her hands away from him. 'I shall miss your sweet little body when we part.'

It sounded like he meant to hurt her, as if to push her away. But it did not work on her—not anymore. Not now that she understood him. All the missing parts were complete and she could see him for who he truly was.

'Cam,' she began gently. 'I am not Jenny. I will not leave you at the altar. I hate that she's turned you into this. But I promise you, I will prove to you that I'm nothing like her.' She didn't know how, but she would find a way.

His jaw ticked, but otherwise he remained unmoved. He was still processing what she had said. But she had to have faith in him. And he had to find that faith in himself. The next part would be the hardest, but it had to be done.

'And now I'm walking away from you, Cam. Not running away. Not forever. Just for now. Because you've taught me that I, too, am worthy.' Going on her tiptoes, she kissed his cheek. 'So when you are ready, come and find me.'

Turning away and leaving Cam was the hardest thing she'd ever had to do in her life. Each step was like slogging through mud, but somehow, she was doing it. She'd done her part, and hopefully, he would know to do his. When she entered the house, she saw Kate was still in the hallway, waiting for her.

'How did it go?'

Trust Kate to know exactly what was going on.

'I've done what I can, but now I must wait.' How long, she didn't know.

'I hope he's worth it.' Kate took her hand. 'In the meantime, what do you think about coming back to Highfield Park?'

She smiled weakly at her friend. 'I think that would be a splendid idea.'

Chapter Twenty-One

'Are we headed back to Mabury Hall, my lord?' John, Cam's footman asked.

'Yes,' Cam replied curtly as he climbed back into his carriage. Taking his hat off, he flung it across the empty seat and sank back into the plush upholstery. Removing his left glove, he pressed a naked palm where Maddie had kissed him on his cheek. The freshly shaven skin was cool and smooth, but he felt as if she had branded him there. And she had branded him—not just on the cheek, but all over.

A damned fool, that's what he was, for not learning his lesson. He would never be enough. He hadn't been for Jenny, and he wasn't for Maddie. Not even she could prove otherwise.

He knocked on the roof of the carriage. As it slowed down, he opened the window. 'John, I've changed my mind.'

'Where shall we go, my lord?'

He thought for a moment. Going back to Mabury Hall was not an option, at least not for now. He did not want to be somewhere that reminded him of Maddie. He needed distraction. An evening of diversions. 'St James's.'

'Where in St James's?'

'Just go, John,' he said impatiently.

'Right away, my lord.'

Cam drummed his fingers on the seat as the carriage sped along. He watched the outside, waiting until they reached the notorious street filled with gaming hells and bordellos and high-end gentlemen's clubs that were just covers for expensive—and legal—gaming hells and bordellos. Tonight, however, he was looking for a particular one.

Why did I not ask my man of business, Atwell, for a damned address?

They drove by a few establishments, but Cam felt they were not the right place. With his patience growing thin, he knocked on the roof. When the coach stopped, he did not bother to wait for John to get the door and instead flung it open, hopping out by himself.

'My lord?'

'I think I shall go for a walk.' John looked like he wanted to protest, but Cam waved him away. 'It's all right. Just wait for me at the corner.'

'Of course, my lord.'

Cam pulled the collar of his shirt over his neck to protect him from the cool, damp London air. He shoved his hands in his coat pockets and began to walk in no particular direction, just following the streets, ignoring the drunken gentlemen stumbling out of bawdy houses and well-dressed women trying to catch his eye as they sauntered by. He was nearing the end of the street when he stopped as something drew his attention.

There.

Up ahead was perhaps the most enormous building Cam had ever seen. It wrapped around the corner and probably took up an entire block, though he could not be certain because the street lamp extended its illumination only so far. That, and the entire structure was black.

If that place was not called The Underworld, Cam would eat his hat.

He hurried over, climbing up the grand black marble steps, then knocked on the heavy, stained oak door. To his surprise, a slot opened up in the middle. A pair of menacing-looking eyes peeped through.

'Password?'

Password? 'I don't know any password.'

The slot slammed shut with a sharp snap.

Undeterred, Cam knocked again.

The slot slid back open. 'Password?'

'I told you, I don't know it. How can I get it?'

'Only members 'ave the password for the day.'

'I'm not a member.'

Slam.

He took a deep breath and rapped his knuckles on the door.

'Pass—'

'I was invited,' Cam quickly said. 'By your owner. Ask him yourself. I'm Cameron, Earl of Balfour.'

'Where's yer invite, then?'

'In—' *Oh.* He reached into his pocket, his fingers searching around. *Damn.* He couldn't remember where he'd placed it. *Murray must have put it awa*y. 'I seem to have lost it.'

Slam.

He knocked his forehead on the door and took a deep, calming breath.

'Sir, do you mind?' came a well-spoken voice from behind.

Cam straightened up and stepped aside. 'Be my guest,' he said to the gentleman on the step behind him. With a frustrated groan, he raked his fingers through his hair and bit out a curse under his breath.

'Are you all right?'

Cam's head shot up. 'I beg your pardon?'

'I asked if you were all right.'

Cam's eyes narrowed at the man. His blond hair was cut in the latest fashion, clothes impeccably tailored and made with expensive materials, which meant he was rich, likely titled. He also had the face of an angel, with fine features and eyes the colour of sapphires. 'I'm fine.'

'On the contrary, you look like you could use a friend.' Those twin sapphires twinkled with amusement.

'We are not friends.'

'You know, I get told that a lot.' He tsked. 'But that has never stopped me. Strangers are just friends you've never met, you know. Devon St. James, Marquess of Ashbrooke.' He held out his hand.

Cam looked at it suspiciously but took it anyway. 'Cameron MacGregor, Earl of Balfour.'

'Scottish, eh?' Ashbrooke said.

'Aye. Will that be a problem?'

'No, no.' Ashbrooke waved him away. 'Not at all. The fact that you're not English actually makes you even more desirable to me as a friend. I've never had a Scottish friend before, you see, so you'll make a fine addition to my collection.'

'Well, show me my place on your shelf and I'll make sure to take my place, then.'

Ashbrooke grinned. 'See? We're already getting along smashingly.'

'So, friend,' Cam began. 'Any chance you can get me in there?' He jerked his thumb at the door.

Ashbrooke frowned. 'You are not a member?'

'Nay.'

'And you do not have the invitation?'

He shook his head.

'Then I cannot bring you in with me, I'm afraid. Rules of The Underworld are strict.'

'Could you somehow get me past the doorman?'

He shuddered. 'You can't pay me enough to try to sneak you inside. If our dear Charon doesn't want you in, believe me, you are not getting in.'

'I— Wait, his name's really Charon?'

'Yes. Maybe. I don't know. That's what most people call him.'

Cam thought for a moment. 'The owner. I was invited by the owner on business. Perhaps you could speak to him and tell him I've misplaced my invitation.'

'Talk to Ransom?' Ashbrooke stared at him as if Cam asked him to cut off his right foot. 'No, thank you. I shall take my chances with Charon.'

Cam rubbed his jaw. 'Damn. There really is no way I'm getting in?'

'Not without an invite.' Ashbrooke took his elbow and guided him down the steps. 'Look, this street has dozens of other establishments where we can carouse all night and forget whatever's troubling you.'

'I suppose you are right.' Cam gestured to the street. 'You seem to know your way around here, Ashbrooke, so lead on.'

'All right, but do call me Ash.' He flashed Cam a roguish smile. 'I think we may become best friends before the night is through. Come!'

As Cam suspected, Ash did indeed know his way around St James's. In fact, he strutted around like he was its lord mayor, waving to the ladies looking out their windows, tipping his hat at all the bouncers, and even stopping to chat with a few suspicious-looking figures scurrying about.

Ash first took Cam to a brothel, but he immediately vetoed the idea. Despite what had happened with Maddie, he could not bring himself to be with another woman. So, Ash led him to a gambling house. Which one it was, Cam didn't know or care, because he spent most of the evening watching Ash play round after round of faro while drinking whatever liquor he was handed. Whatever it was, it was ghastly, but he didn't care, as long as it dulled his mind and senses.

'Well, the standards here really must have slipped if they're letting the likes of you in here.'

The sound of that voice was enough to get Cam's blood boiling. Rising to his feet, he shoved his chair back and spun around. He staggered as the world wobbled beneath his feet but braced himself against the faro table. 'You.'

Viscount Palmer glared at him. 'You think you're so clever, Balfour? Stealing Miss DeVries from right under my nose?'

Cam ground his teeth. 'It's not my fault she prefers me.'

'I need her more,' the Viscount snarled.

'Her dowry, maybe,' Cam slurred. His tongue felt thick and unwieldy.

'You're already wealthy. Why couldn't you let the rest of us have a chance?'

'Gentlemen,' Ash interrupted, getting up from his game and standing between them. 'Is there a problem here?'

'Step aside, Ashbrooke. This is not of your concern.' Palmer's hateful stare never left Cam's. 'I didn't want her, anyway. Who would want someone like her?'

Cam made a fist with his hand. 'You'd better watch what you say next.'

He huffed. 'Tell me, is it true what they say about plain and homely girls? Are they as eager to please in bed? Because from her looks, I bet she's probably giving you a grand old time.'

Rage fuelled Cam as he shoved Ash aside and lunged for Palmer. His fist connected with the Viscount's nose with a satisfying *crack.*

'You broke my nose!'

'I'll break more than that!' Cam reached for him again but, with his senses dulled, missed completely. Seeing an opening, Palmer grabbed him by the shoulder and pulled, then punched him in the jaw. Cam's head ricocheted back and he fell to the floor, but not before he managed to drag Palmer down with him. The Viscount landed on top, and they scrambled on the floor, trying to get the advantage.

Shouts and screams rang around them, along with breaking glass, smashing chairs, and general havoc. Palmer managed another blow to Cam's cheek, but he could hardly feel the pain anymore. With one last push, he rolled the Viscount under him, then let his fists fly once more.

'How. Dare. You!' he bellowed, punctuating his blows with every word. 'She is an Amazon goddess and you are not fit to speak her name!' He punched him one more time, and Palmer let out a pained moan before his head knocked back on the floor.

'Damn it, Balfour!' Ash cursed as he helped Cam to his feet. 'This was all about a woman?'

'Aye,' he slurred. *Maddie.* 'S-sorry about the fight. And ruining your evening.'

He let out a *pfft*. 'Evenings at St James's are pretty much the same night after night. At least you've provided some novel entertainment, though just to inform you, a fist-fight at a gambling den hadn't been on my list of things to do tonight.'

Ash guided Cam outside, away from the chaos. Cam hissed and lifted a hand to his face as the sun dug into his eyes like claws. 'What the—What time is it?'

'I don't know. Seven? Eight?' Ash hailed a passing hackney cab. 'Are you renting a terrace somewhere? Or staying with family or friends?'

'Mabury Hall. In Mayfair.'

'Mabury—as in the Duke of Mabury?' Ash looked at him disbelievingly. 'You're staying with my best friend?'

'I thought I was your best friend, Ash? *Oi!*' he protested as Ash packed him in the cab and climbed in. 'Where are we going?'

'I'm taking you to Sebastian.'

Cam frowned. 'I don't want to go back.'

'Whyever not?'

Because she is there. Cam leaned back into the cab's seat, feeling the rush of energy from the fight drain away from his body. His jaw hurt and blood trickled down from a cut above his eye, but he didn't care. *Punching Viscount Odious was definitely worth it.* Especially after what he'd said about Maddie. If there was anyone who didn't deserve her, it was Palmer, who couldn't see how beautiful and magnificent she was.

The lurching motion of the cab made Cam's head spin, so he closed his eyes. The alcohol still numbed his senses, so the next few minutes blurred together. Before he knew it, he was being ushered past a confused-looking Eames across the Mabury House threshold and into the Duke's private study.

'Where the hell— Ash?' Mabury's face turned comically confused. 'What are you doing here?'

'I met a new friend.' Ash gestured to Cam. 'Who's apparently a friend to you, too.'

Mabury sighed. 'Bring him to the sofa. I'll send for coffee and some hot towels and bandages.' He called out and a footman immediately entered.

As the Duke whispered instructions to his footman, Ash assisted Cam to the dark leather sofa, then headed to the mantel to pour himself a drink. 'I know it's early for a drink, but—' He stopped as he took a sip. 'This is divine. Whisky, eh?'

'The finest,' Cam interjected. 'Single malt scotch.' The room spun as he tried to lift his head, so he lay back down once again.

Mabury walked over and knelt by Cam. 'What the hell happened, Ash?'

'Do you want the short or long version?' The Duke lifted a dark brow. 'Right. Well, after Cam and I met outside The Underworld, we decided to band together for a night of carousing and general mischief. Then he got stinking drunk, started a fist-fight, all the while screaming about some Amazon goddess.'

'He deserved it, that bastard,' Cam spat. '*Ouch!*' Pain throbbed on the left side of his face.

'Started a fist-fight—' Mabury gritted his teeth. 'What the hell were you thinking, Balfour?'

'It was Viscount Odious—*Palmer.*'

'I see.' The Duke's obsidian eyes turned even darker. 'I hope you made him hurt.'

Cam grinned. 'I did.'

Mabury stretched up to his full height and smoothed his hands down his trousers. 'So, this is about Maddie. I should have guessed. What happened between you two?'

'None of your business.'

'It is my business, Balfour, because she's my guest and

therefore under my protection, and more importantly, it has upset my wife.' Dark eyes blazed with a quiet anger. 'Kate was tight-lipped about it, so you'd better tell me now what's going on.'

'We had a fight.'

'So you go off and get drunk and start a different fight,' Mabury said sarcastically. 'How did that work out for you?'

'Bloody well great, thank you very much.' Cam attempted to sit up. 'Now, if you don't mind, I shall—'

Mabury pushed him back down. 'No, you will not ignore Maddie, nor pretend nothing happened. You're going to get cleaned up and dressed and make up with her.'

'Why on God's green earth would I do that?'

'Because for some reason, she's in love with you, you nitwit,' Mabury roared. 'Anyone with eyes could have seen that.'

'Then I advise you get some spectacles, Your Grace, because there is no way she is in love with me.' Bitterness coated his tongue. 'Why would she be?'

'A pitiful fool you are, Balfour. Why don't you think she is?'

Cam's mouth pulled back. Was Mabury really going to make him lay out all his flaws? Did he need to list all the reasons why someone smart and beautiful like Maddie would not want him? 'She needs more than I can give her.' *More than I am.* 'I told her she should find someone else.'

Mabury huffed. 'And why the hell would you do that?'

'Because I am not enough for her!' he snarled. 'That's why she could not possibly love me. She told me herself she needed more than I can give her.'

'Is that so? What made her say that?'

His head pounded and all he wanted was to lie down

in a bed in a dark room and never emerge. 'All this time, I thought she didn't care about my title, but just last night at the dinner party, she was playing the part of the perfect society lady. I thought it was just the stress of the wedding planning, but when I tried to get her to leave with me, she told me that everything had to be perfect. And that I had to step up and give *more*. Then when I told her I couldn't give her more, she walked away from me.'

'Balfour, you idiot!'

All three men paused, then looked towards the source of the voice.

Kate, Duchess of Mabury, who had apparently been standing by the doorway the entire time, came down on them like an avenging angel. She dropped the tray of towels and bandages on the coffee table with a loud bang that made Cam's head pound.

'Your Grace, how lovely you look this morning,' Ash greeted cheerfully. 'Even lovelier than usual. Did you do something with your hair? New gown? Or perhaps it's the seething rage you're channelling to my best friend?'

'I thought I was your best friend,' Mabury said.

'New best friend,' Ash qualified. 'I'm allowed more than one.'

'Your Grace,' Cam said to the Duchess. 'I would stand, but as you can see, I am injured.'

'Good.' Her blue eyes blazed with fury. 'And to think I was worried about you. But now I know you're just a numbskull!'

'Maybe you are right, Your Grace. Otherwise, Maddie would have stayed.'

'You told her that she should find someone else.'

'And then she ran away from me.'

'She did not—' The Duchess threw her hands up in the air. 'Were you not listening to her? Or were you so

caught up in pitying yourself that you did not comprehend what she was trying to tell you?'

'Aye, I was there, remember? And, as I recall, Your
Grace, you were not.'

'She told me everything about what happened.' She
plopped down ungracefully on the armchair across from
him. 'Maddie was doing all that for *you*. The big society wedding. The tea parties. The gossip. Kissing up to
that puckered old Dowager. Maddie hated every minute
of it, but she did it so the ton would look favourably on
her and, in turn, you and your family.'

Disbelief struck him like another blow to the head.
'Why would she do that?'

'So that Persephone may have a successful season and
then you can fulfil your mother's dying wish.'

'You are— Wait, you know of that?'

'Yes, your sister told us. And when dear, sweet Maddie found out, her first thought was how she would help
you fulfil that promise.'

A sense of dread pooled in his chest. Of course that's
what Maddie would do. She'd done it all for him. 'That's
preposterous. She didn't need to take on that burden.'

'That's what I said.'

'And I never asked her to—' He shot to his feet, ignoring the pain on the left side of his face. 'I thought… I
thought she was doing it because she wanted her mother's
approval. Lord, I've been an idiot.'

'I'm glad we agree,' Mabury added.

Maddie thought he was pushing her away because she
was like Jenny. In what way, exactly? In no way. Jenny
could not compare to her.

*But I promise you, I will prove to you that I'm noth-
ing like her.*

He let out a laugh. Prove to him? What a joke. She had nothing to prove to him.

Cam turned to the Duchess. 'I must speak with her.'

'She's not here.'

'Not here?'

'She's gone.'

No. His throat burned as if he'd swallowed a bad batch of whisky. 'Where is she? Did she go back to America? I must find her!'

'She did not leave England,' the Duchess said. 'Only to Highfield Park. She and Mama left at around dawn. I was supposed to join them, but I had to delay because of a problem at the factory.'

Relief swept over him. 'Thank God. I'll call my carriage and leave at once.'

'Not like that, you won't.' Mabury wrinkled his nose. 'You look like death and smell like a public house. And Eames told me this morning your carriage had not returned.'

'Damn.' He had forgotten about the instructions he'd given his footman. 'My carriage should be somewhere in St James's.'

'I'll have Eames send someone to find them,' the Duke offered.

'And I'll call Murray so he can draw you a bath and prepare some fresh clothes,' the Duchess added.

'And I'll stay here and drink more of this fine whisky,' Ash quipped.

Cam looked at Mabury. 'Is he always like this?'

'Worse,' was the Duke's only answer.

Cam excused himself and headed up to his room. Maddie had probably arrived in Surrey by now. He wished she hadn't left, wished he'd come to his senses sooner, and wished he hadn't let her walk away last night. But after everything, he now understood why she'd had to do that. It was not to teach him a lesson or make him chase after her. No—by walking away, she was telling him that she deserved more. That she now had confidence in herself and she would no longer accept anything less from him.

But at the same time, she also told him to come seek her out when he was ready because she trusted he, too, would have confidence in himself. That he was more than just a charmer with no substance.

Maddie had walked away because she believed in him. He just hoped he could prove her right.

Maddie was in the orangery at Highfield Park, enjoying the warm, citrus-scented air wafting up through the iron grates on the floor. How she loved this place, with its lovely brickwork walls, high glass ceiling, tiled paths, and abundance of exotic plants.

She and the Dowager had arrived at Highfield Park early that morning from London. After napping for a few hours, she'd had a cold lunch in her room then decided to go to the orangery. This place reminded her of another world, which was one of the reasons she went there. Here, she could imagine she was someplace else.

Still, she could not quite enjoy the peace and tranquillity—not with the turmoil inside her.

Please, she said in silent prayer. *Please, make him understand what I was trying to say.* How long that would take—if he realised it all—she didn't know, but hopefully it wouldn't be too long. She hated leaving him, but she'd done this for him and for herself.

The sound of footsteps from behind made her pause. Who could be here? *Perhaps it was the gardener.* She hurried deeper into the orangery, hoping to avoid whoever it was so as not to disturb their work, but the footsteps followed her. Frowning, she halted and turned around. 'Who's— Cam?'

Her heart stopped beating as she soaked in the sight of him standing a few feet away, golden hair glinting in the sunlight, emerald eyes bright. Then she noticed the cuts and bruises on his face. 'Oh, heavens! What happened to you?'

'It doesn't matter, darling,' he said in that soft burr that smoothed over her like velvet. 'I'm here.'

'You're here,' she breathed.

He took slow, unsure steps towards her. 'You said I should come find you when I'm ready.'

She barely managed a whisper. 'Are you?'

'I'm not sure I'm that man you think I am,' he said. 'Not yet, anyway. But walking away from me was the right thing to do. However, know this. I will always come after you. You could walk halfway across the world and I would be right behind you.'

A breath hitched in her throat, and she clutched a hand to her chest.

'You're not Jenny,' he continued. 'Never were, never could be. But her actions wounded me so deeply, I couldn't see what was happening before my very eyes.'

'And what was that?'

'That slowly, carefully, you were getting past my defences and making me fall in love with you.'

Did he really say...?

'Cam...'

'I was scared, plain and simple. That you, too, would run away from me. But you have nothing to prove to me. In fact, I should be the one proving myself worthy of you.'

She lifted a hand towards him. 'I shouldn't have said—'

'I was wrong.' He caught her hand and pressed it to

his bristly cheek. 'I have done you wrong, Maddie. Accusing you of awful things when all you wanted to do was help me fulfil my promise to my ma.'

'I just want Persephone to have the London season your mother envisioned.'

'I didn't know that's what you were doing. Maddie, you don't have to do anything you don't want, especially if it makes you miserable.'

'I wanted to do it for you.'

'And I just want you to be happy.'

Tears gathered in the corners of her eyes at his words. 'I am happy.' She knew now that was the truth. 'Because of you.'

'Ma would have loved you, you know.' He kissed her palm, then turned his beautiful emerald eyes to her. 'And I do. Love you.'

This wonderful, beautiful, broken man. Cam challenged her and made her look at herself through his eyes and built her confidence. How could he not see himself in the same way? She searched for the right words, to tell him what he needed to hear.

When she finally did speak, she said, 'Iron pyrite.'

'I beg your pardon?'

'Iron. Pyrite. That's what fool's gold is called.' Her teeth sank into her lower lip. 'Cam, you're not iron pyrite. And you're no fool.' She cupped his face with both her hands. 'You're smart, in your own way. After all, you've managed your business and estate by yourself, I presume? Your fortunes haven't disappeared, nor has the distillery gone bankrupt?'

He shook his head.

'There are different kinds of intelligence, according to my father. Some people can calculate figures in their head, others can repair machinery. Then there are those who inspire others, true leaders who make others want to follow in their lead. Trust me, Cam. Those kinds of skills are worth their weight in gold. So no, you are not without substance.'

'How can you—'

'I'm a metallurgist—trust me.'

The corner of his mouth quirked up.

She continued, 'The day you proposed, you asked me if wanting you was reason enough to marry you. I realise now what you were really asking me.' Maddie felt as if she were standing at the edge of a cliff, not knowing what was below, though in this case, she didn't know if her hunch was correct. 'What you were really asking me is if *you* were enough.' Her throat tightened and her heart pounded so loudly she was nearly deaf, but she forged on. 'And the answer is yes, you are enough, Cam. Enough for me, for a lifetime. For two lifetimes, even. I've fallen in love with you, you see.'

'Maddie, I love you, too,' he said in a hoarse voice. 'And I will tell you and show you every day, until the last breath leaves my body.'

Arms came around her, pulling her close to his chest before his mouth came down on hers. His firm mouth moved over hers, caressing her softly before it turned deeper. Maddie tipped her head back to give him full access, opening up to him and basking in the love he showered on her as his kisses overwhelmed her. This kiss was not their first, and certainly not their last, but to Maddie it felt like something special.

It felt like true happiness.

Epilogue

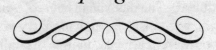

The incredible beauty of the Scottish Highlands, with their rolling hills, verdant valleys, and wild landscapes, was a sight to behold.

At least, that's what Maddie heard, because she had yet to leave the master bedroom of Kinlaly Castle, her new home since taking the title of Countess of Balfour.

'Cam?'

'Hmm?'

'Cam!' She playfully grabbed a handful of his hair to get his attention.

Cam looked up at her from between her legs, annoyed. '*Oi*. I was busy with something.'

She giggled. 'Not that I don't appreciate your efforts, but don't you think it's time we left the room?'

'Nay,' was his answer, and he proceeded with the work she had interrupted. Maddie mewled and moaned until pleasure wracked her body and she lay back on the pillows, wrung out and boneless.

Cam crawled up her body, trailing kisses upwards over her belly, stopping not so briefly at her breasts, nibbling at her neck before finally capturing her mouth with a deep kiss.

'Satisfied, wife?' he asked with a cheeky grin.

'Very.'

Maddie could hardly believe they were finally married. After he'd come to her in Highfield Park, he'd offered to delay the wedding, if only to relieve the pressure on her. However, Maddie would not hear of it. So instead, they'd compromised with a smaller wedding held in Highfield Park. Frankly, it had been even more beautiful and meaningful to Maddie than some society wedding, especially since all the people they cared about had been there, including all three of Cam and Persephone's brothers.

A week after the wedding, she, Cam, and her—now hers, too, she supposed—brothers made the trip back to Scotland. Persephone opted to stay behind to finish out the season under the sponsorship of the Dowager. Maddie was thrilled for her, though puzzled—Cam had asked Persephone if she wanted to come back home with them and try again next season, but for some reason she wanted to remain in London.

Maddie was sad to be away from her friend, but then they wouldn't be parted for too long, because they had more reason to return to London, not just with Glenbaire business. The construction of the DeVries London Furnace and Ironworks would be finished in a few months and they would begin operations soon. Her father had asked her to return to help, and of course, she'd said yes.

So it seemed the DeVrieses would be in England for a while longer, much to the delight of Mama and Caroline. Despite her antics, Maddie had no ill will towards her sister, as she'd decided to focus on her own happiness with Cam rather than spend time and energy on her sister's bile. However, during the wedding breakfast, Caroline had attempted to steal the limelight from Maddie by orchestrating a fist-fight between Viscount Gilbey and Lord Finlay over her.

Thankfully, Cam and the Duke of Mabury were able to stop them in time. However, when Caroline's involvement had been discovered, Papa had finally put his foot down and given her an ultimatum: there would be no more stringing along an endless parade of gentlemen. She would have to either settle down or decline all her current suitors and wait for the next season. Papa had warned her, however, that the next one would be her last, and if she didn't find a husband, he would send her back to America. By the time they'd left, Caroline had not decided, but knowing her sister, she would not pass up a chance to have another year of balls and new gowns and suitors. But Maddie still had hope that perhaps her sister would somehow mature before then and, somehow, find happiness, if not satisfaction and peace.

'You seem far away,' Cam said as he positioned himself beside her so they lay face to face. 'What's on your mind, darling? And how can I make you forget it so that you're only thinking of me?'

How she loved the way his burr had become more pronounced as soon as they'd got here. 'I am always thinking of you.'

A hand traced up her hip, all the way to her breasts, to the brass object that lay between them—the assayer's blowpipe that Cam had given her. While she was out shopping with Kate one day, she had found a thin gold chain at a jewellery shop and threaded it through the pipe so she could wear it close to her heart.

'You know I could buy you jewellery worth thousands more than this, right?'

'I know,' she said. 'But this is a special piece. It's the first gift you ever gave me.'

'An apology gift,' he reminded her jokingly. 'A reminder of our fake courtship.'

'Which became a real marriage.'

'True. *Hmm*. I think it's time we put it to the test.'

'Test?'

'Aye, I was told it was useful in finding precious metals.' Scooting closer, he took the pipe and placed one
end over the left side of her chest, then the other end by
his ear.

'That's not how that works, Cam,' she pointed out.

'Shh... I'm doing serious work here.' His brows drew
together as if he were in serious thought. 'Yes... Mmm-
hmm... Just as I thought.'

'Really? What does it say?'

Bright emerald-green eyes looked back at her, filled
with love and happiness. 'That you, darling, are priceless.'

* * * * *

MILLS & BOON

Desire

Indulge in secrets and scandal, intense drama and plenty of sizzling hot action with powerful and passionate heroes who have it all: wealth, status, good looks…everything but the right woman.

LET'S TALK
Romance

For exclusive extracts, competitions
and special offers, find us online:

f MillsandBoon

𝕏 @MillsandBoon

◎ @MillsandBoonUK

♪ @MillsandBoonUK

Get in touch on 01413 063 232

MILLS & BOON

THE HEART OF ROMANCE

A ROMANCE FOR EVERY READER

MODERN

Prepare to be swept off your feet by sophisticated, sexy and seductive heroes, in some of the world's most glamourous and romantic locations, where power and passion collide.

HISTORICAL

Escape with historical heroes from time gone by. Whether your passion is for wicked Regency Rakes, muscled Vikings or rugged Highlanders, awaken the romance of the past.

MEDICAL

Set your pulse racing with dedicated, delectable doctors in the high-pressure world of medicine, where emotions run high and passion, comfort and love are the best medicine.

True Love

Celebrate true love with tender stories of heartfelt romance, from the rush of falling in love to the joy a new baby can bring, and a focus on the emotional heart of a relationship.

Desire

Indulge in secrets and scandal, intense drama and sizzling hot action with heroes who have it all: wealth, status, good looks...everything but the right woman.

HEROES

The excitement of a gripping thriller, with intense romance at its heart. Resourceful, true-to-life women and strong, fearless men face danger and desire - a killer combination!

To see which titles are coming soon, please visit

millsandboon.co.uk/nextmonth